PIGS MIGHT FLY

NICK ABADZIS
JEREL DYE

Color by Laurel Lynn Leake
and Alex Campbell

:01
First Second
New York

"Dogs look up to man. Cats look down to man. But a pig will look us in the eye and see an equal."

—Winston Churchill

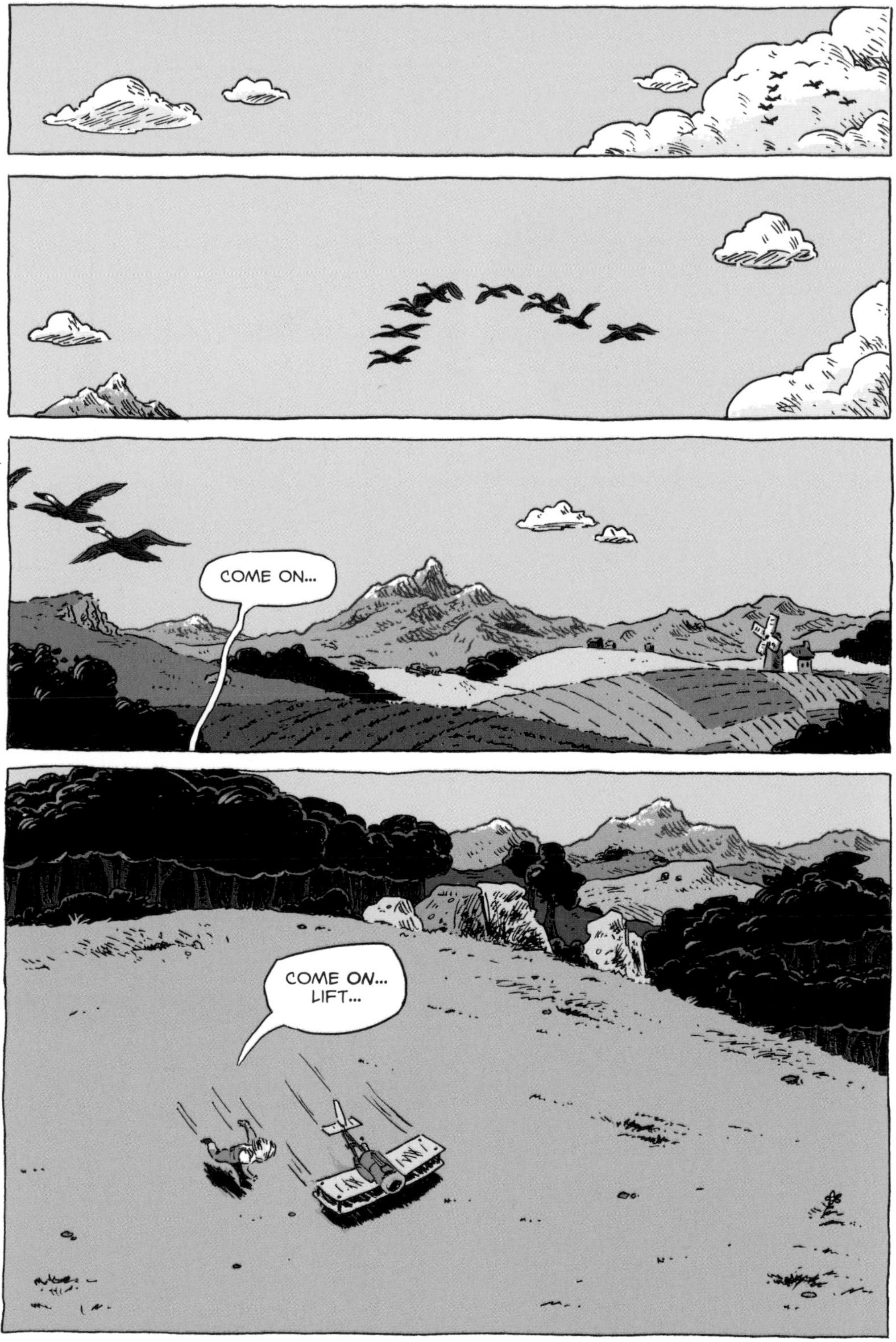
COME ON...
COME ON...
LIFT...

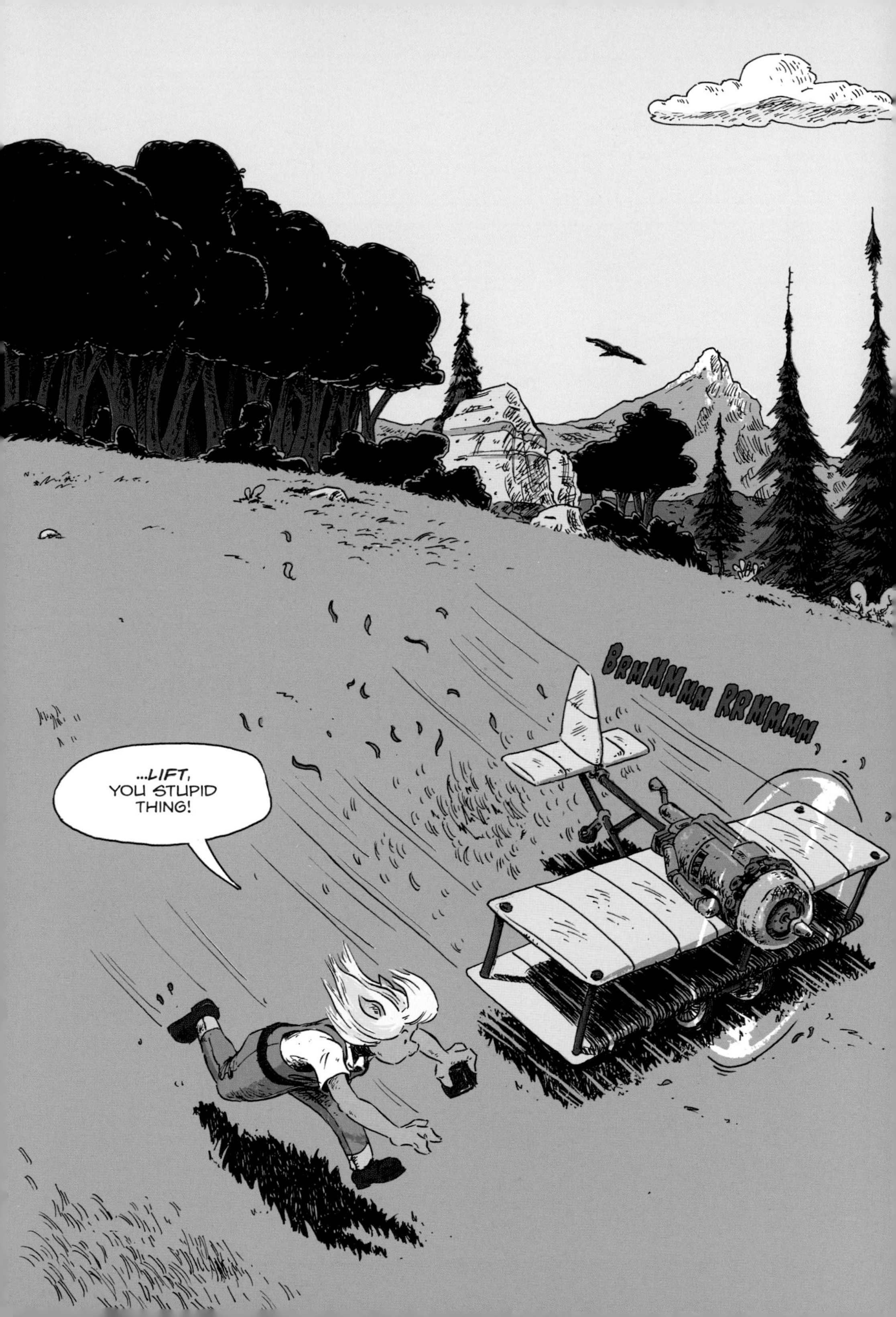
...LIFT, YOU STUPID THING!
BRMMMmm RRMMMM,

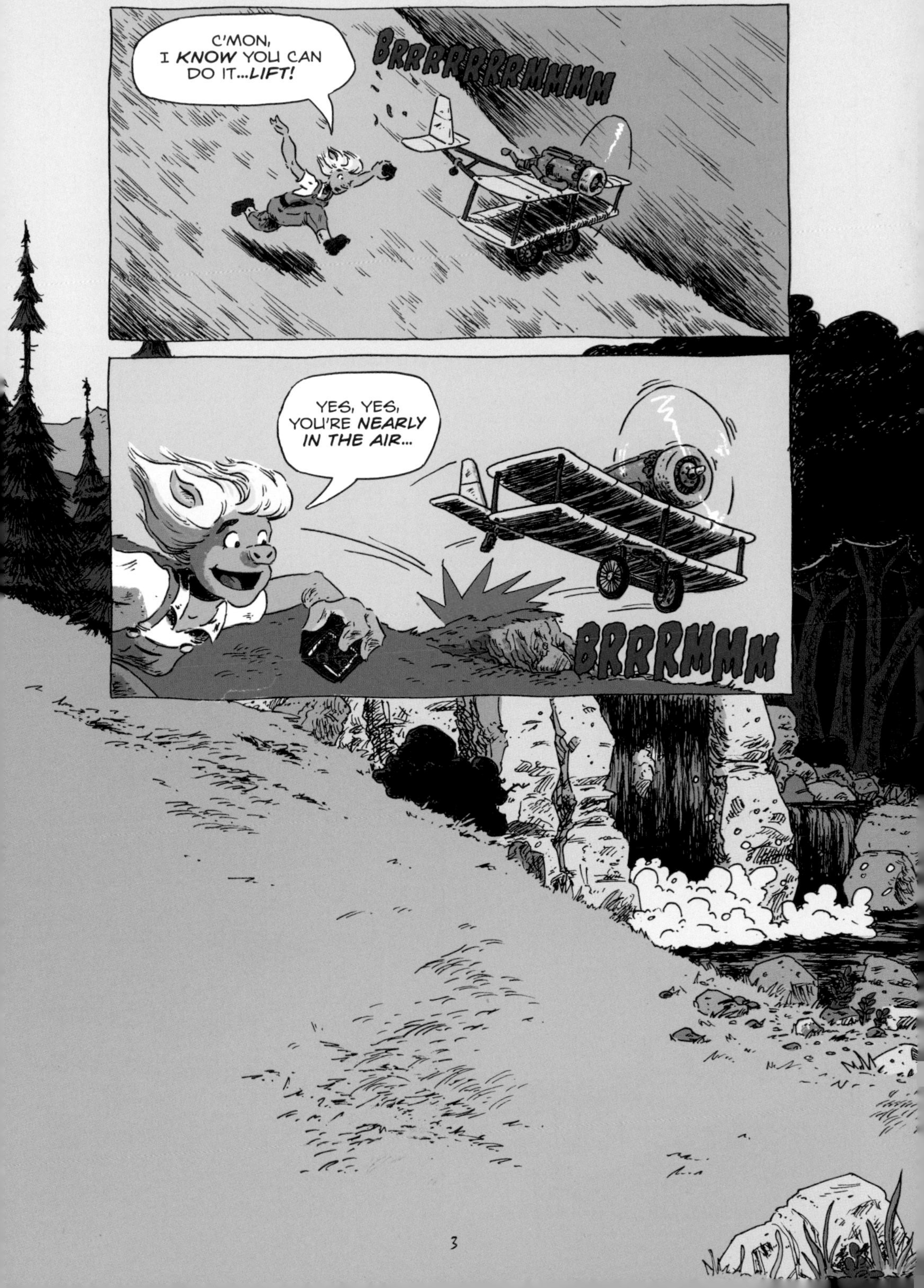
C'MON, I KNOW YOU CAN DO IT...LIFT!
BRRRRRRRRMMMMM
YES, YES, YOU'RE NEARLY IN THE AIR...
BRRRMMM

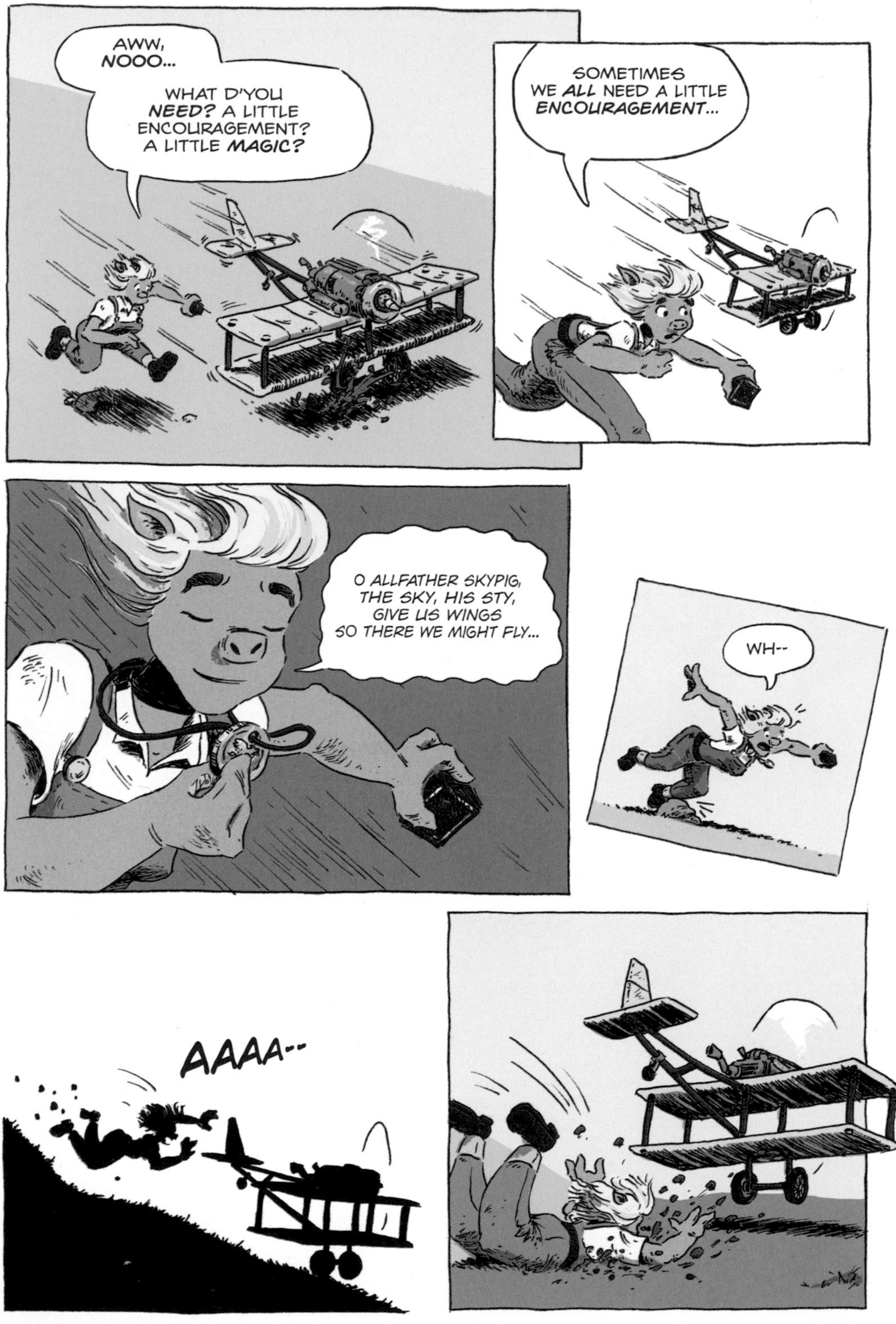
AWW, NOOO...
WHAT D'YOU NEED? A LITTLE ENCOURAGEMENT? A LITTLE MAGIC?
SOMETIMES WE ALL NEED A LITTLE ENCOURAGEMENT...
O ALLFATHER SKYPIG, THE SKY, HIS STY, GIVE US WINGS SO THERE WE MIGHT FLY...
WH--
AAAA--

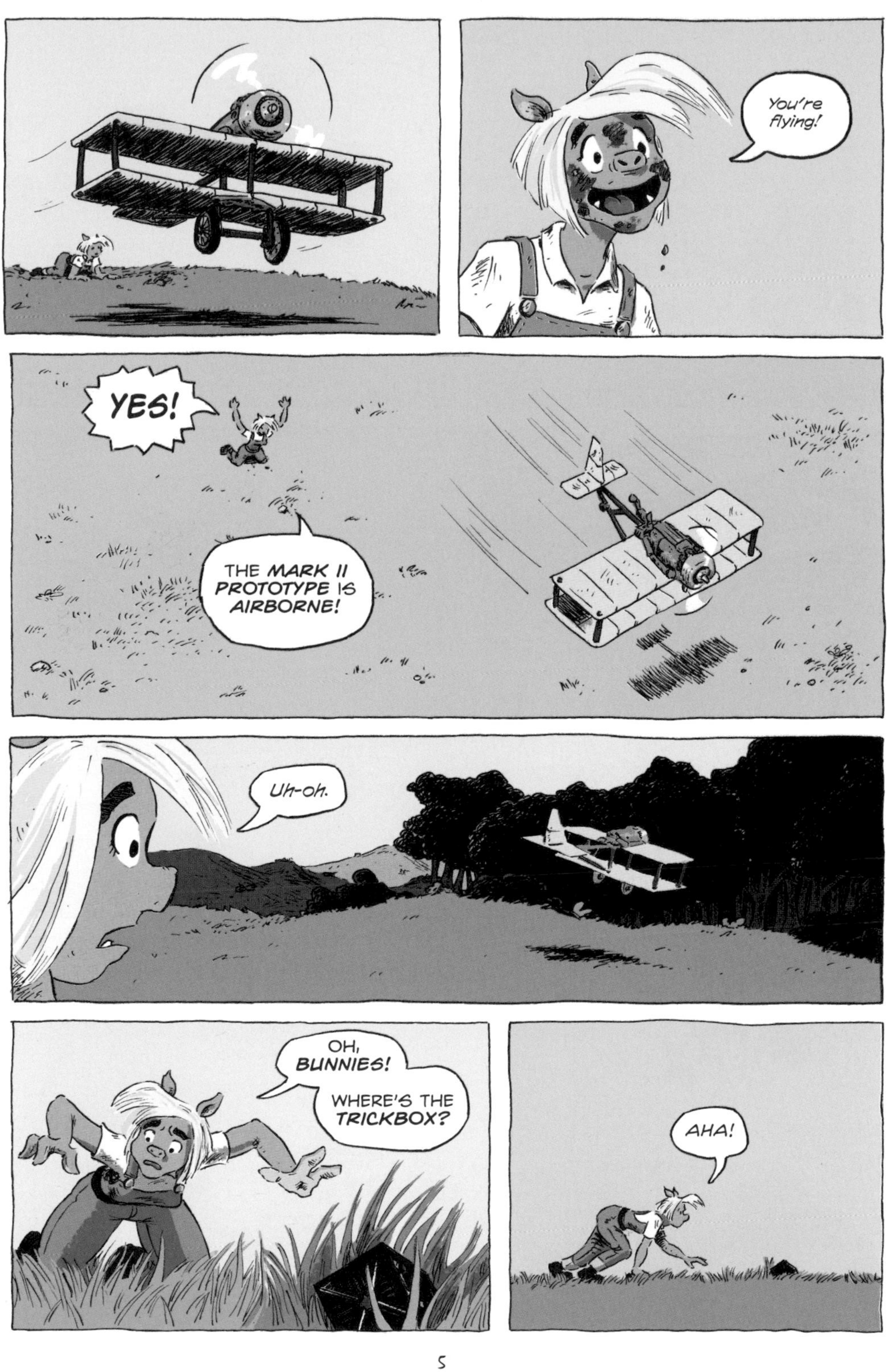
You're flying!
YES!
THE MARK II PROTOTYPE IS AIRBORNE!
Uh-oh.
OH, BUNNIES!
WHERE'S THE TRICKBOX?
AHA!

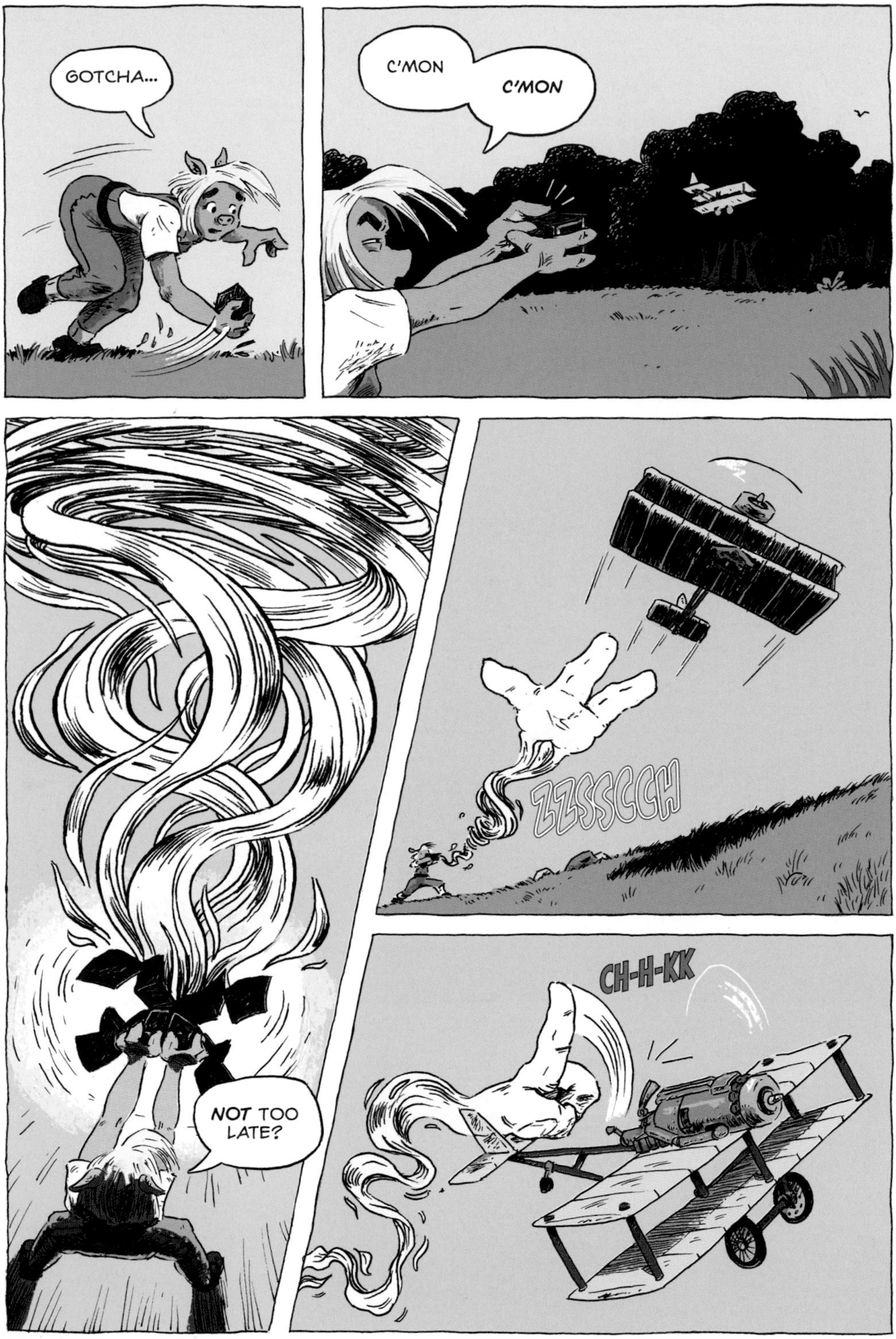
GOTCHA...
C'MON
C'MON
ZZSSCCH
NOT TOO LATE?
CH-H-KK

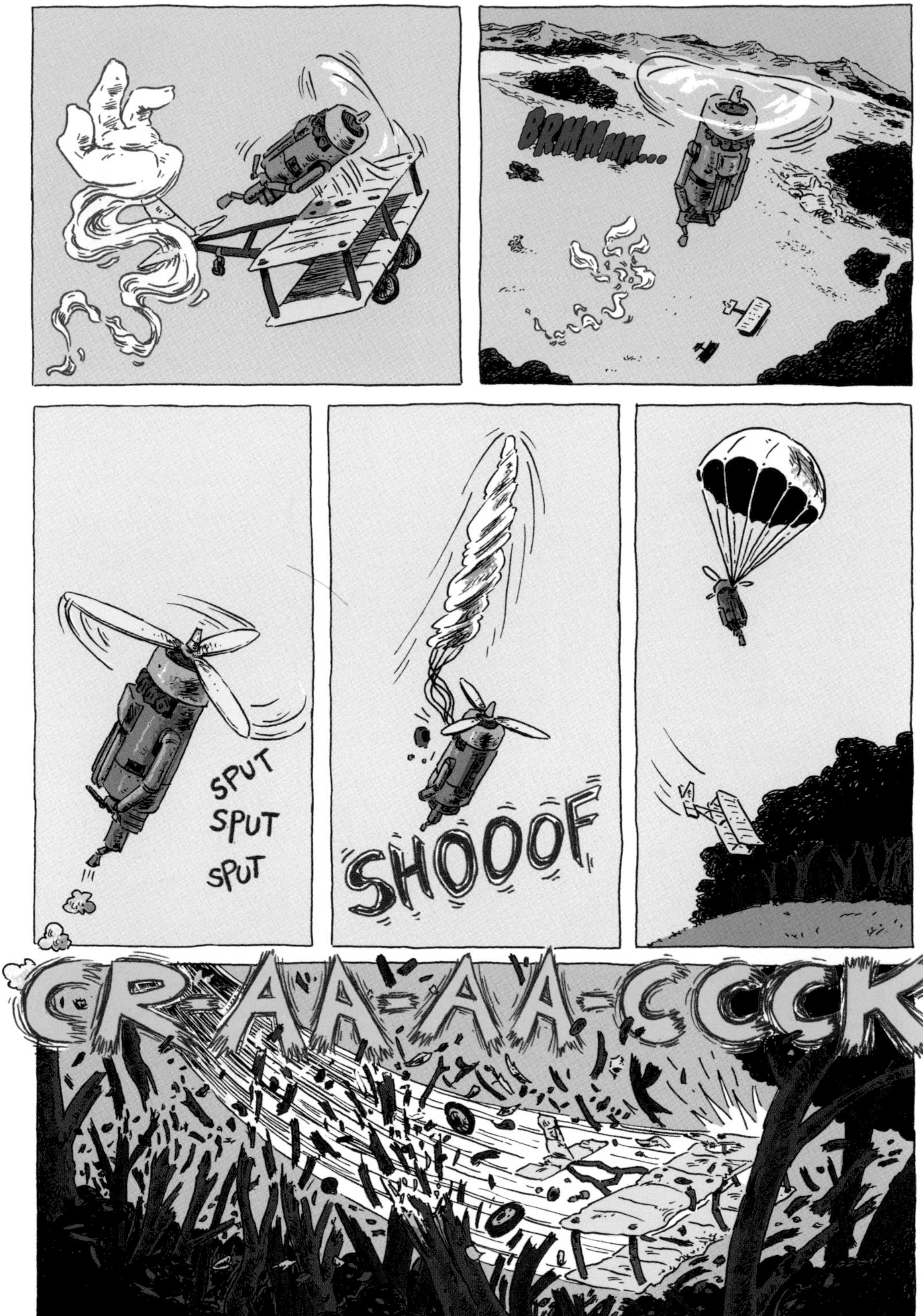
BRMMMM...
SPUT
SPUT
SPUT
SHOOOF
CR-A-A-A-CCCK

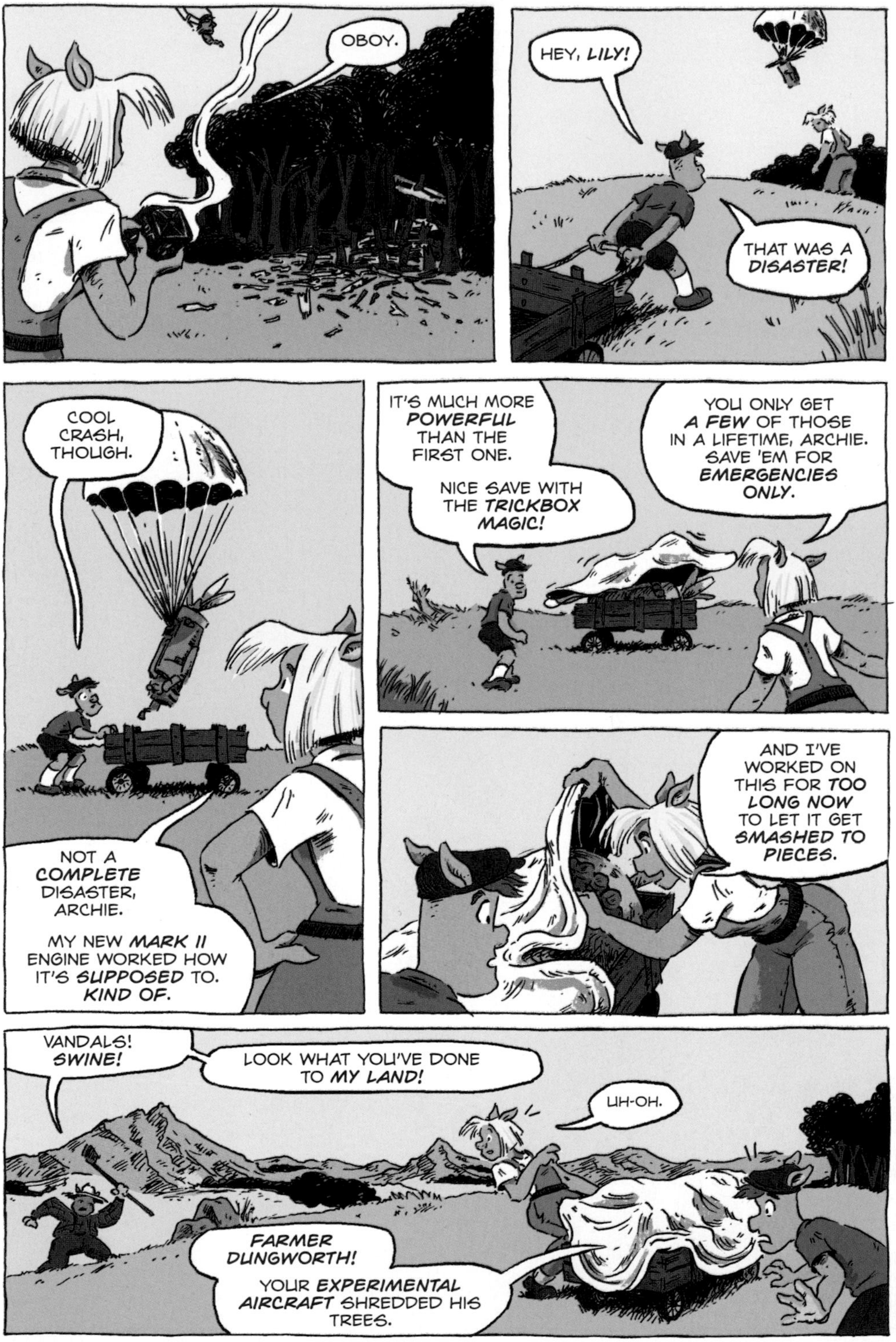
OBOY.
HEY, LILY!
THAT WAS A DISASTER!
COOL CRASH, THOUGH.
NOT A COMPLETE DISASTER, ARCHIE.
MY NEW MARK II ENGINE WORKED HOW IT'S SUPPOSED TO. KIND OF.
IT'S MUCH MORE POWERFUL THAN THE FIRST ONE.
NICE SAVE WITH THE TRICKBOX MAGIC!
YOU ONLY GET A FEW OF THOSE IN A LIFETIME, ARCHIE. SAVE 'EM FOR EMERGENCIES ONLY.
AND I'VE WORKED ON THIS FOR TOO LONG NOW TO LET IT GET SMASHED TO PIECES.
VANDALS! SWINE!
LOOK WHAT YOU'VE DONE TO MY LAND!
UH-OH.
FARMER DUNGWORTH!
YOUR EXPERIMENTAL AIRCRAFT SHREDDED HIS TREES.

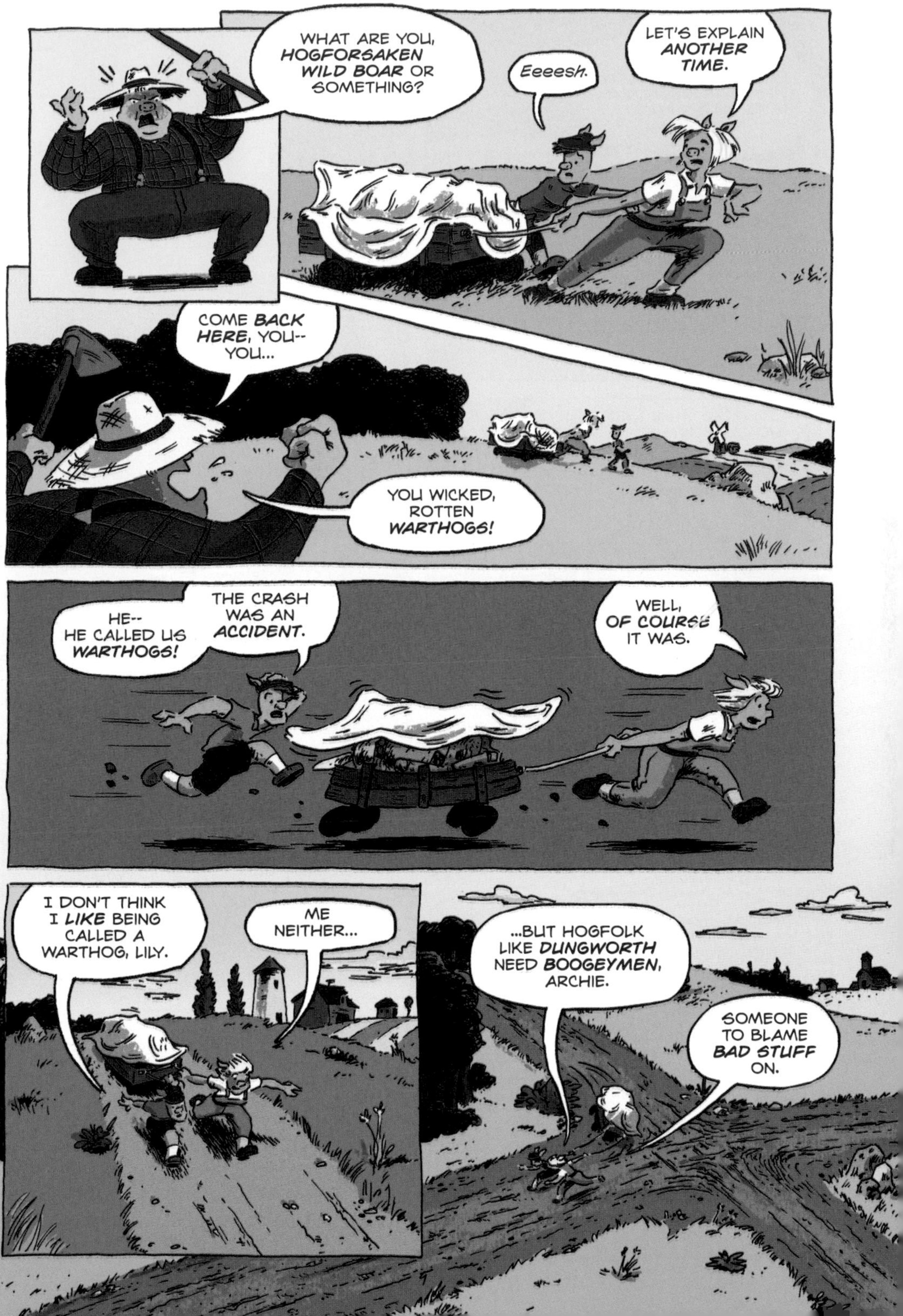
WHAT ARE YOU, HOGFORSAKEN WILD BOAR OR SOMETHING?
Eeeesh.
LET'S EXPLAIN ANOTHER TIME.
COME BACK HERE, YOU-- YOU...
YOU WICKED, ROTTEN WARTHOGS!
HE-- HE CALLED US WARTHOGS!
THE CRASH WAS AN ACCIDENT.
WELL, OF COURSE IT WAS.
I DON'T THINK I LIKE BEING CALLED A WARTHOG, LILY.
ME NEITHER...
...BUT HOGFOLK LIKE DUNGWORTH NEED BOOGEYMEN, ARCHIE.
SOMEONE TO BLAME BAD STUFF ON.

Whew

I'M SURE EVEN THE **WARTHOGS** HAVE THEIR OWN **MONSTERS** TO SCARE THEIR KIDS WITH.

HAS ANYONE EVER EVEN **SEEN A** WARTHOG?

DUNNO.

LISTEN, I DON'T WANT TO GET YOU INTO ANY MORE **TROUBLE** TODAY. GO ON, GO HOME.

AW, LILY...

I CAN GET THE PROPELLER HOME FROM HERE. THANKS FOR ALL YOUR **HELP** TODAY.

I KNOW WHAT YOU'RE **DOING**, LILY...

YOU RECKON DUNGWORTH WILL THINK THAT THE **WRECKAGE** OF YOUR AIRCRAFT IS ONE OF **YOUR FATHER'S** FLYING MACHINES...

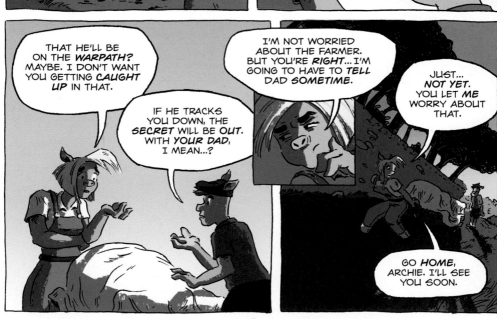

THAT HE'LL BE ON THE **WARPATH**? MAYBE. I DON'T WANT YOU GETTING **CAUGHT UP** IN THAT.

IF HE TRACKS YOU DOWN, THE **SECRET** WILL BE **OUT**. WITH **YOUR DAD**, I MEAN...?

I'M NOT WORRIED ABOUT THE FARMER. BUT YOU'RE **RIGHT**... I'M GOING TO HAVE TO **TELL** DAD **SOMETIME**.

JUST... **NOT YET**. YOU LET **ME** WORRY ABOUT THAT.

GO **HOME**, ARCHIE. I'LL SEE YOU SOON.

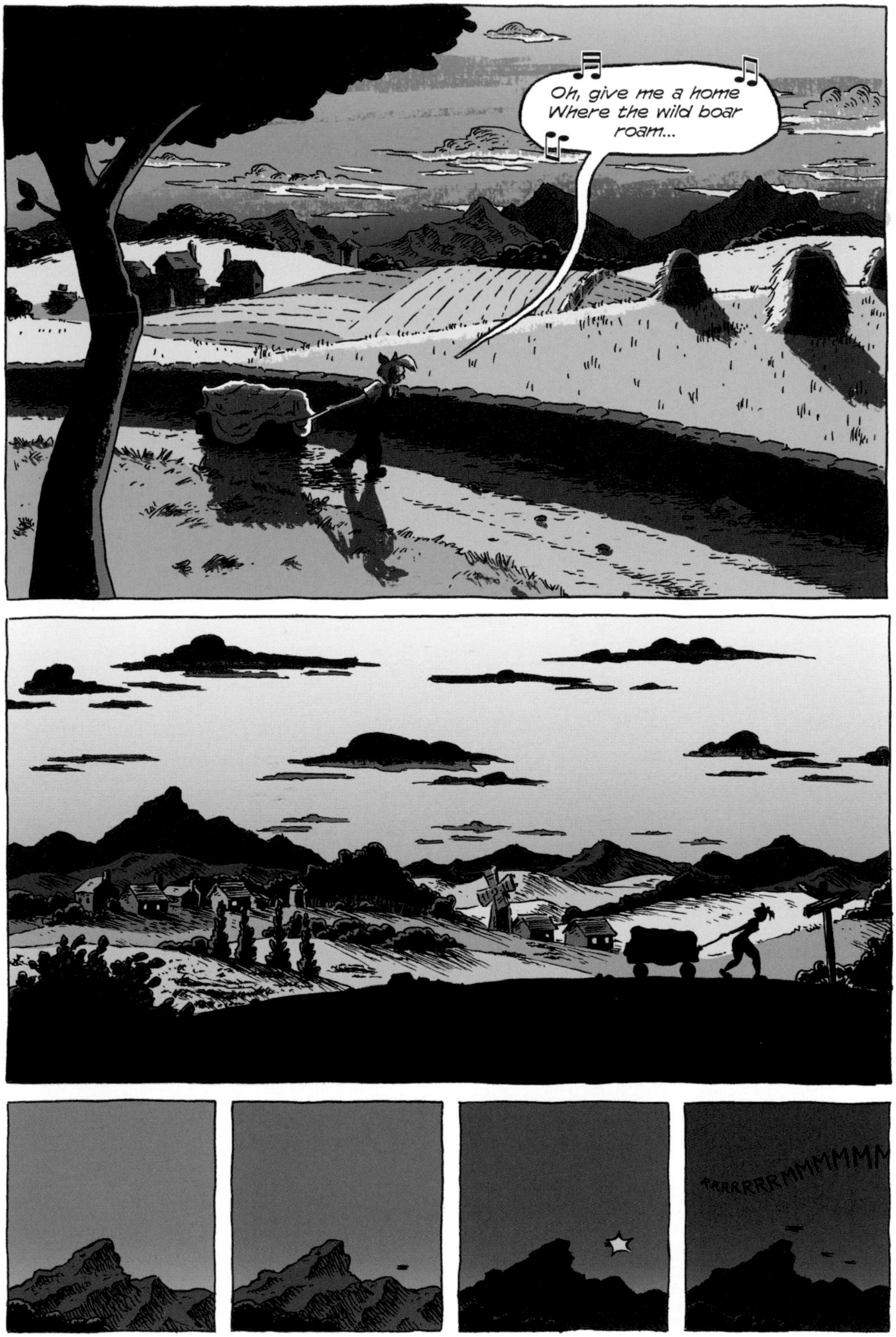
Oh, give me a home
Where the wild boar
roam...
RRRRRRRMMMMMM

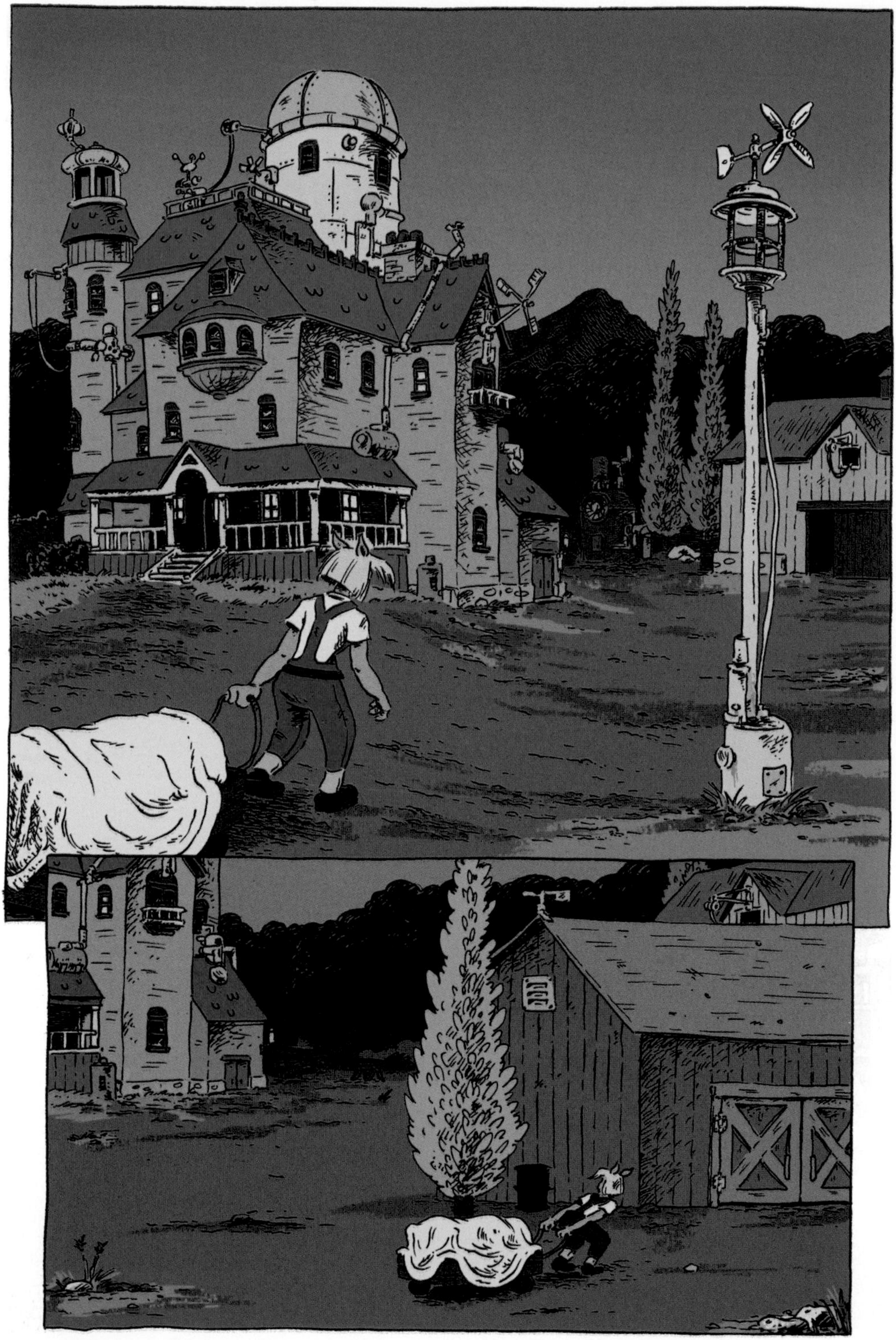

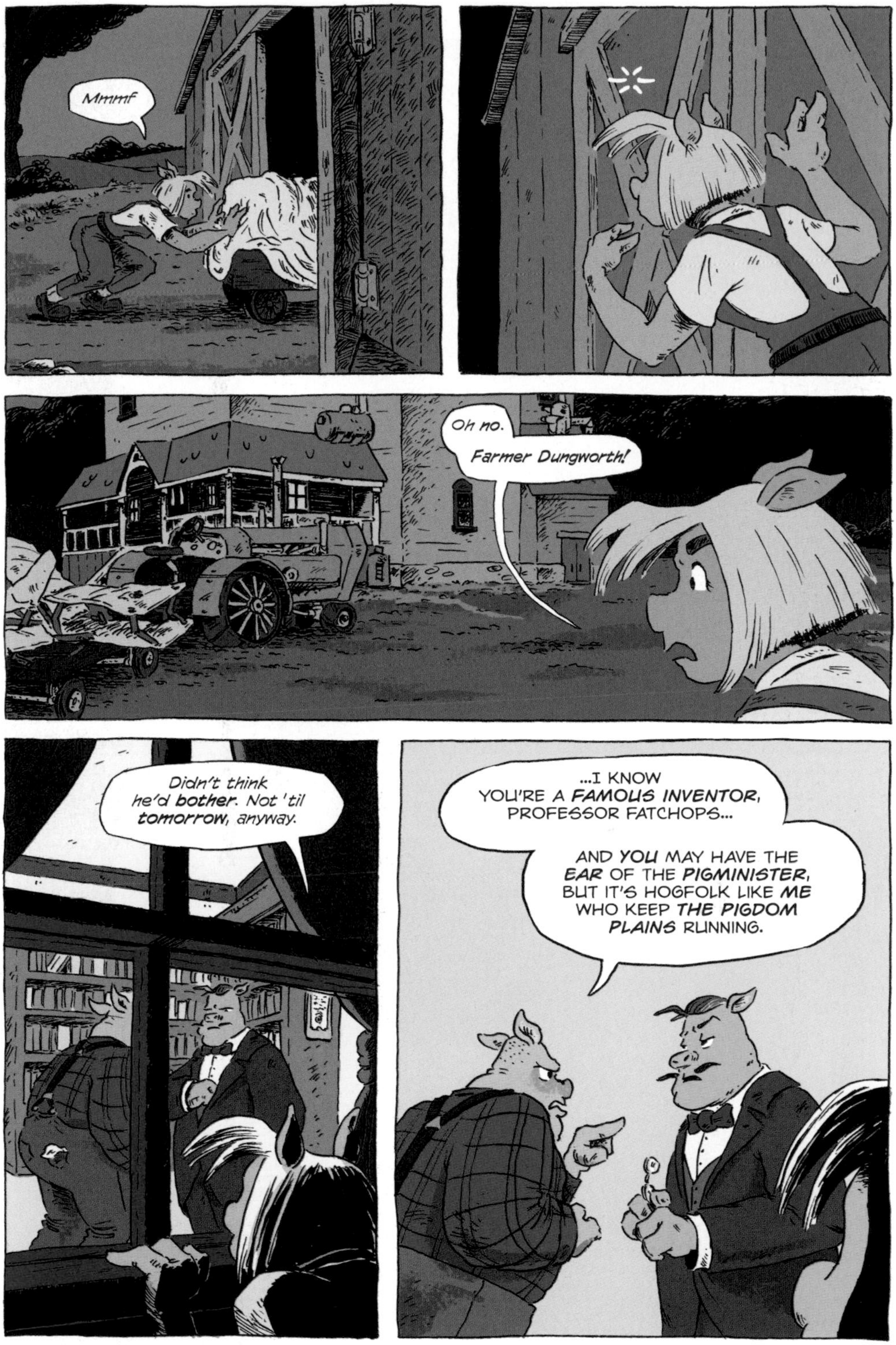
Mmmf
Oh no.
Farmer Dungworth!
Didn't think he'd **bother**. Not 'til **tomorrow**, anyway.
...I KNOW YOU'RE A ***FAMOUS INVENTOR***, PROFESSOR FATCHOPS...
AND ***YOU*** MAY HAVE THE ***EAR*** OF THE ***PIGMINISTER***, BUT IT'S HOGFOLK LIKE ***ME*** WHO KEEP ***THE PIGDOM PLAINS*** RUNNING.

14

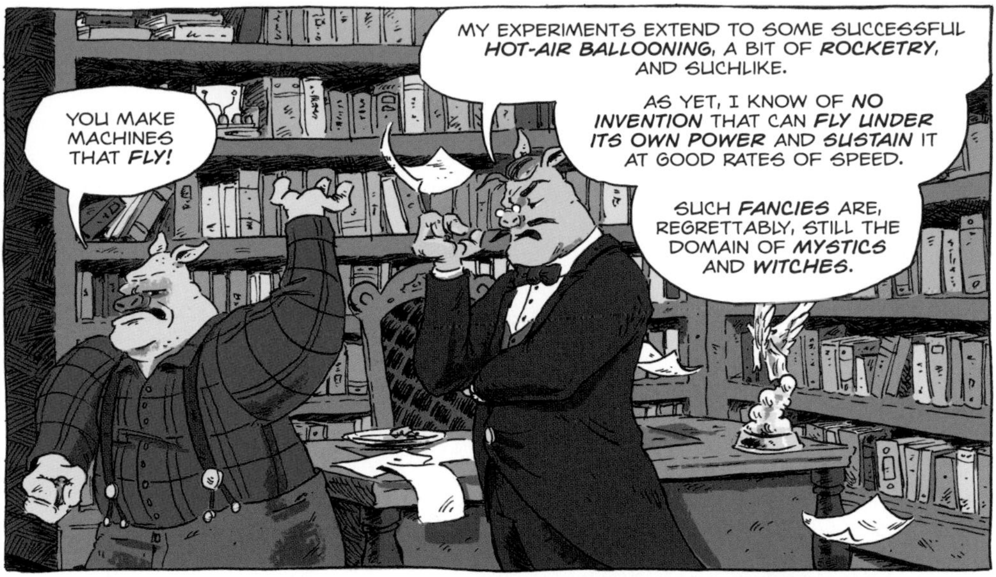
YOU MAKE MACHINES THAT *FLY!*
MY EXPERIMENTS EXTEND TO SOME SUCCESSFUL *HOT-AIR BALLOONING*, A BIT OF *ROCKETRY*, AND SUCHLIKE.
AS YET, I KNOW OF *NO INVENTION* THAT CAN *FLY UNDER ITS OWN POWER* AND *SUSTAIN* IT AT GOOD RATES OF SPEED.
SUCH *FANCIES* ARE, REGRETTABLY, STILL THE DOMAIN OF *MYSTICS* AND *WITCHES*.

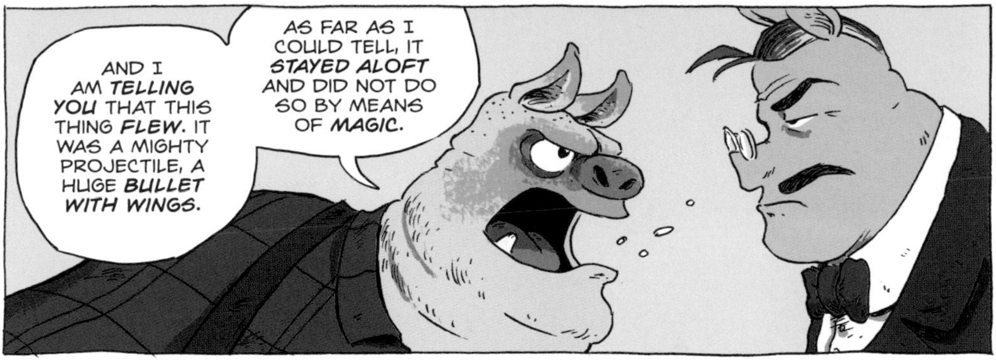
AND I AM *TELLING YOU* THAT THIS THING *FLEW*. IT WAS A MIGHTY PROJECTILE, A HUGE *BULLET WITH WINGS*.
AS FAR AS I COULD TELL, IT *STAYED ALOFT* AND DID NOT DO SO BY MEANS OF *MAGIC*.

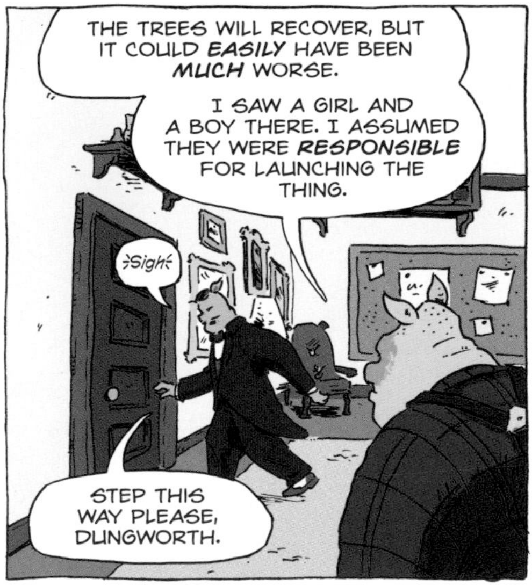
THE TREES WILL RECOVER, BUT IT COULD *EASILY* HAVE BEEN *MUCH* WORSE.
I SAW A GIRL AND A BOY THERE. I ASSUMED THEY WERE *RESPONSIBLE* FOR LAUNCHING THE THING.
Sigh
STEP THIS WAY PLEASE, DUNGWORTH.

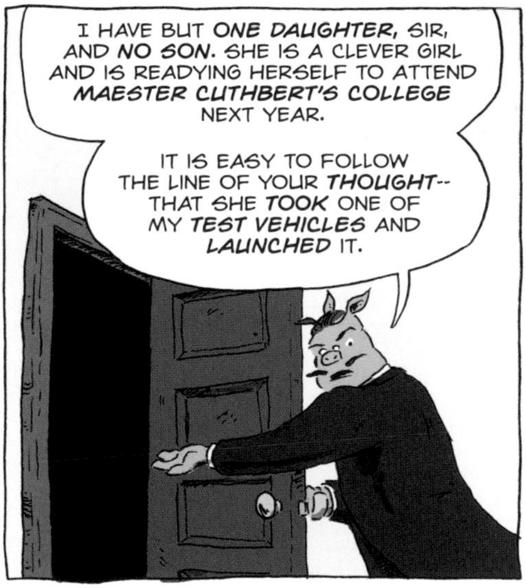
I HAVE BUT *ONE DAUGHTER*, SIR, AND *NO SON*. SHE IS A CLEVER GIRL AND IS READYING HERSELF TO ATTEND *MAESTER CUTHBERT'S COLLEGE* NEXT YEAR.
IT IS EASY TO FOLLOW THE LINE OF YOUR *THOUGHT*-- THAT SHE *TOOK* ONE OF MY *TEST VEHICLES* AND *LAUNCHED* IT.

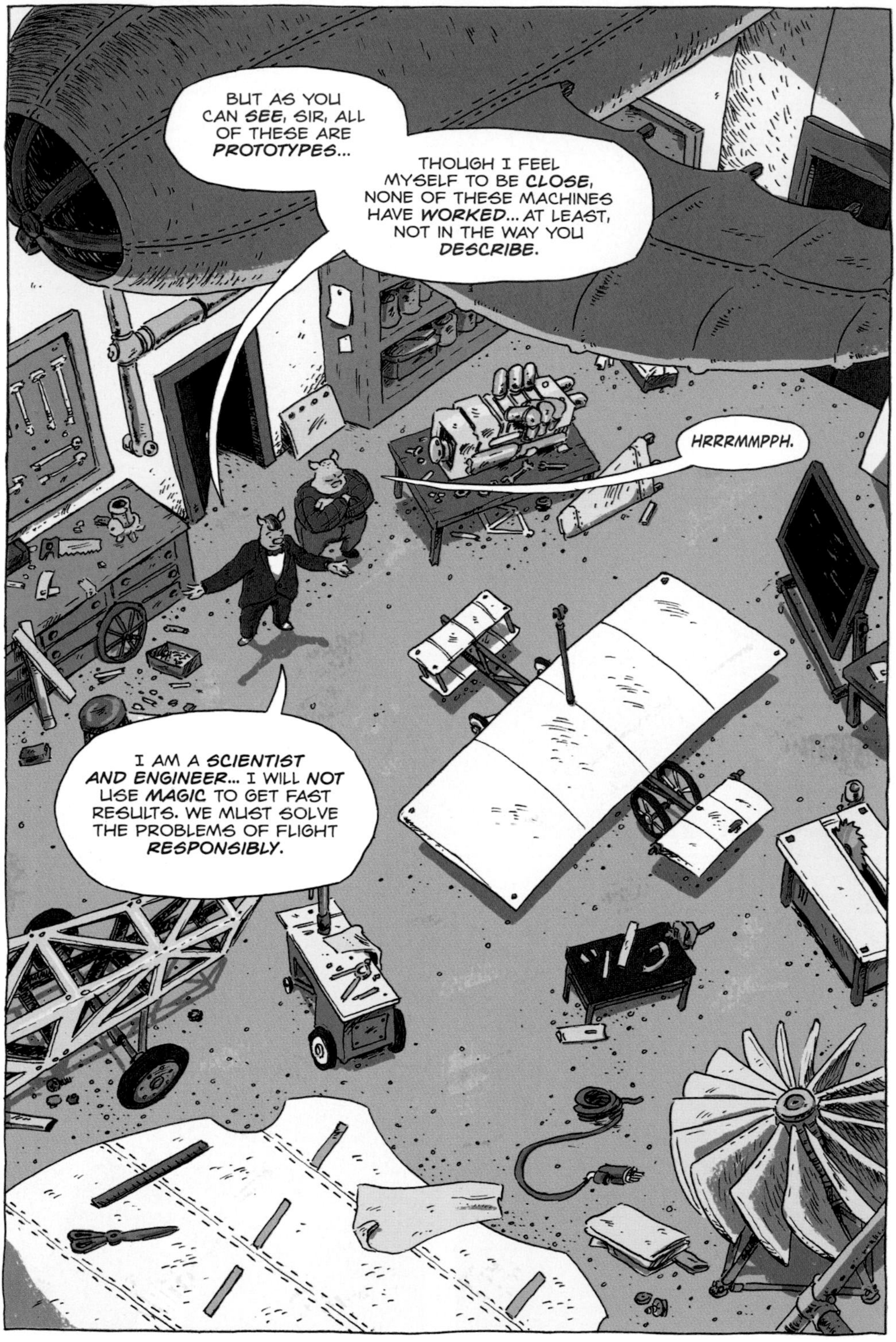
BUT AS YOU CAN SEE, SIR, ALL OF THESE ARE PROTOTYPES...
THOUGH I FEEL MYSELF TO BE CLOSE, NONE OF THESE MACHINES HAVE WORKED... AT LEAST, NOT IN THE WAY YOU DESCRIBE.
HRRRMMPPH.
I AM A SCIENTIST AND ENGINEER... I WILL NOT USE MAGIC TO GET FAST RESULTS. WE MUST SOLVE THE PROBLEMS OF FLIGHT RESPONSIBLY.

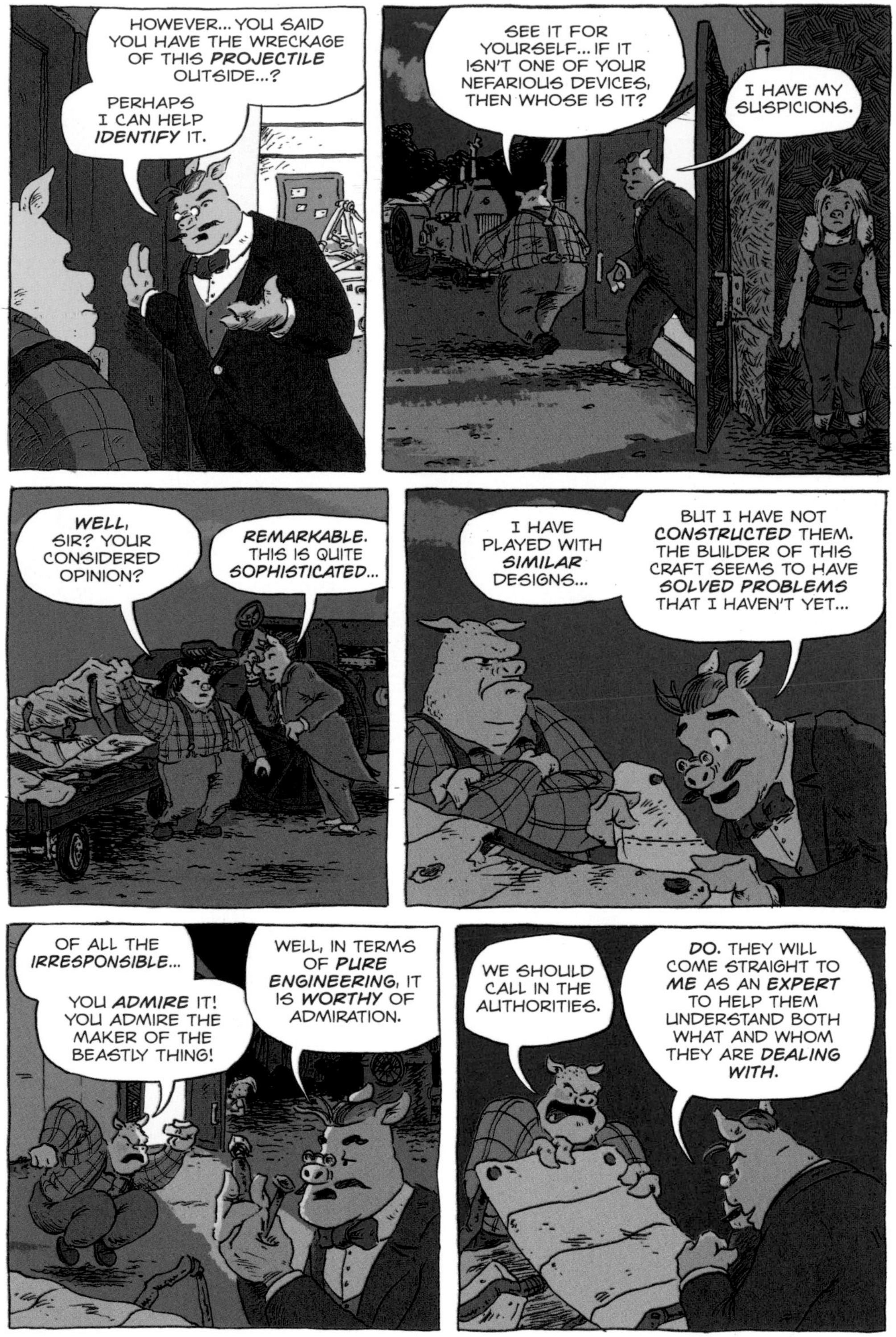
HOWEVER... YOU SAID YOU HAVE THE WRECKAGE OF THIS PROJECTILE OUTSIDE...?
PERHAPS I CAN HELP IDENTIFY IT.
SEE IT FOR YOURSELF... IF IT ISN'T ONE OF YOUR NEFARIOUS DEVICES, THEN WHOSE IS IT?
I HAVE MY SUSPICIONS.
WELL, SIR? YOUR CONSIDERED OPINION?
REMARKABLE. THIS IS QUITE SOPHISTICATED...
I HAVE PLAYED WITH SIMILAR DESIGNS...
BUT I HAVE NOT CONSTRUCTED THEM. THE BUILDER OF THIS CRAFT SEEMS TO HAVE SOLVED PROBLEMS THAT I HAVEN'T YET...
OF ALL THE IRRESPONSIBLE...
YOU ADMIRE IT! YOU ADMIRE THE MAKER OF THE BEASTLY THING!
WELL, IN TERMS OF PURE ENGINEERING, IT IS WORTHY OF ADMIRATION.
WE SHOULD CALL IN THE AUTHORITIES.
DO. THEY WILL COME STRAIGHT TO ME AS AN EXPERT TO HELP THEM UNDERSTAND BOTH WHAT AND WHOM THEY ARE DEALING WITH.

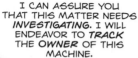

I CAN ASSURE YOU THAT THIS MATTER NEEDS *INVESTIGATING*. I WILL ENDEAVOR TO *TRACK* THE *OWNER* OF THIS MACHINE.

IN THE INTERESTS OF *SINCERE NEIGHBORLY CIVILITY*, ISN'T THAT AN *ENTIRELY REASONABLE* AND *EQUITABLE OFFER* TO MAKE, FARMER DUNGWORTH...?

I HOPE IT WILL *SATISFY* YOU. I WILL REPORT MY FINDINGS TO YOU AND ANY *RELEVANT AUTHORITIES*.

HRRRMPH

PROFESSOR FATCHOPS, I'M A *PRACTICAL PIG*... A *HUMBLE FARMER*.

ALTHOUGH I'VE GROWN *RICH* FROM THE *FAT OF THE LAND*, I WORK *HARD* FOR A LIVING.

I WILL ADMIT THAT I AM NOT A *GREATLY LEARNED HOG*, SO FAR BE IT FROM *ME* TO THINK THAT *I* KNOW HOW HOGKIND SHOULD LIVE.

BUT I KNOW *THIS* MUCH...

...IF PIGS WERE SUPPOSED TO FLY...

RRRMM

...WE'D ALREADY HAVE WINGS.

PHUT PHUT PHUT

OWOOOOH OWOOOOHOWOOOOH

PHUT PHUT

WOOOOHOWOOOOHO

WHAT IN SEVEN SHADES OF SWILL IS THAT?

THAT IS THE WARNING SIREN.

OHOWOOOO

WARNING SIREN? FOR WHAT?

FOR A WARTHOG ATTACK.

WARTHOGS? IT CAN'T BE. IT'S BEEN DECADES...

LISTEN-- THAT SOUND, OVER THE SIREN...

COMING CLOSER...

19

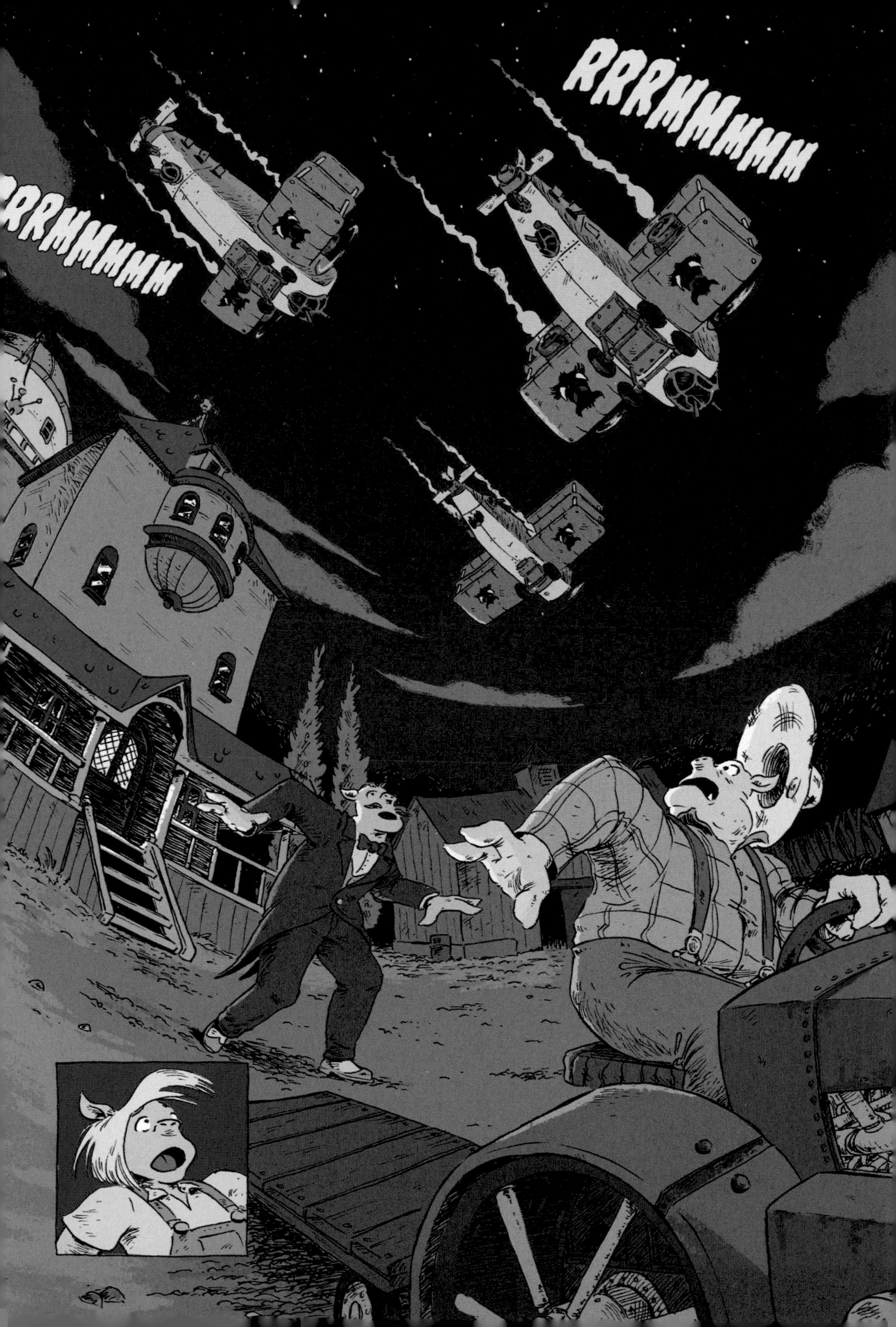
RRRMMMMMM
RRRMMMMMM

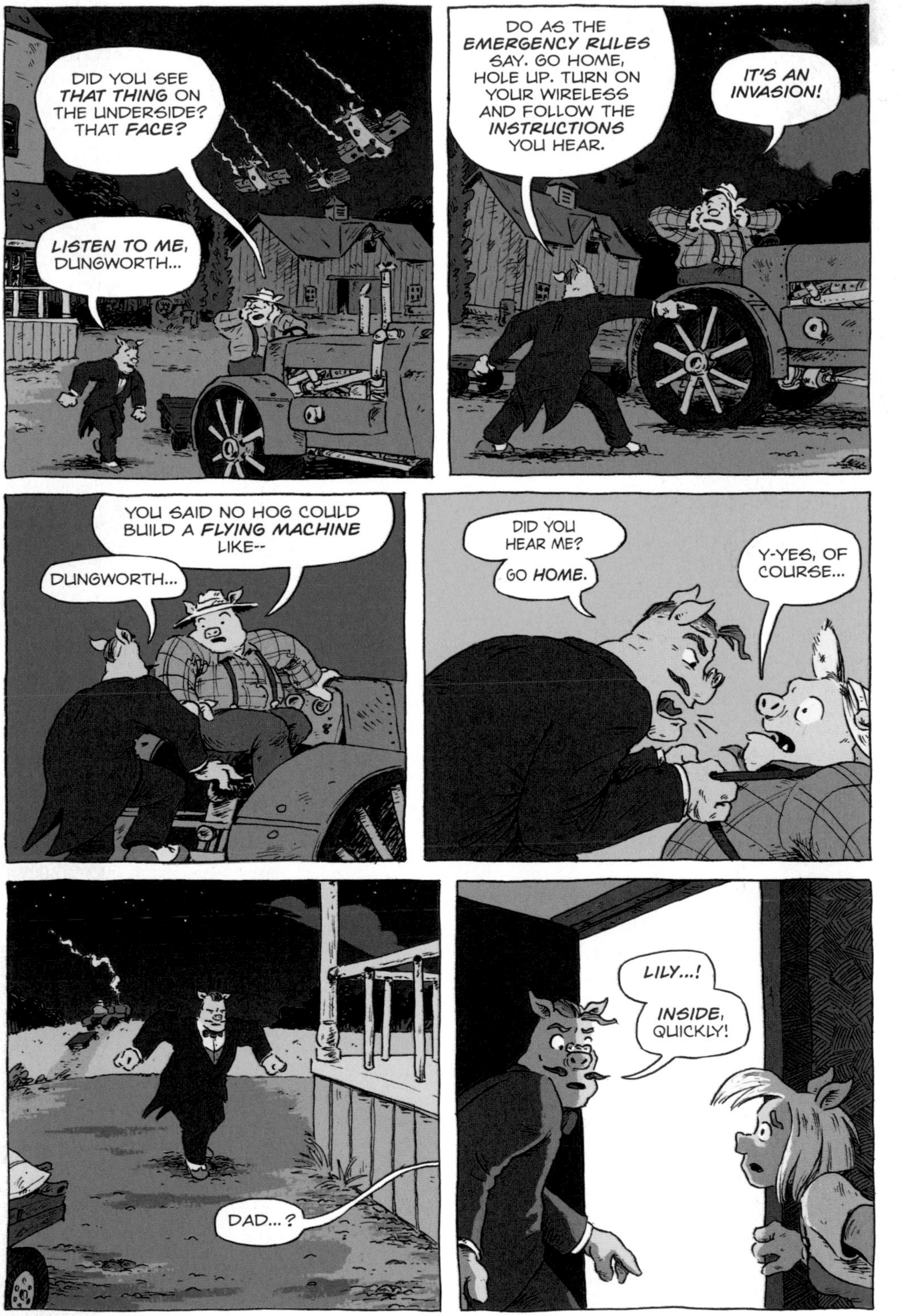
DID YOU SEE THAT THING ON THE UNDERSIDE? THAT FACE?
LISTEN TO ME, DUNGWORTH...
DO AS THE EMERGENCY RULES SAY. GO HOME, HOLE UP. TURN ON YOUR WIRELESS AND FOLLOW THE INSTRUCTIONS YOU HEAR.
IT'S AN INVASION!
YOU SAID NO HOG COULD BUILD A FLYING MACHINE LIKE--
DUNGWORTH...
DID YOU HEAR ME?
GO HOME.
Y-YES, OF COURSE...
DAD...?
LILY...!
INSIDE, QUICKLY!

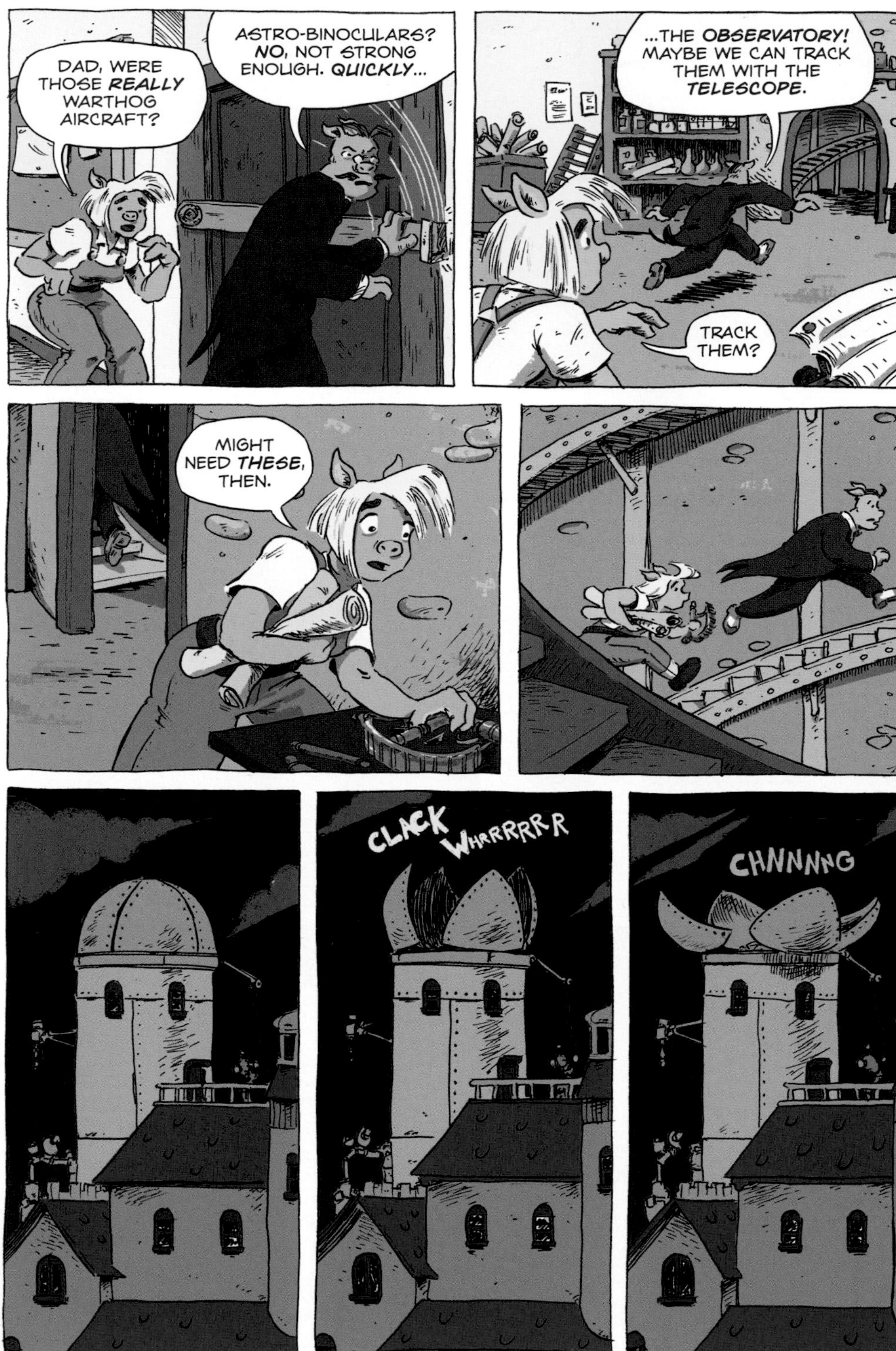

DAD, WERE THOSE *REALLY* WARTHOG AIRCRAFT?
ASTRO-BINOCULARS? *NO*, NOT STRONG ENOUGH. *QUICKLY*...
...THE *OBSERVATORY!* MAYBE WE CAN TRACK THEM WITH THE *TELESCOPE*.
TRACK THEM?
MIGHT NEED *THESE*, THEN.
CLACK
WHRRRRRR
CHNNNNG

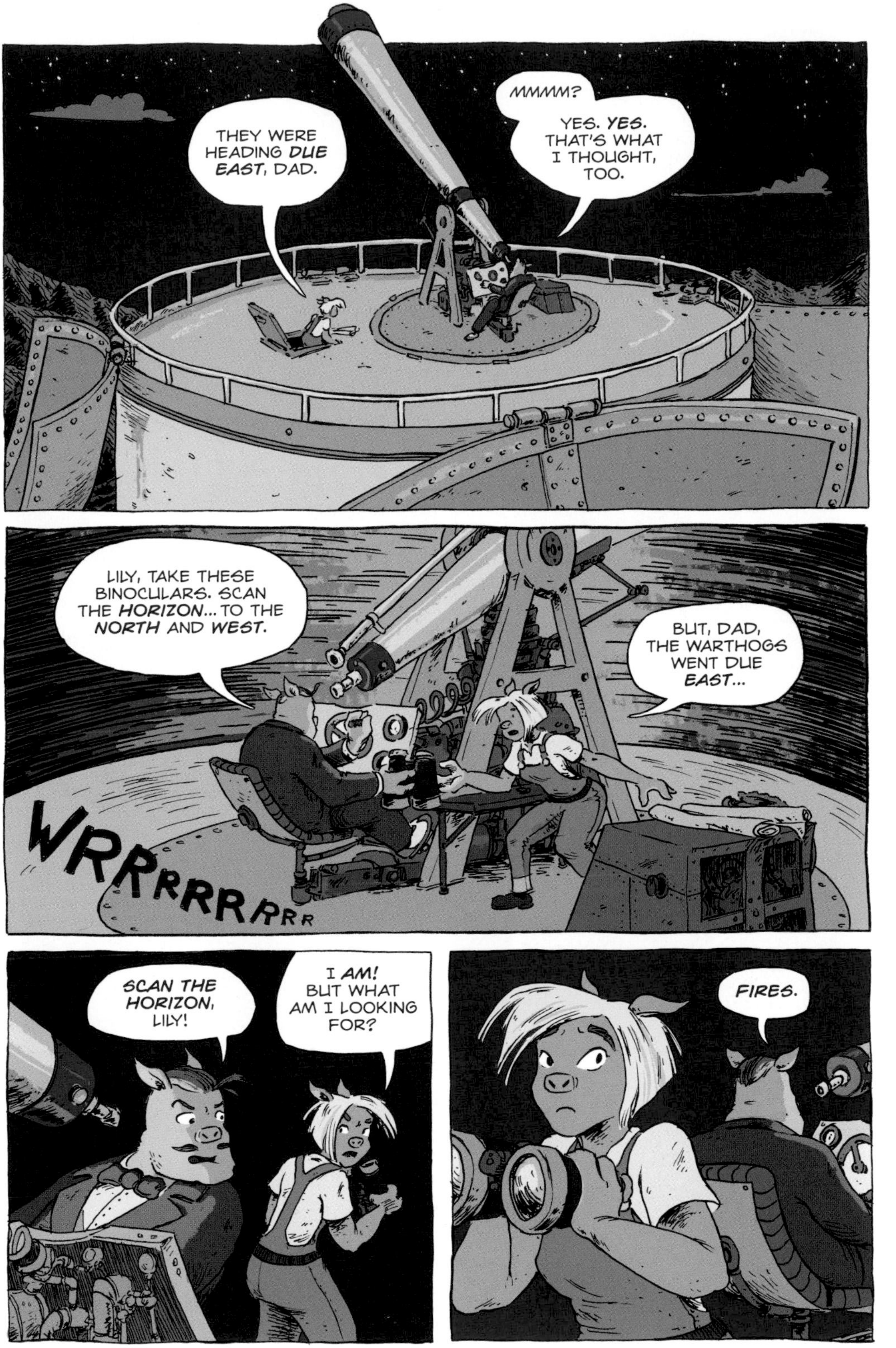
THEY WERE HEADING DUE EAST, DAD.
MMMM?
YES. YES. THAT'S WHAT I THOUGHT, TOO.
LILY, TAKE THESE BINOCULARS. SCAN THE HORIZON... TO THE NORTH AND WEST.
BUT, DAD, THE WARTHOGS WENT DUE EAST...
WRRRRRRRRR
SCAN THE HORIZON, LILY!
I AM! BUT WHAT AM I LOOKING FOR?
FIRES.

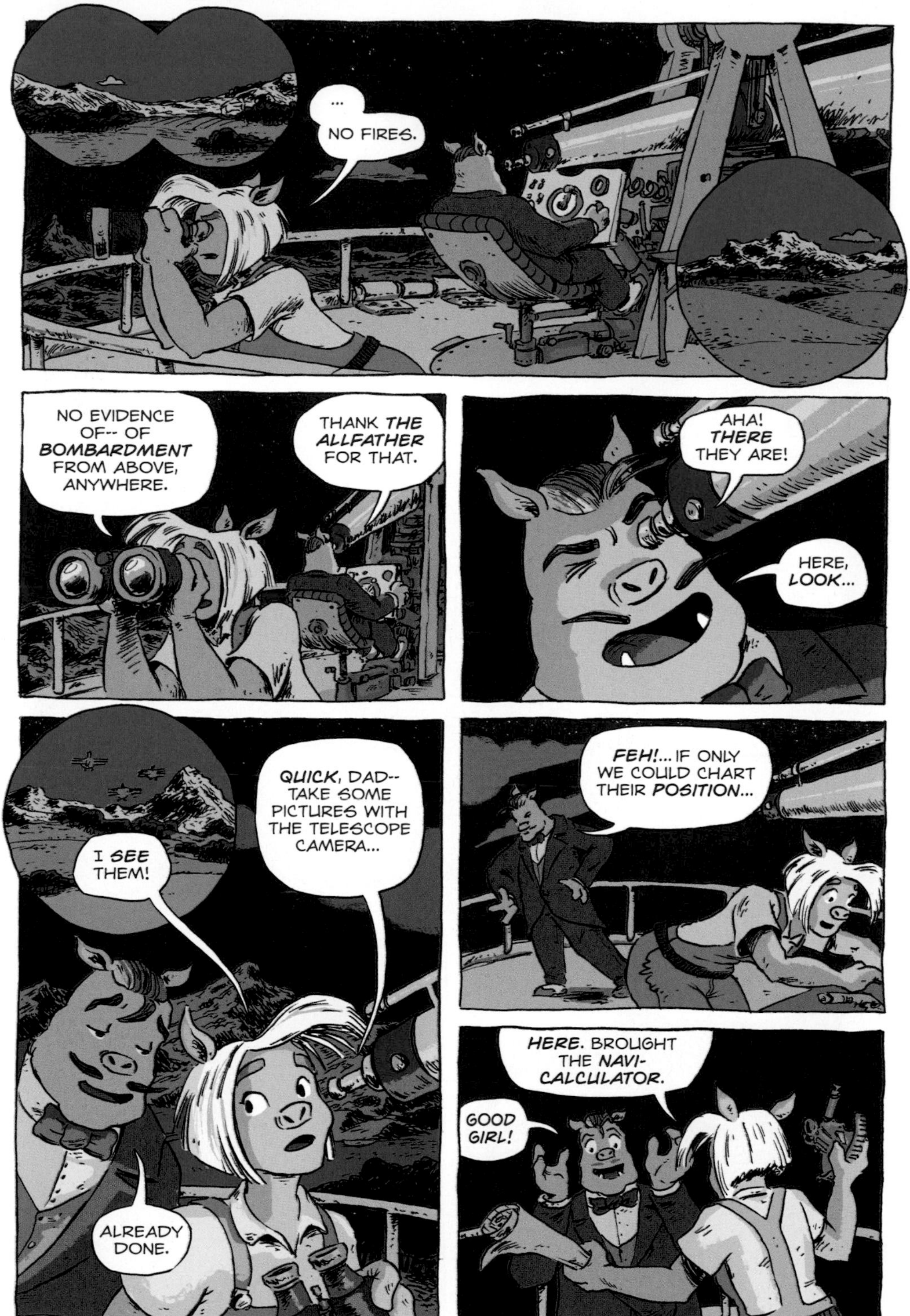

...
NO FIRES.
NO EVIDENCE OF-- OF BOMBARDMENT FROM ABOVE, ANYWHERE.
THANK THE ALLFATHER FOR THAT.
AHA! THERE THEY ARE!
HERE, LOOK...
I SEE THEM!
QUICK, DAD-- TAKE SOME PICTURES WITH THE TELESCOPE CAMERA...
ALREADY DONE.
FEH!... IF ONLY WE COULD CHART THEIR POSITION...
HERE. BROUGHT THE NAVI-CALCULATOR.
GOOD GIRL!

THEY'RE OVER *OINKSBURY*, HEADING FOR OLD *HAMTON PALACE*.

THEY WERE ALREADY COMING BACK AROUND WHEN THEY FLEW OVER US.

BY *TROTTSTY'S BEARD!* YOU'RE *RIGHT*.

THEY'RE ON A *CIRCULAR COURSE...*

INDEED!

THEY'RE HEADING BACK TO WHEREVER THEY CAME FROM... OVER THE *MOUNTAINS*, IN THE *WILDBOAR WILDERNESS...*

THAT WAS A *SCOUTING RUN*.

TO CHECK OUT THE *PIGDOM*... OUR *RESOURCES*, OUR *DEFENSES...*

AND PROBABLY TO SEE HOW GOOD THEIR AIRCRAFTS' *RANGE* IS...

I THINK THEY WANTED TO ANNOUNCE THEIR PRESENCE, TO *SCARE* US... NOT *SPY* ON US.

IT *WORKED*. DID YOU SEE DUNGWORTH?

BUT THREE AIRCRAFT AREN'T EXACTLY AN *INVASION FORCE*. THEY COULD JUST BE *PIRATES*.

PERHAPS.

WHATEVER THEY WERE UP TO, WE'RE *NOT* READY.

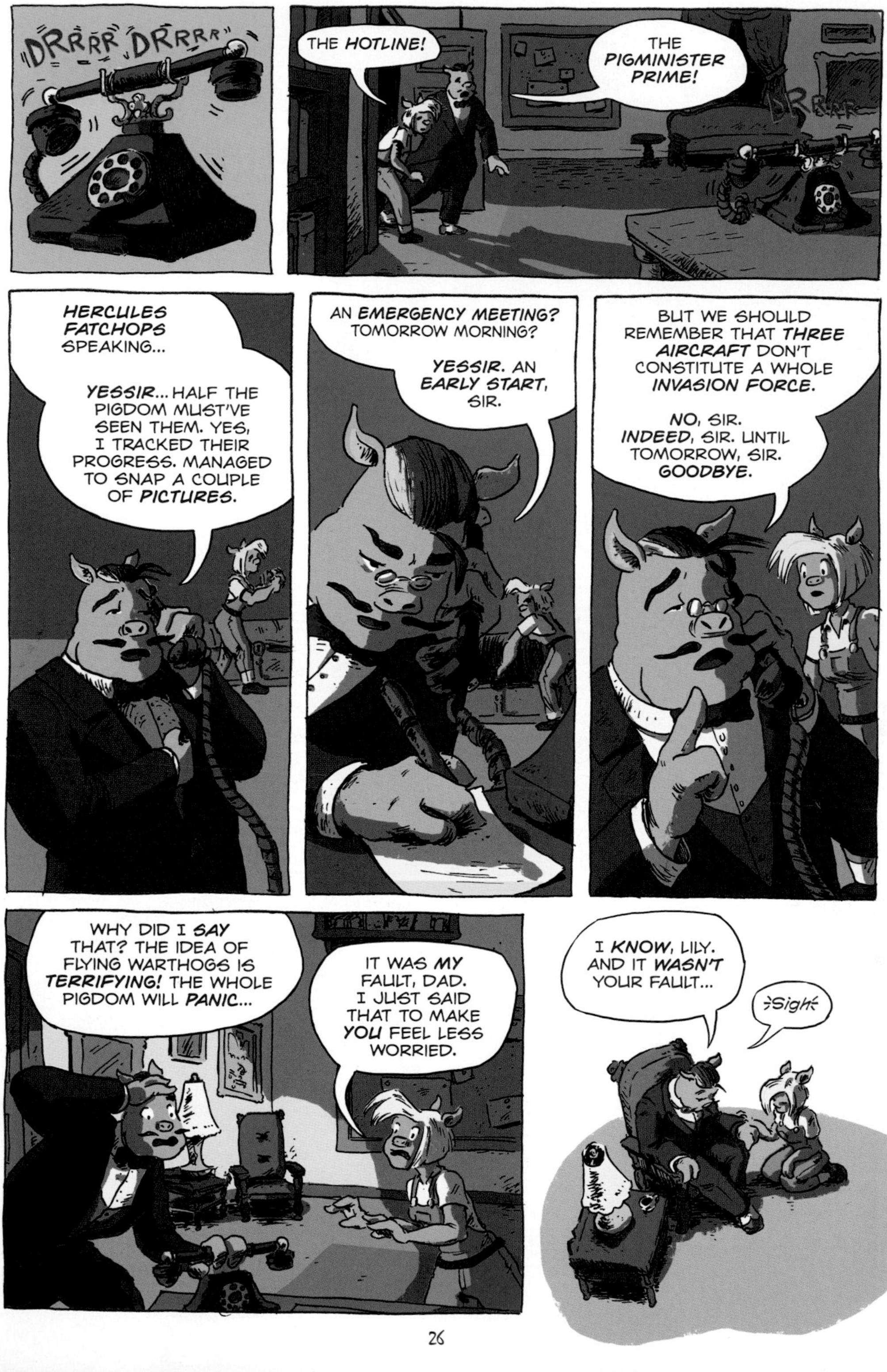
DRRRR DRRRR
THE HOTLINE!
THE PIGMINISTER PRIME!
HERCULES FATCHOPS SPEAKING...
YESSIR... HALF THE PIGDOM MUST'VE SEEN THEM. YES, I TRACKED THEIR PROGRESS. MANAGED TO SNAP A COUPLE OF PICTURES.
AN EMERGENCY MEETING? TOMORROW MORNING?
YESSIR. AN EARLY START, SIR.
BUT WE SHOULD REMEMBER THAT THREE AIRCRAFT DON'T CONSTITUTE A WHOLE INVASION FORCE.
NO, SIR. INDEED, SIR. UNTIL TOMORROW, SIR. GOODBYE.
WHY DID I SAY THAT? THE IDEA OF FLYING WARTHOGS IS TERRIFYING! THE WHOLE PIGDOM WILL PANIC...
IT WAS MY FAULT, DAD. I JUST SAID THAT TO MAKE YOU FEEL LESS WORRIED.
I KNOW, LILY. AND IT WASN'T YOUR FAULT...
Sigh

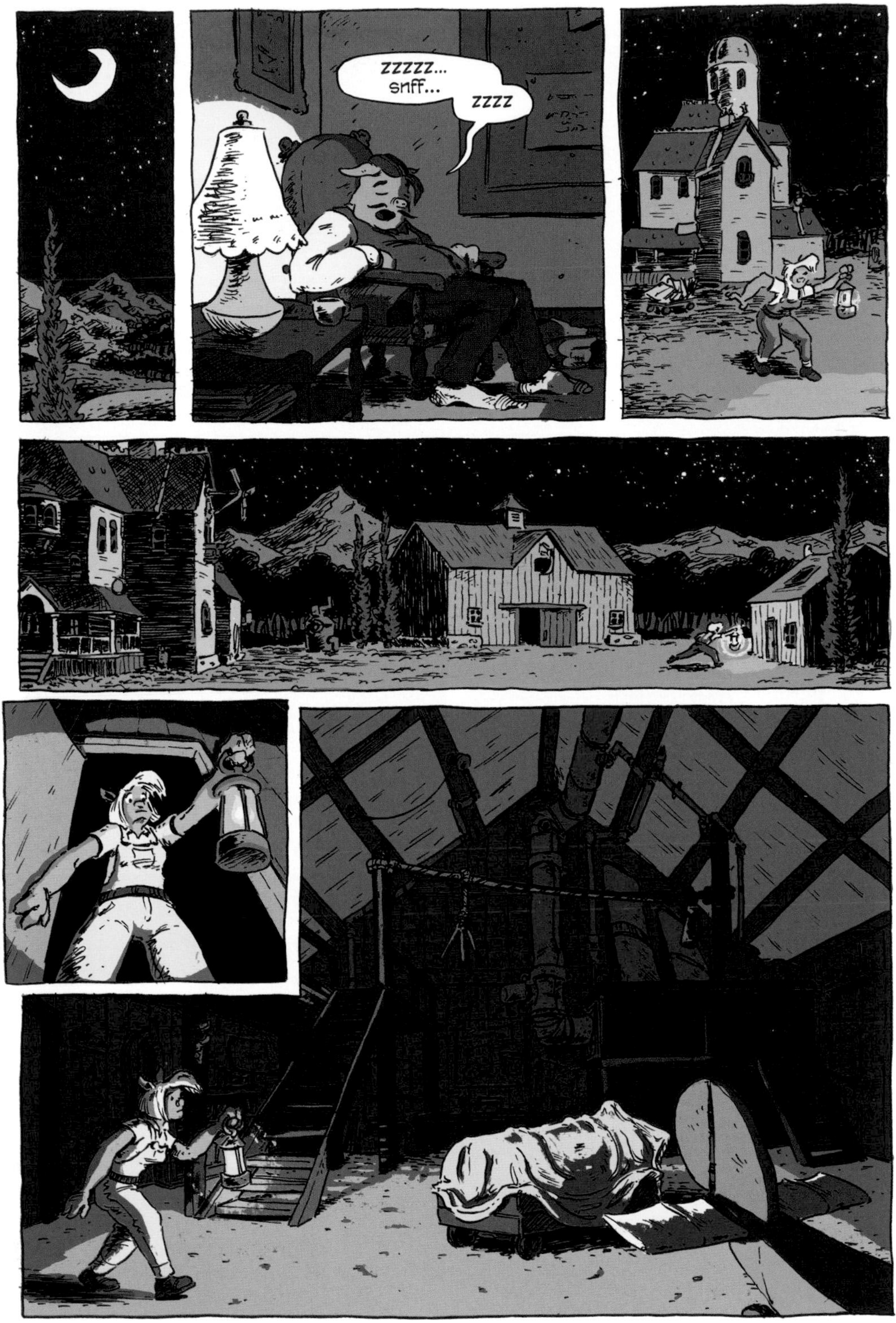
ZZZZZ...
SNFF...
ZZZZ

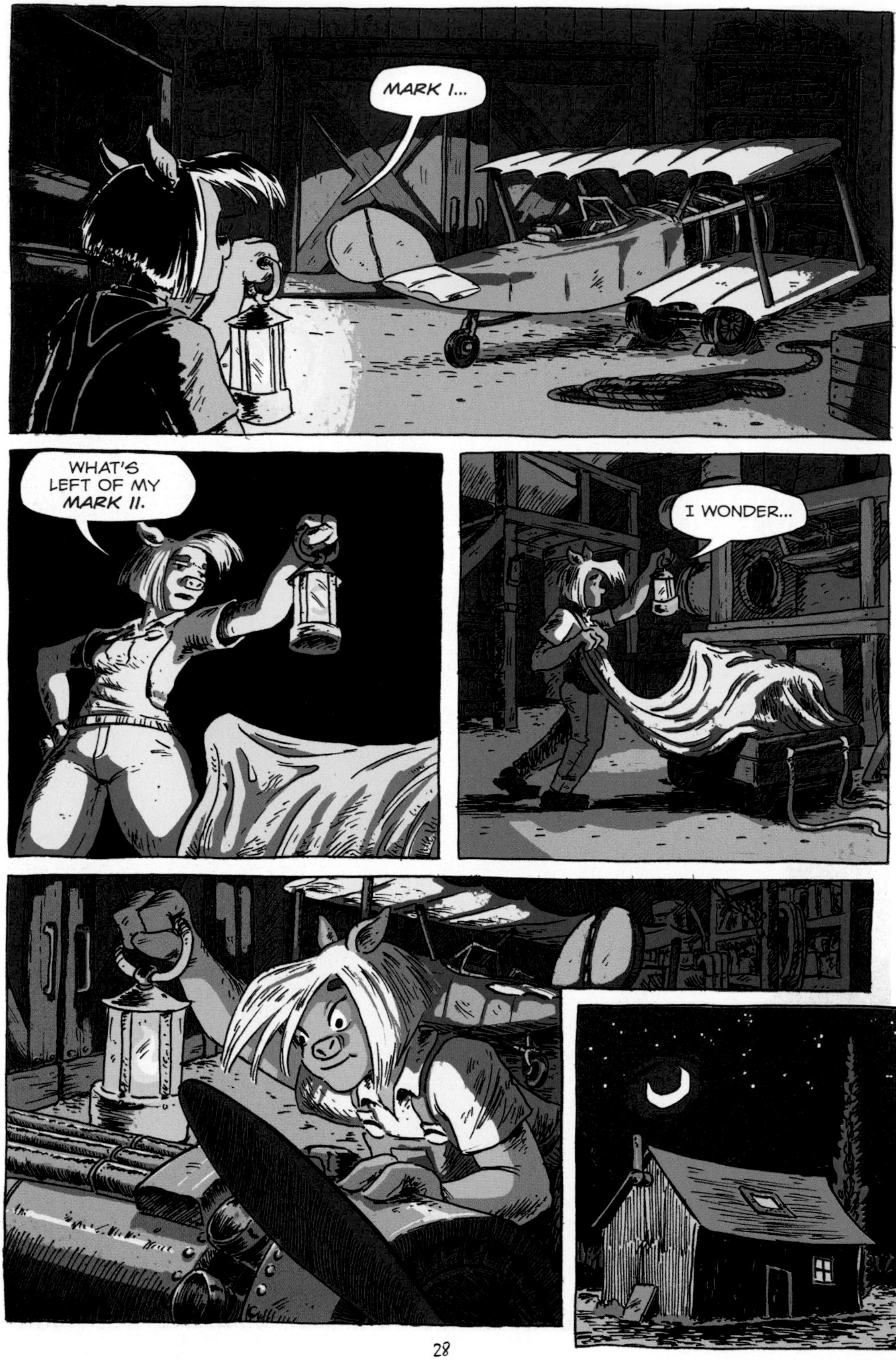
MARK I...
WHAT'S LEFT OF MY MARK II.
I WONDER...

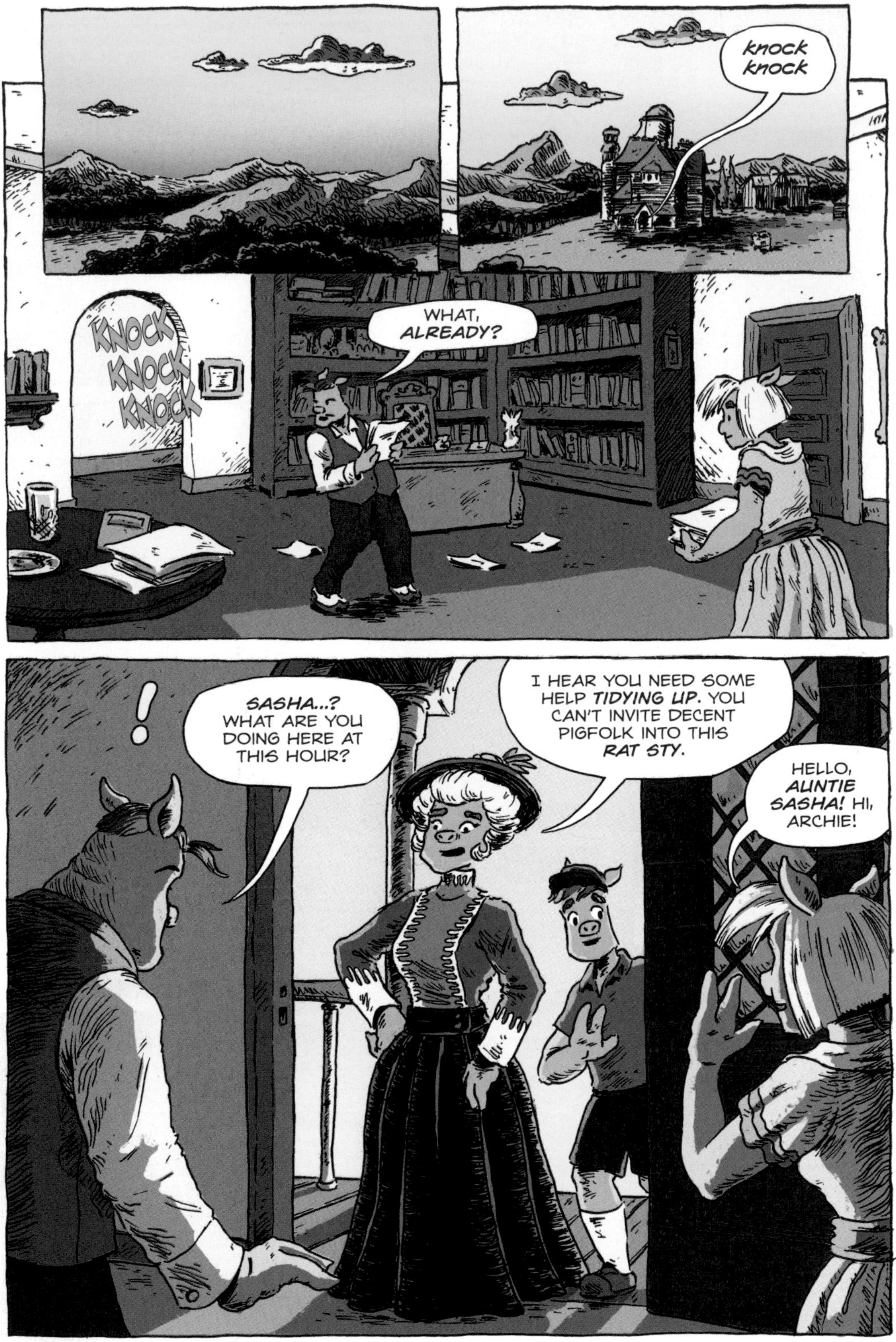
knock knock
KNOCK KNOCK KNOCK
WHAT, ALREADY?
!
SASHA...? WHAT ARE YOU DOING HERE AT THIS HOUR?
I HEAR YOU NEED SOME HELP TIDYING UP. YOU CAN'T INVITE DECENT PIGFOLK INTO THIS RAT STY.
HELLO, AUNTIE SASHA! HI, ARCHIE!

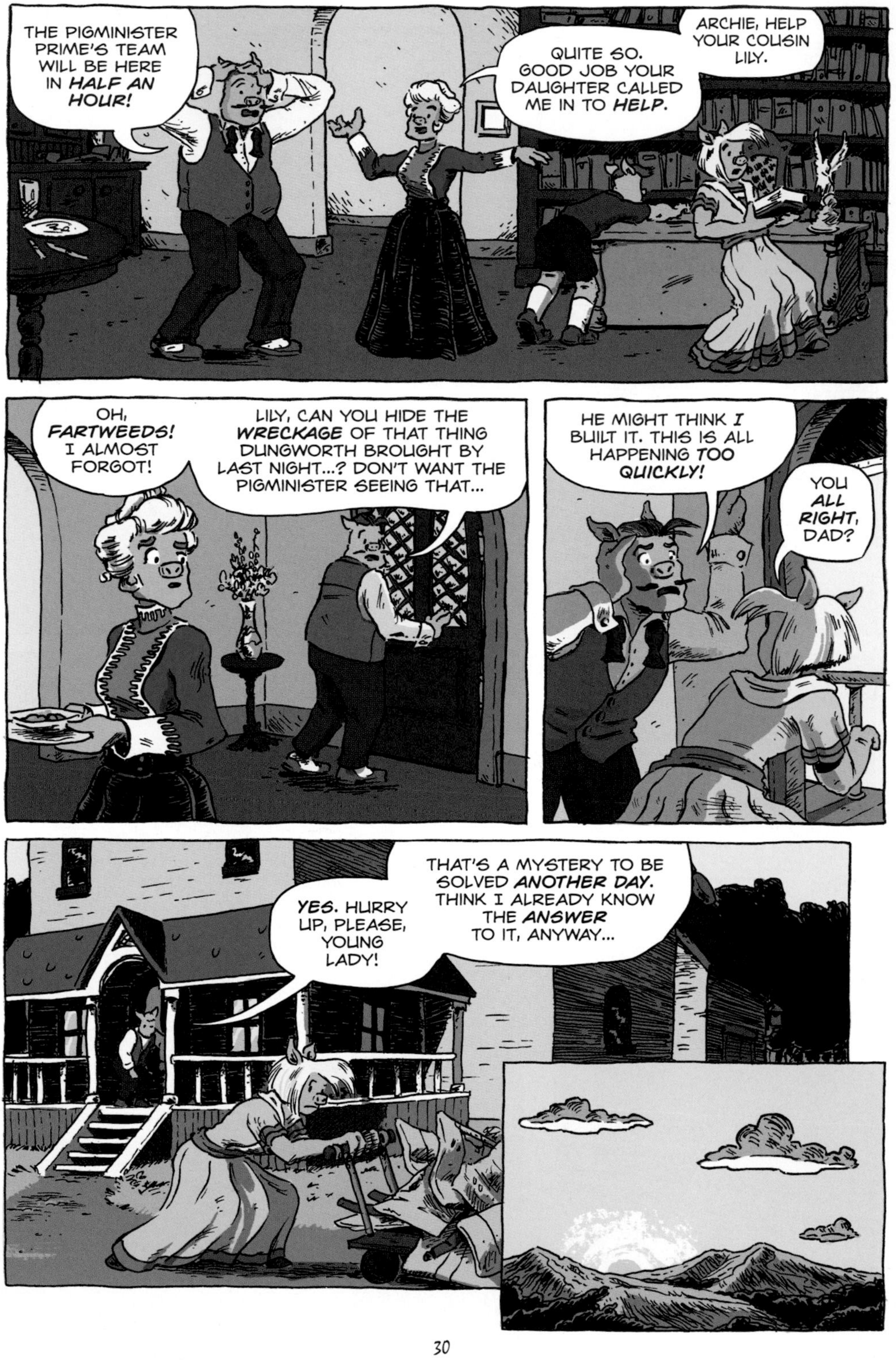
THE PIGMINISTER PRIME'S TEAM WILL BE HERE IN **HALF AN HOUR!**
QUITE SO. GOOD JOB YOUR DAUGHTER CALLED ME IN TO **HELP**.
ARCHIE, HELP YOUR COUSIN LILY.
OH, **FARTWEEDS!** I ALMOST FORGOT!
LILY, CAN YOU HIDE THE **WRECKAGE** OF THAT THING DUNGWORTH BROUGHT BY LAST NIGHT...? DON'T WANT THE PIGMINISTER SEEING THAT...
HE MIGHT THINK ***I*** BUILT IT. THIS IS ALL HAPPENING **TOO QUICKLY!**
YOU **ALL RIGHT**, DAD?
YES. HURRY UP, PLEASE, YOUNG LADY!
THAT'S A MYSTERY TO BE SOLVED **ANOTHER DAY**. THINK I ALREADY KNOW THE **ANSWER** TO IT, ANYWAY...

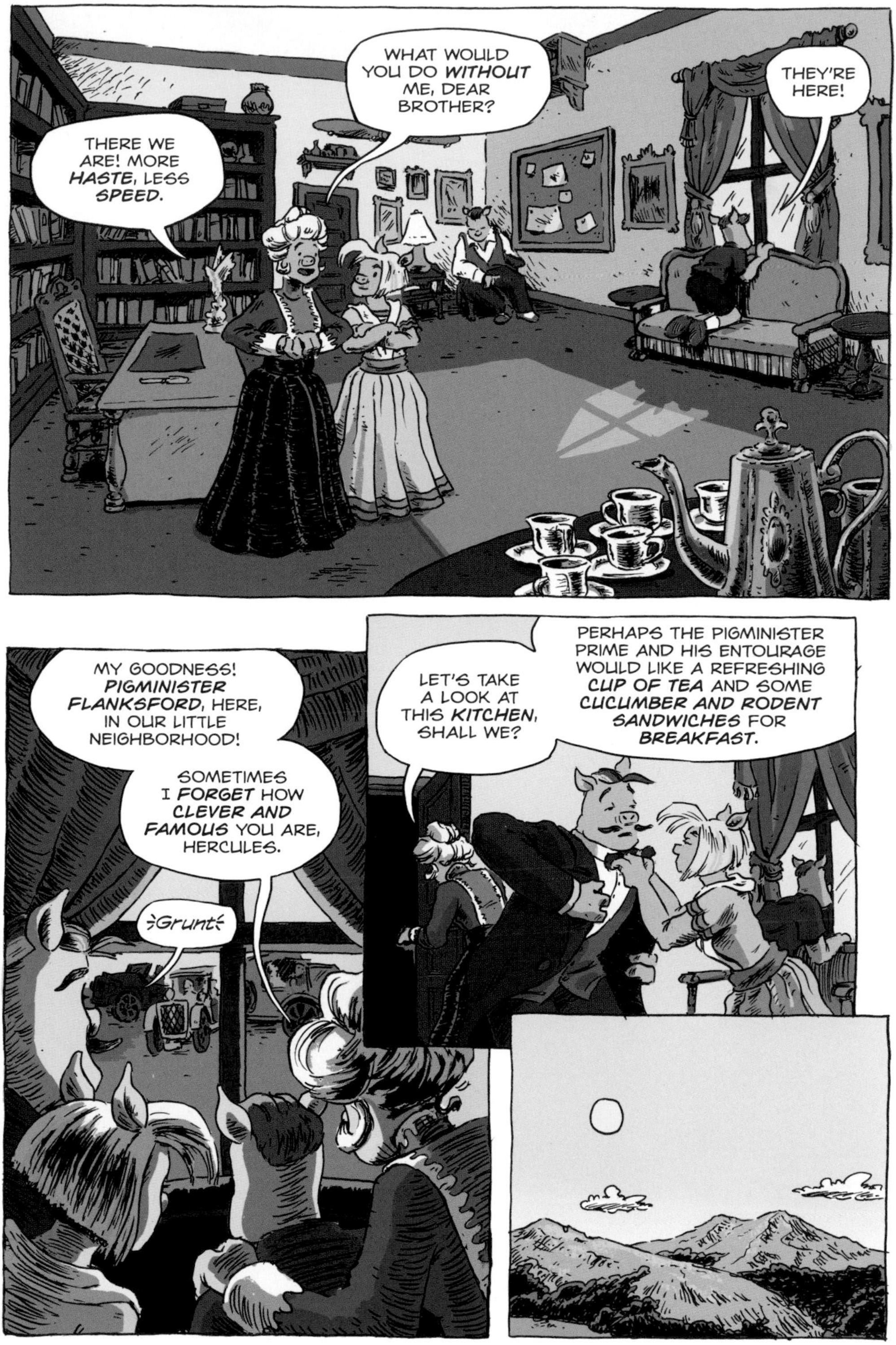
THERE WE ARE! MORE HASTE, LESS SPEED.
WHAT WOULD YOU DO WITHOUT ME, DEAR BROTHER?
THEY'RE HERE!
MY GOODNESS! PIGMINISTER FLANKSFORD, HERE, IN OUR LITTLE NEIGHBORHOOD!
SOMETIMES I FORGET HOW CLEVER AND FAMOUS YOU ARE, HERCULES.
Grunt
LET'S TAKE A LOOK AT THIS KITCHEN, SHALL WE?
PERHAPS THE PIGMINISTER PRIME AND HIS ENTOURAGE WOULD LIKE A REFRESHING CUP OF TEA AND SOME CUCUMBER AND RODENT SANDWICHES FOR BREAKFAST.

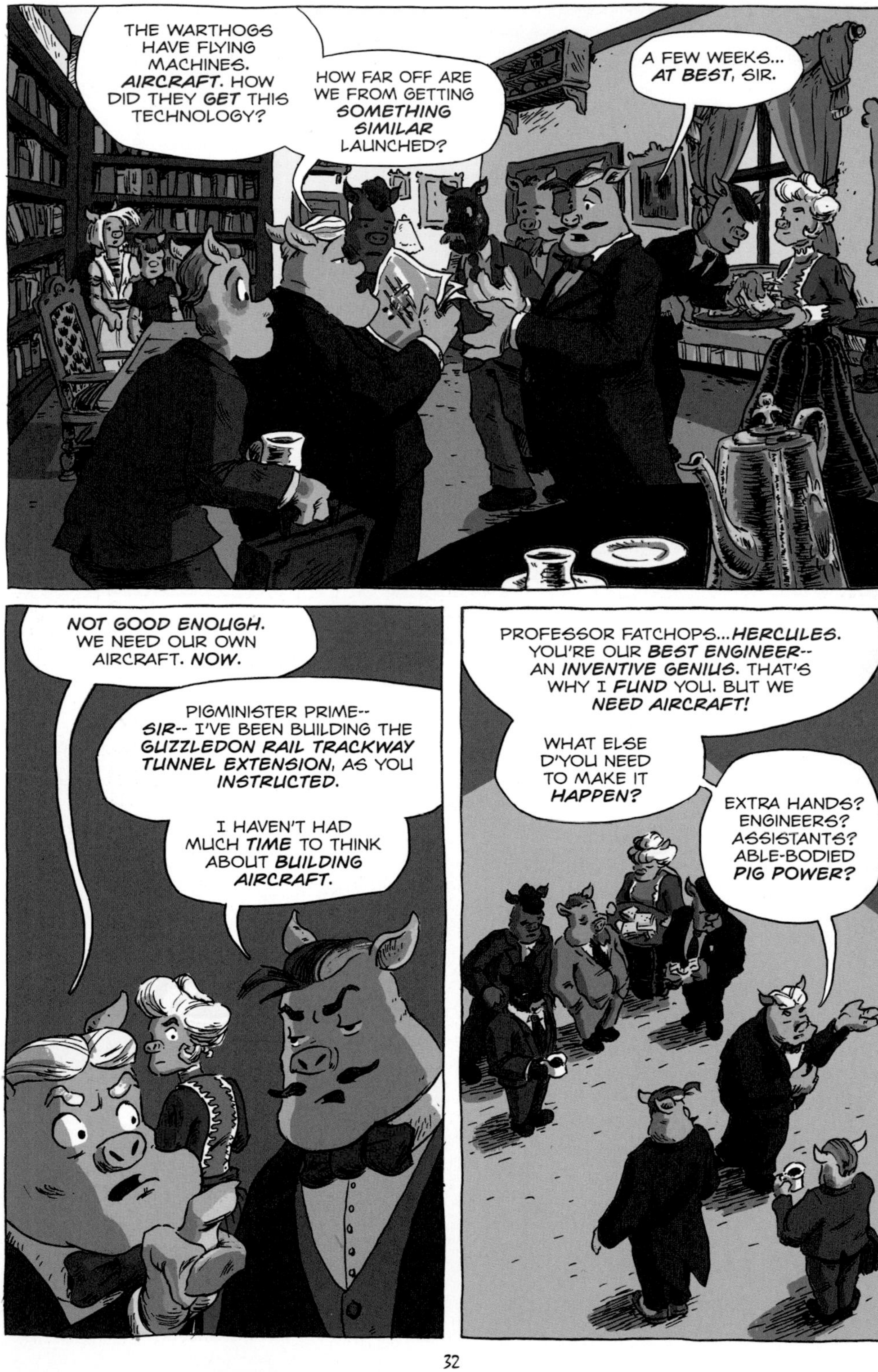
THE WARTHOGS HAVE FLYING MACHINES. AIRCRAFT. HOW DID THEY GET THIS TECHNOLOGY?
HOW FAR OFF ARE WE FROM GETTING SOMETHING SIMILAR LAUNCHED?
A FEW WEEKS... AT BEST, SIR.
NOT GOOD ENOUGH. WE NEED OUR OWN AIRCRAFT. NOW.
PIGMINISTER PRIME-- SIR-- I'VE BEEN BUILDING THE GUZZLEDON RAIL TRACKWAY TUNNEL EXTENSION, AS YOU INSTRUCTED.
I HAVEN'T HAD MUCH TIME TO THINK ABOUT BUILDING AIRCRAFT.
PROFESSOR FATCHOPS...HERCULES. YOU'RE OUR BEST ENGINEER-- AN INVENTIVE GENIUS. THAT'S WHY I FUND YOU. BUT WE NEED AIRCRAFT!
WHAT ELSE D'YOU NEED TO MAKE IT HAPPEN?
EXTRA HANDS? ENGINEERS? ASSISTANTS? ABLE-BODIED PIG POWER?

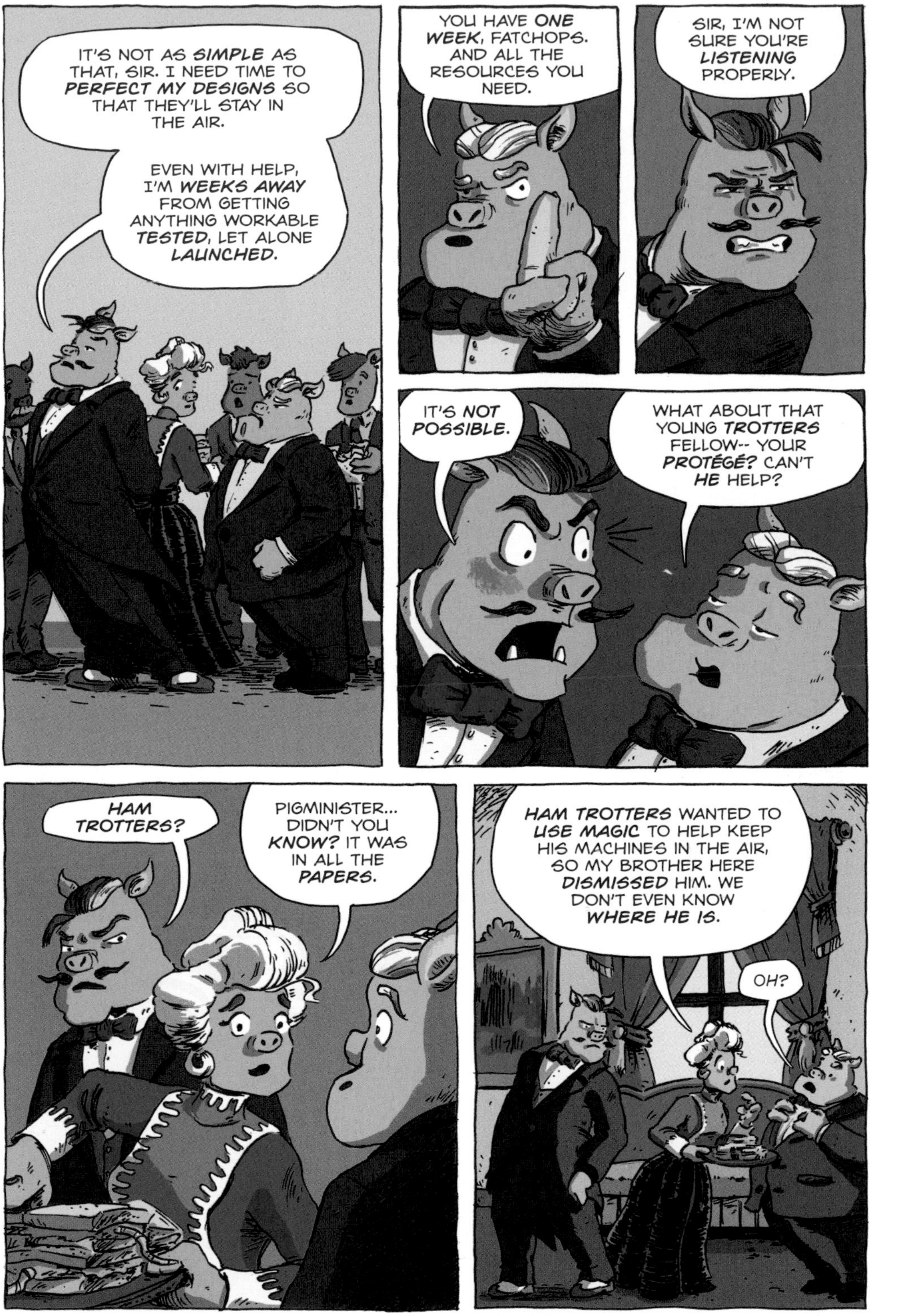
IT'S NOT AS SIMPLE AS THAT, SIR. I NEED TIME TO PERFECT MY DESIGNS SO THAT THEY'LL STAY IN THE AIR.
EVEN WITH HELP, I'M WEEKS AWAY FROM GETTING ANYTHING WORKABLE TESTED, LET ALONE LAUNCHED.
YOU HAVE ONE WEEK, FATCHOPS. AND ALL THE RESOURCES YOU NEED.
SIR, I'M NOT SURE YOU'RE LISTENING PROPERLY.
IT'S NOT POSSIBLE.
WHAT ABOUT THAT YOUNG TROTTERS FELLOW-- YOUR PROTÉGÉ? CAN'T HE HELP?
HAM TROTTERS?
PIGMINISTER... DIDN'T YOU KNOW? IT WAS IN ALL THE PAPERS.
HAM TROTTERS WANTED TO USE MAGIC TO HELP KEEP HIS MACHINES IN THE AIR, SO MY BROTHER HERE DISMISSED HIM. WE DON'T EVEN KNOW WHERE HE IS.
OH?

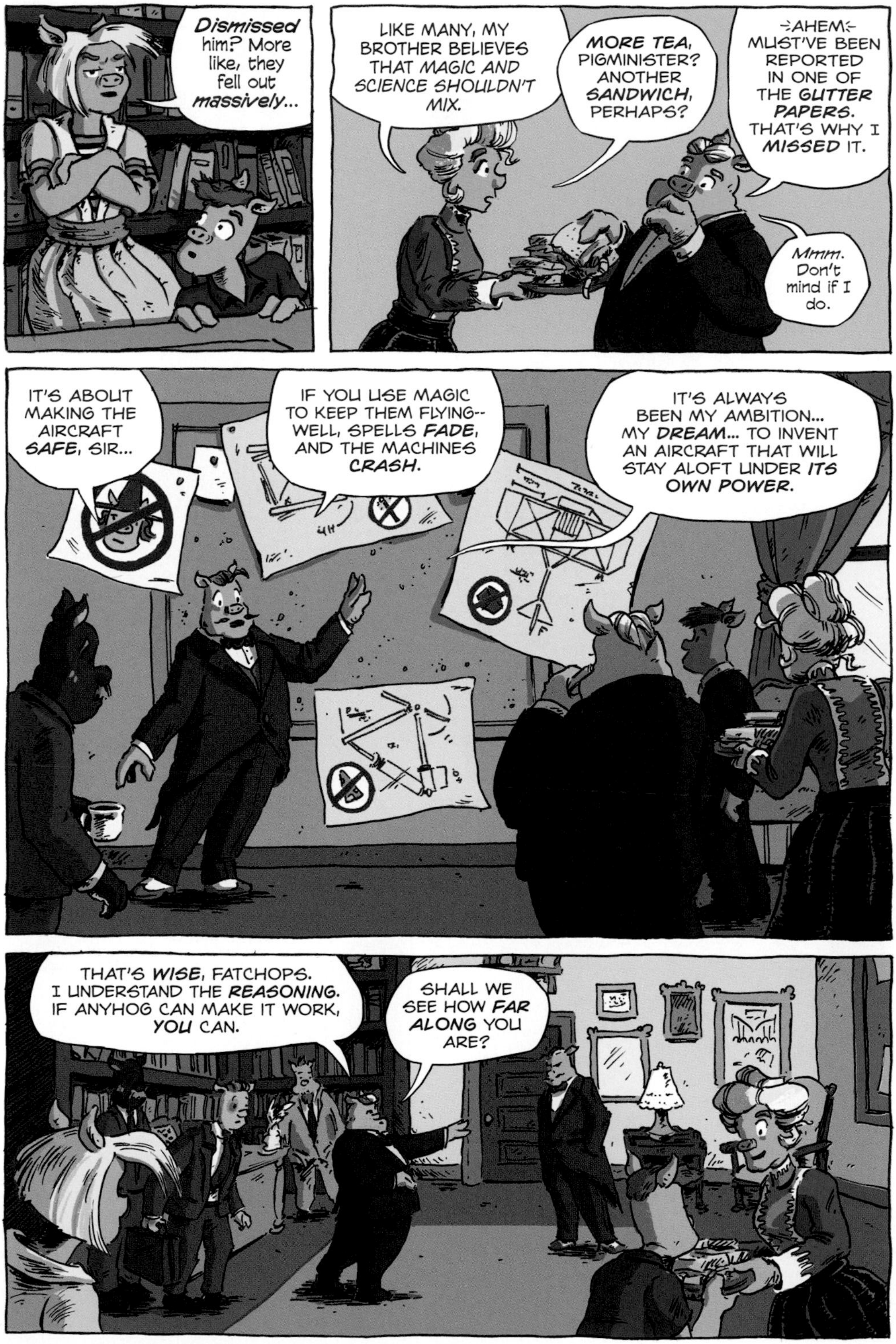
Dismissed him? More like, they fell out massively...
LIKE MANY, MY BROTHER BELIEVES THAT MAGIC AND SCIENCE SHOULDN'T MIX.
MORE TEA, PIGMINISTER? ANOTHER SANDWICH, PERHAPS?
AHEM MUST'VE BEEN REPORTED IN ONE OF THE GUTTER PAPERS. THAT'S WHY I MISSED IT.
Mmm. Don't mind if I do.
IT'S ABOUT MAKING THE AIRCRAFT SAFE, SIR...
IF YOU USE MAGIC TO KEEP THEM FLYING-- WELL, SPELLS FADE, AND THE MACHINES CRASH.
IT'S ALWAYS BEEN MY AMBITION... MY DREAM... TO INVENT AN AIRCRAFT THAT WILL STAY ALOFT UNDER ITS OWN POWER.
THAT'S WISE, FATCHOPS. I UNDERSTAND THE REASONING. IF ANYHOG CAN MAKE IT WORK, YOU CAN.
SHALL WE SEE HOW FAR ALONG YOU ARE?

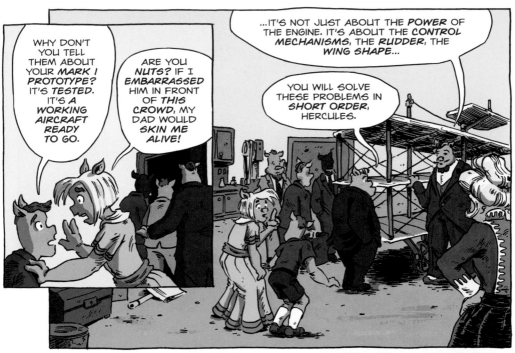

WHY DON'T YOU TELL THEM ABOUT YOUR **MARK I** PROTOTYPE? IT'S **TESTED.** IT'S **A WORKING AIRCRAFT READY TO GO.**

ARE YOU **NUTS?** IF I EMBARRASSED HIM IN FRONT OF **THIS CROWD,** MY DAD WOULD **SKIN ME ALIVE!**

...IT'S NOT JUST ABOUT THE **POWER** OF THE ENGINE. IT'S ABOUT THE **CONTROL MECHANISMS,** THE **RUDDER,** THE **WING SHAPE...**

YOU WILL SOLVE THESE PROBLEMS IN **SHORT ORDER,** HERCULES.

IF YOU USE YOUR **MARK II MOTOR** ON THE MARK I AIRCRAFT, IT'LL BE EVEN MORE **POWERFUL.** IT SURE WORKED YESTERDAY ONCE IT GOT GOING!

ARCHIE... SHUT **UP.**

YOU'RE JUST BEING **STUBBORN!** WE **KNOW** IT **WORKS...**

WHAT WORKS?

UHH... THE **MANGLE** IN THE **LAUNDRY ROOM.** LILY **FIXED** IT.

I didn't know it was *broken*.

PIGMINISTER FLANKSFORD, SIR! **MORE WARTHOG AIRCRAFT** HAVE BEEN **SIGHTED** OVER SWILLINGTON!

AN **ATTACK?**

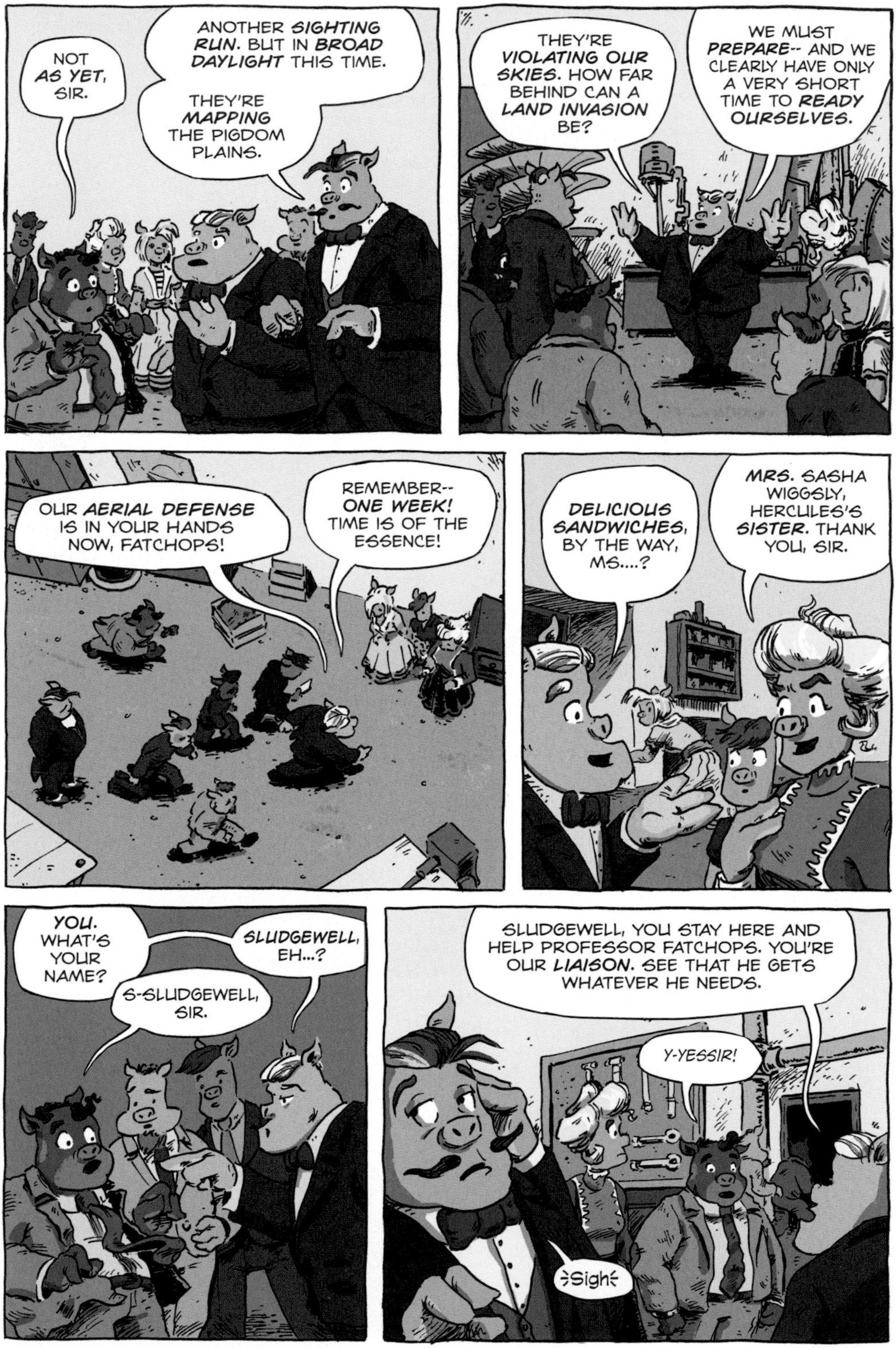
NOT AS YET, SIR.
ANOTHER SIGHTING RUN. BUT IN BROAD DAYLIGHT THIS TIME.
THEY'RE MAPPING THE PIGDOM PLAINS.
THEY'RE VIOLATING OUR SKIES. HOW FAR BEHIND CAN A LAND INVASION BE?
WE MUST PREPARE-- AND WE CLEARLY HAVE ONLY A VERY SHORT TIME TO READY OURSELVES.
OUR AERIAL DEFENSE IS IN YOUR HANDS NOW, FATCHOPS!
REMEMBER-- ONE WEEK! TIME IS OF THE ESSENCE!
DELICIOUS SANDWICHES, BY THE WAY, MS....?
MRS. SASHA WIGGSLY, HERCULES'S SISTER. THANK YOU, SIR.
YOU. WHAT'S YOUR NAME?
S-SLUDGEWELL, SIR.
SLUDGEWELL, EH...?
SLUDGEWELL, YOU STAY HERE AND HELP PROFESSOR FATCHOPS. YOU'RE OUR LIAISON. SEE THAT HE GETS WHATEVER HE NEEDS.
Y-YESSIR!
Sigh

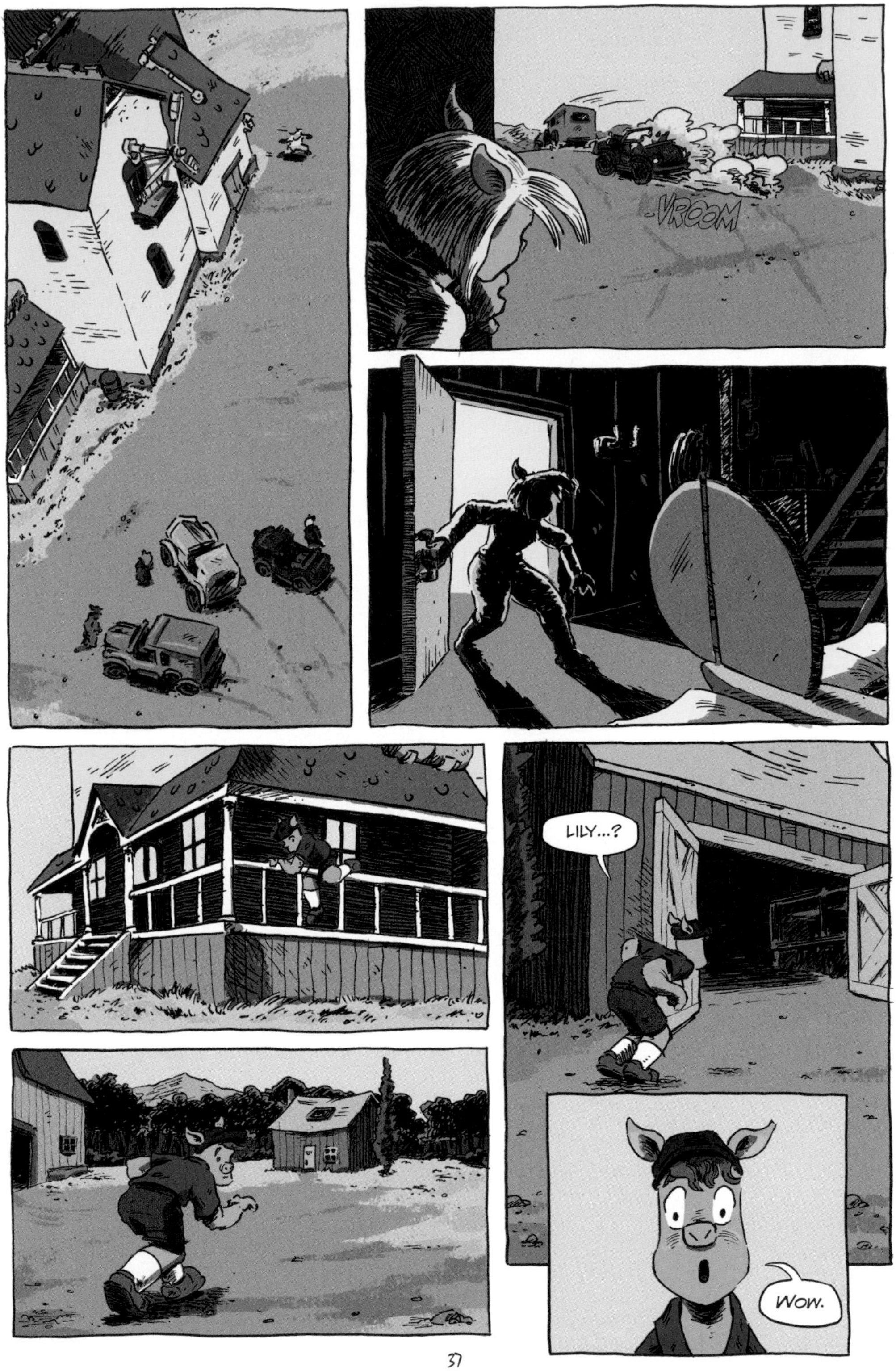
VROOM
LILY...?
WOW.

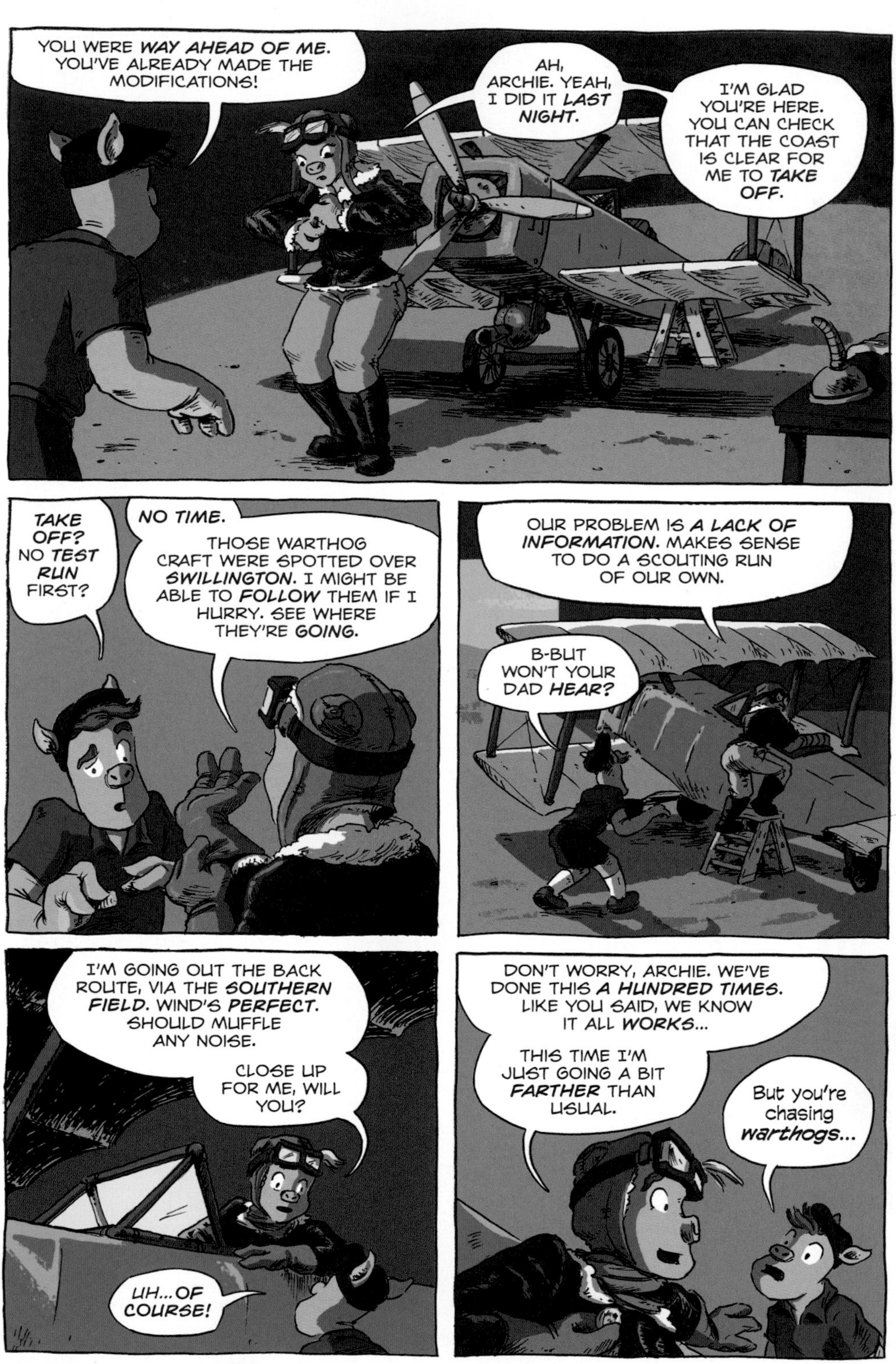
YOU WERE WAY AHEAD OF ME. YOU'VE ALREADY MADE THE MODIFICATIONS!
AH, ARCHIE. YEAH, I DID IT LAST NIGHT.
I'M GLAD YOU'RE HERE. YOU CAN CHECK THAT THE COAST IS CLEAR FOR ME TO TAKE OFF.
TAKE OFF? NO TEST RUN FIRST?
NO TIME.
THOSE WARTHOG CRAFT WERE SPOTTED OVER SWILLINGTON. I MIGHT BE ABLE TO FOLLOW THEM IF I HURRY. SEE WHERE THEY'RE GOING.
OUR PROBLEM IS A LACK OF INFORMATION. MAKES SENSE TO DO A SCOUTING RUN OF OUR OWN.
B-BUT WON'T YOUR DAD HEAR?
I'M GOING OUT THE BACK ROUTE, VIA THE SOUTHERN FIELD. WIND'S PERFECT. SHOULD MUFFLE ANY NOISE.
CLOSE UP FOR ME, WILL YOU?
UH...OF COURSE!
DON'T WORRY, ARCHIE. WE'VE DONE THIS A HUNDRED TIMES. LIKE YOU SAID, WE KNOW IT ALL WORKS...
THIS TIME I'M JUST GOING A BIT FARTHER THAN USUAL.
But you're chasing warthogs...

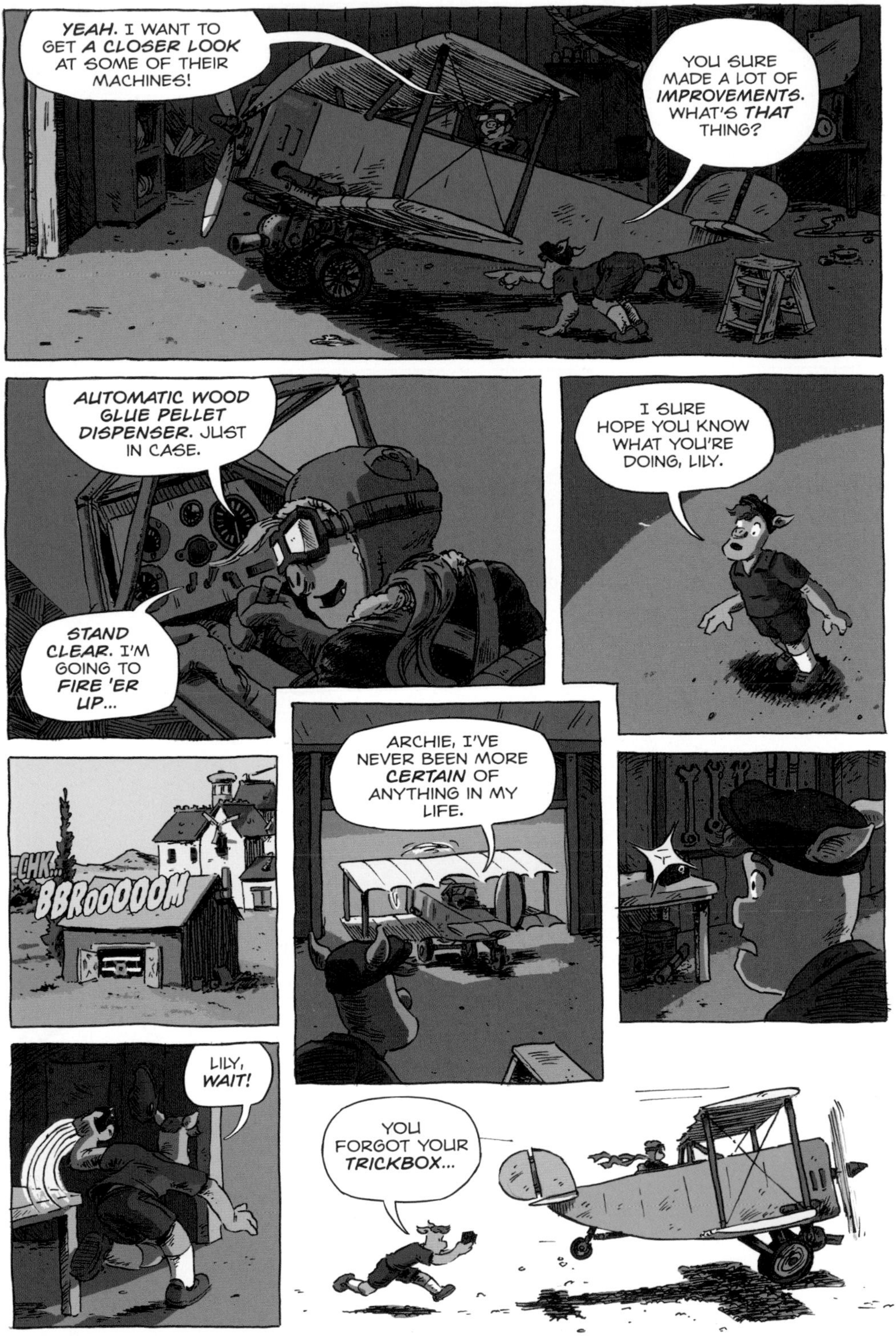
YEAH. I WANT TO GET A CLOSER LOOK AT SOME OF THEIR MACHINES!
YOU SURE MADE A LOT OF IMPROVEMENTS. WHAT'S THAT THING?
AUTOMATIC WOOD GLUE PELLET DISPENSER. JUST IN CASE.
STAND CLEAR. I'M GOING TO FIRE 'ER UP...
I SURE HOPE YOU KNOW WHAT YOU'RE DOING, LILY.
CHK...
BBROOOOOOM
ARCHIE, I'VE NEVER BEEN MORE CERTAIN OF ANYTHING IN MY LIFE.
LILY, WAIT!
YOU FORGOT YOUR TRICKBOX...

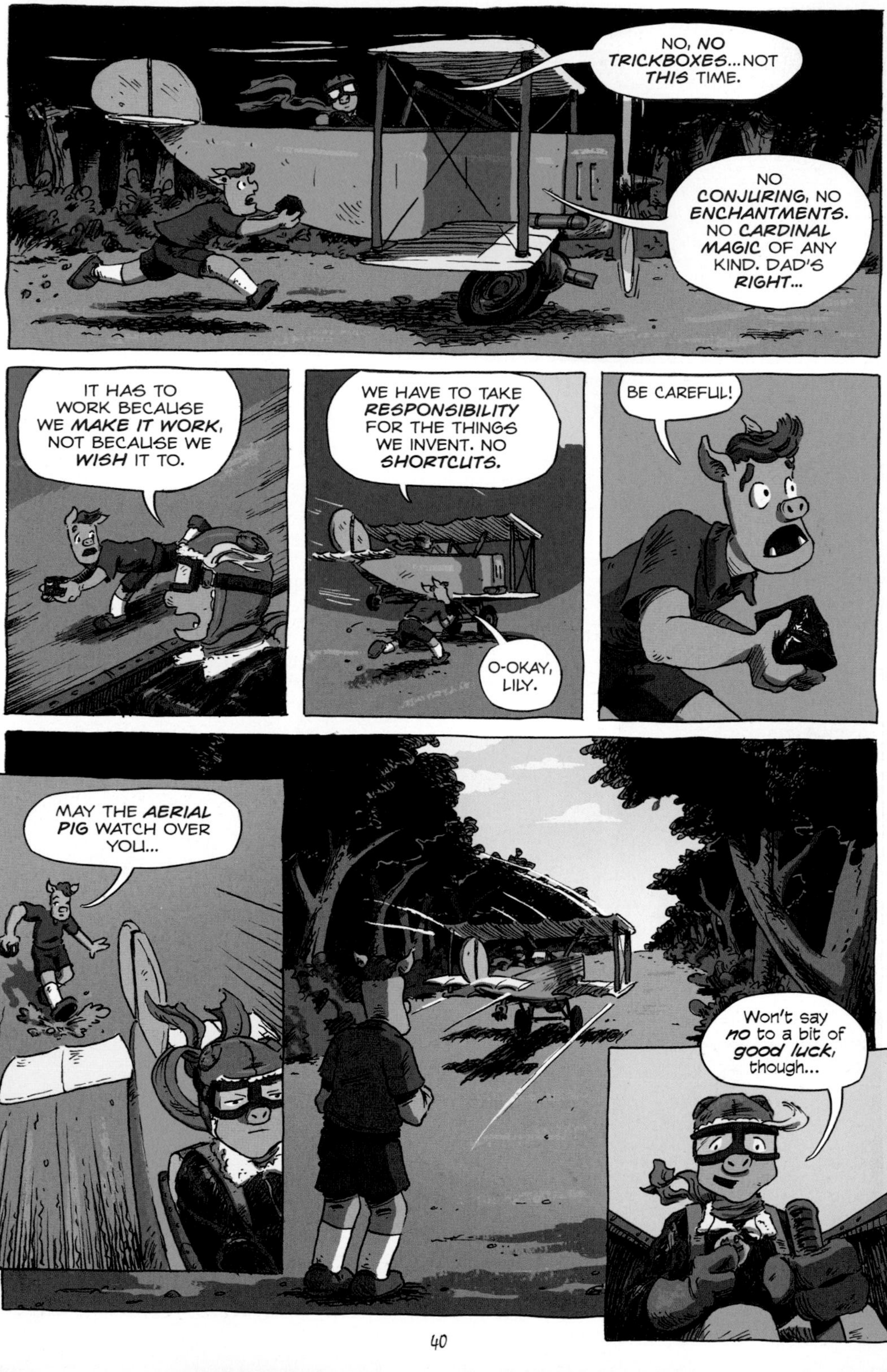
NO, NO TRICKBOXES...NOT THIS TIME.
NO CONJURING, NO ENCHANTMENTS. NO CARDINAL MAGIC OF ANY KIND. DAD'S RIGHT...
IT HAS TO WORK BECAUSE WE MAKE IT WORK, NOT BECAUSE WE WISH IT TO.
WE HAVE TO TAKE RESPONSIBILITY FOR THE THINGS WE INVENT. NO SHORTCUTS.
O-OKAY, LILY.
BE CAREFUL!
MAY THE AERIAL PIG WATCH OVER YOU...
Won't say no to a bit of good luck, though...

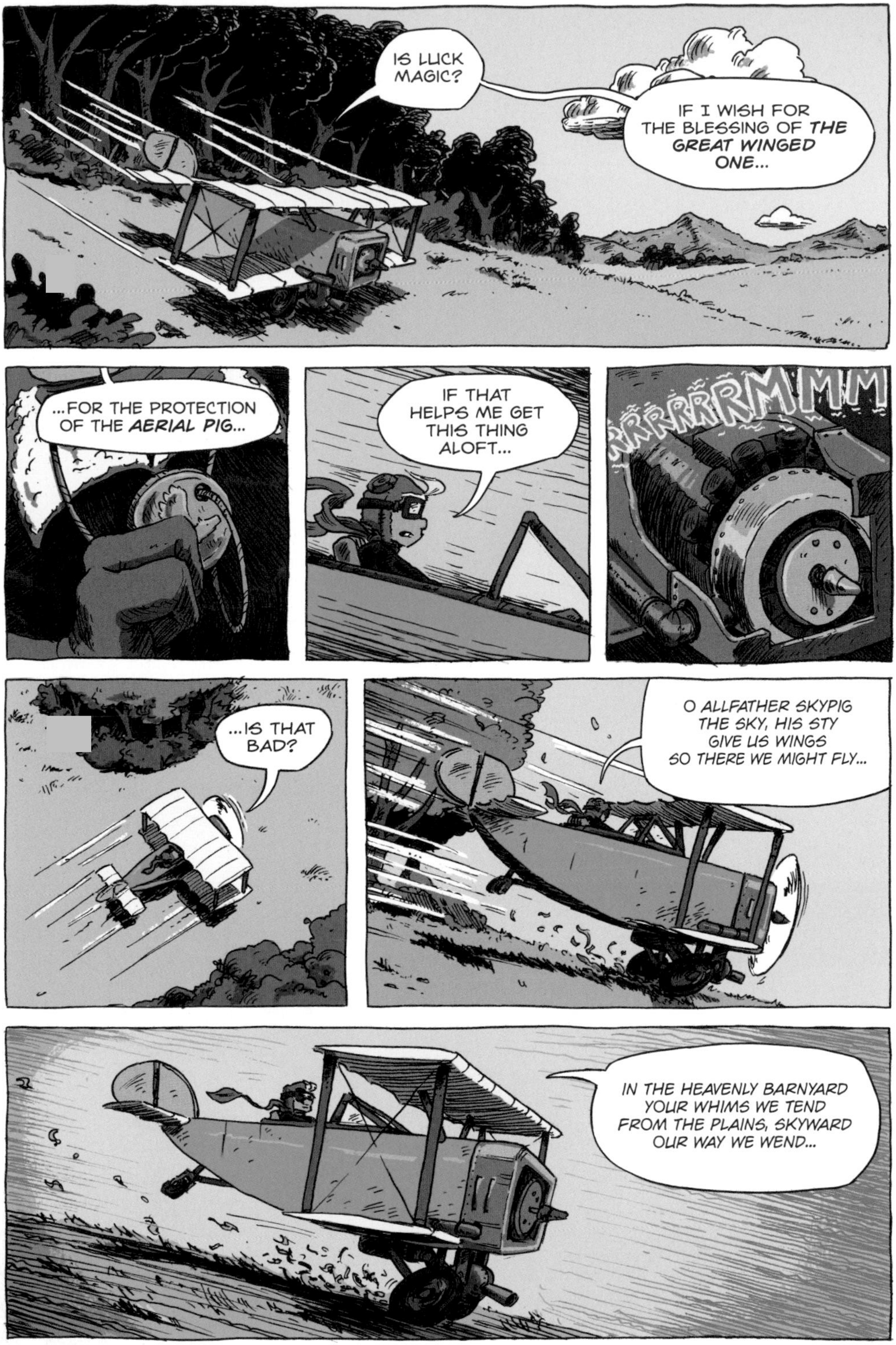
IS LUCK MAGIC?
IF I WISH FOR THE BLESSING OF ***THE GREAT WINGED*** ONE...
...FOR THE PROTECTION OF THE ***AERIAL PIG***...
IF THAT HELPS ME GET THIS THING ALOFT...
RRRRRRRMMMM
...IS THAT BAD?
O ALLFATHER SKYPIG THE SKY, HIS STY GIVE US WINGS SO THERE WE MIGHT FLY...
IN THE HEAVENLY BARNYARD YOUR WHIMS WE TEND FROM THE PLAINS, SKYWARD OUR WAY WE WEND...

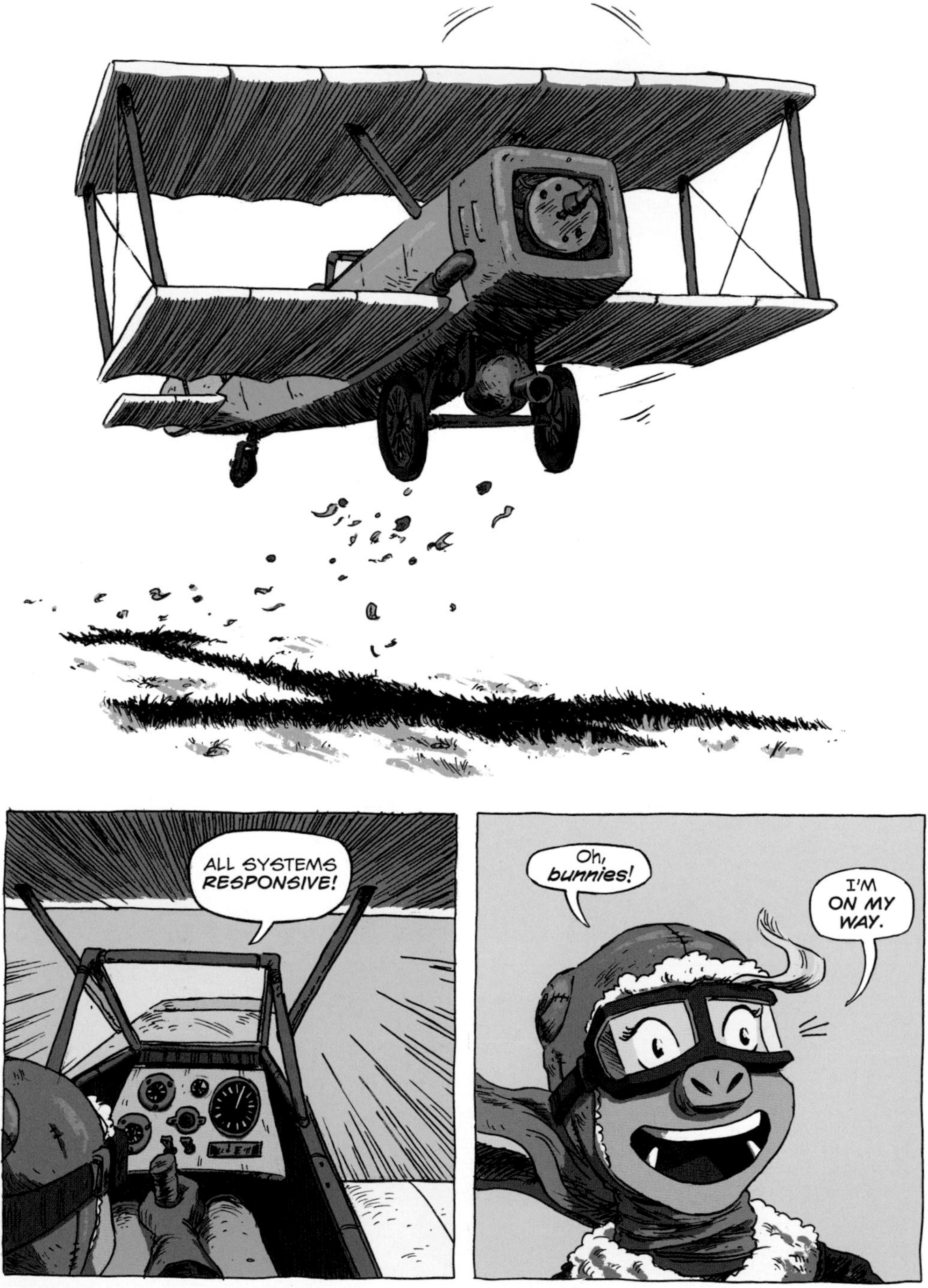
ALL SYSTEMS RESPONSIVE!
Oh, bunnies!
I'M ON MY WAY.

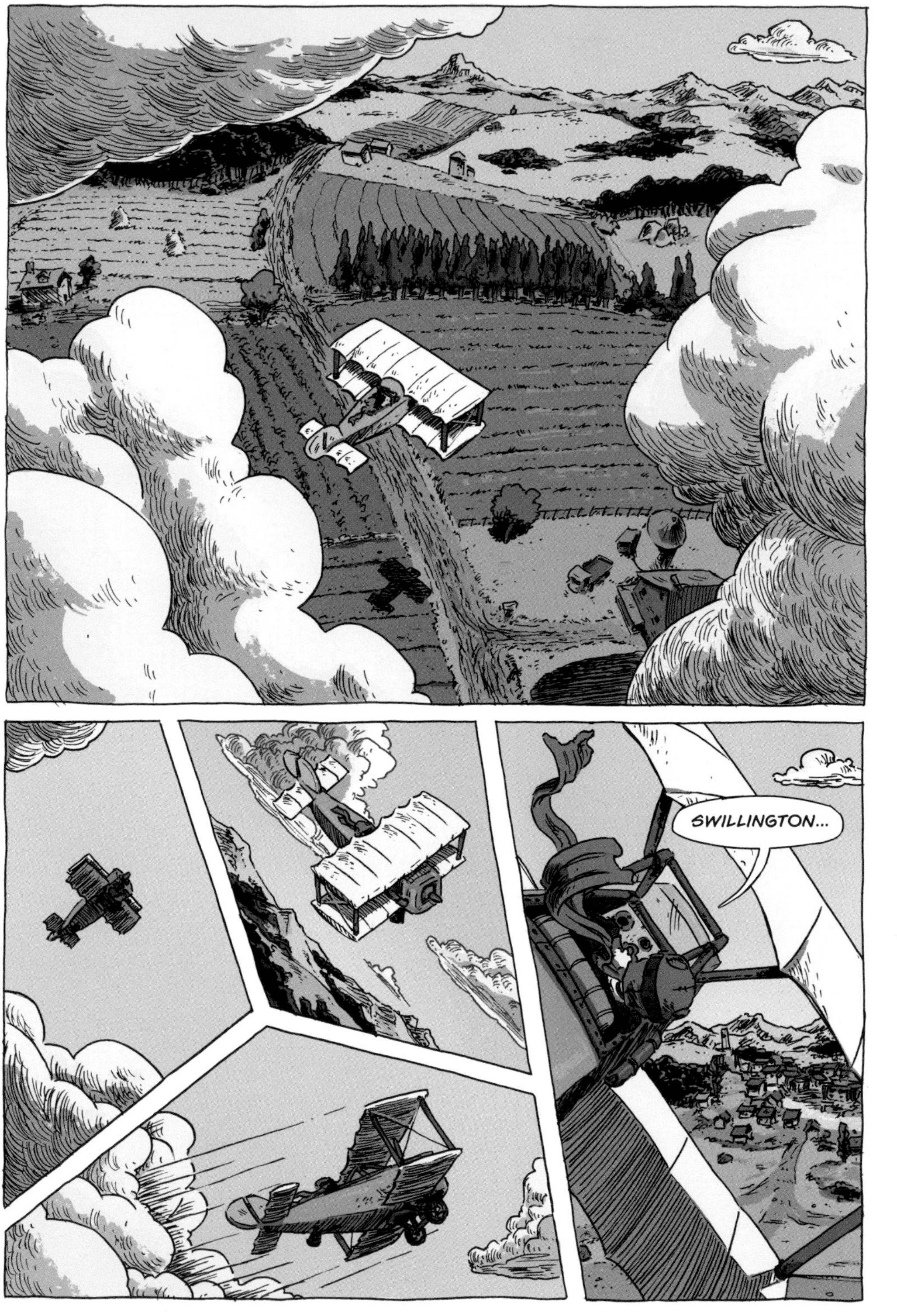
SWILLINGTON...

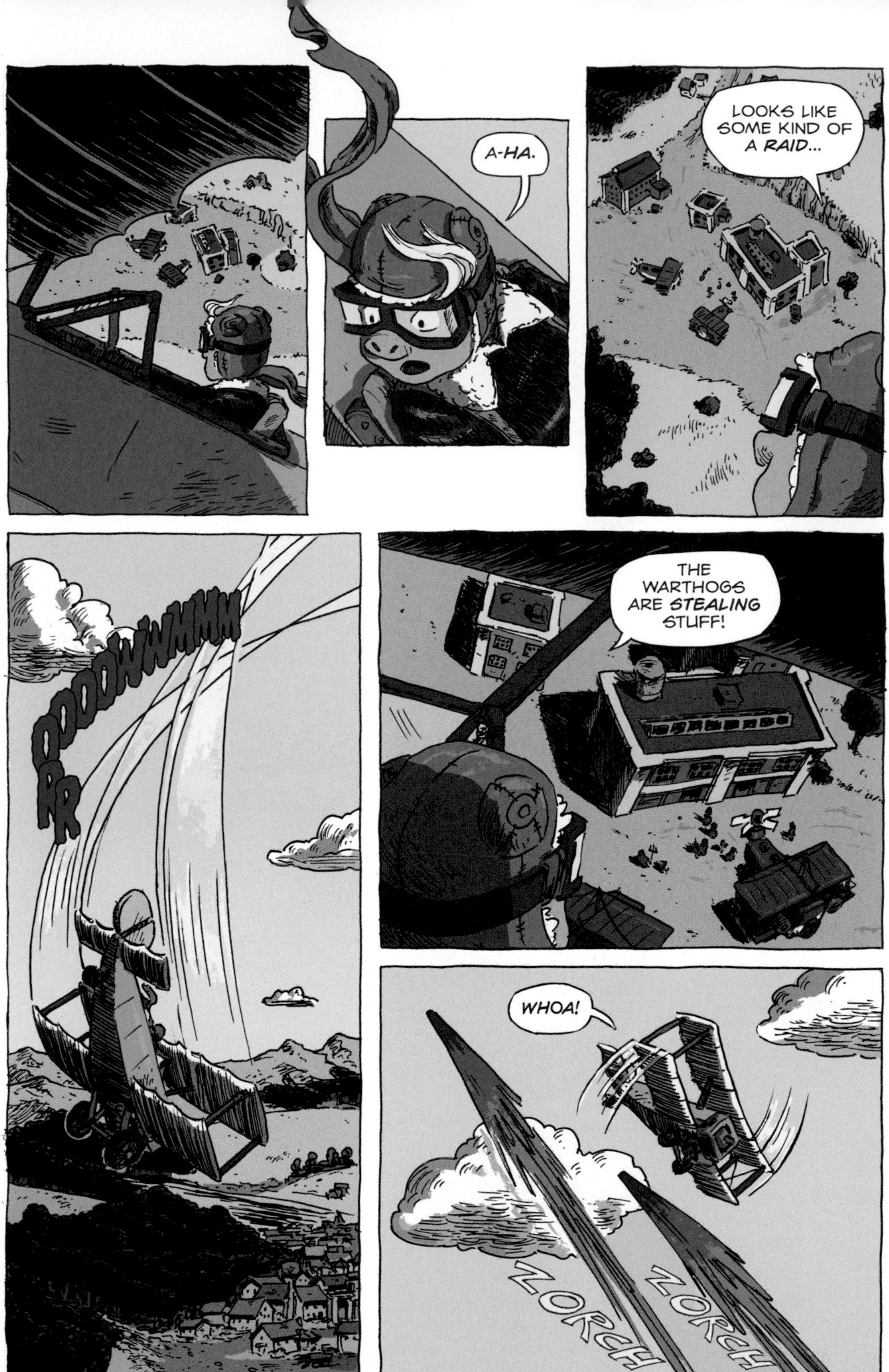
A-HA.
LOOKS LIKE SOME KIND OF A RAID...
RRRRRROOOOWWMMMM
THE WARTHOGS ARE STEALING STUFF!
WHOA!
ZORCH
ZORCH

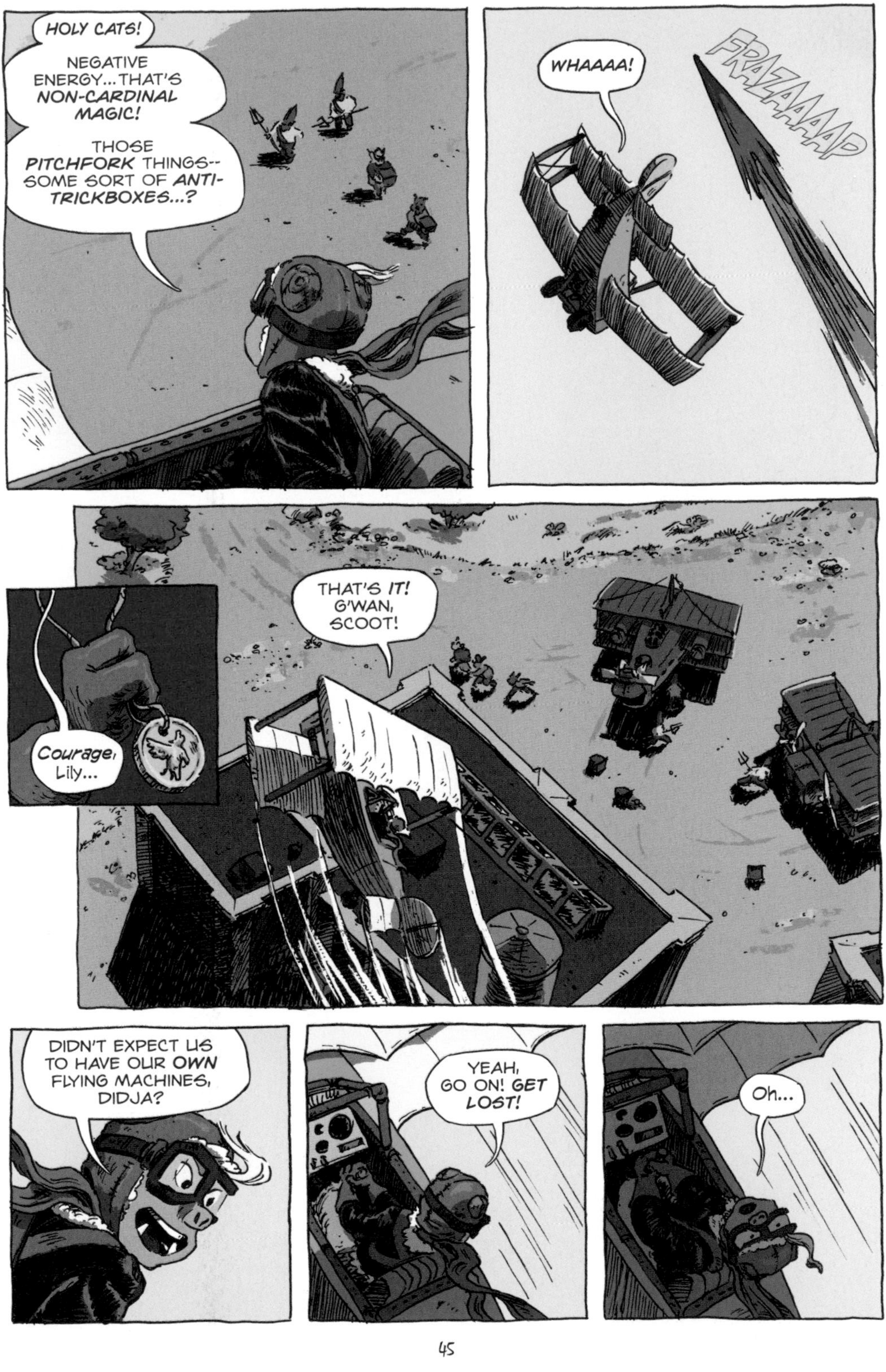
HOLY CATS!
NEGATIVE ENERGY...THAT'S NON-CARDINAL MAGIC!
THOSE PITCHFORK THINGS-- SOME SORT OF ANTI-TRICKBOXES...?
WHAAAA!
FRAZAAAAP
THAT'S IT! G'WAN, SCOOT!
Courage, Lily...
DIDN'T EXPECT US TO HAVE OUR OWN FLYING MACHINES, DIDJA?
YEAH, GO ON! GET LOST!
Oh...

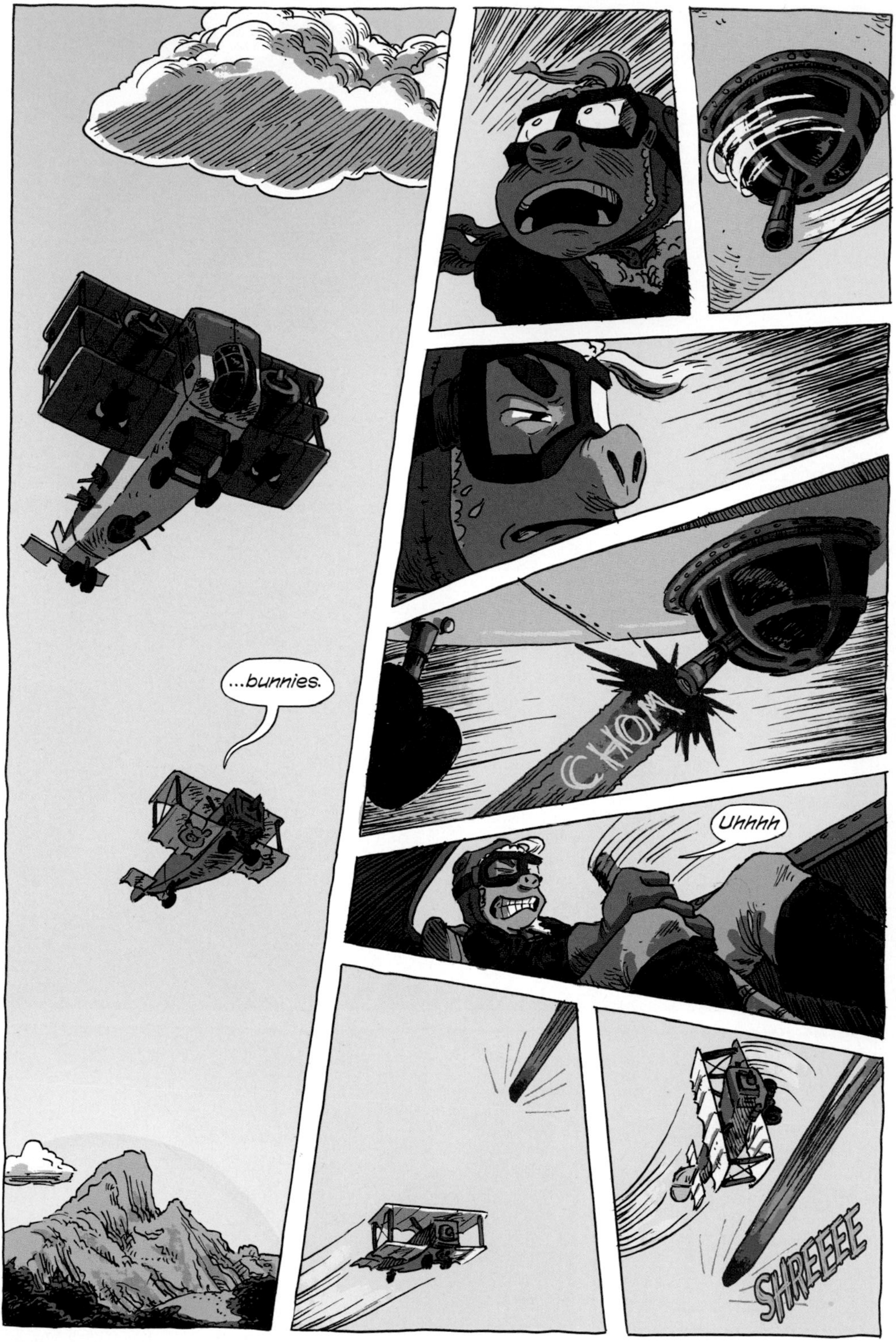
...bunnies.
CHOM
Uhhhh
SHREEEE

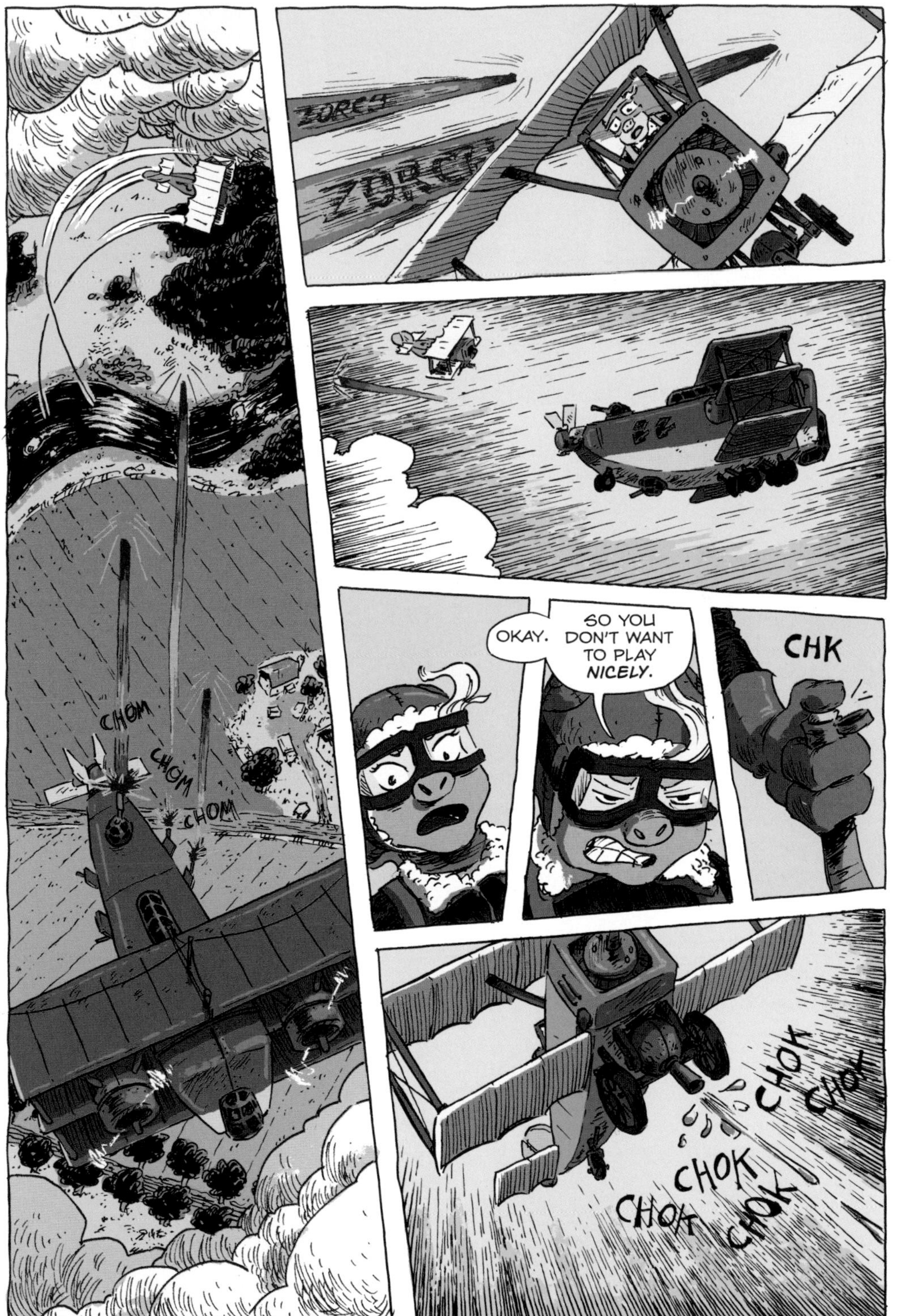
ZORCH
ZORCH
CHOM
CHOM
CHOM
OKAY.
SO YOU DON'T WANT TO PLAY *NICELY*.
CHK
CHOK
CHOK
CHOK
CHOK
CHOK

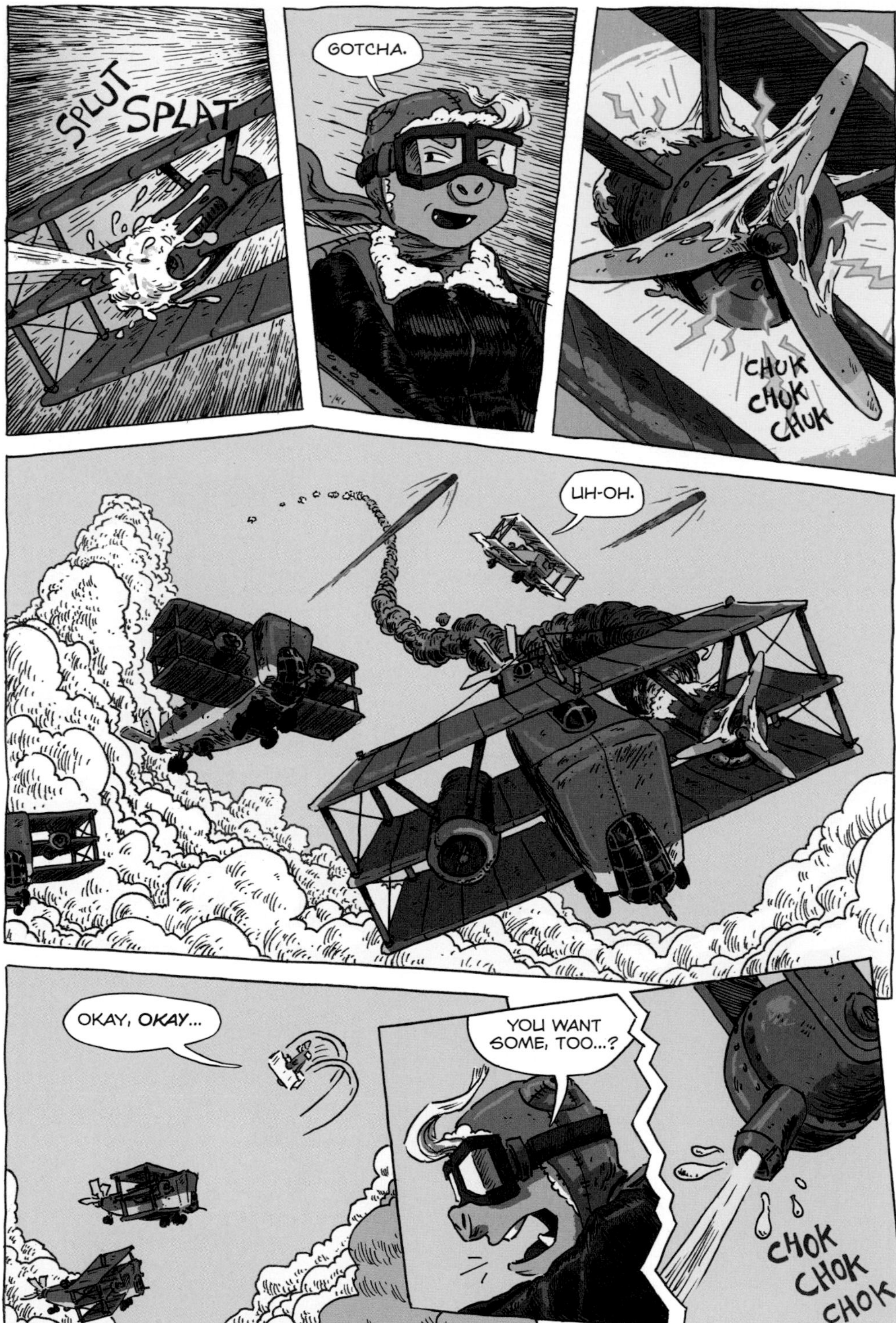
SPLUT SPLAT
GOTCHA.
CHUK CHUK CHUK
UH-OH.
OKAY, OKAY...
YOU WANT SOME, TOO...?
CHOK CHOK CHOK

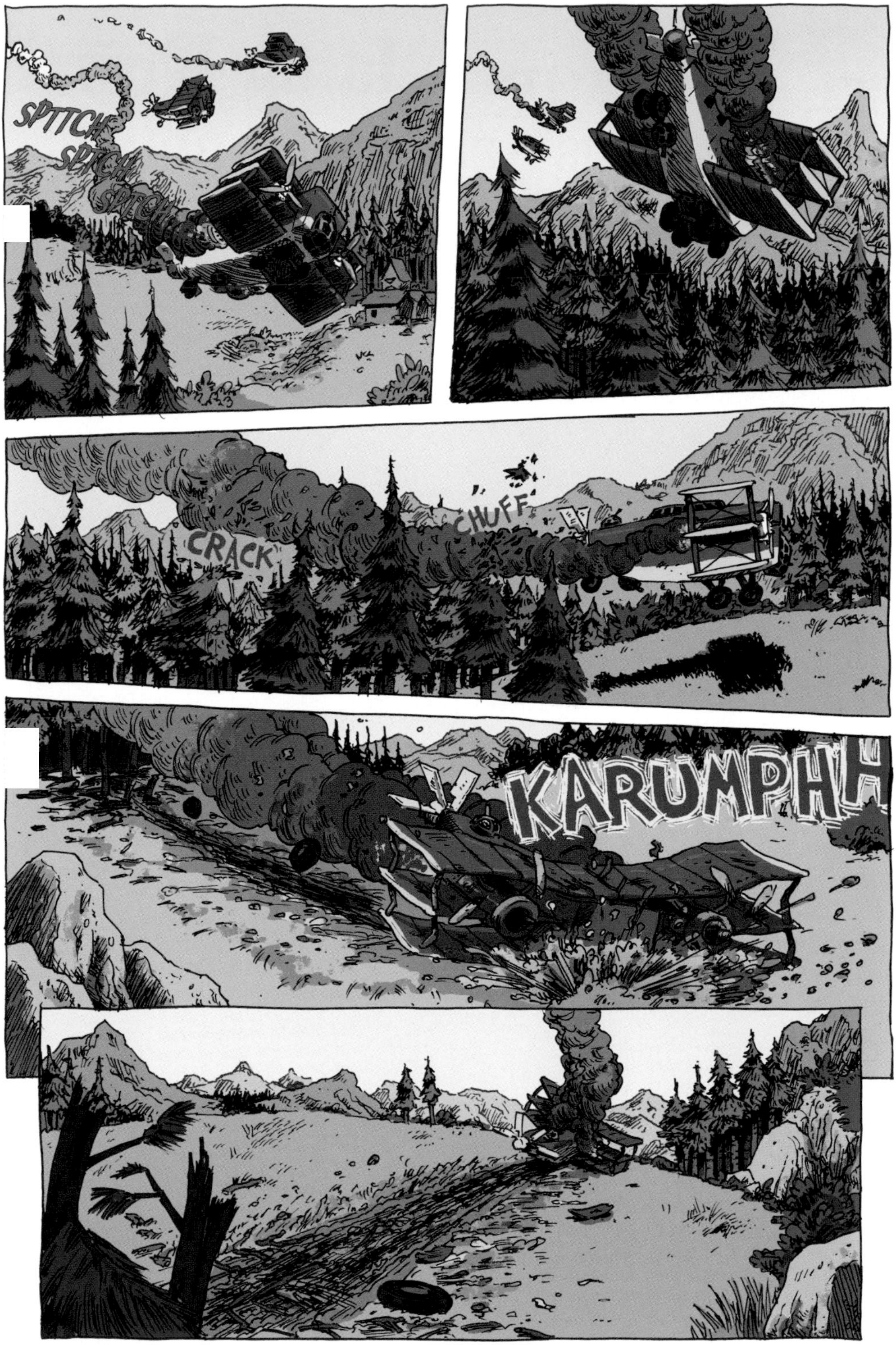
SPTTCH
SPTTCH
SPTTCH
CRACK
CHUFF
KARUMPHH

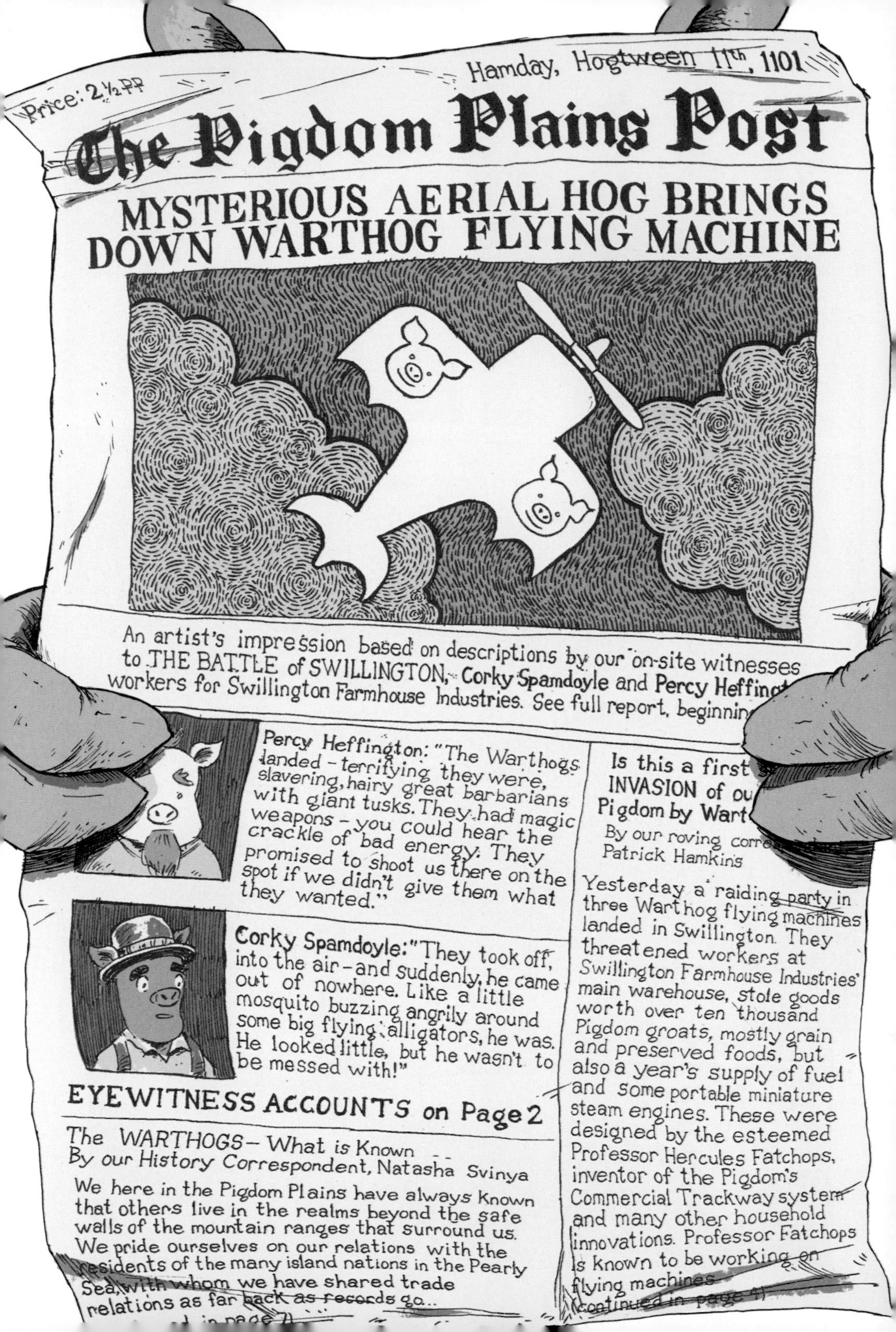

Price: 2½ PP

Hamday, Hogtween 11th, 1101

The Pigdom Plains Post

MYSTERIOUS AERIAL HOG BRINGS DOWN WARTHOG FLYING MACHINE

An artist's impression based on descriptions by our on-site witnesses to THE BATTLE of SWILLINGTON, **Corky Spamdoyle** and **Percy Heffing**[t]... workers for Swillington Farmhouse Industries. See full report, beginning...

Percy Heffington: "The Warthogs landed – terrifying they were, slavering, hairy great barbarians with giant tusks. They had magic weapons – you could hear the crackle of bad energy. They promised to shoot us there on the spot if we didn't give them what they wanted."

Corky Spamdoyle: "They took off, into the air – and suddenly, he came out of nowhere. Like a little mosquito buzzing angrily around some big flying alligators, he was. He looked little, but he wasn't to be messed with!"

EYEWITNESS ACCOUNTS on Page 2

The WARTHOGS – What is Known
By our History Correspondent, Natasha Svinya

We here in the Pigdom Plains have always known that others live in the realms beyond the safe walls of the mountain ranges that surround us. We pride ourselves on our relations with the residents of the many island nations in the Pearly Sea, with whom we have shared trade relations as far back as records go...
...in page 4

Is this a first INVASION of ou[r] Pigdom by Wart[hogs]

By our roving corre[spondent] Patrick Hamkins

Yesterday a raiding party in three Warthog flying machines landed in Swillington. They threatened workers at Swillington Farmhouse Industries' main warehouse, stole goods worth over ten thousand Pigdom groats, mostly grain and preserved foods, but also a year's supply of fuel and some portable miniature steam engines. These were designed by the esteemed Professor Hercules Fatchops, inventor of the Pigdom's Commercial Trackway system and many other household innovations. Professor Fatchops is known to be working on flying machines
(continued in page 4)

"...THE CREW OF THE DOWNED WARTHOG AIRCRAFT ESCAPED BEFORE PIGDOM AUTHORITIES COULD REACH IT. THEY WERE TRACKED TO A PASS OVER THE WARTHOG MOUNTAINS, EVIDENTLY MAKING FOR THEIR OWN TERRITORY..."

-PSHAW!-

IDIOTS! THEY LET THE CREW *ESCAPE?* THEY'D HAVE TOLD US EVERYTHING WE NEED TO KNOW...

AS FOR THIS MYSTERIOUS "*AERIAL HOG*"...

YOU'RE JUST *ANGRY* BECAUSE SOMEHOG GOT *AIRBORNE* BEFORE *YOU.*

HE BROUGHT THAT WARTHOG MACHINE *DOWN* AND *CHASED THE OTHERS AWAY.*

YES! *YES,* I AM!

IF THAT *IDIOT* FLANKSFORD HADN'T HAD ME *DIGGING TUNNELS,* I'D HAVE FINISHED A PROTOTYPE AIRCRAFT *YEARS* AGO!

DAD... I COULD *HELP.*

YOU CAN INVENT *A WHOLE NEW WORLD*...TRACKWAYS, TRAMS, ENGINES, COMMUNICATIONS, AND WHAT *THANKS* D'YOU GET?

"WE NEED A FLYING MACHINE IN A WEEK." *ONE WEEK!*

IDIOTS!

DAD, LET ME HELP YOU!

NO, LILY.

DON'T WANT YOU INVOLVED WITH THESE *IMBECILIC* GOVERNMENT TYPES...

BUT I'D BE HELPING *YOU.* I'M NOT A *PIGLET* ANYMORE, DAD.

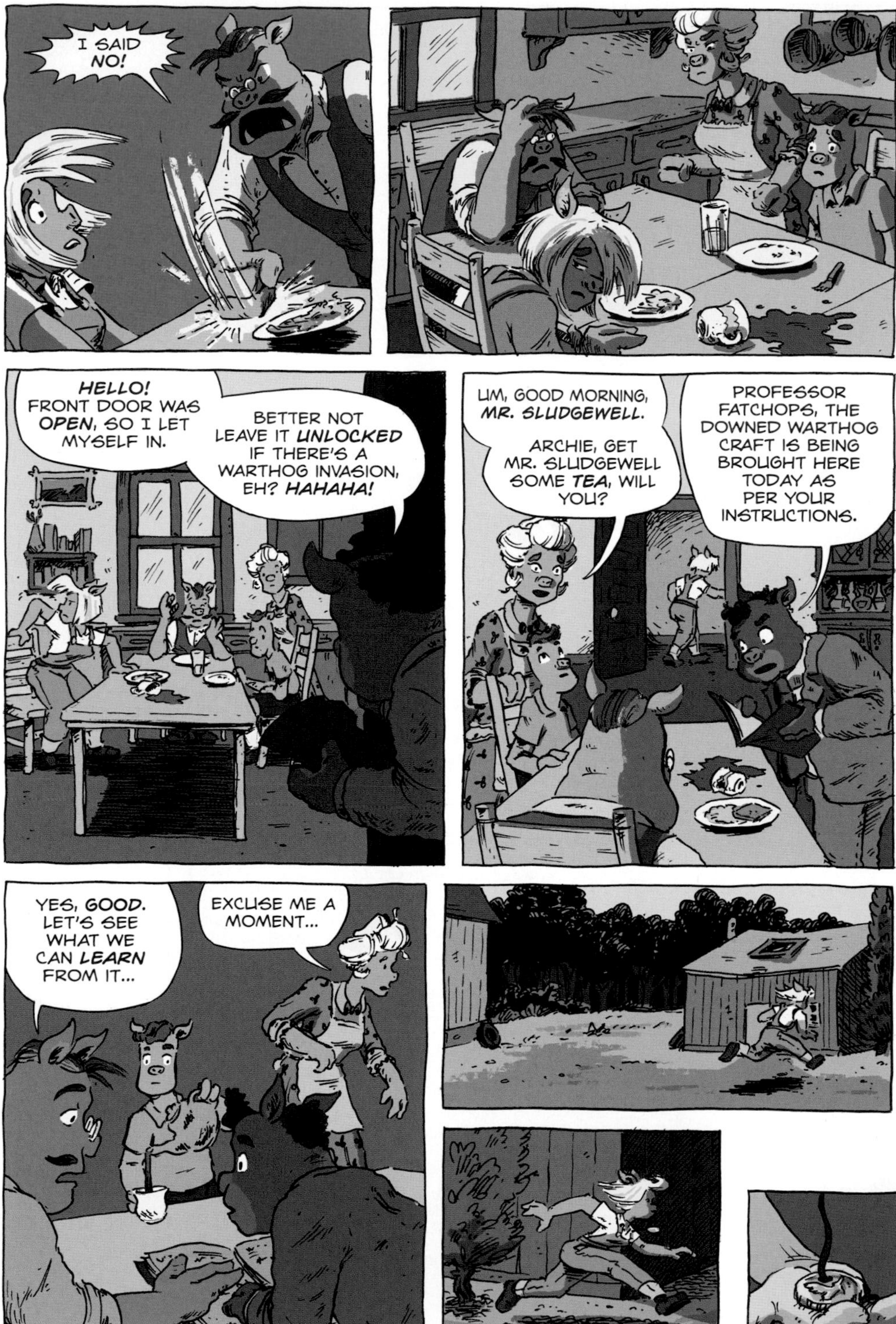

I SAID NO!
HELLO! FRONT DOOR WAS OPEN, SO I LET MYSELF IN.
BETTER NOT LEAVE IT UNLOCKED IF THERE'S A WARTHOG INVASION, EH? HAHAHA!
UM, GOOD MORNING, MR. SLUDGEWELL.
ARCHIE, GET MR. SLUDGEWELL SOME TEA, WILL YOU?
PROFESSOR FATCHOPS, THE DOWNED WARTHOG CRAFT IS BEING BROUGHT HERE TODAY AS PER YOUR INSTRUCTIONS.
YES, GOOD. LET'S SEE WHAT WE CAN LEARN FROM IT...
EXCUSE ME A MOMENT...

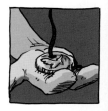

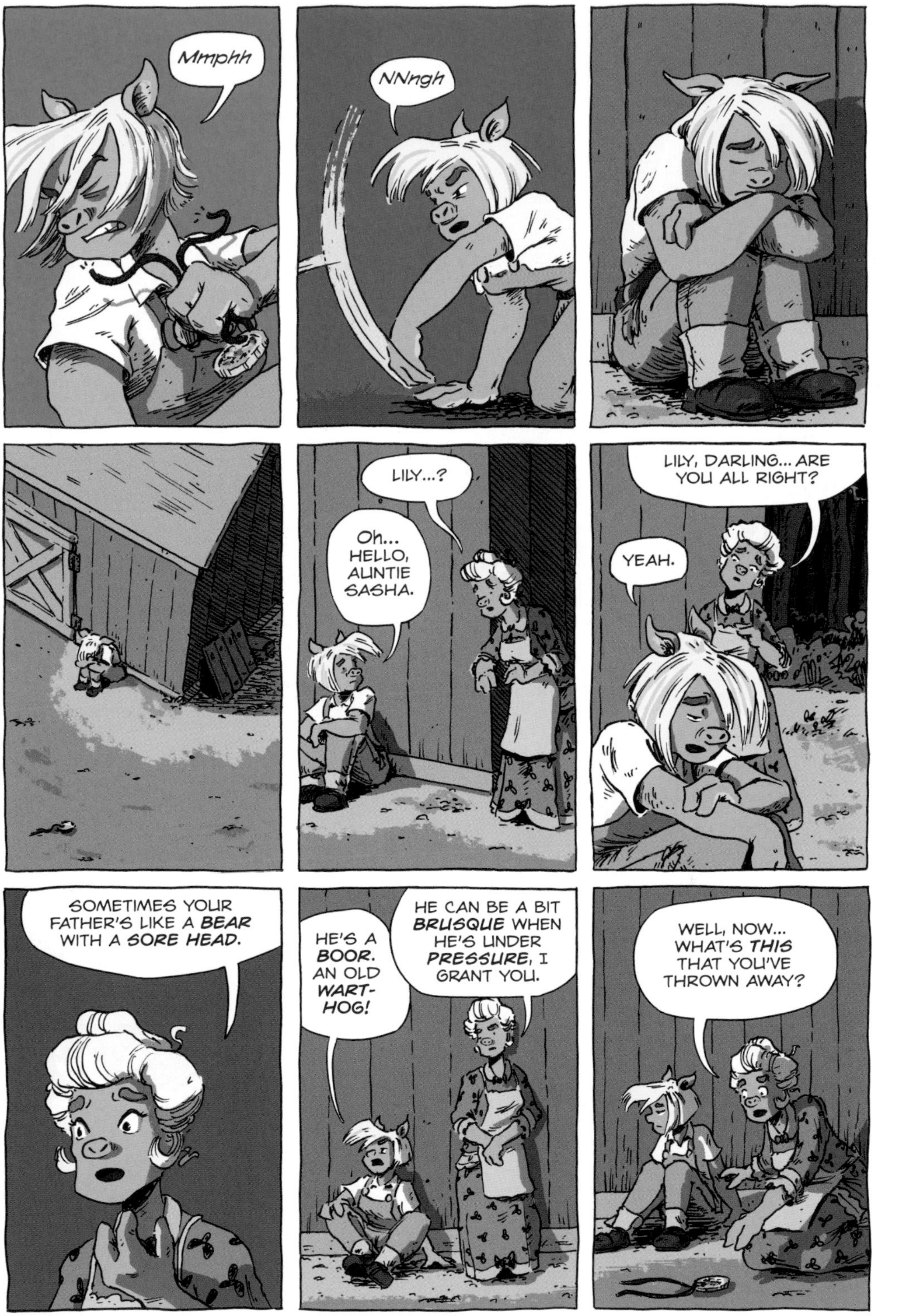
Mmphh
NNngh
LILY...?
Oh... HELLO, AUNTIE SASHA.
LILY, DARLING... ARE YOU ALL RIGHT?
YEAH.
SOMETIMES YOUR FATHER'S LIKE A BEAR WITH A SORE HEAD.
HE'S A BOOR. AN OLD WART-HOG!
HE CAN BE A BIT BRUSQUE WHEN HE'S UNDER PRESSURE, I GRANT YOU.
WELL, NOW... WHAT'S THIS THAT YOU'VE THROWN AWAY?

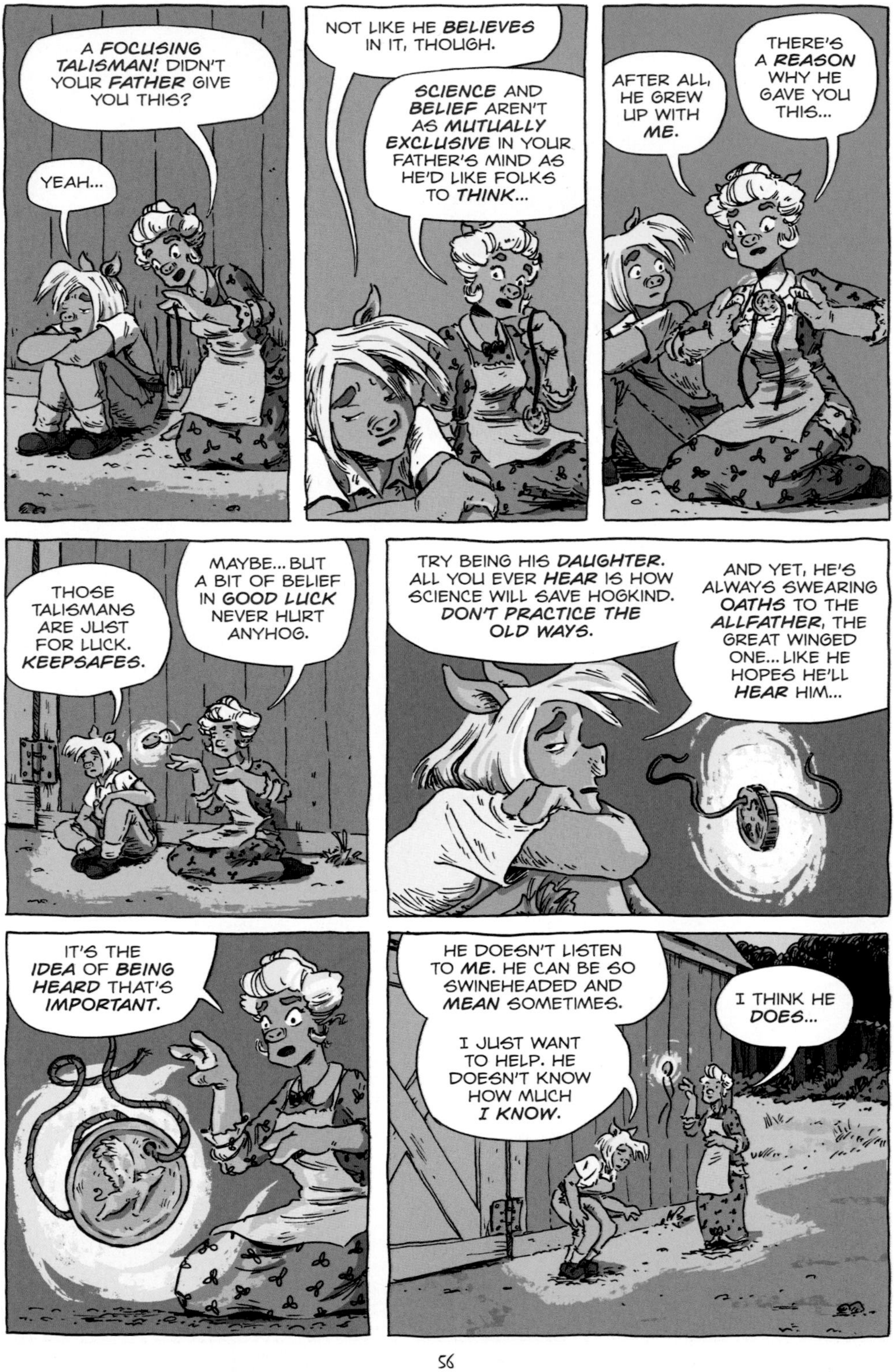
A FOCUSING TALISMAN! DIDN'T YOUR FATHER GIVE YOU THIS?
YEAH...
NOT LIKE HE BELIEVES IN IT, THOUGH.
SCIENCE AND BELIEF AREN'T AS MUTUALLY EXCLUSIVE IN YOUR FATHER'S MIND AS HE'D LIKE FOLKS TO THINK...
AFTER ALL, HE GREW UP WITH ME.
THERE'S A REASON WHY HE GAVE YOU THIS...
THOSE TALISMANS ARE JUST FOR LUCK. KEEPSAFES.
MAYBE... BUT A BIT OF BELIEF IN GOOD LUCK NEVER HURT ANYHOG.
TRY BEING HIS DAUGHTER. ALL YOU EVER HEAR IS HOW SCIENCE WILL SAVE HOGKIND. DON'T PRACTICE THE OLD WAYS.
AND YET, HE'S ALWAYS SWEARING OATHS TO THE ALLFATHER, THE GREAT WINGED ONE... LIKE HE HOPES HE'LL HEAR HIM...
IT'S THE IDEA OF BEING HEARD THAT'S IMPORTANT.
HE DOESN'T LISTEN TO ME. HE CAN BE SO SWINEHEADED AND MEAN SOMETIMES.
I JUST WANT TO HELP. HE DOESN'T KNOW HOW MUCH I KNOW.
I THINK HE DOES...

...HE JUST DOESN'T WANT YOU FALLING INTO THE SAME *TRAP* HE DID, WORKING FOR ALL THOSE FAT-BOTTOMED, SELF-IMPORTANT FOOLS...

HE WANTS SOMETHING *BETTER* FOR YOU.

IT MIGHT SOUND *CORNY*, LILY, BUT *YOU* ARE WHAT HE *BELIEVES* IN.

FUNNY WAY OF *SHOWING* IT.

AND WHAT ABOUT *YOU*, LILY LEANCHOPS? WHAT DO *YOU* BELIEVE? DO YOU STILL HAVE THAT TRICKBOX *I* GAVE YOU?

OF *COURSE!* I WOULDN'T PART WITH *THAT* FOR *ANYTHING!*

THAT'S NICE TO KNOW. THAT'S *MY* KEEPSAFE TO YOU. YOU *KNOW* HOW MUCH I LOVE YOU, LILY. I DON'T WANT ANYTHING EVER TO *HAPPEN* TO YOU.

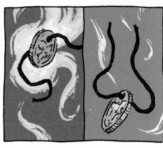

Oh, AUNTIE SASHA... WHAT WOULD I *DO* WITHOUT YOU?

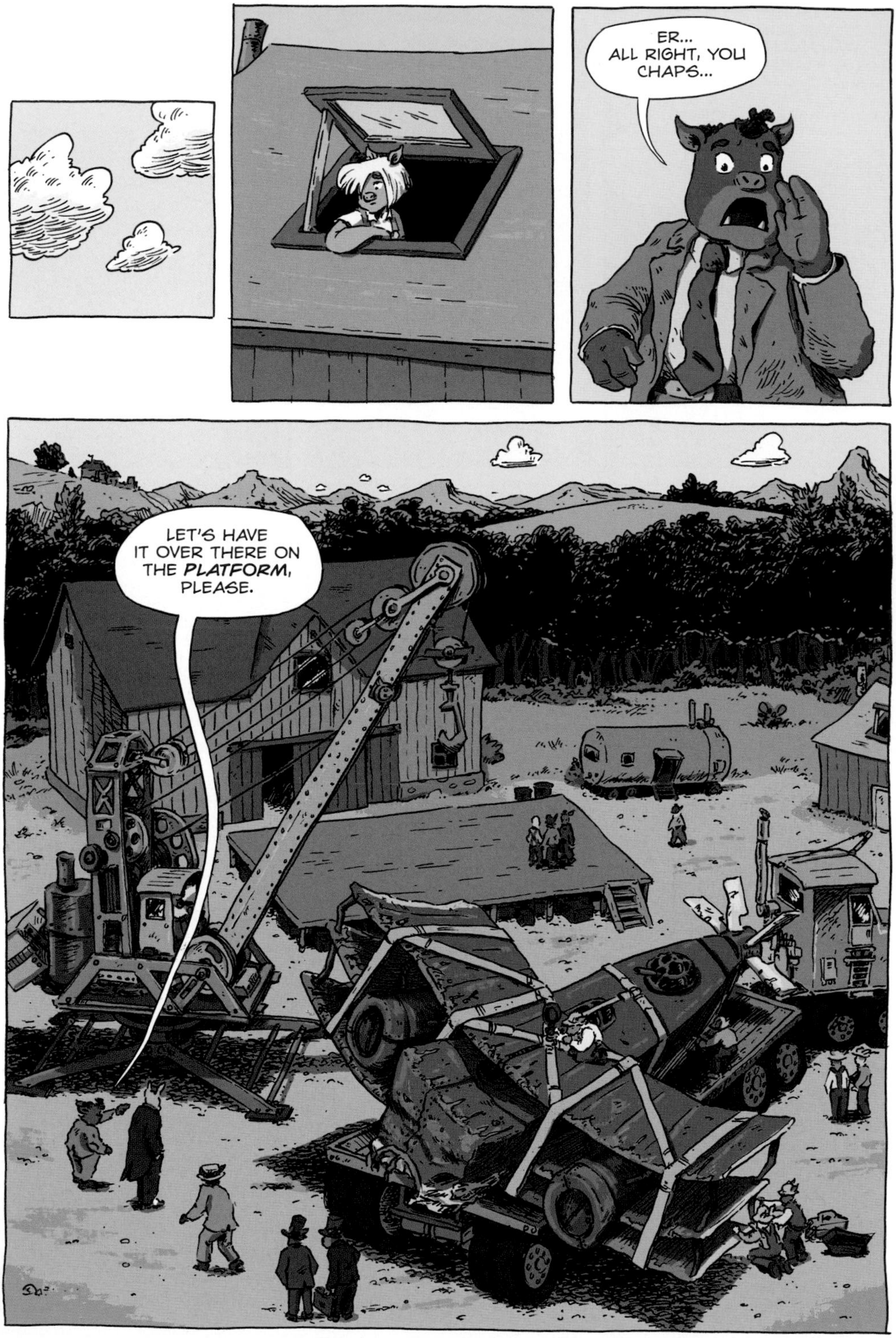
ER... ALL RIGHT, YOU CHAPS...
LET'S HAVE IT OVER THERE ON THE *PLATFORM*, PLEASE.

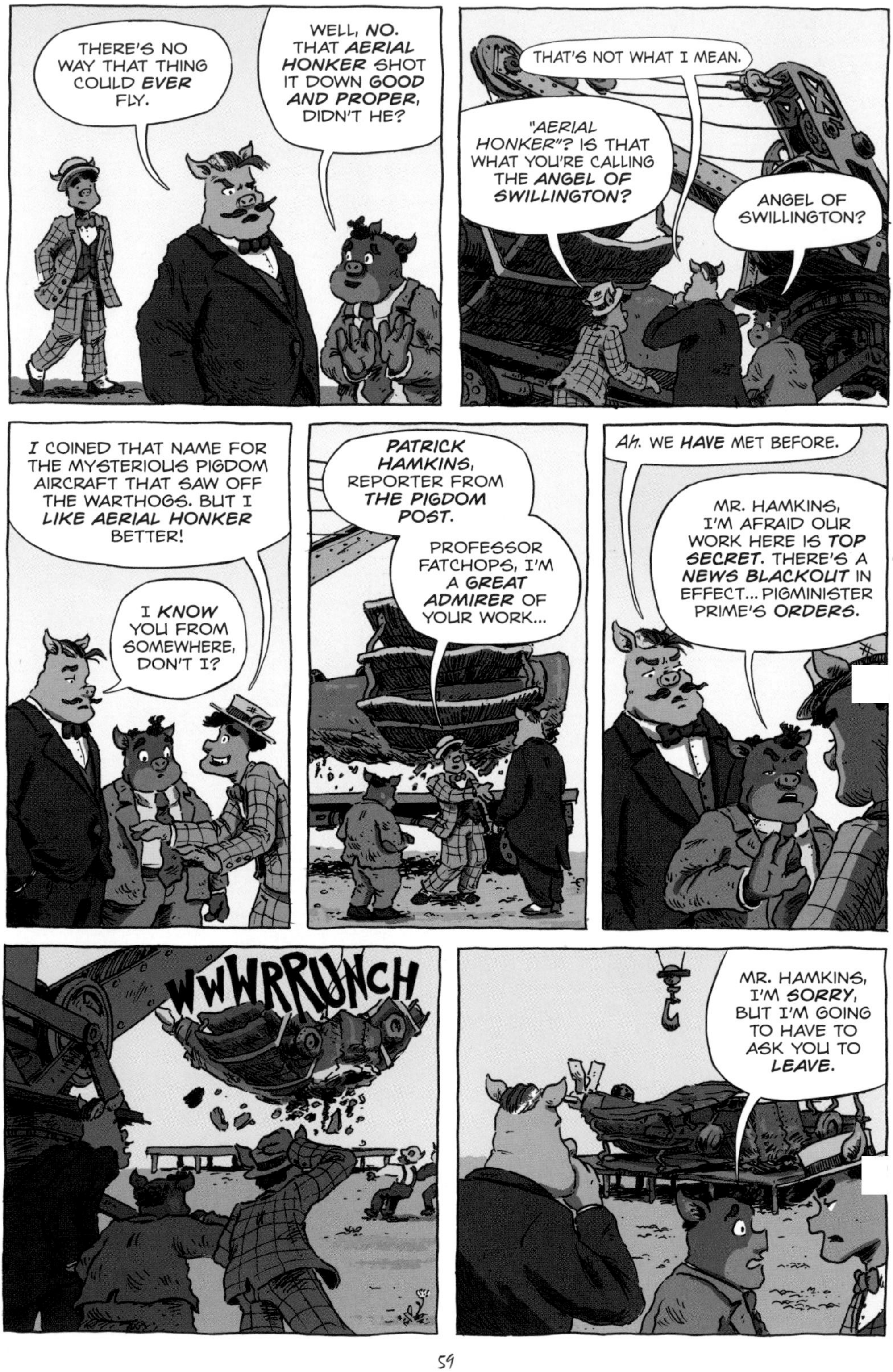
THERE'S NO WAY THAT THING COULD EVER FLY.
WELL, NO. THAT AERIAL HONKER SHOT IT DOWN GOOD AND PROPER, DIDN'T HE?
THAT'S NOT WHAT I MEAN.
"AERIAL HONKER"? IS THAT WHAT YOU'RE CALLING THE ANGEL OF SWILLINGTON?
ANGEL OF SWILLINGTON?
I COINED THAT NAME FOR THE MYSTERIOUS PIGDOM AIRCRAFT THAT SAW OFF THE WARTHOGS. BUT I LIKE AERIAL HONKER BETTER!
I KNOW YOU FROM SOMEWHERE, DON'T I?
PATRICK HAMKINS, REPORTER FROM THE PIGDOM POST.
PROFESSOR FATCHOPS, I'M A GREAT ADMIRER OF YOUR WORK...
Ah. WE HAVE MET BEFORE.
MR. HAMKINS, I'M AFRAID OUR WORK HERE IS TOP SECRET. THERE'S A NEWS BLACKOUT IN EFFECT... PIGMINISTER PRIME'S ORDERS.
WWWRRUNCH
MR. HAMKINS, I'M SORRY, BUT I'M GOING TO HAVE TO ASK YOU TO LEAVE.

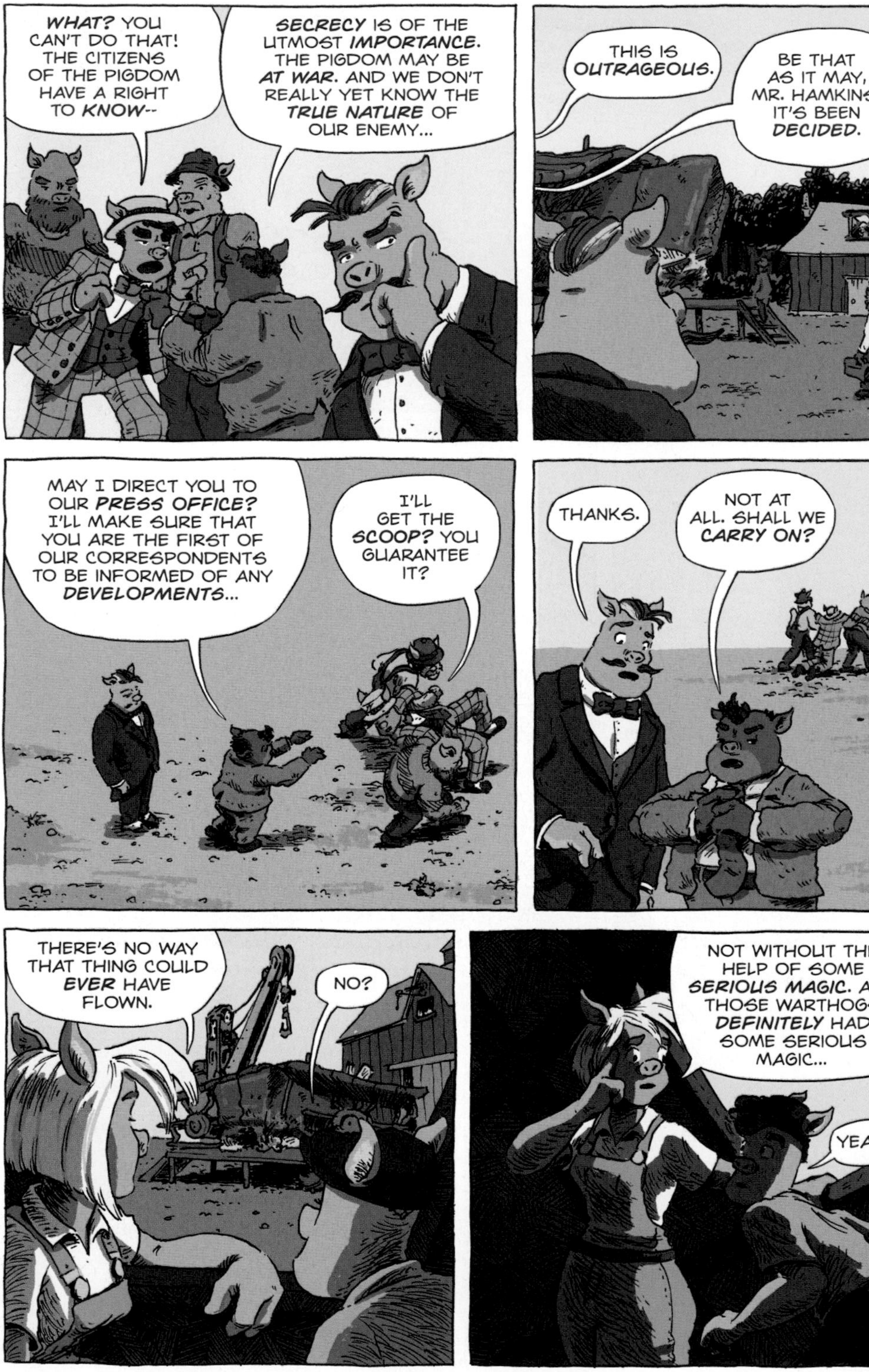
WHAT? YOU CAN'T DO THAT! THE CITIZENS OF THE PIGDOM HAVE A RIGHT TO KNOW--
SECRECY IS OF THE UTMOST IMPORTANCE. THE PIGDOM MAY BE AT WAR. AND WE DON'T REALLY YET KNOW THE TRUE NATURE OF OUR ENEMY...
THIS IS OUTRAGEOUS.
BE THAT AS IT MAY, MR. HAMKINS. IT'S BEEN DECIDED.
MAY I DIRECT YOU TO OUR PRESS OFFICE? I'LL MAKE SURE THAT YOU ARE THE FIRST OF OUR CORRESPONDENTS TO BE INFORMED OF ANY DEVELOPMENTS...
I'LL GET THE SCOOP? YOU GUARANTEE IT?
THANKS.
NOT AT ALL. SHALL WE CARRY ON?
THERE'S NO WAY THAT THING COULD EVER HAVE FLOWN.
NO?
NOT WITHOUT THE HELP OF SOME SERIOUS MAGIC. AND THOSE WARTHOGS DEFINITELY HAD SOME SERIOUS MAGIC...
YEAH.

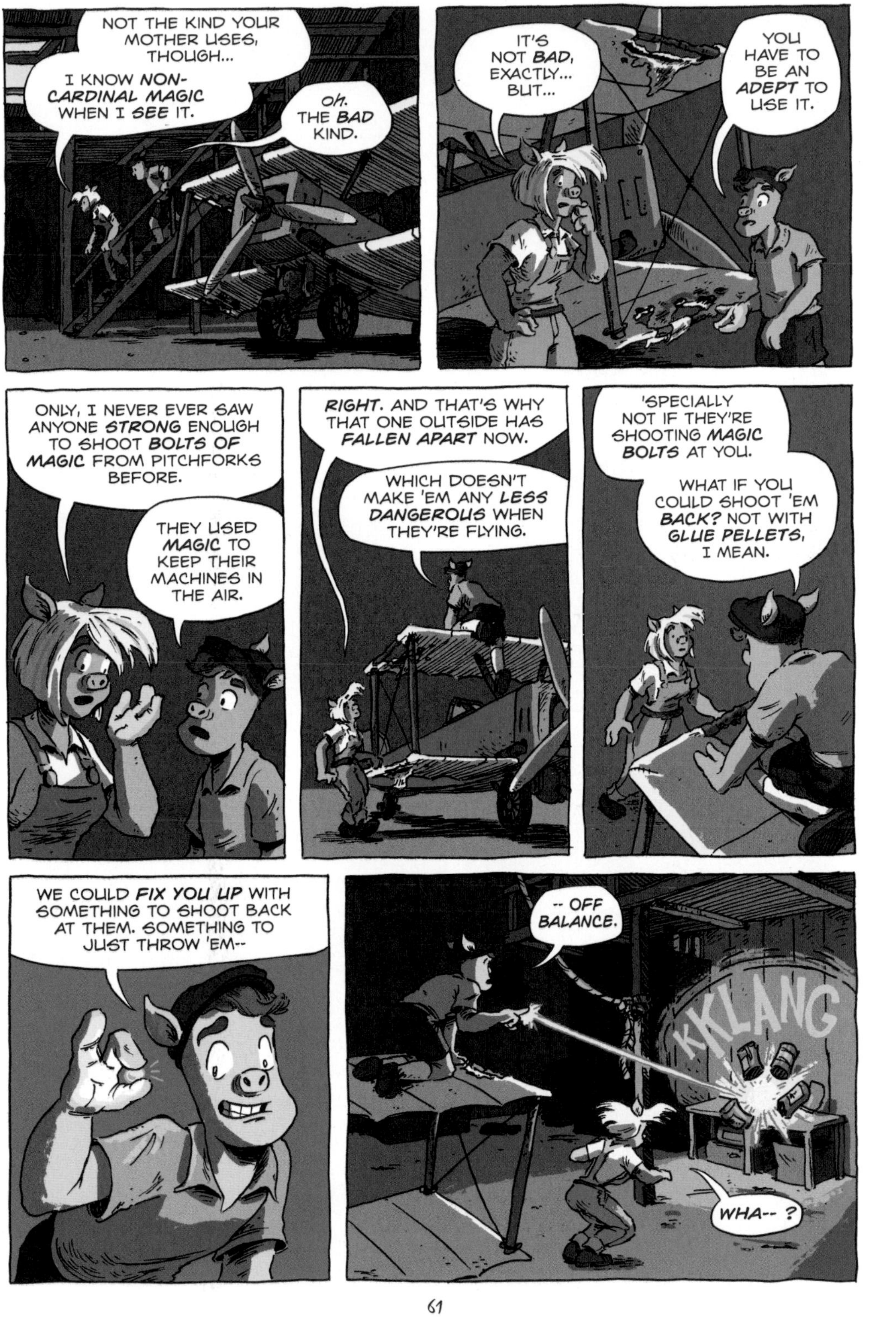
NOT THE KIND YOUR MOTHER USES, THOUGH...
I KNOW NON-CARDINAL MAGIC WHEN I SEE IT.
Oh. THE BAD KIND.
IT'S NOT BAD, EXACTLY... BUT...
YOU HAVE TO BE AN ADEPT TO USE IT.
ONLY, I NEVER EVER SAW ANYONE STRONG ENOUGH TO SHOOT BOLTS OF MAGIC FROM PITCHFORKS BEFORE.
THEY USED MAGIC TO KEEP THEIR MACHINES IN THE AIR.
RIGHT. AND THAT'S WHY THAT ONE OUTSIDE HAS FALLEN APART NOW.
WHICH DOESN'T MAKE 'EM ANY LESS DANGEROUS WHEN THEY'RE FLYING.
'SPECIALLY NOT IF THEY'RE SHOOTING MAGIC BOLTS AT YOU.
WHAT IF YOU COULD SHOOT 'EM BACK? NOT WITH GLUE PELLETS, I MEAN.
WE COULD FIX YOU UP WITH SOMETHING TO SHOOT BACK AT THEM. SOMETHING TO JUST THROW 'EM--
-- OFF BALANCE.
KKLANG
WHA-- ?

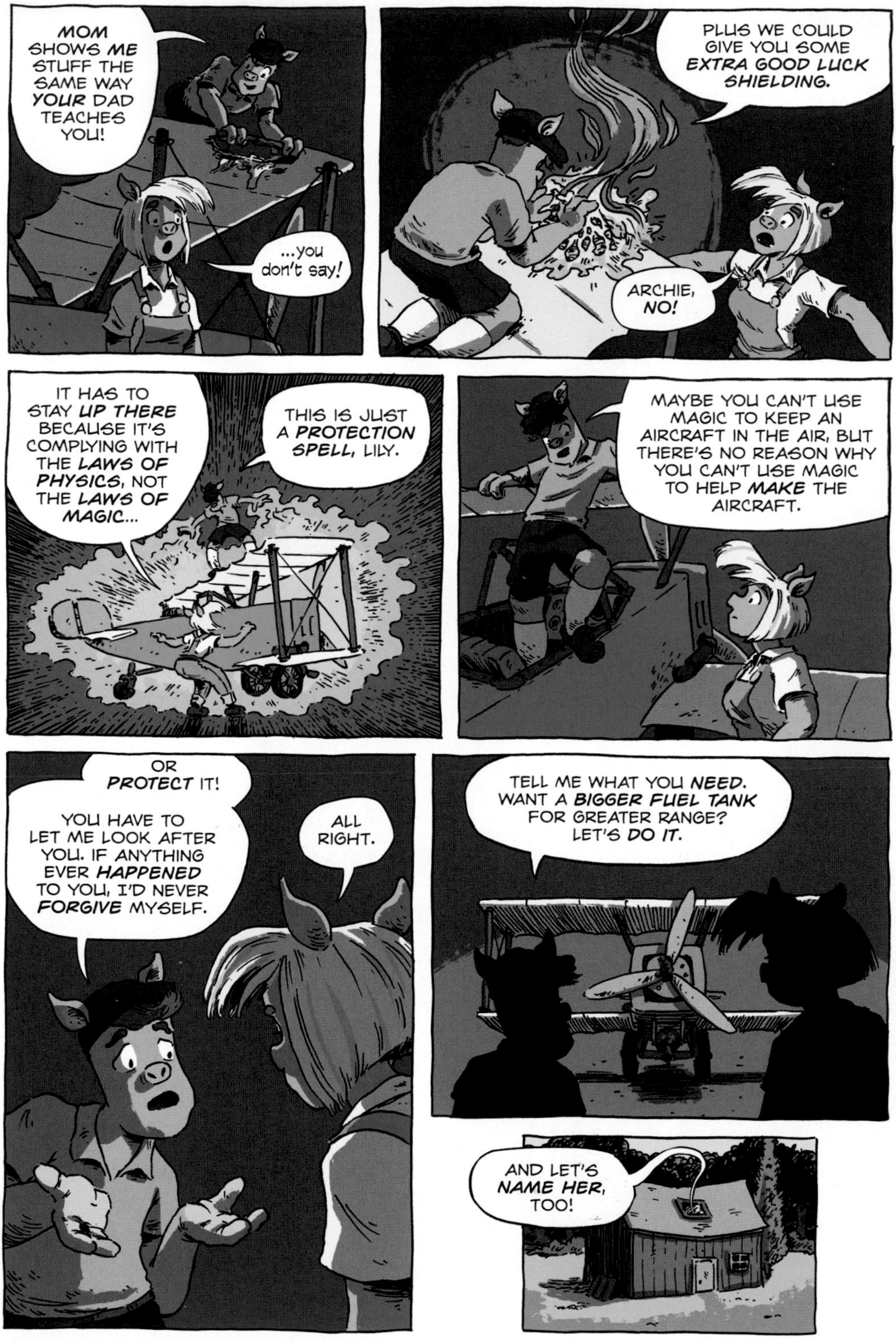
MOM SHOWS ME STUFF THE SAME WAY YOUR DAD TEACHES YOU!
...you don't say!
PLUS WE COULD GIVE YOU SOME EXTRA GOOD LUCK SHIELDING.
ARCHIE, NO!
IT HAS TO STAY UP THERE BECAUSE IT'S COMPLYING WITH THE LAWS OF PHYSICS, NOT THE LAWS OF MAGIC...
THIS IS JUST A PROTECTION SPELL, LILY.
MAYBE YOU CAN'T USE MAGIC TO KEEP AN AIRCRAFT IN THE AIR, BUT THERE'S NO REASON WHY YOU CAN'T USE MAGIC TO HELP MAKE THE AIRCRAFT.
OR PROTECT IT!
YOU HAVE TO LET ME LOOK AFTER YOU. IF ANYTHING EVER HAPPENED TO YOU, I'D NEVER FORGIVE MYSELF.
ALL RIGHT.
TELL ME WHAT YOU NEED. WANT A BIGGER FUEL TANK FOR GREATER RANGE? LET'S DO IT.
AND LET'S NAME HER, TOO!

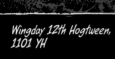

Wingday 12th Hogtween, 1101 YH

The past few days have been both _intolerable_ and _intoxicating_. I felt overcome by a deep despair in confronting the apparent impossibility of the task I've been given.

And yet, by drawing on all my past ideas and designs, we are shaping the possibility of building something that might actually prove to be _serviceable_. There is _something_ _in the air_, a sense of timing and _possibility_ that is helping make this venture cohere.

To my surprise, I have found an ally in _Horace Sludgewell_, the ministerial aide assigned to me. I thought he would be pugnacious, interfering, power-hungry, and unreasonable, like all the political types I know. He is not the unimaginative, vulgarian dullard I feared. Indeed, he handles the workers well and has gone out of his way to be both supportive and efficient.

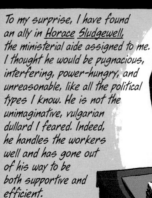

One thing really _bothers me_-- the mysterious _Angel of Swillington_, as Patrick Hamkins dubbed it. Hamkins is a swine and a hack, but his snout for a good story is not in doubt. Perhaps he suspects that I fear that this "Aerial Hog" may prove to be my ex-apprentice, _Ham Trotters_, but there is nothing I can find in the reports of the craft's appearance that point to Trotters's trademark laziness of design.

My instincts tell me that I am missing something entirely _obvious_ here. Who is this valiant and strange vigilante of the skies? I don't, unfortunately, have time to ponder this. My attention must be on the project at hand...

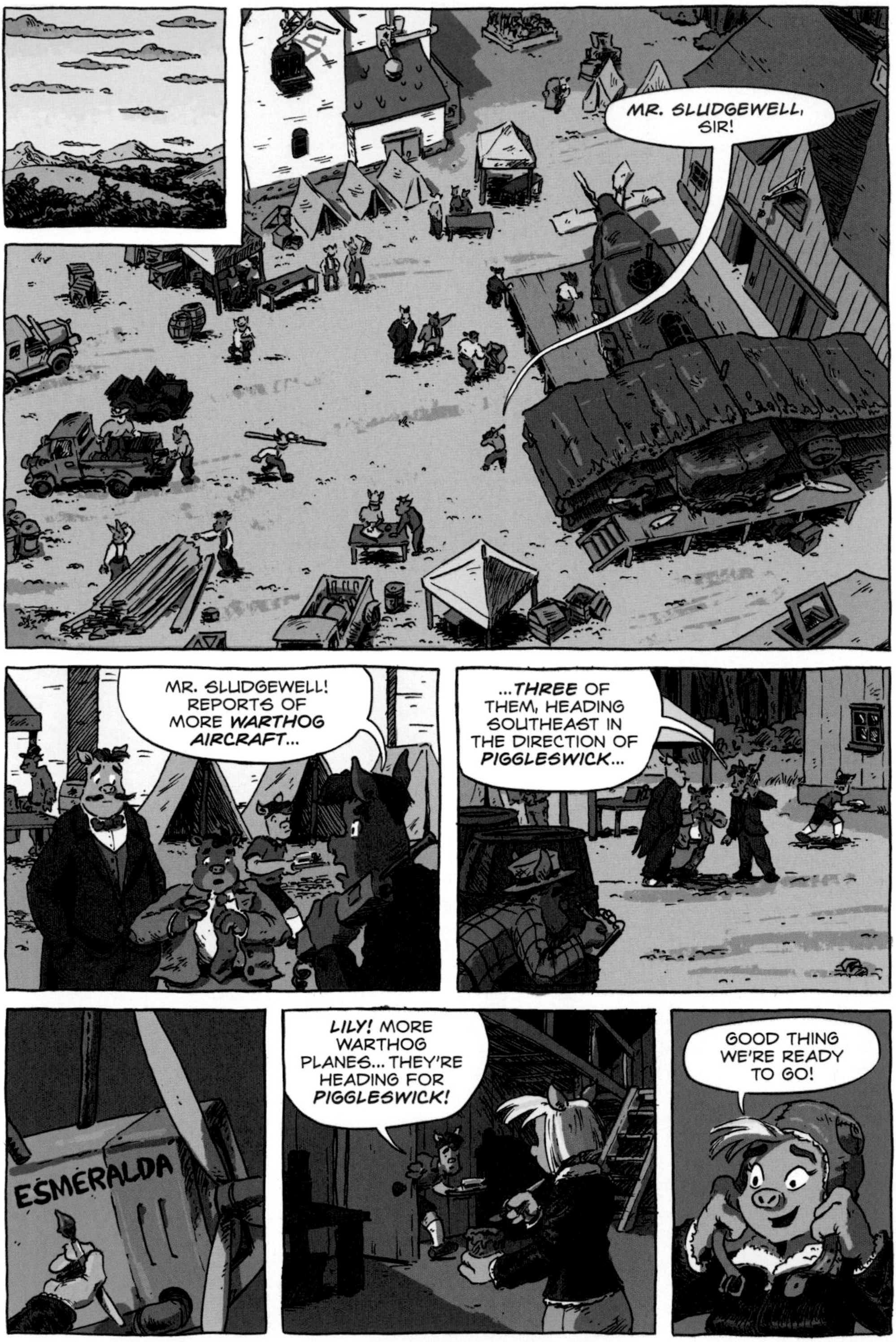
MR. SLUDGEWELL, SIR!
MR. SLUDGEWELL! REPORTS OF MORE WARTHOG AIRCRAFT...
...THREE OF THEM, HEADING SOUTHEAST IN THE DIRECTION OF PIGGLESWICK...
ESMERALDA
LILY! MORE WARTHOG PLANES... THEY'RE HEADING FOR PIGGLESWICK!
GOOD THING WE'RE READY TO GO!

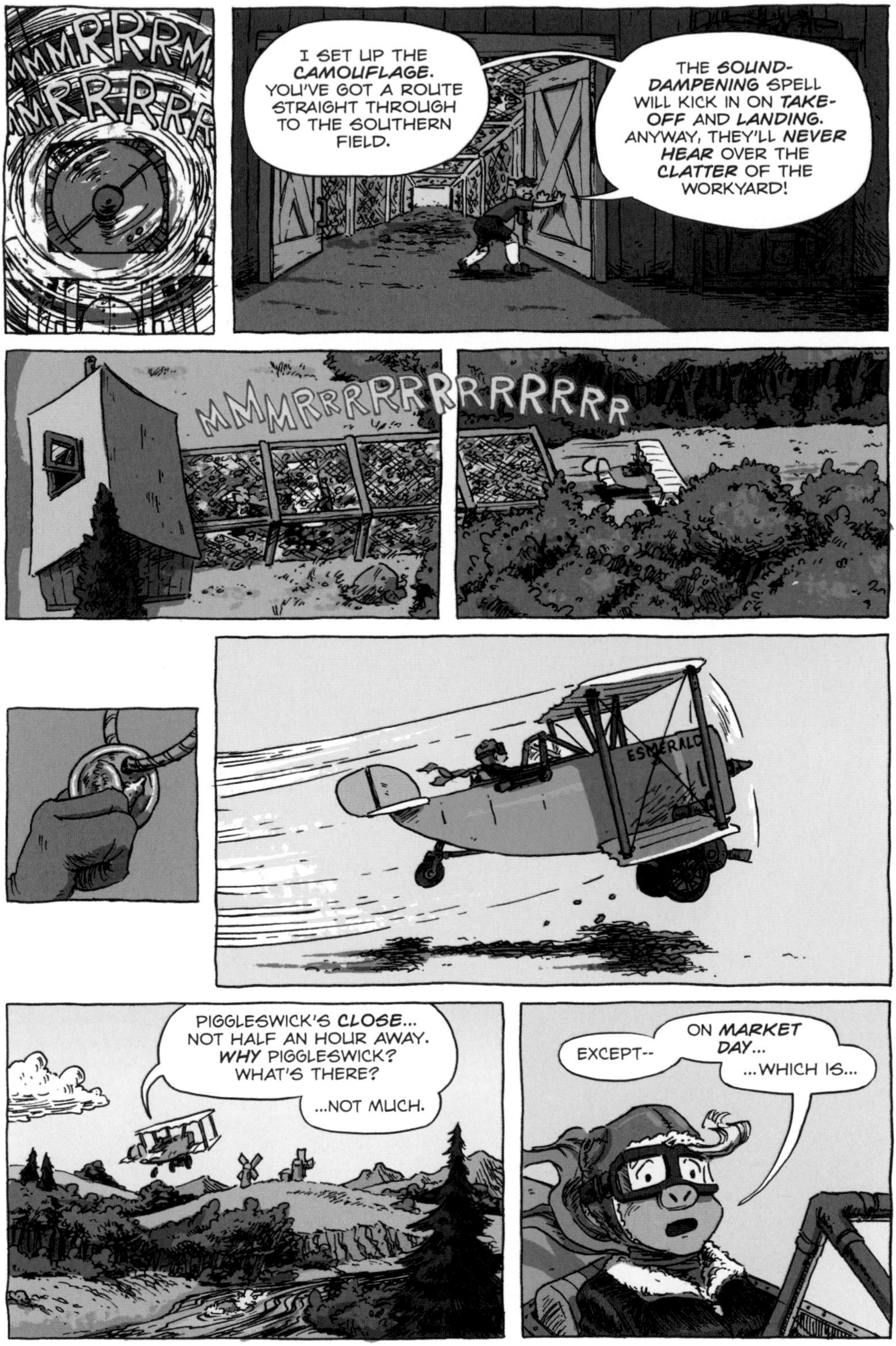
MMMRRRRM
MMRRRRR
I SET UP THE CAMOUFLAGE. YOU'VE GOT A ROUTE STRAIGHT THROUGH TO THE SOUTHERN FIELD.
THE SOUND-DAMPENING SPELL WILL KICK IN ON TAKE-OFF AND LANDING. ANYWAY, THEY'LL NEVER HEAR OVER THE CLATTER OF THE WORKYARD!
MMMRRRRRRRRRRRRR
ESMERALD
PIGGLESWICK'S CLOSE... NOT HALF AN HOUR AWAY. WHY PIGGLESWICK? WHAT'S THERE?
...NOT MUCH.
EXCEPT--
ON MARKET DAY...
...WHICH IS...

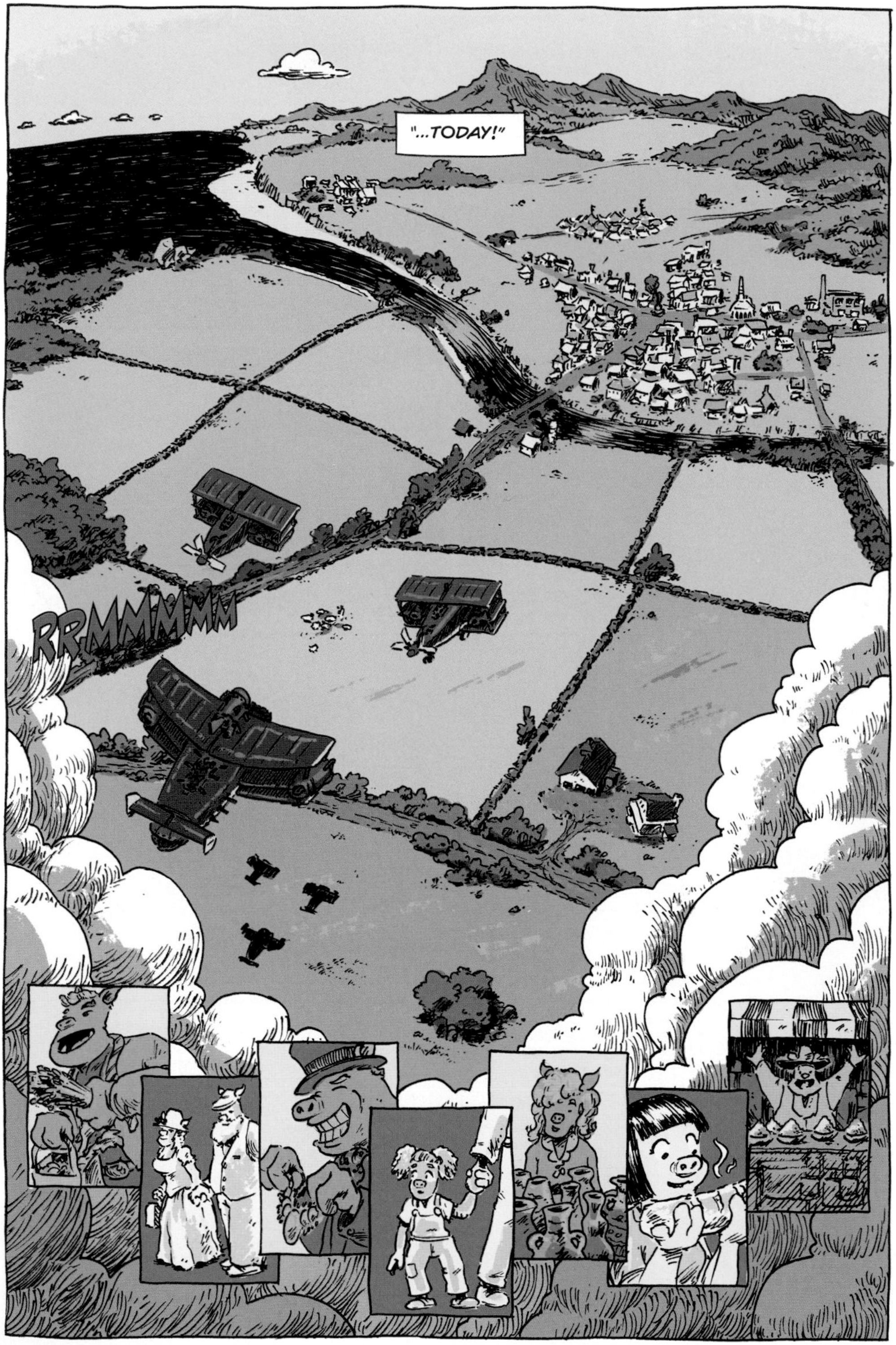
"...TODAY!"
RRMMMMM

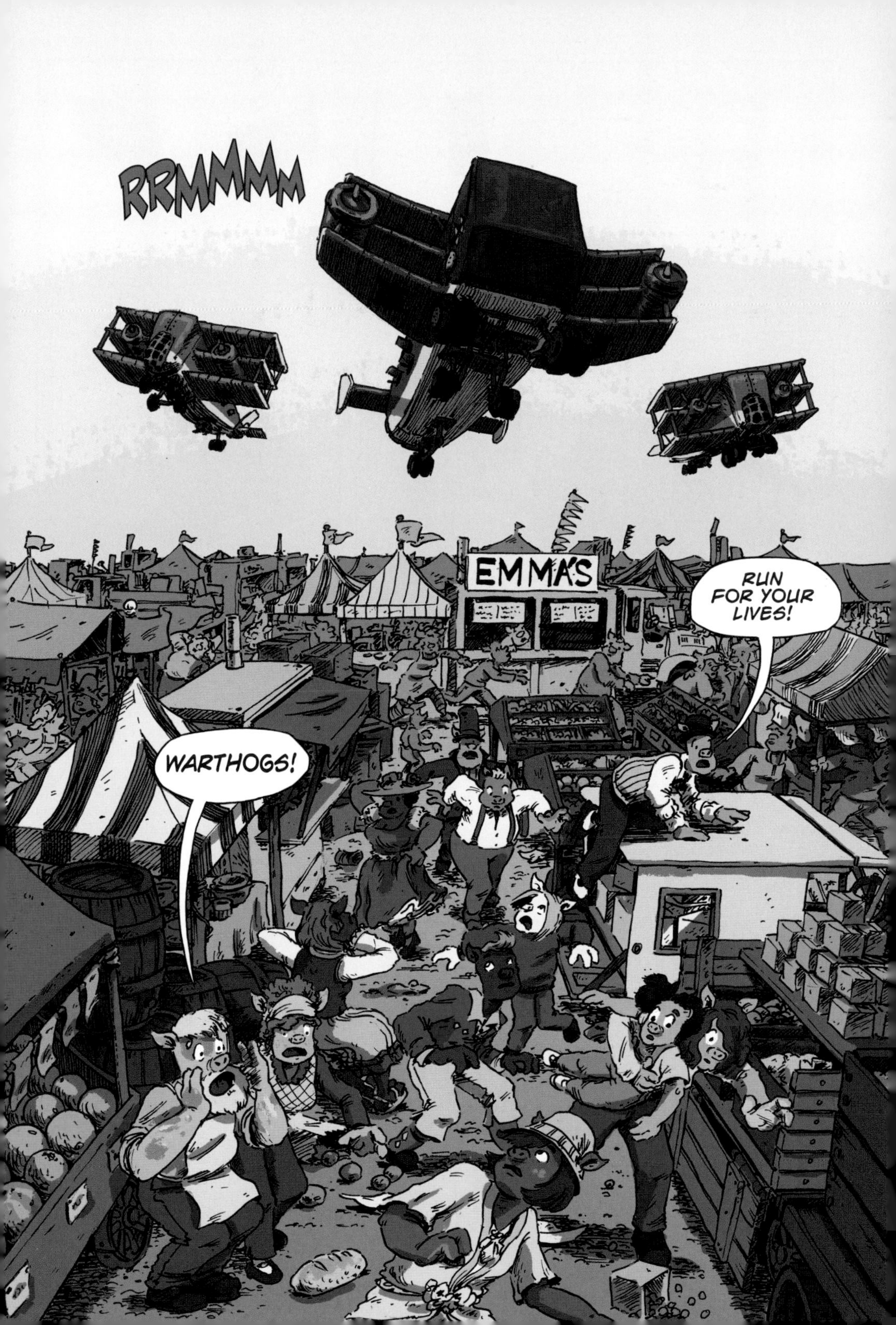
RRMMMM
EMMA'S
RUN FOR YOUR LIVES!
WARTHOGS!

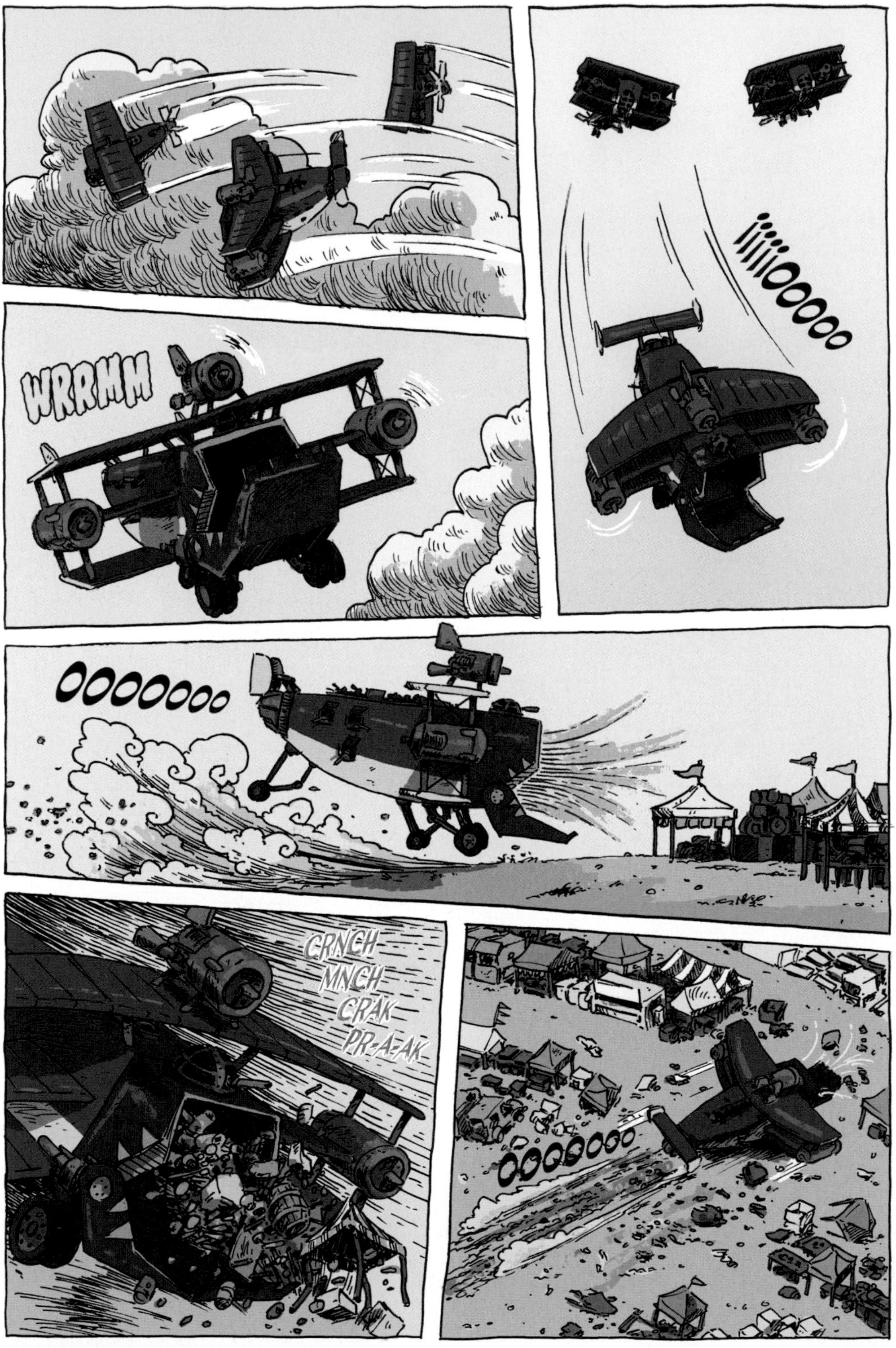

iiiiiiOOOOOO
WRRMM
OOOOOOO
CRNCH
MNCH
CRAK
PR-A-AK
OOOOOOO

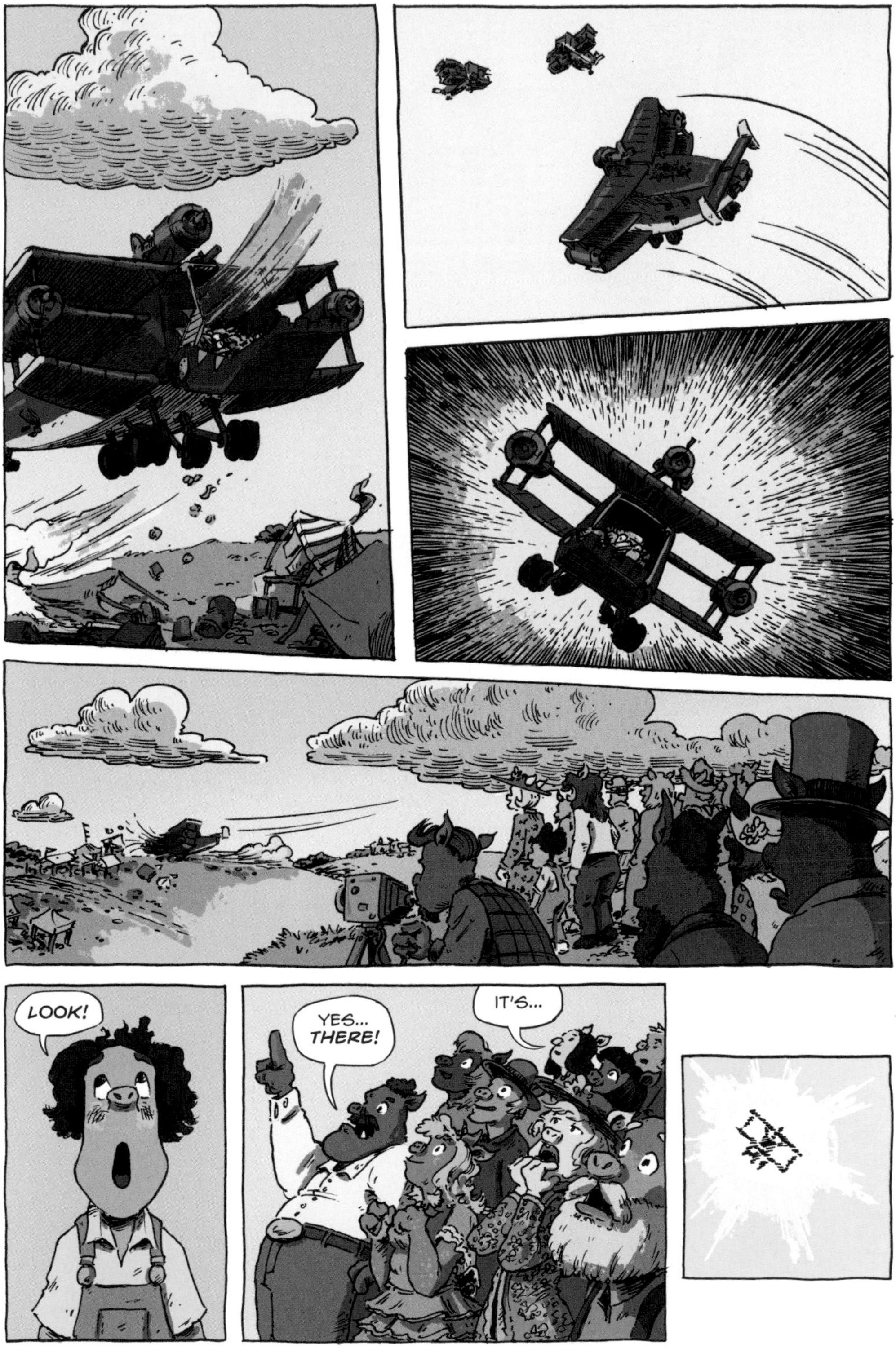
LOOK!
YES... THERE!
IT'S...

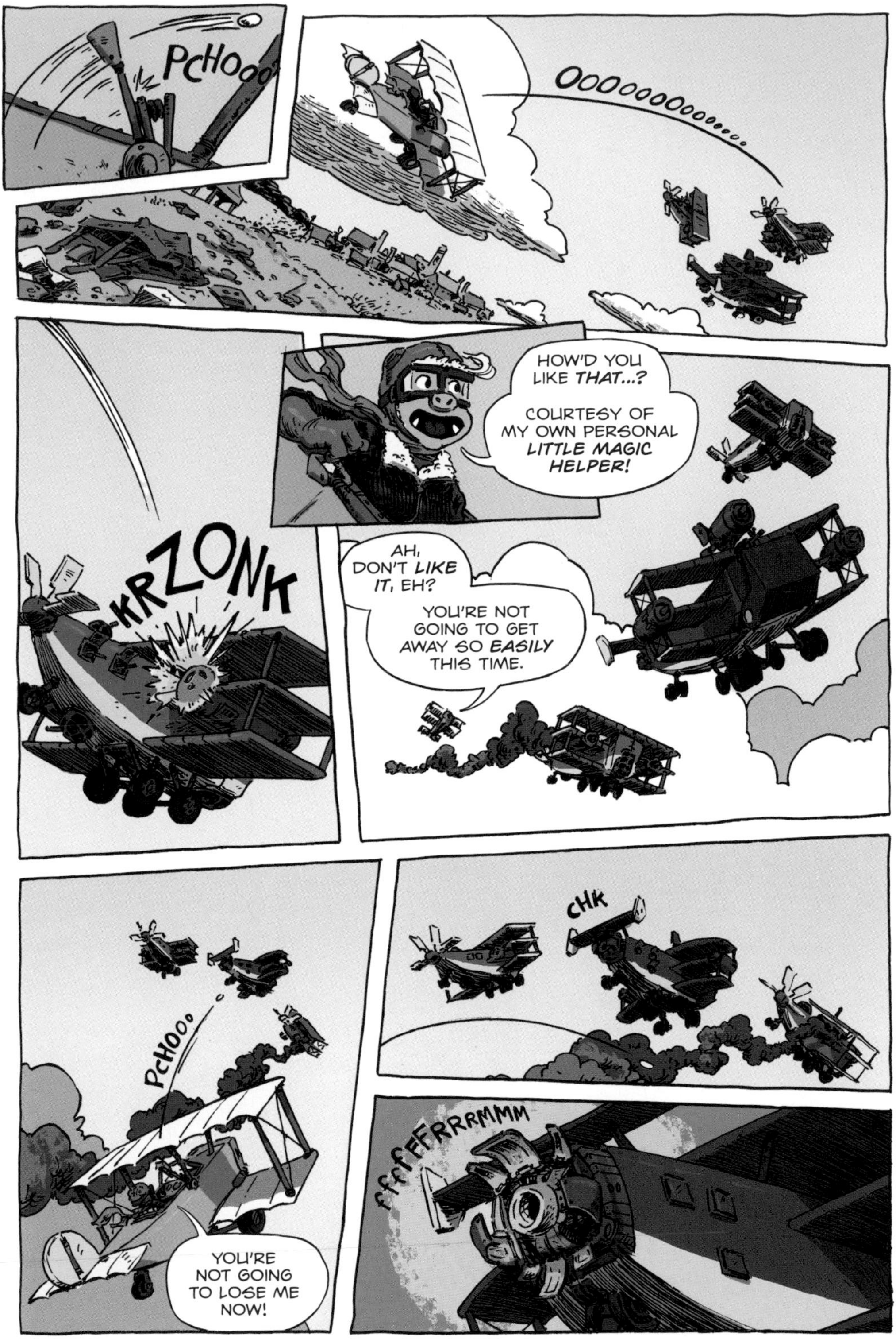
PCHOOO
OOOOOOOOOOOOOO
HOW'D YOU LIKE *THAT...?*
COURTESY OF MY OWN PERSONAL *LITTLE MAGIC HELPER!*
KRZONK
AH, DON'T *LIKE IT*, EH?
YOU'RE NOT GOING TO GET AWAY SO *EASILY* THIS TIME.
PCHOOO
YOU'RE NOT GOING TO LOSE ME NOW!
CHK
FFFFFFRRRMMM

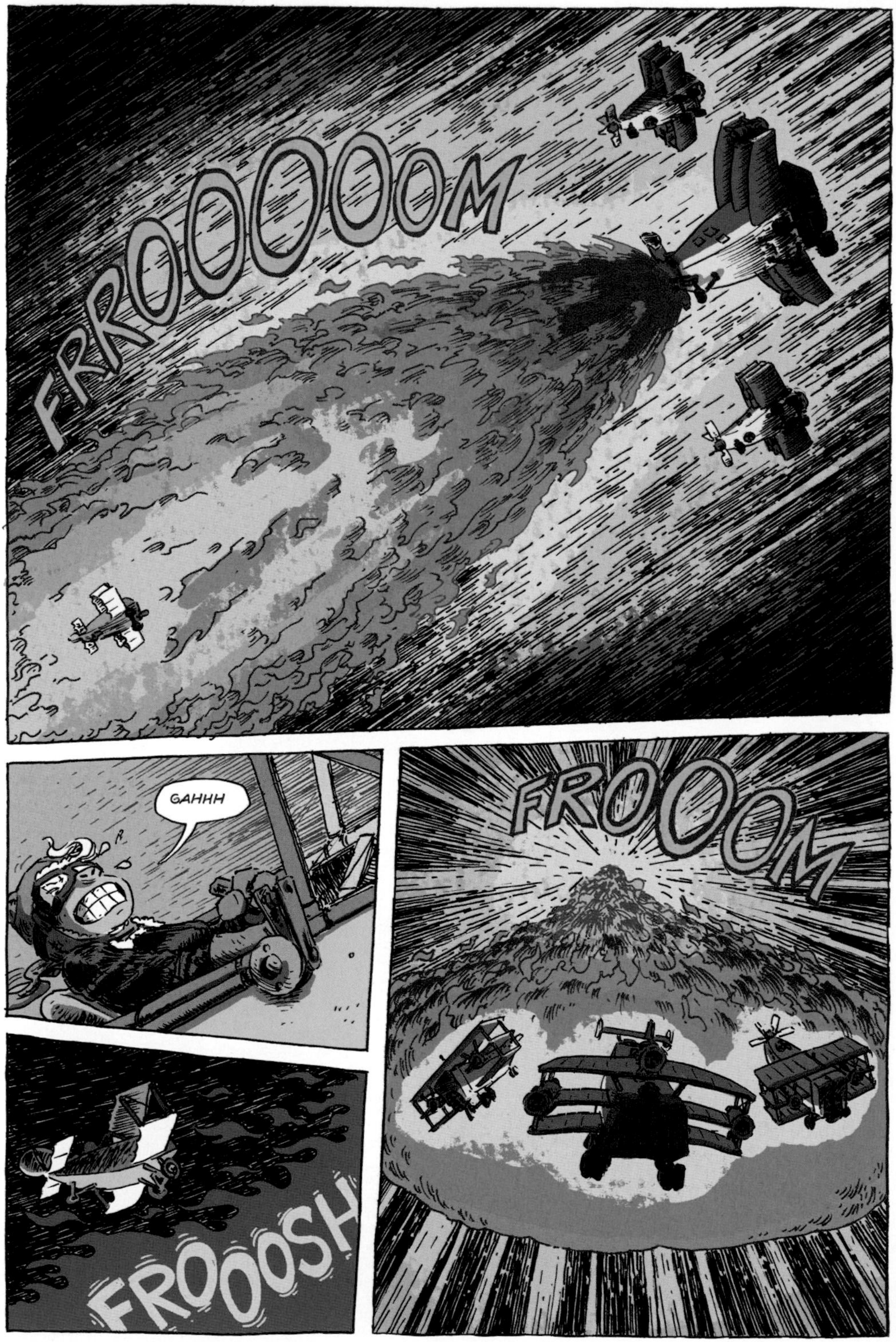
FRROOOOOM
GAHHH
FROOOM
FROOOSH

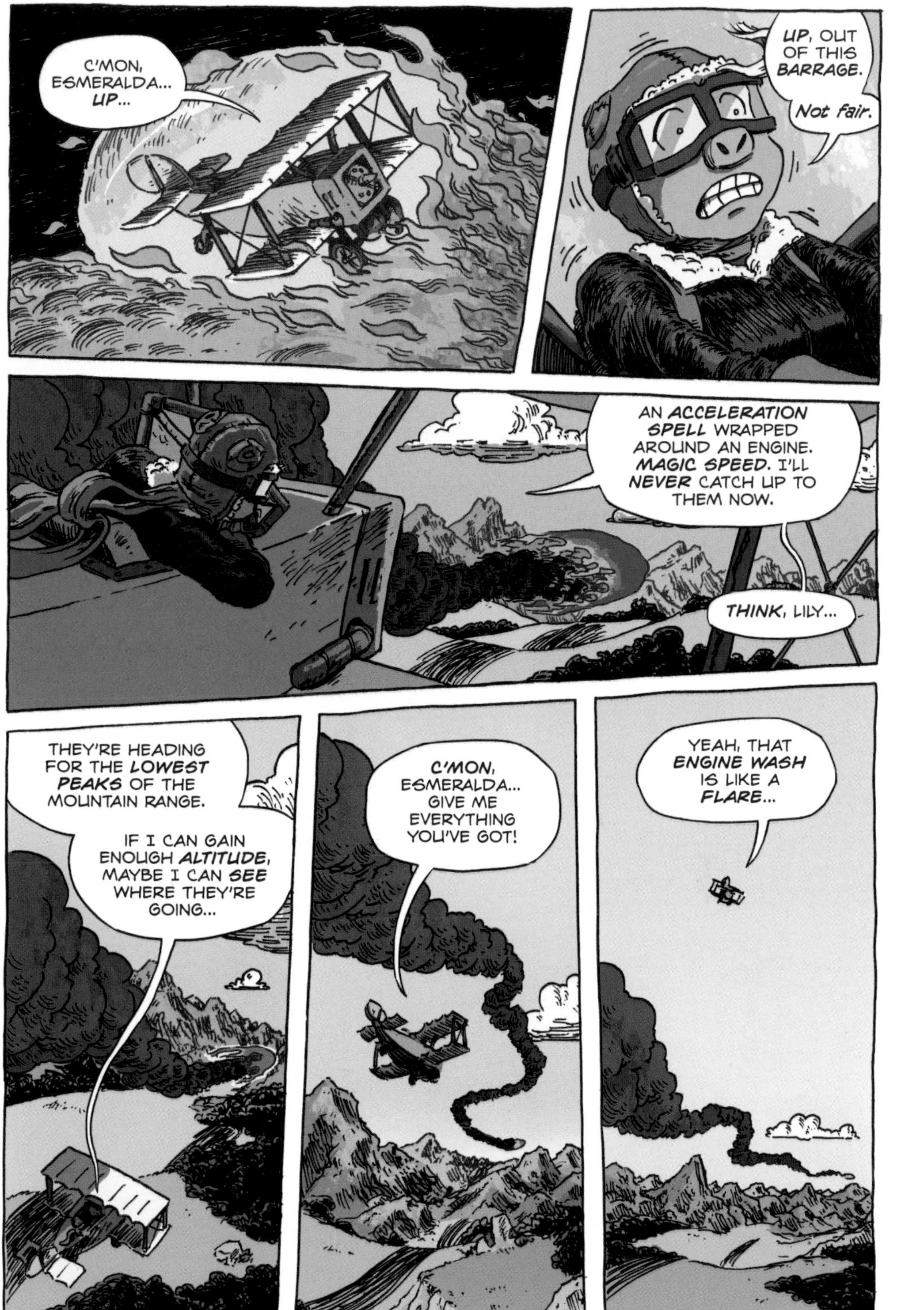
C'MON, ESMERALDA... UP...
UP, OUT OF THIS BARRAGE.
Not fair.
AN ACCELERATION SPELL WRAPPED AROUND AN ENGINE. MAGIC SPEED. I'LL NEVER CATCH UP TO THEM NOW.
THINK, LILY...
THEY'RE HEADING FOR THE LOWEST PEAKS OF THE MOUNTAIN RANGE.
IF I CAN GAIN ENOUGH ALTITUDE, MAYBE I CAN SEE WHERE THEY'RE GOING...
C'MON, ESMERALDA... GIVE ME EVERYTHING YOU'VE GOT!
YEAH, THAT ENGINE WASH IS LIKE A FLARE...

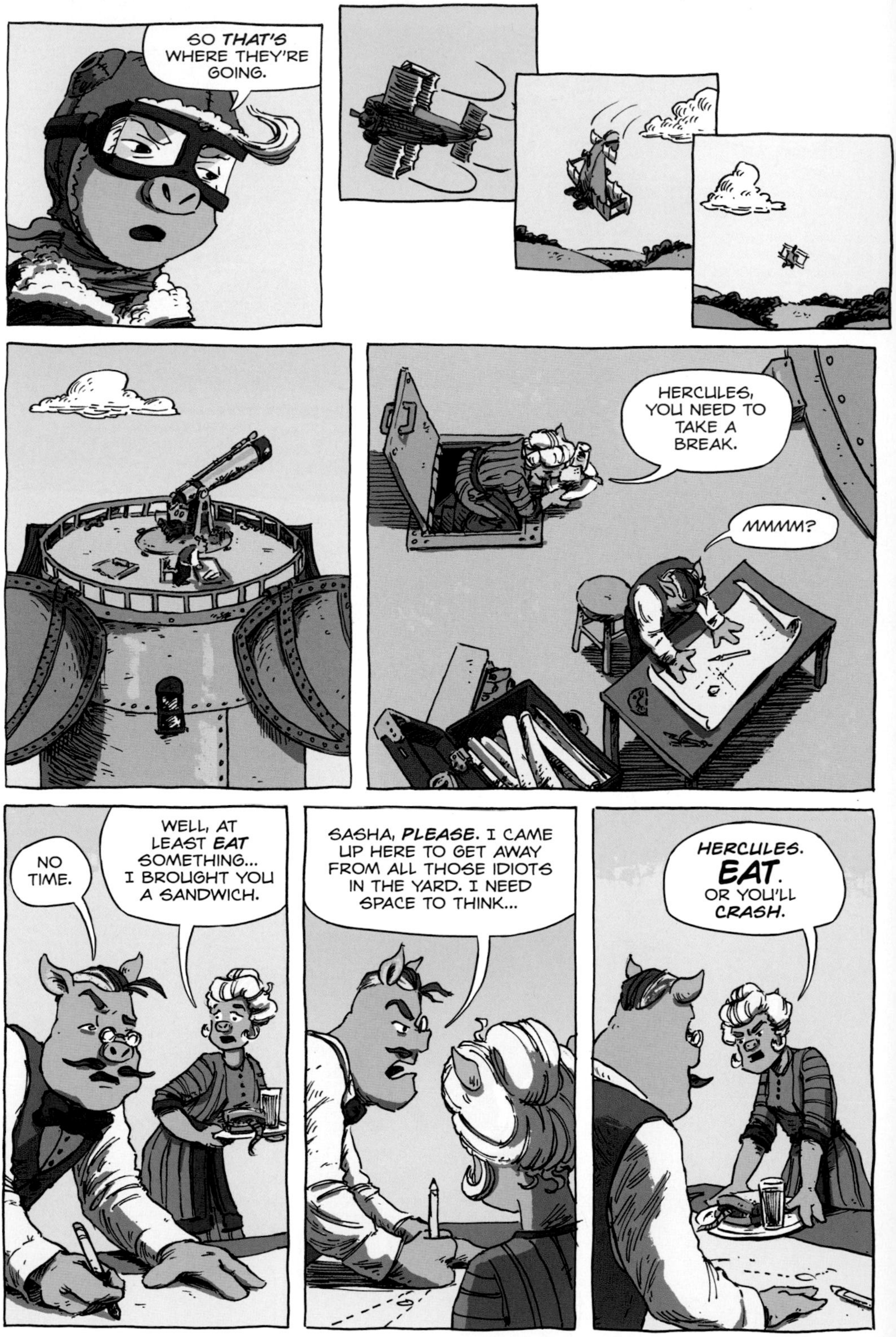

SO THAT'S WHERE THEY'RE GOING.
HERCULES, YOU NEED TO TAKE A BREAK.
MMMM?
NO TIME.
WELL, AT LEAST EAT SOMETHING... I BROUGHT YOU A SANDWICH.
SASHA, PLEASE. I CAME UP HERE TO GET AWAY FROM ALL THOSE IDIOTS IN THE YARD. I NEED SPACE TO THINK...
HERCULES. EAT. OR YOU'LL CRASH.

≋Munch≋

WHAT...
IS THAT?

WELCOME
HOME, AERIAL
HONKER!

RRRMMM

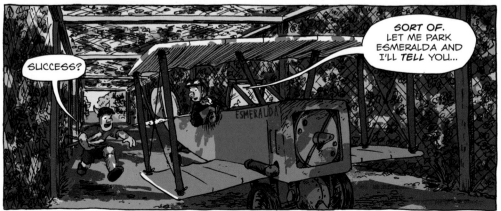

SUCCESS?

SORT OF.
LET ME PARK
ESMERALDA AND
I'LL **TELL** YOU...

ESMERALDA

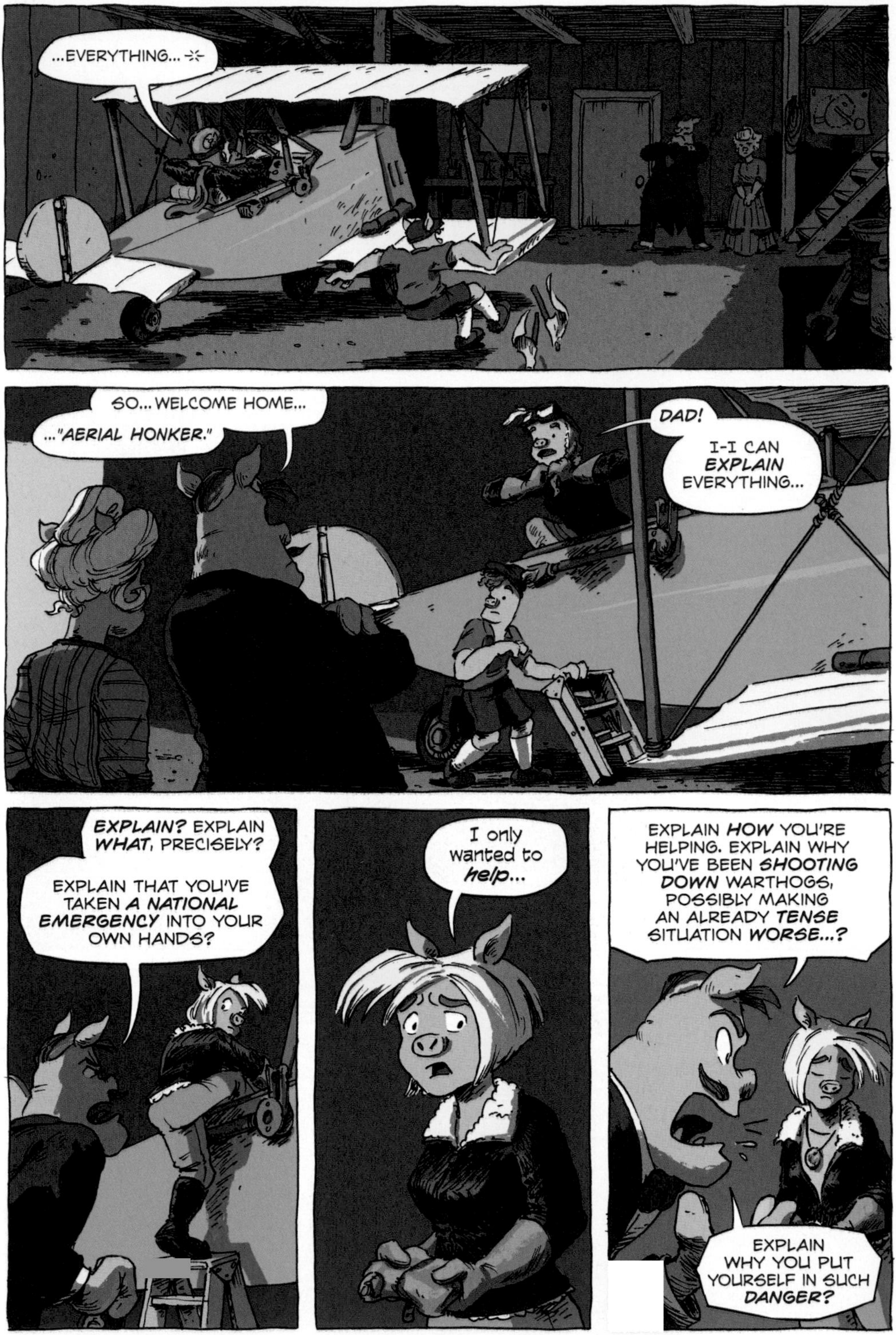
...EVERYTHING...
SO... WELCOME HOME...
..."AERIAL HONKER."
DAD!
I-I CAN EXPLAIN EVERYTHING...
EXPLAIN? EXPLAIN WHAT, PRECISELY?
EXPLAIN THAT YOU'VE TAKEN A NATIONAL EMERGENCY INTO YOUR OWN HANDS?
I only wanted to help...
EXPLAIN HOW YOU'RE HELPING. EXPLAIN WHY YOU'VE BEEN SHOOTING DOWN WARTHOGS, POSSIBLY MAKING AN ALREADY TENSE SITUATION WORSE...?
EXPLAIN WHY YOU PUT YOURSELF IN SUCH DANGER?

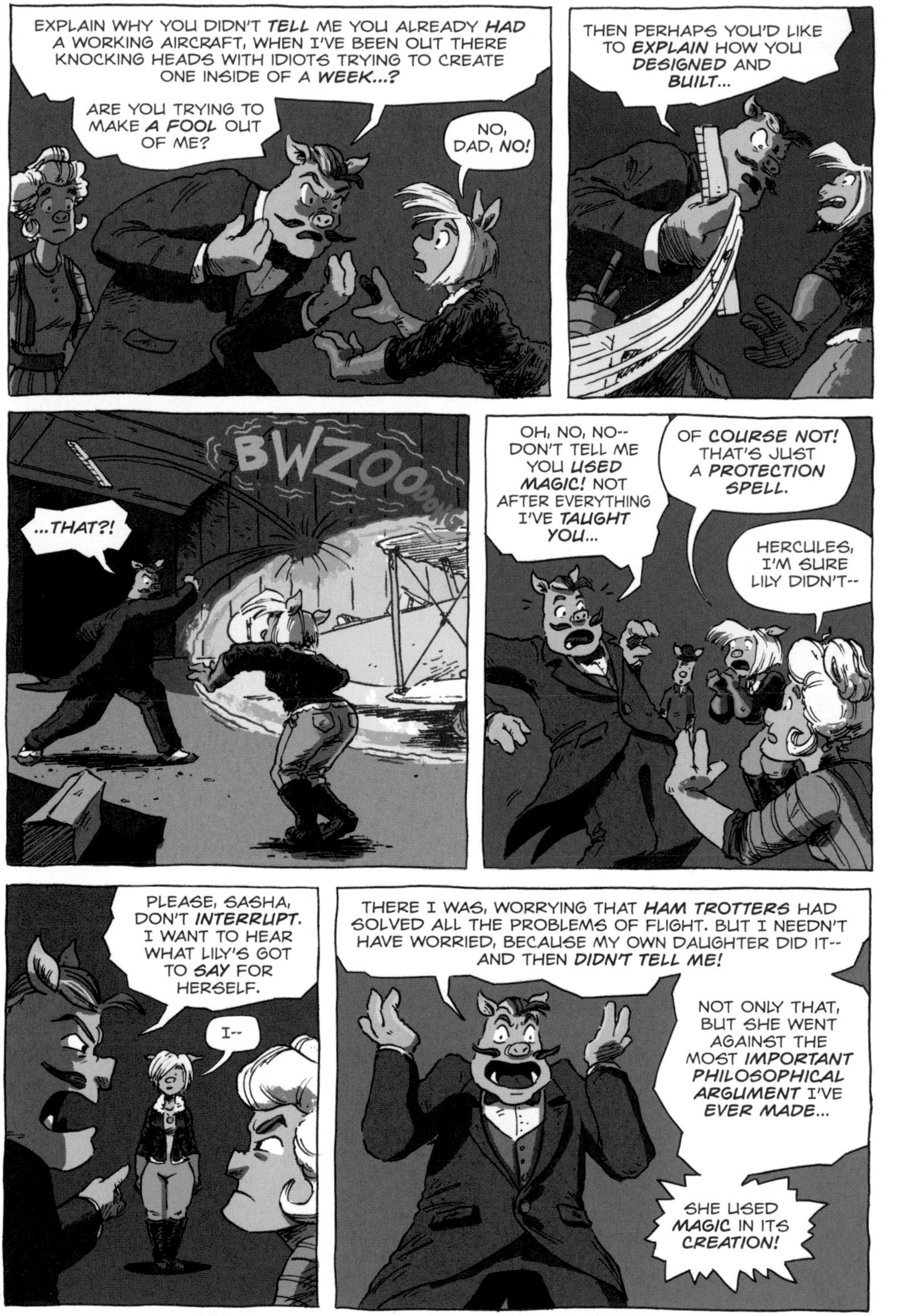
EXPLAIN WHY YOU DIDN'T TELL ME YOU ALREADY HAD A WORKING AIRCRAFT, WHEN I'VE BEEN OUT THERE KNOCKING HEADS WITH IDIOTS TRYING TO CREATE ONE INSIDE OF A WEEK...?
ARE YOU TRYING TO MAKE A FOOL OUT OF ME?
NO, DAD, NO!
THEN PERHAPS YOU'D LIKE TO EXPLAIN HOW YOU DESIGNED AND BUILT...
BWZOOOOOOING
...THAT?!
OH, NO, NO-- DON'T TELL ME YOU USED MAGIC! NOT AFTER EVERYTHING I'VE TAUGHT YOU...
OF COURSE NOT! THAT'S JUST A PROTECTION SPELL.
HERCULES, I'M SURE LILY DIDN'T--
PLEASE, SASHA, DON'T INTERRUPT. I WANT TO HEAR WHAT LILY'S GOT TO SAY FOR HERSELF.
I--
THERE I WAS, WORRYING THAT HAM TROTTERS HAD SOLVED ALL THE PROBLEMS OF FLIGHT. BUT I NEEDN'T HAVE WORRIED, BECAUSE MY OWN DAUGHTER DID IT-- AND THEN DIDN'T TELL ME!
NOT ONLY THAT, BUT SHE WENT AGAINST THE MOST IMPORTANT PHILOSOPHICAL ARGUMENT I'VE EVER MADE...
SHE USED MAGIC IN ITS CREATION!

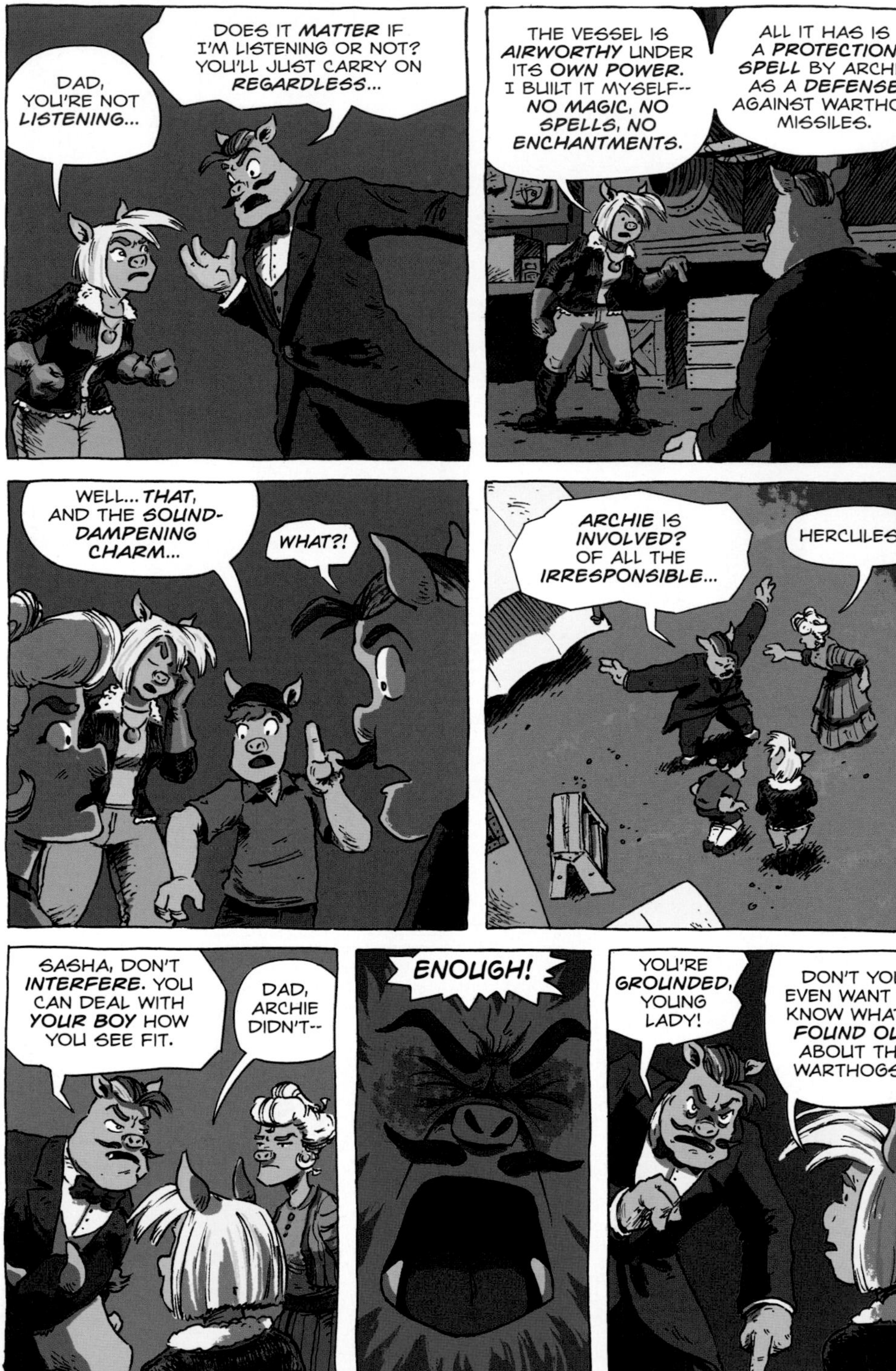
DAD, YOU'RE NOT LISTENING...
DOES IT MATTER IF I'M LISTENING OR NOT? YOU'LL JUST CARRY ON REGARDLESS...
THE VESSEL IS AIRWORTHY UNDER ITS OWN POWER. I BUILT IT MYSELF-- NO MAGIC, NO SPELLS, NO ENCHANTMENTS.
ALL IT HAS IS A PROTECTION SPELL BY ARCHIE AS A DEFENSE AGAINST WARTHOG MISSILES.
WELL... THAT, AND THE SOUND-DAMPENING CHARM...
WHAT?!
ARCHIE IS INVOLVED? OF ALL THE IRRESPONSIBLE...
HERCULES...
SASHA, DON'T INTERFERE. YOU CAN DEAL WITH YOUR BOY HOW YOU SEE FIT.
DAD, ARCHIE DIDN'T--
ENOUGH!
YOU'RE GROUNDED, YOUNG LADY!
DON'T YOU EVEN WANT TO KNOW WHAT I FOUND OUT ABOUT THE WARTHOGS?

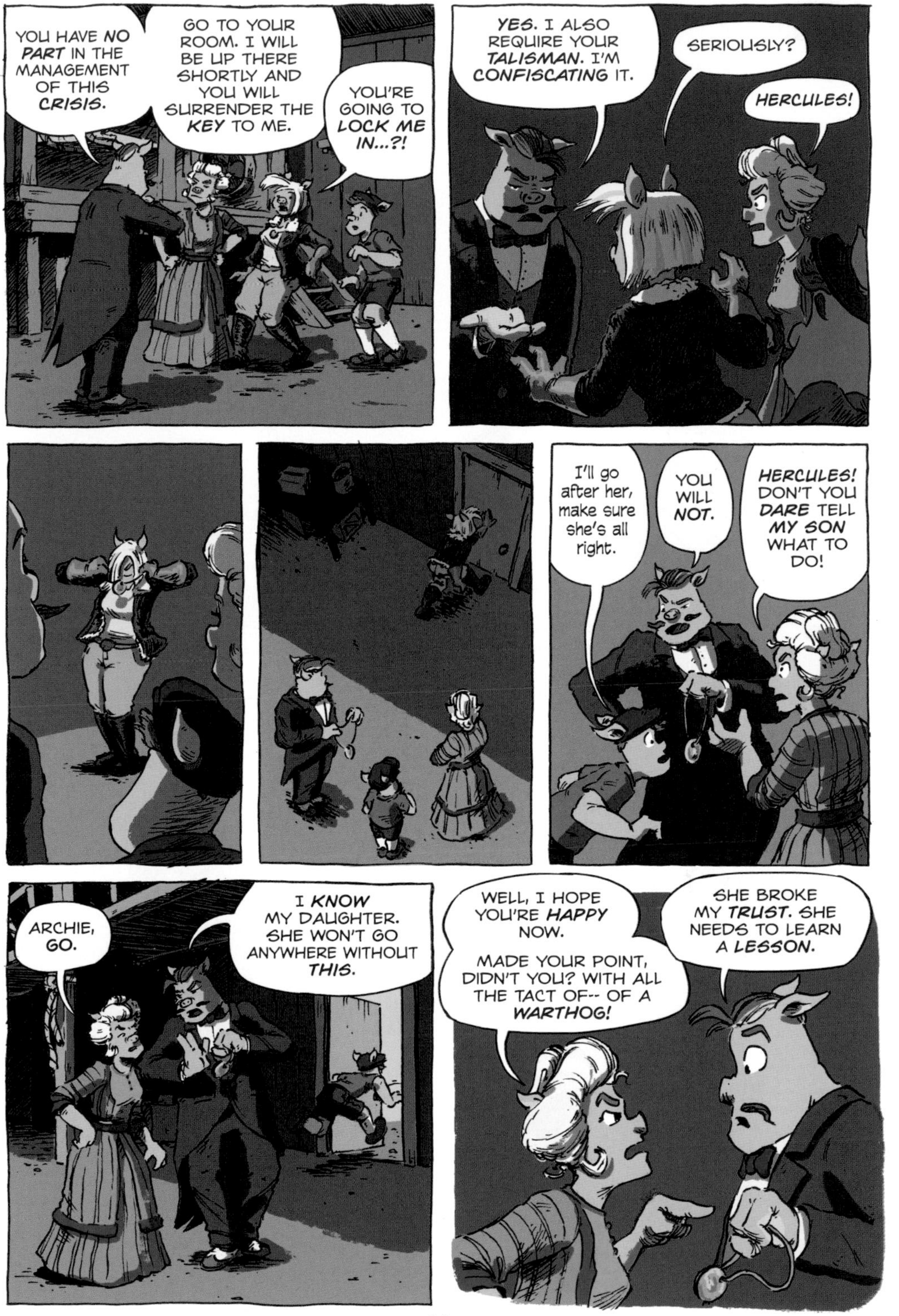
YOU HAVE NO PART IN THE MANAGEMENT OF THIS CRISIS.
GO TO YOUR ROOM. I WILL BE UP THERE SHORTLY AND YOU WILL SURRENDER THE KEY TO ME.
YOU'RE GOING TO LOCK ME IN...?!
YES. I ALSO REQUIRE YOUR TALISMAN. I'M CONFISCATING IT.
SERIOUSLY?
HERCULES!
I'll go after her, make sure she's all right.
YOU WILL NOT.
HERCULES! DON'T YOU DARE TELL MY SON WHAT TO DO!
ARCHIE, GO.
I KNOW MY DAUGHTER. SHE WON'T GO ANYWHERE WITHOUT THIS.
WELL, I HOPE YOU'RE HAPPY NOW.
MADE YOUR POINT, DIDN'T YOU? WITH ALL THE TACT OF-- OF A WARTHOG!
SHE BROKE MY TRUST. SHE NEEDS TO LEARN A LESSON.

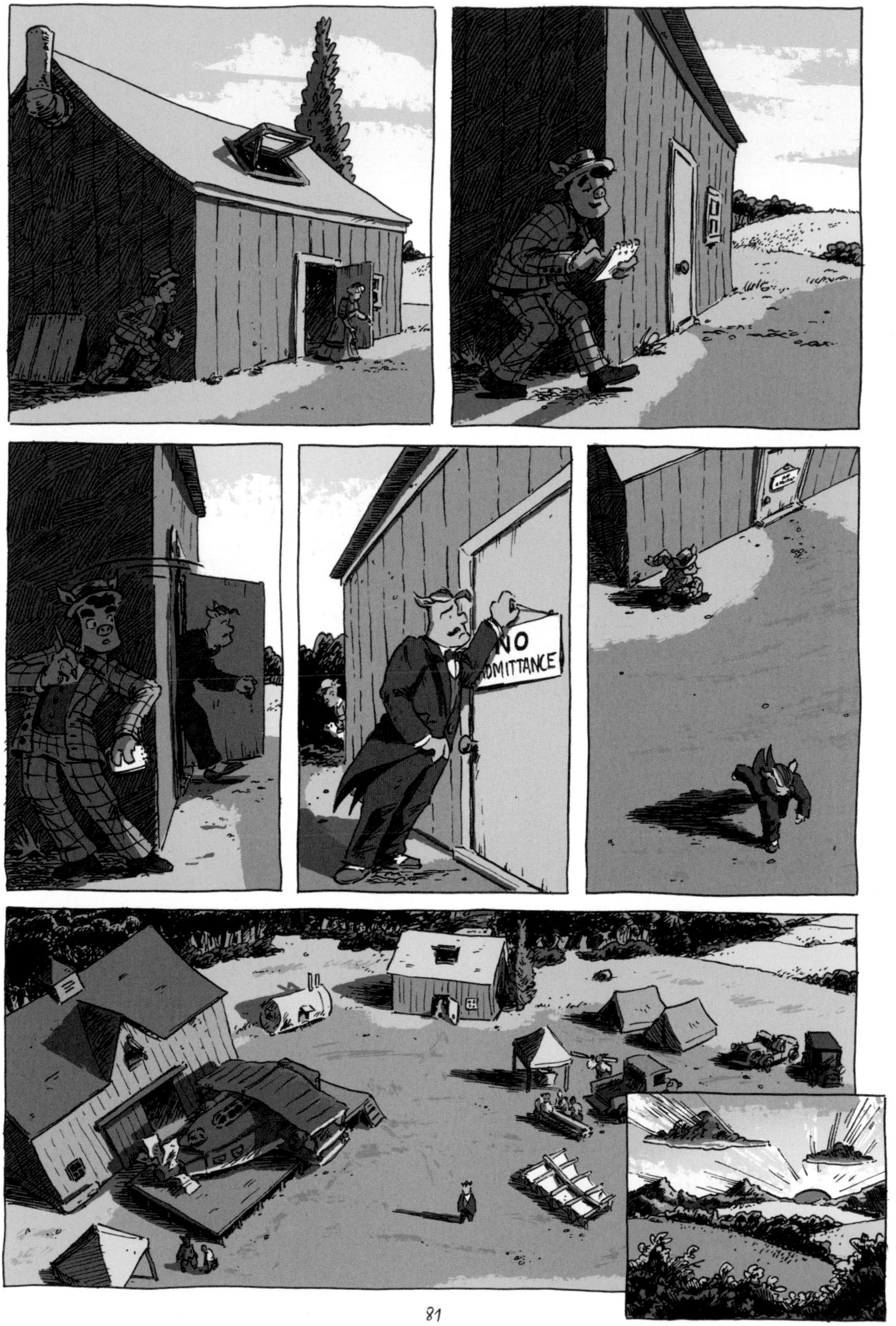
NO
ADMITTANCE

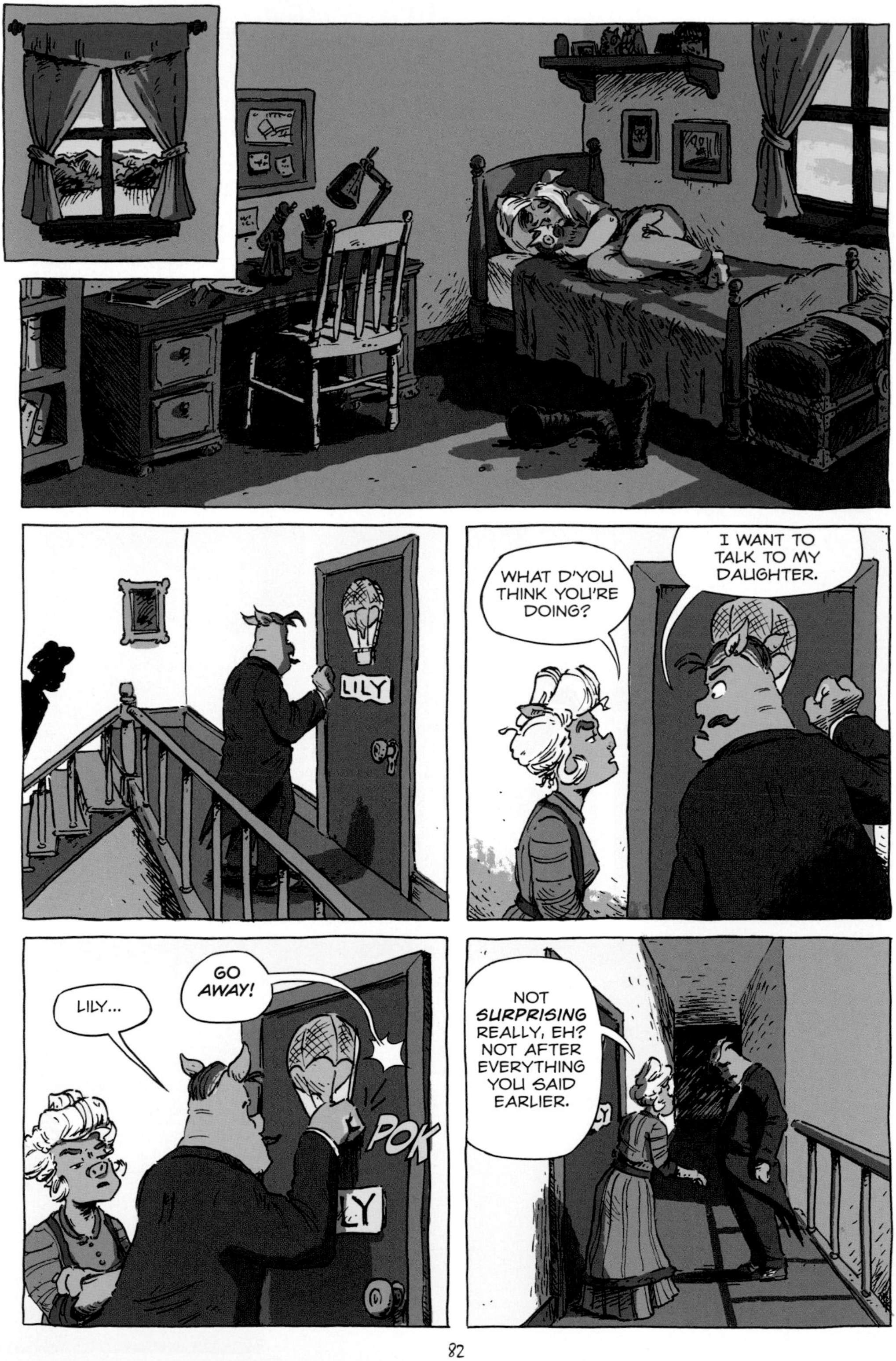
LILY
WHAT D'YOU THINK YOU'RE DOING?
I WANT TO TALK TO MY DAUGHTER.
LILY...
GO AWAY!
POK
LY
NOT SURPRISING REALLY, EH? NOT AFTER EVERYTHING YOU SAID EARLIER.

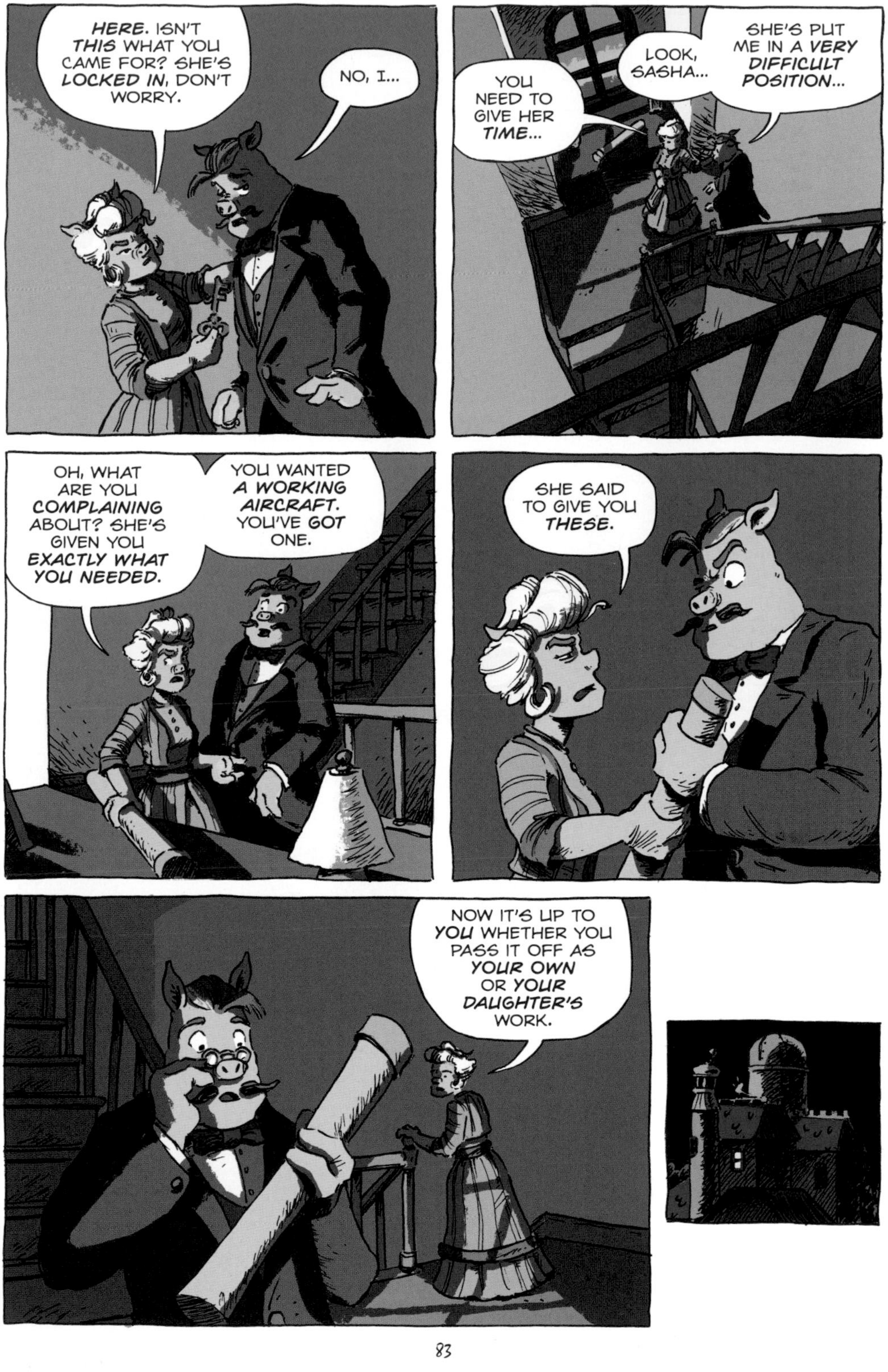
HERE. ISN'T THIS WHAT YOU CAME FOR? SHE'S LOCKED IN, DON'T WORRY.
NO, I...
YOU NEED TO GIVE HER TIME...
LOOK, SASHA...
SHE'S PUT ME IN A VERY DIFFICULT POSITION...
OH, WHAT ARE YOU COMPLAINING ABOUT? SHE'S GIVEN YOU EXACTLY WHAT YOU NEEDED.
YOU WANTED A WORKING AIRCRAFT. YOU'VE GOT ONE.
SHE SAID TO GIVE YOU THESE.
NOW IT'S UP TO YOU WHETHER YOU PASS IT OFF AS YOUR OWN OR YOUR DAUGHTER'S WORK.

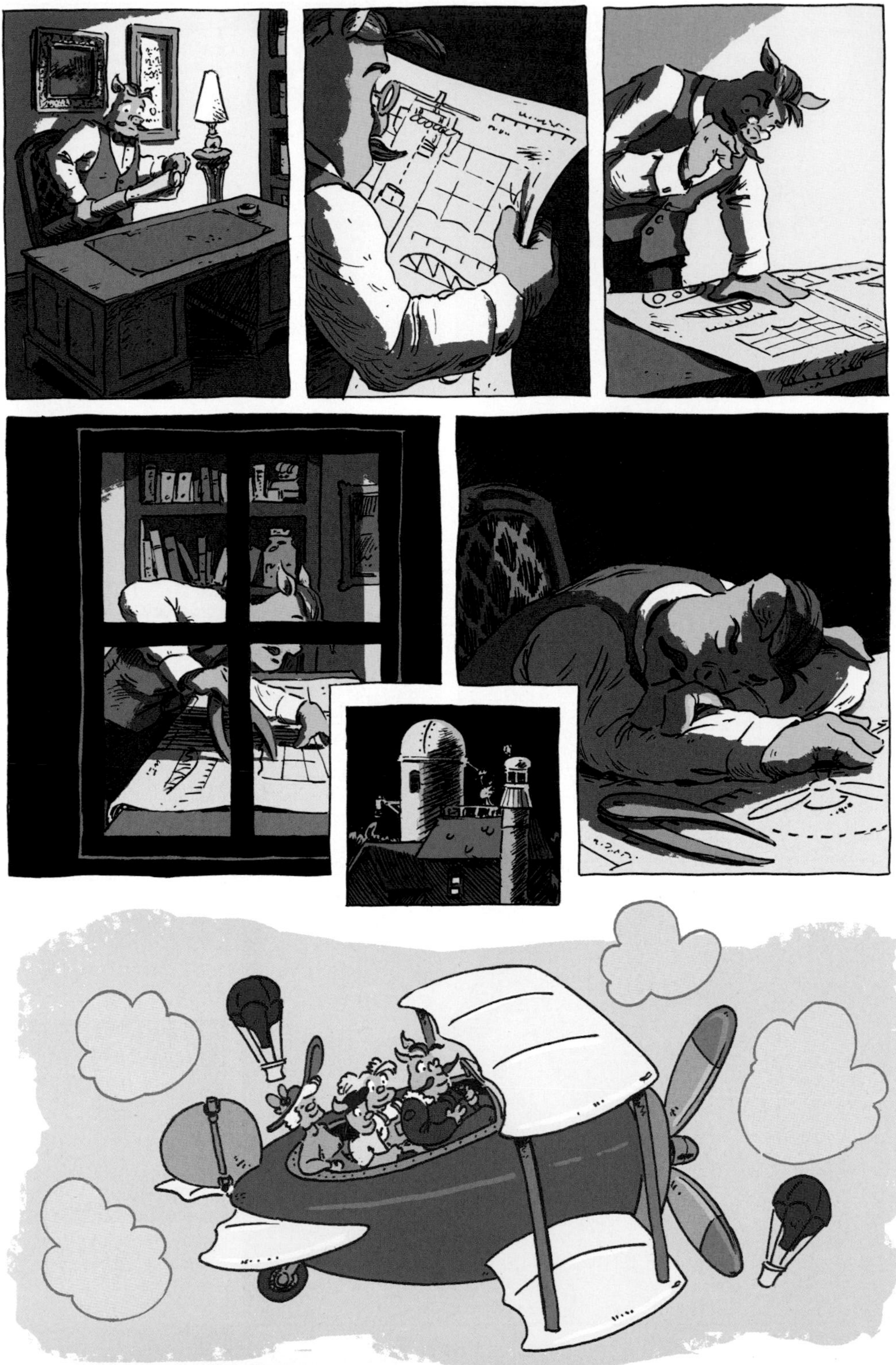

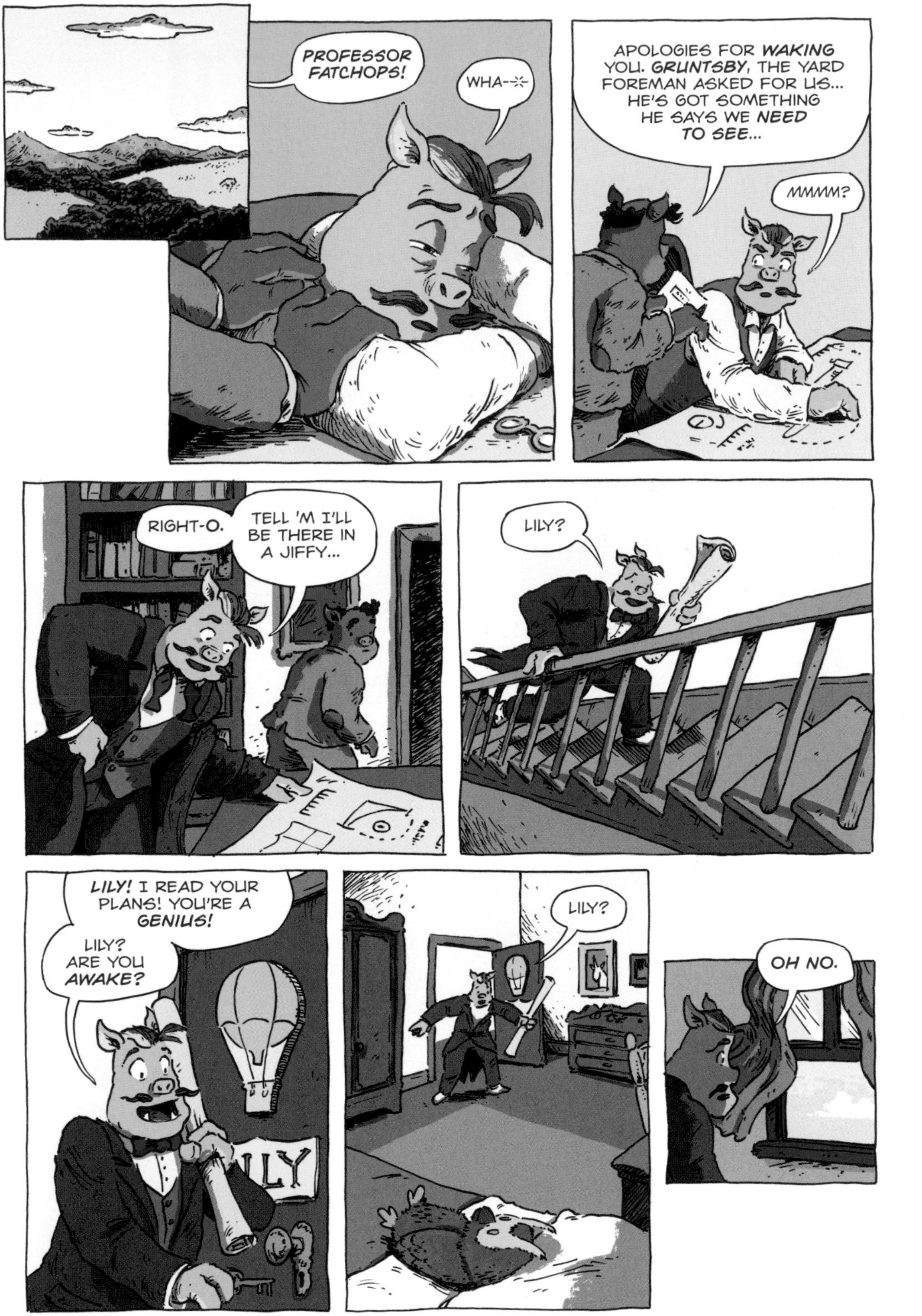
PROFESSOR FATCHOPS!
WHA--
APOLOGIES FOR WAKING YOU. GRUNTSBY, THE YARD FOREMAN ASKED FOR US... HE'S GOT SOMETHING HE SAYS WE NEED TO SEE...
MMMM?
RIGHT-O.
TELL 'M I'LL BE THERE IN A JIFFY...
LILY?
LILY! I READ YOUR PLANS! YOU'RE A GENIUS!
LILY? ARE YOU AWAKE?
LILY
LILY?
OH NO.

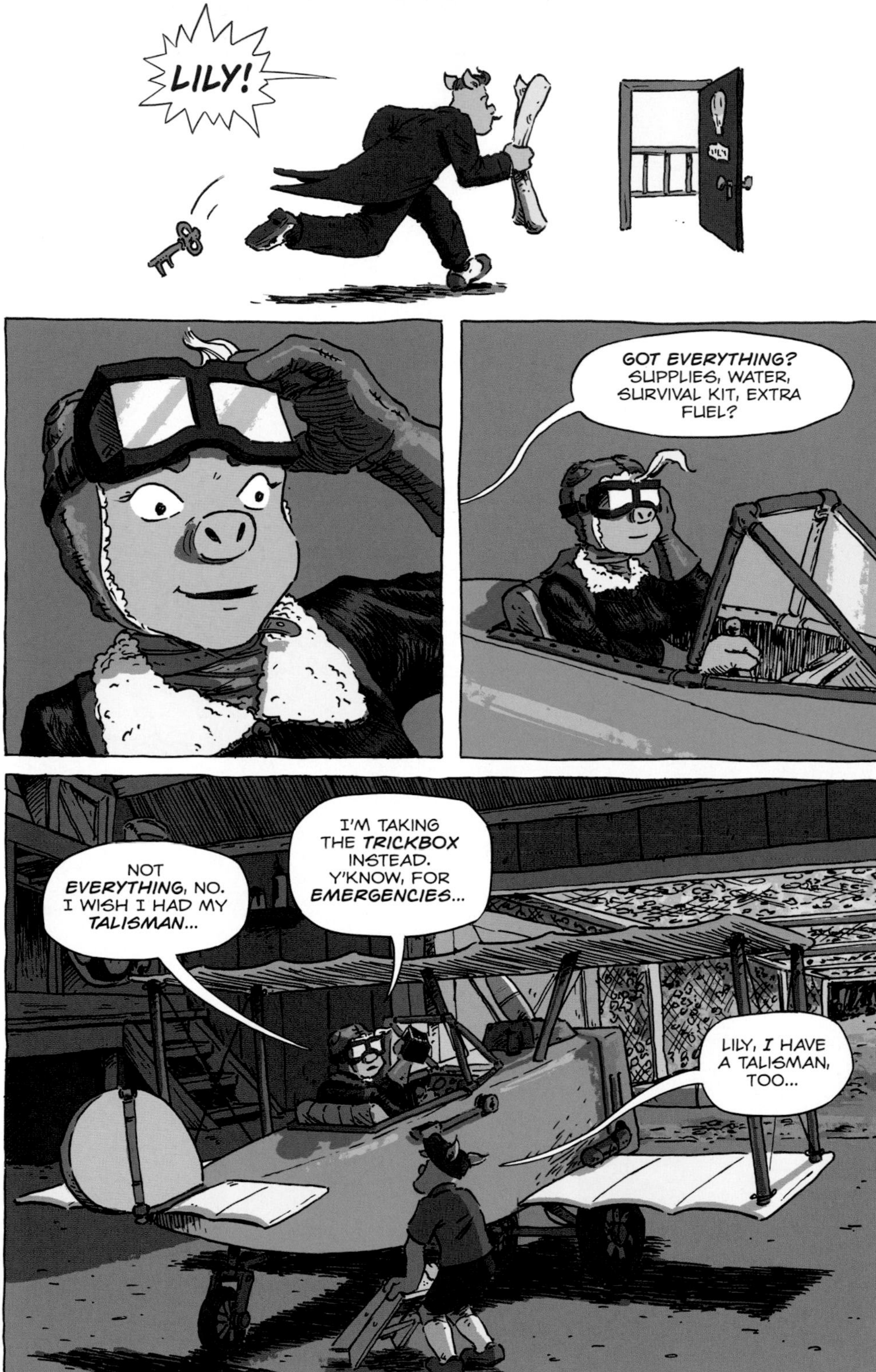
LILY!
GOT EVERYTHING? SUPPLIES, WATER, SURVIVAL KIT, EXTRA FUEL?
NOT EVERYTHING, NO. I WISH I HAD MY TALISMAN...
I'M TAKING THE TRICKBOX INSTEAD. Y'KNOW, FOR EMERGENCIES...
LILY, I HAVE A TALISMAN, TOO...

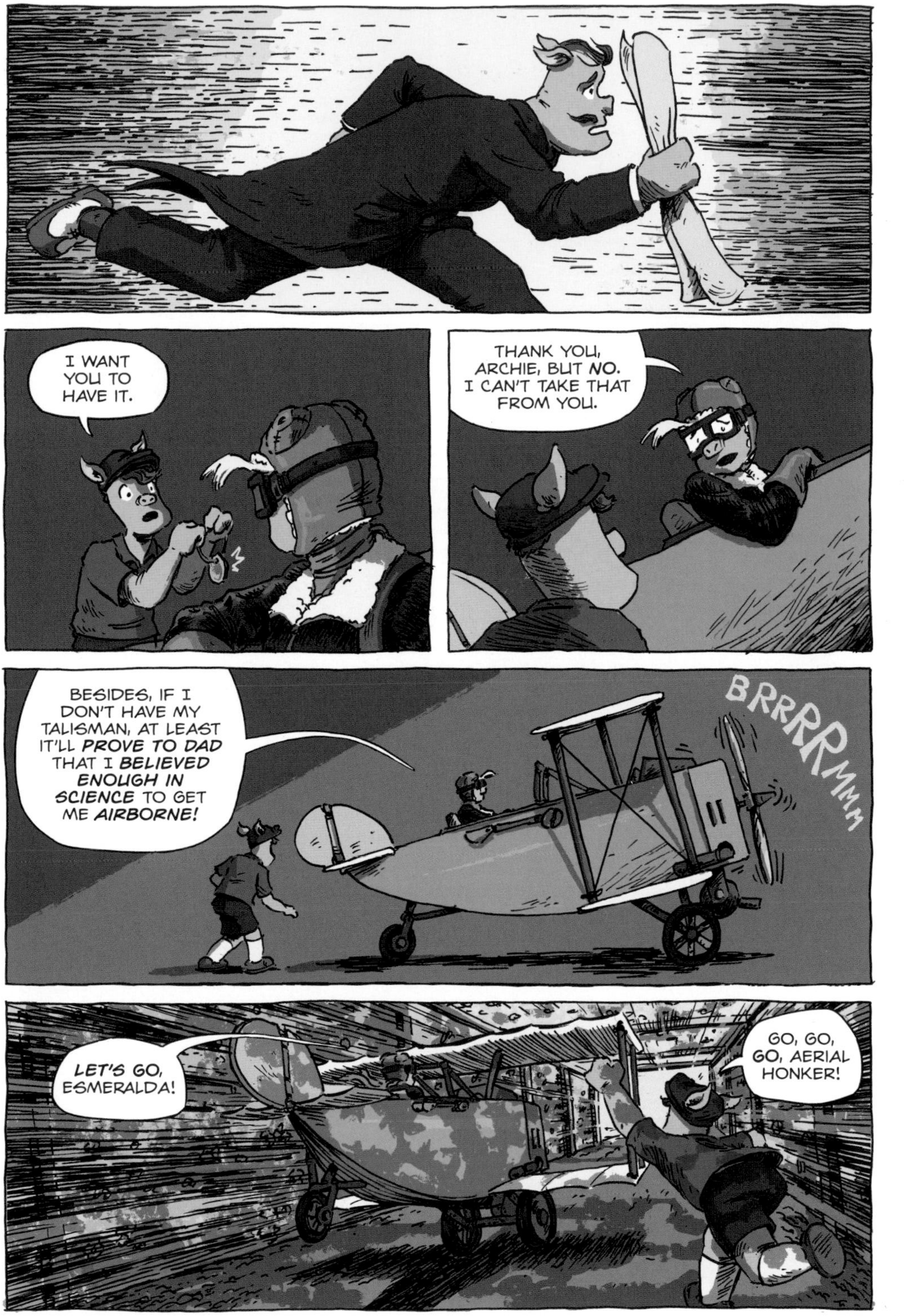
I WANT YOU TO HAVE IT.
THANK YOU, ARCHIE, BUT NO. I CAN'T TAKE THAT FROM YOU.
BESIDES, IF I DON'T HAVE MY TALISMAN, AT LEAST IT'LL PROVE TO DAD THAT I BELIEVED ENOUGH IN SCIENCE TO GET ME AIRBORNE!
BRRRRRMMMM
LET'S GO, ESMERALDA!
GO, GO, GO, AERIAL HONKER!

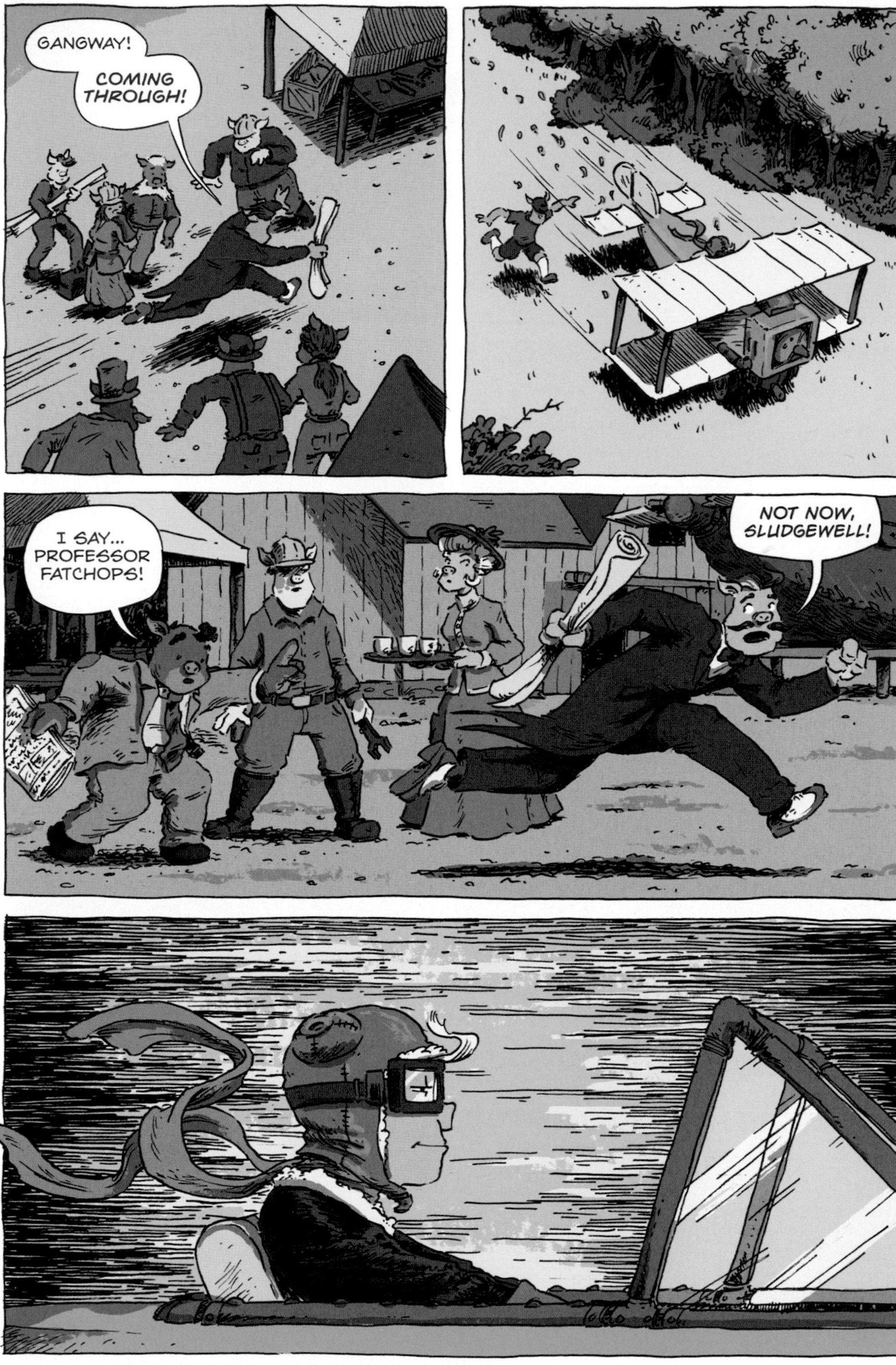
GANGWAY!
COMING THROUGH!
I SAY... PROFESSOR FATCHOPS!
NOT NOW, SLUDGEWELL!

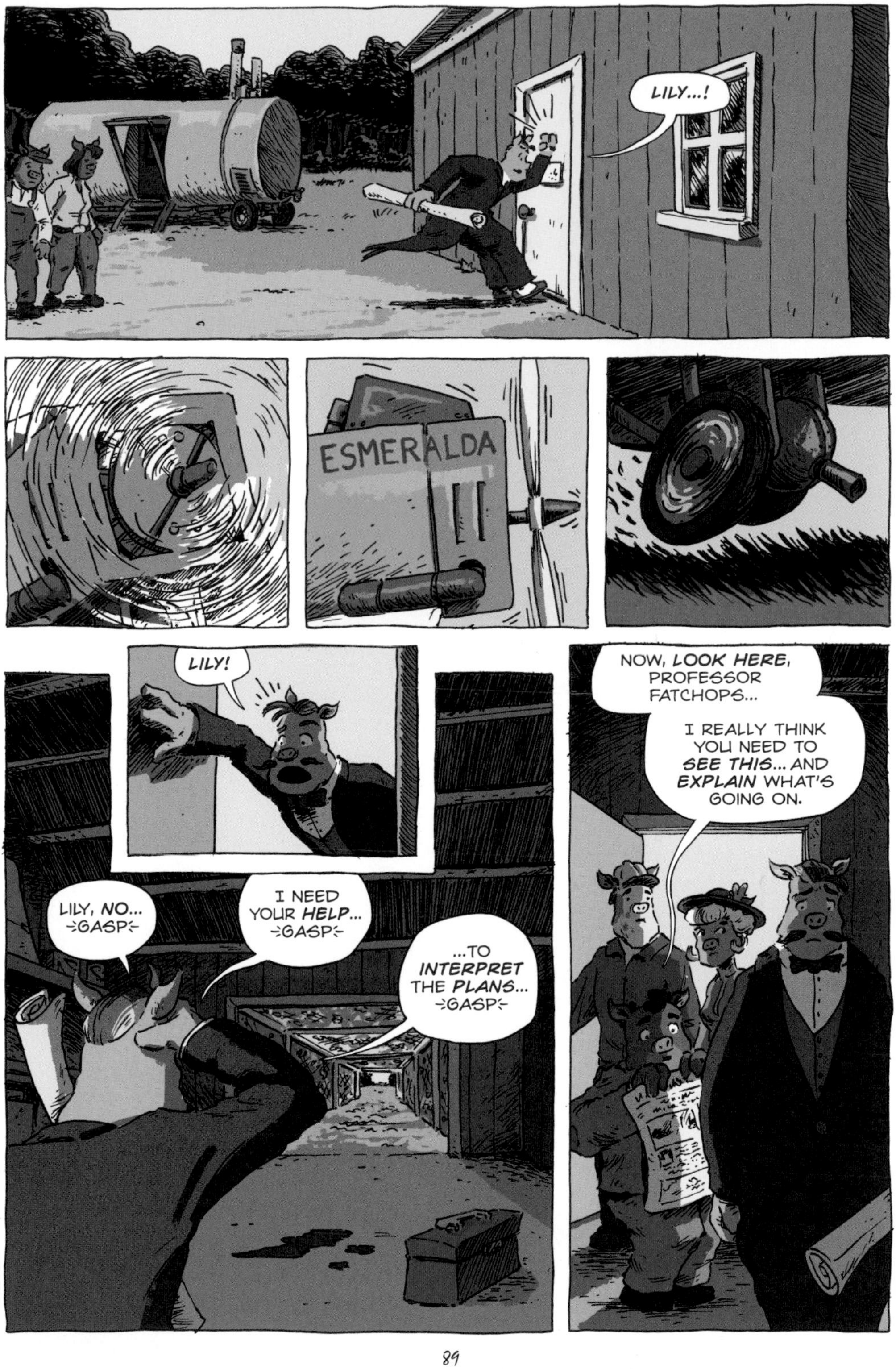
LILY...!
ESMERALDA
LILY!
LILY, NO... GASP
I NEED YOUR HELP... GASP
...TO INTERPRET THE PLANS... GASP
NOW, LOOK HERE, PROFESSOR FATCHOPS...
I REALLY THINK YOU NEED TO SEE THIS... AND EXPLAIN WHAT'S GOING ON.

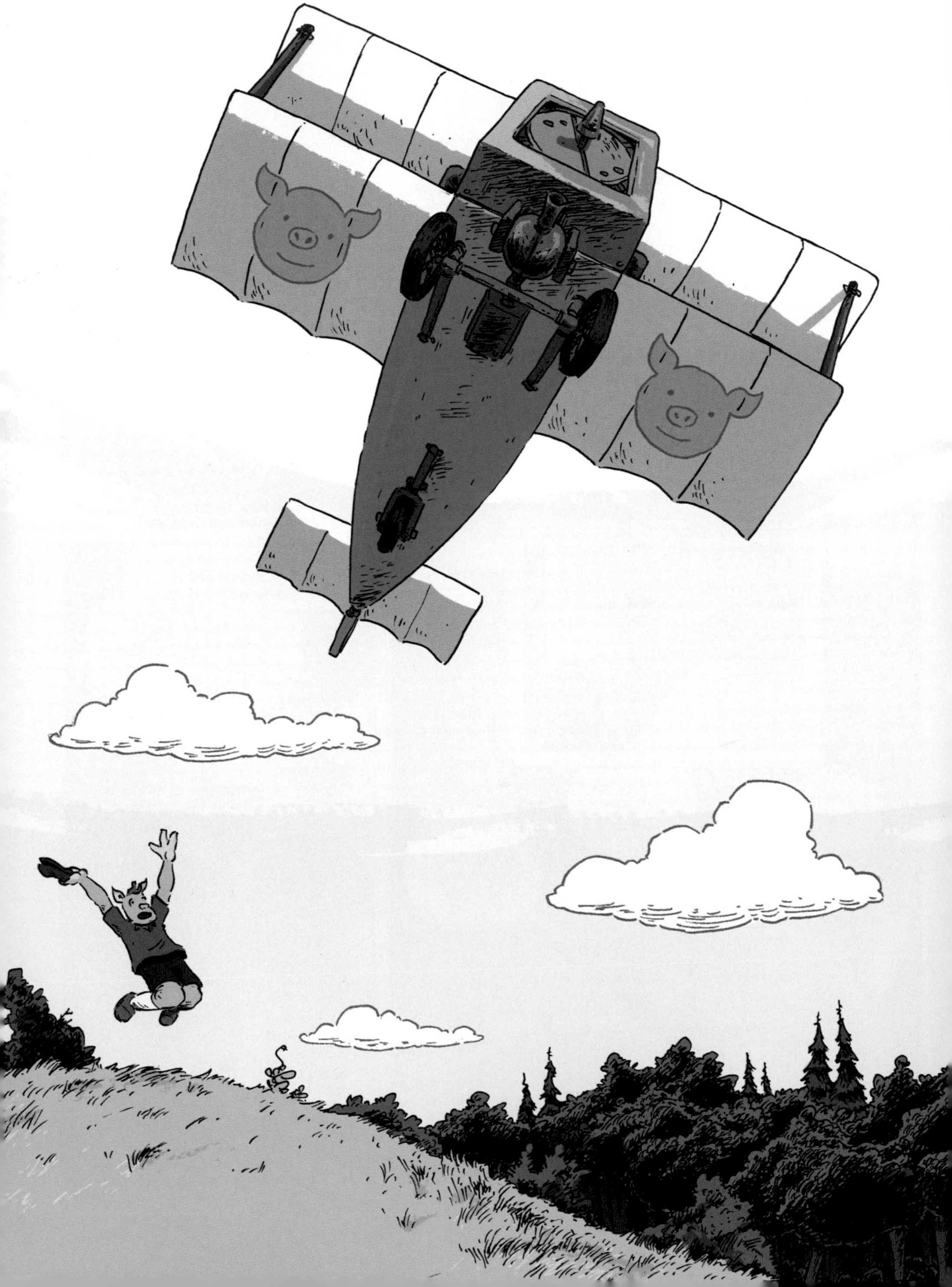

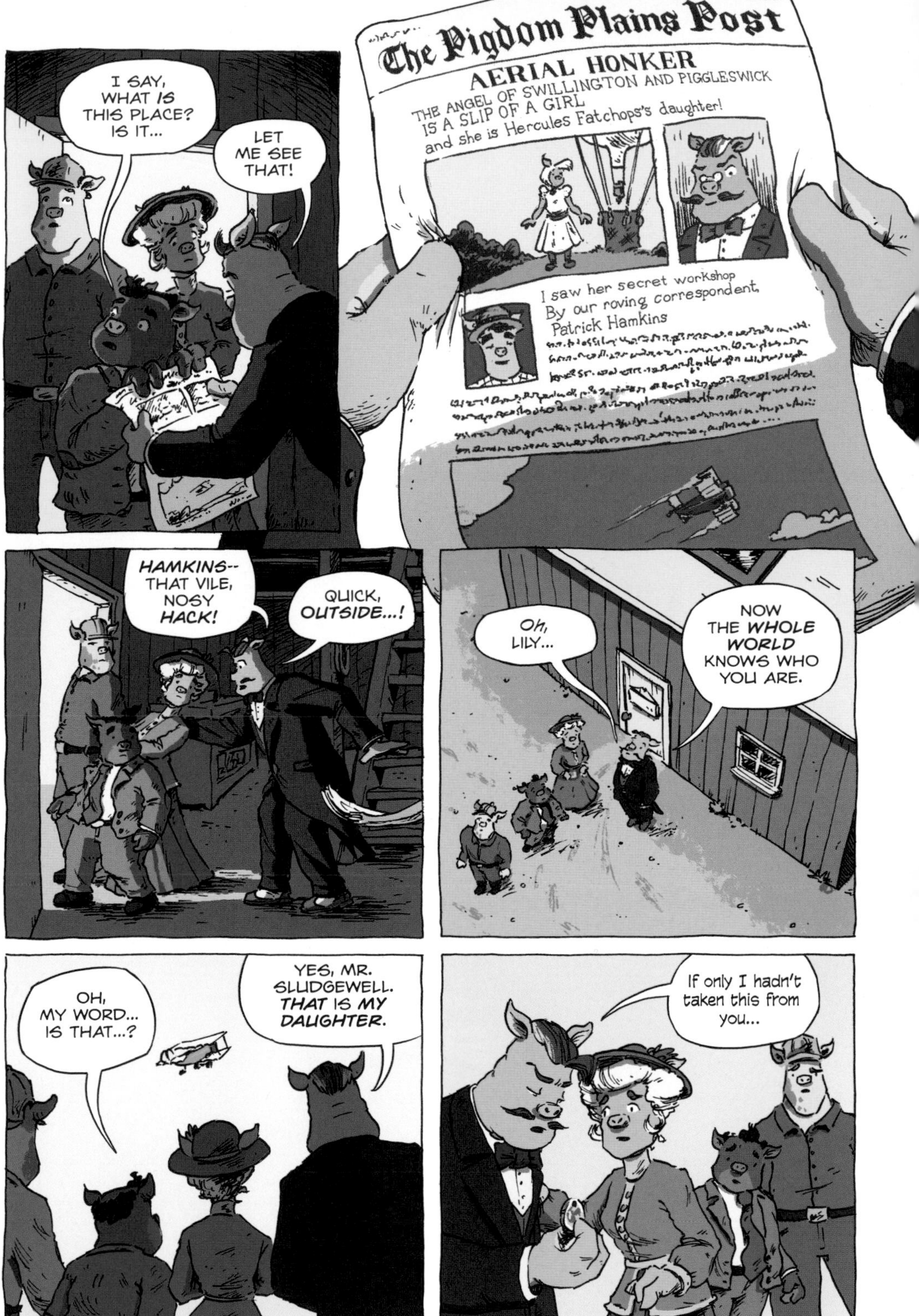
I SAY, WHAT IS THIS PLACE? IS IT...
LET ME SEE THAT!
The Pigdom Plains Post
AERIAL HONKER
THE ANGEL OF SWILLINGTON AND PIGGLESWICK IS A SLIP OF A GIRL
and she is Hercules Fatchops's daughter!
I saw her secret workshop
By our roving correspondent,
Patrick Hamkins
HAMKINS-- THAT VILE, NOSY HACK!
QUICK, OUTSIDE...!
Oh, LILY...
NOW THE WHOLE WORLD KNOWS WHO YOU ARE.
OH, MY WORD... IS THAT...?
YES, MR. SLUDGEWELL. THAT IS MY DAUGHTER.
If only I hadn't taken this from you...

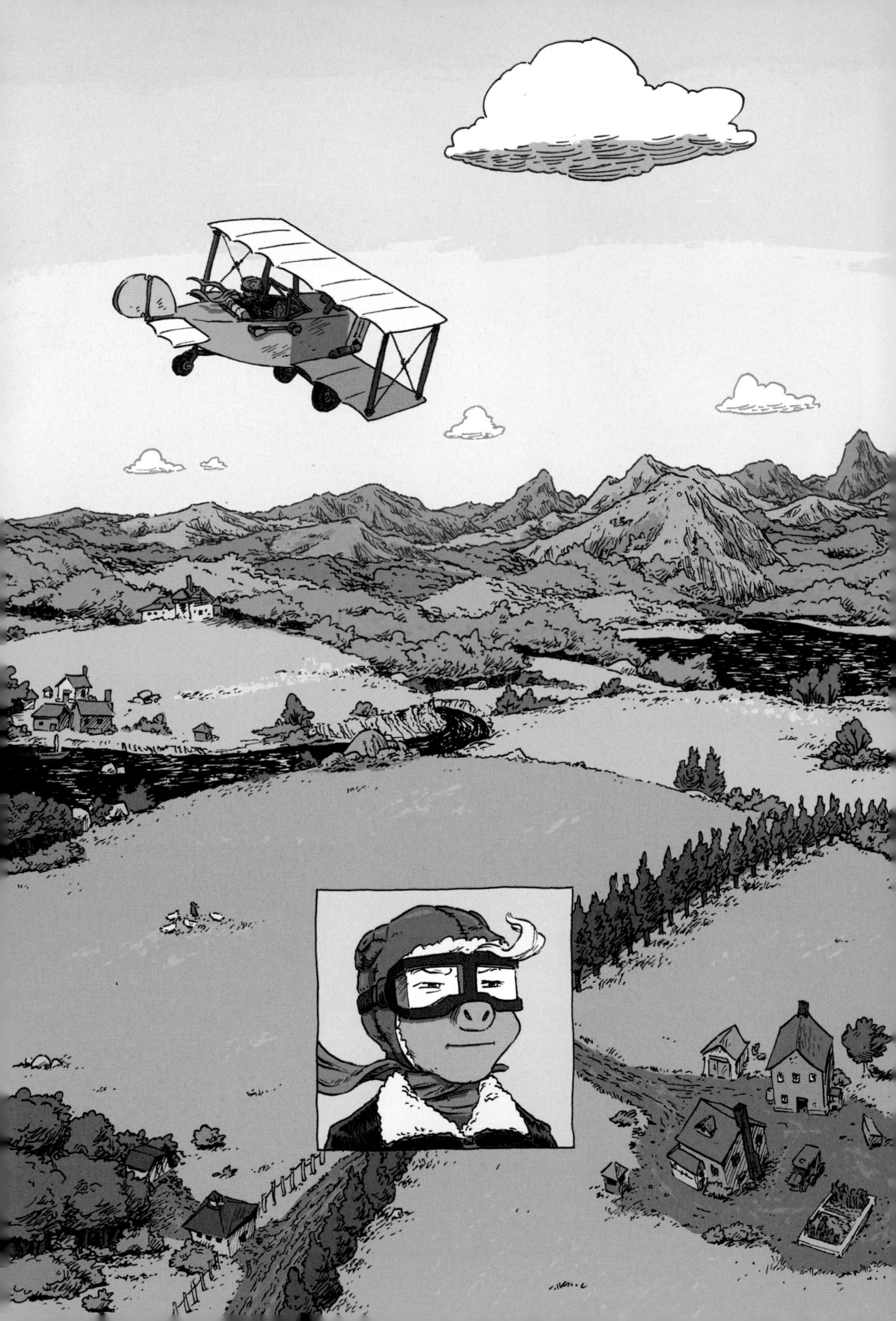

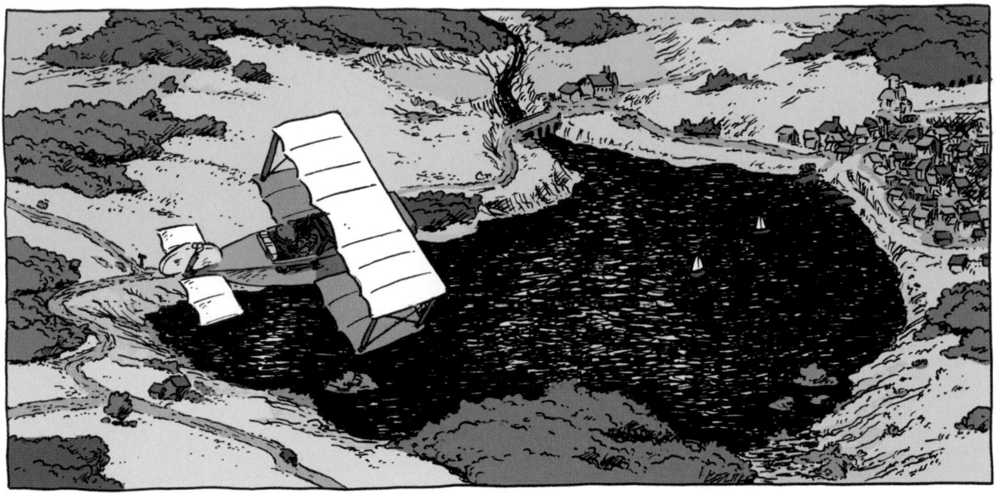

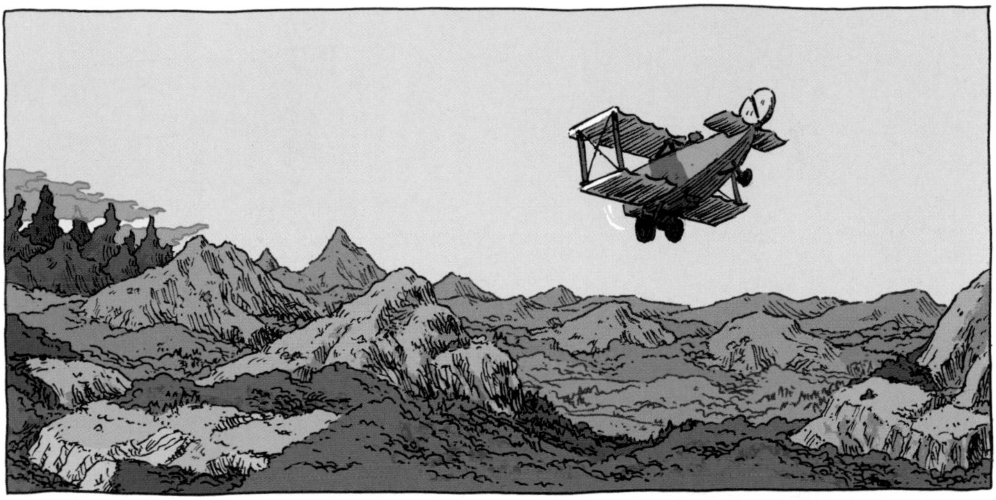

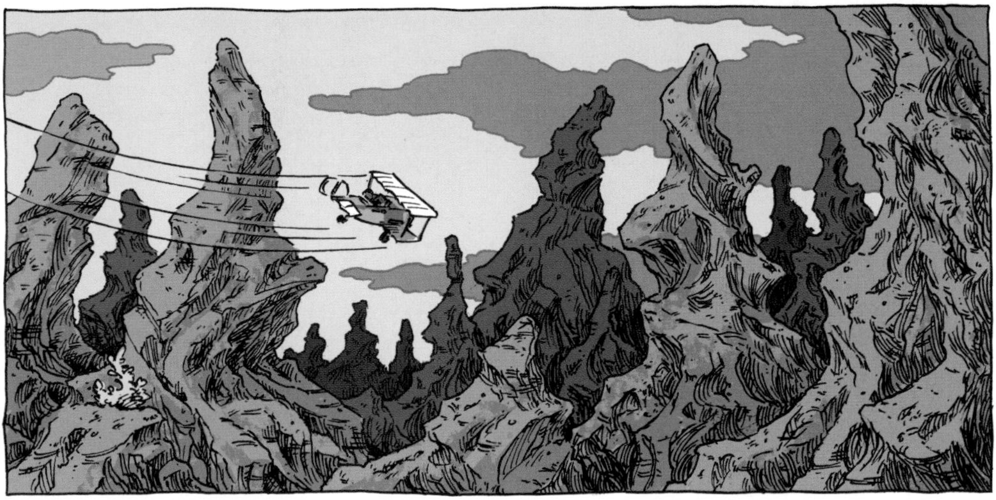

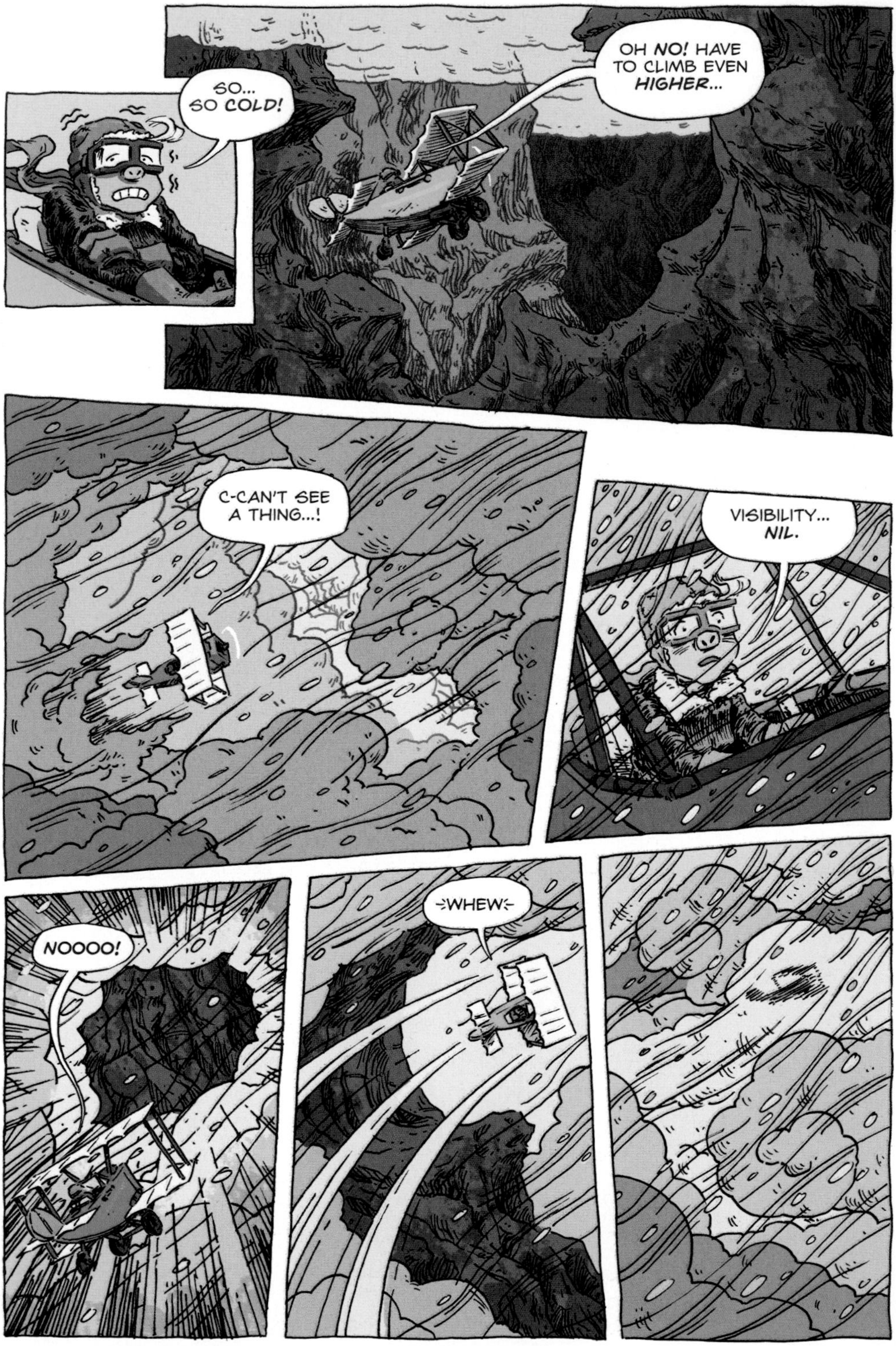
SO... SO COLD!
OH NO! HAVE TO CLIMB EVEN HIGHER...
C-CAN'T SEE A THING...!
VISIBILITY... NIL.
NOOOO!
WHEW

THIS PASSAGE IS GETTING THINNER AND *THINNER*...

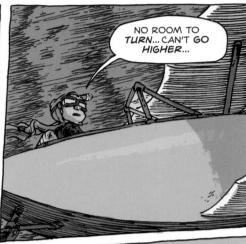

NO ROOM TO *TURN*... CAN'T GO *HIGHER*...

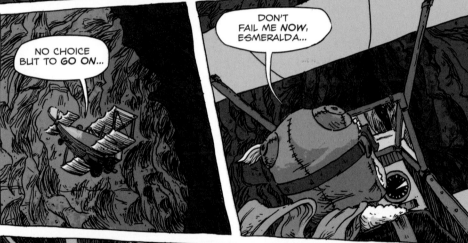

NO CHOICE BUT TO GO ON...

DON'T FAIL ME *NOW*, ESMERALDA...

WRRRRROOOAM

WRAOWW

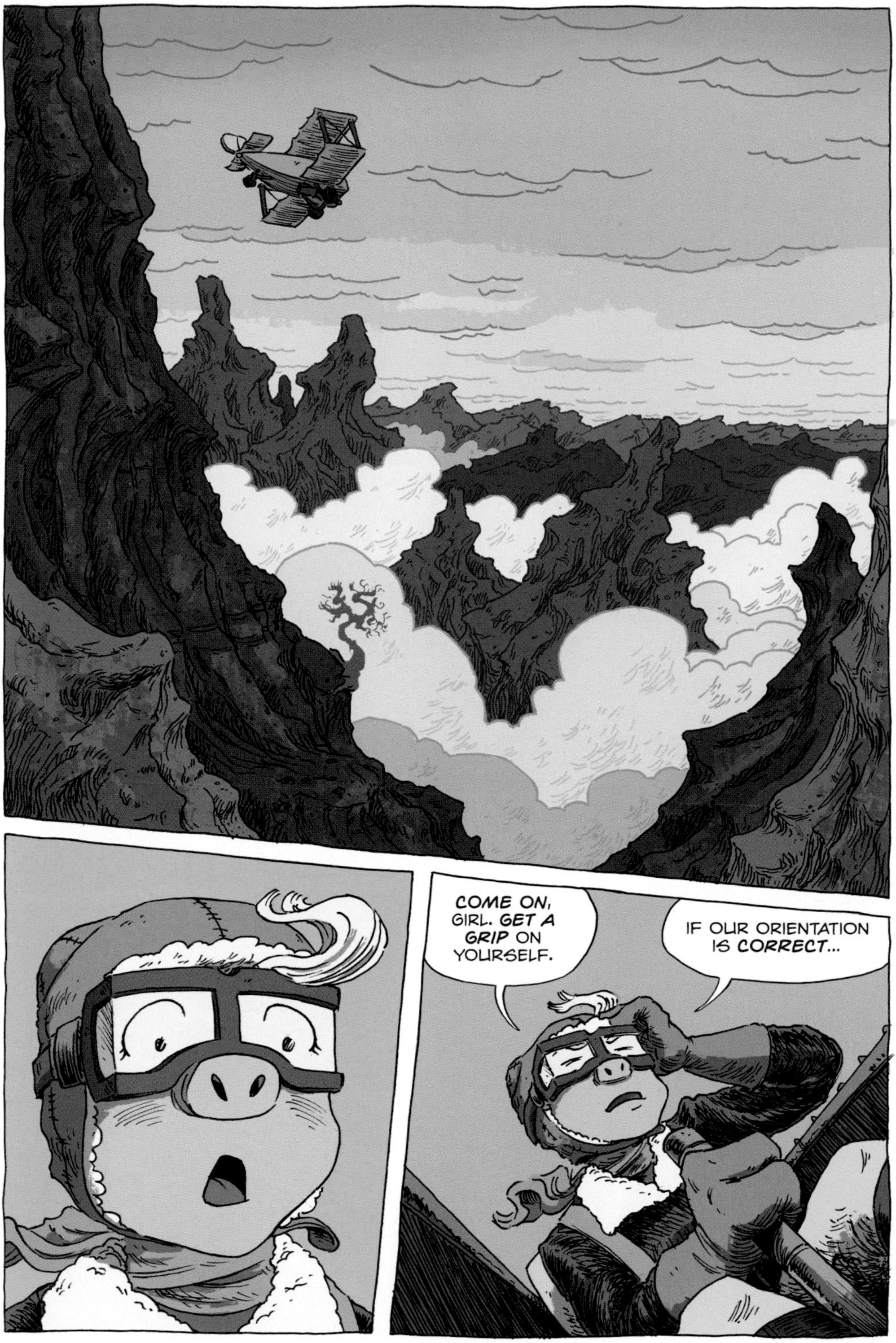
COME ON, GIRL. GET A GRIP ON YOURSELF.
IF OUR ORIENTATION IS CORRECT...

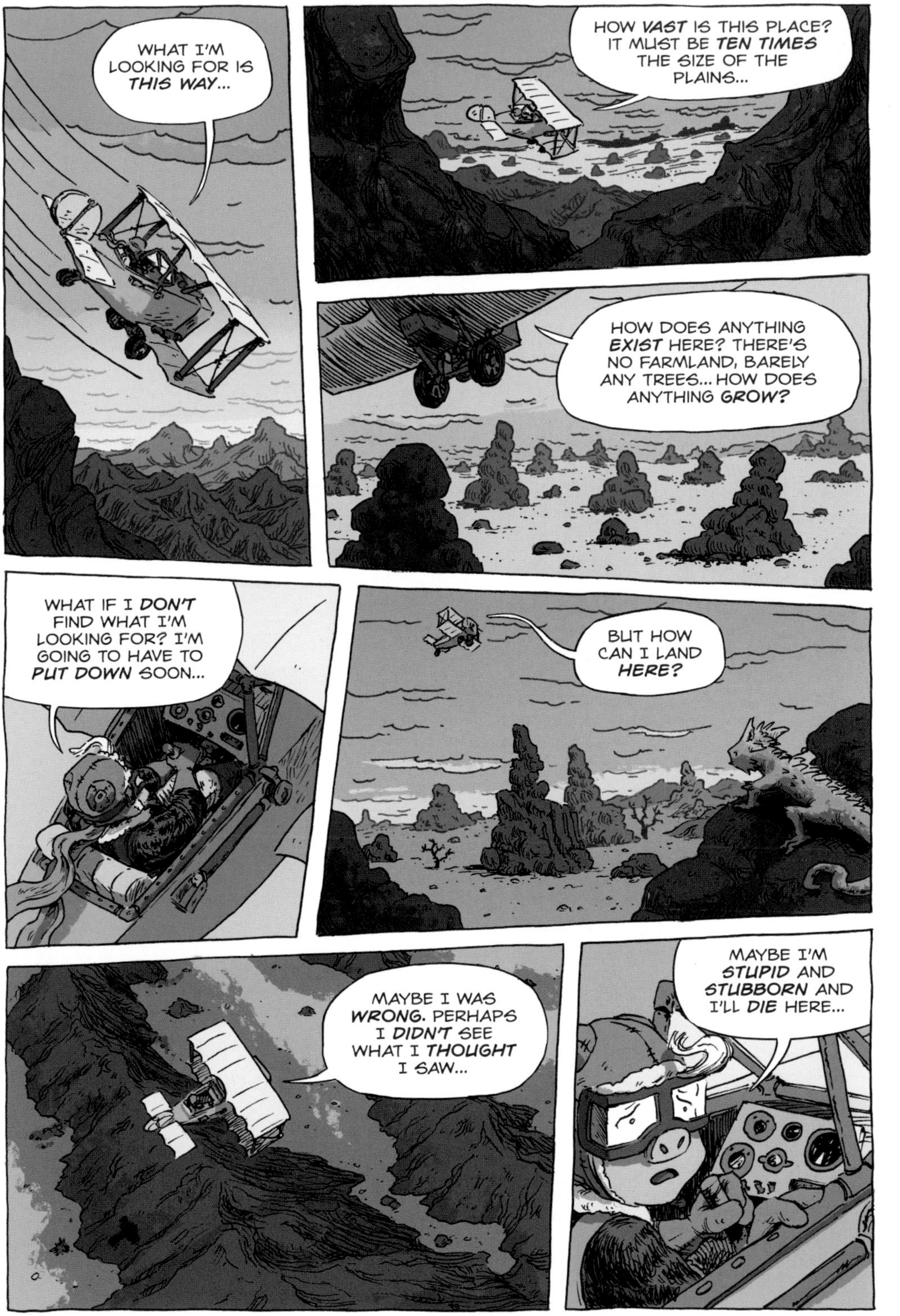
WHAT I'M LOOKING FOR IS THIS WAY...
HOW VAST IS THIS PLACE? IT MUST BE TEN TIMES THE SIZE OF THE PLAINS...
HOW DOES ANYTHING EXIST HERE? THERE'S NO FARMLAND, BARELY ANY TREES... HOW DOES ANYTHING GROW?
WHAT IF I DON'T FIND WHAT I'M LOOKING FOR? I'M GOING TO HAVE TO PUT DOWN SOON...
BUT HOW CAN I LAND HERE?
MAYBE I WAS WRONG. PERHAPS I DIDN'T SEE WHAT I THOUGHT I SAW...
MAYBE I'M STUPID AND STUBBORN AND I'LL DIE HERE...

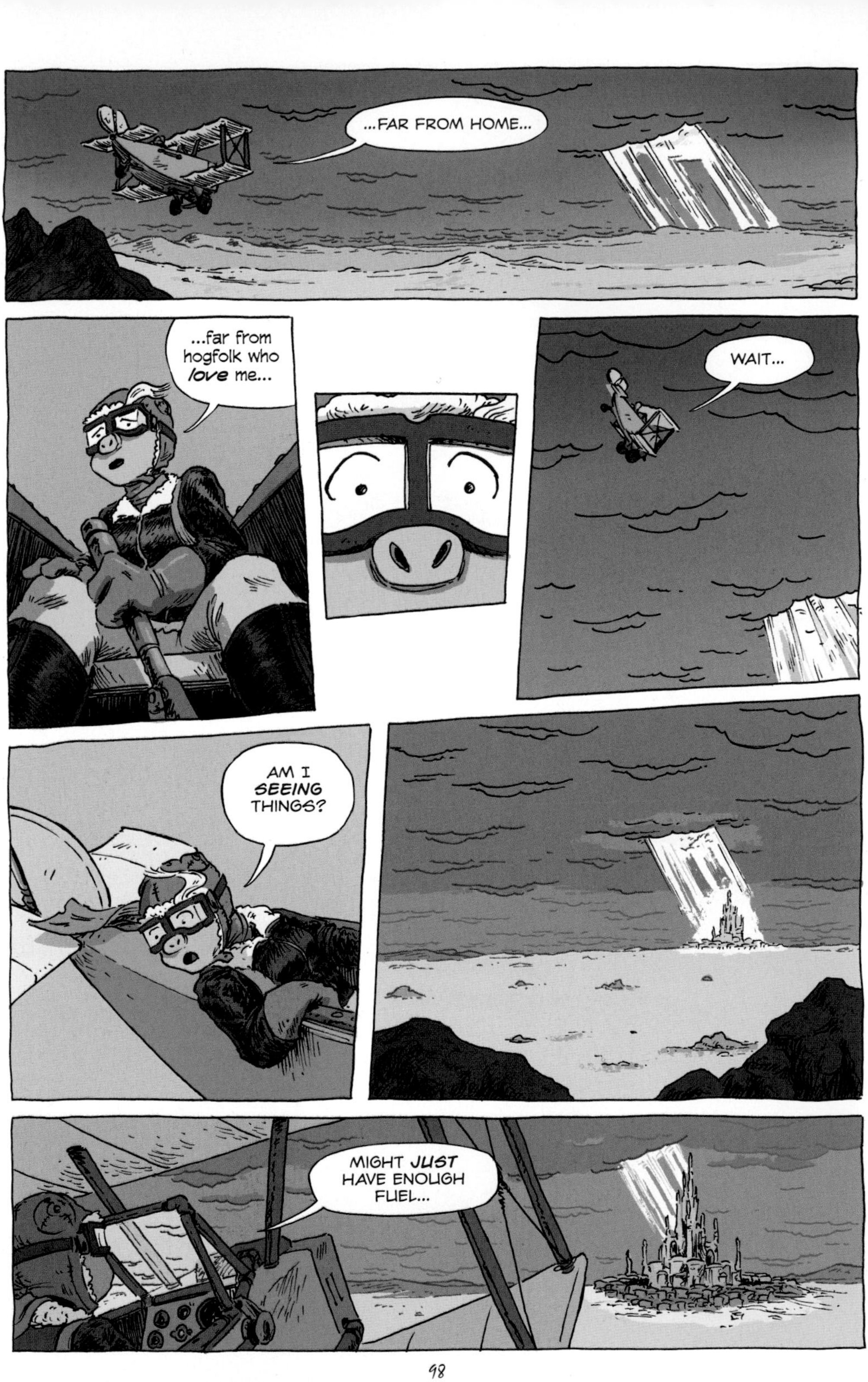
...FAR FROM HOME...
...far from hogfolk who *love* me...
WAIT...
AM I **SEEING** THINGS?
MIGHT **JUST** HAVE ENOUGH FUEL...

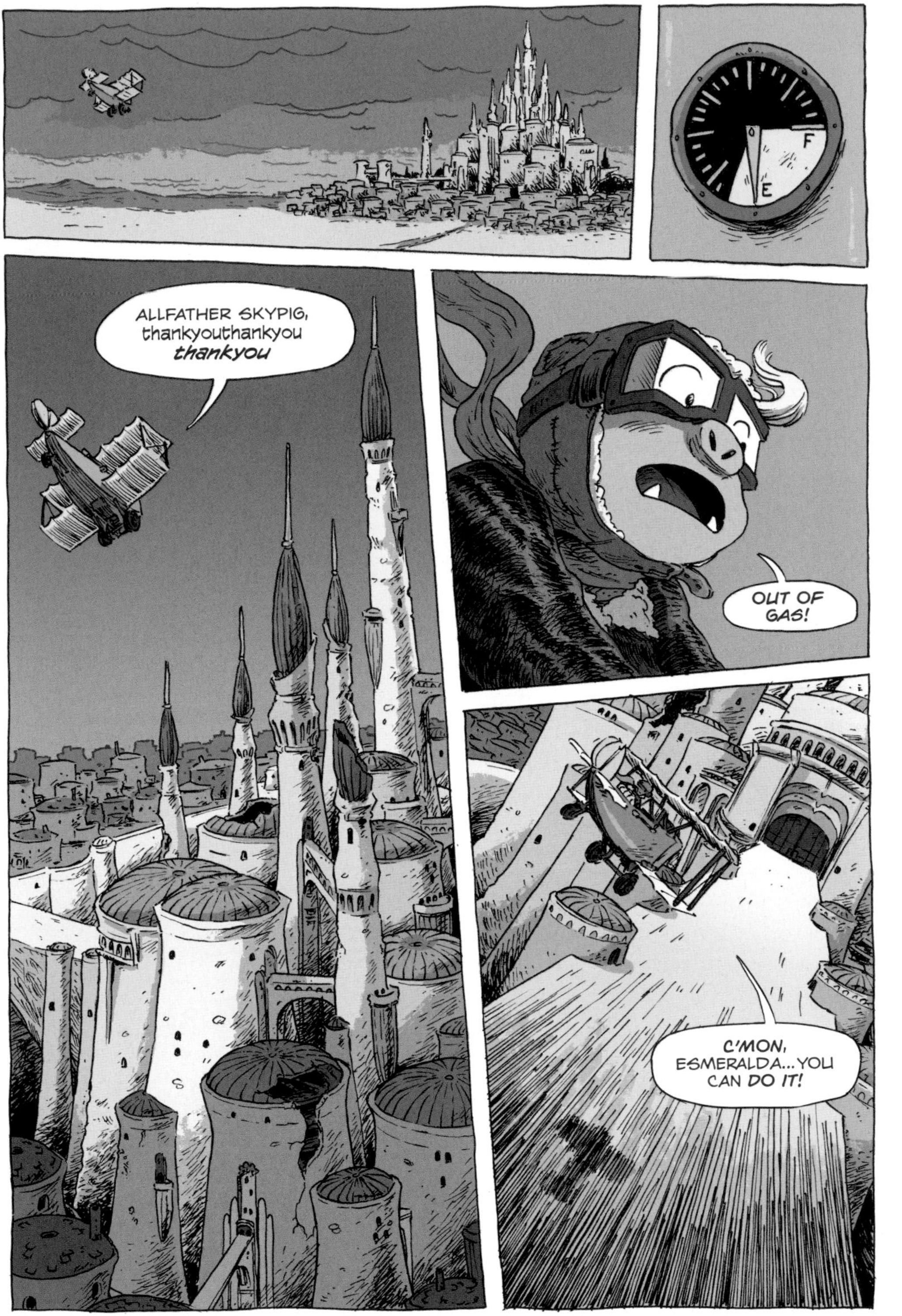
F
E
ALLFATHER SKYPIG, thankyouthankyou *thankyou*
OUT OF GAS!
C'MON, ESMERALDA...YOU CAN *DO IT!*

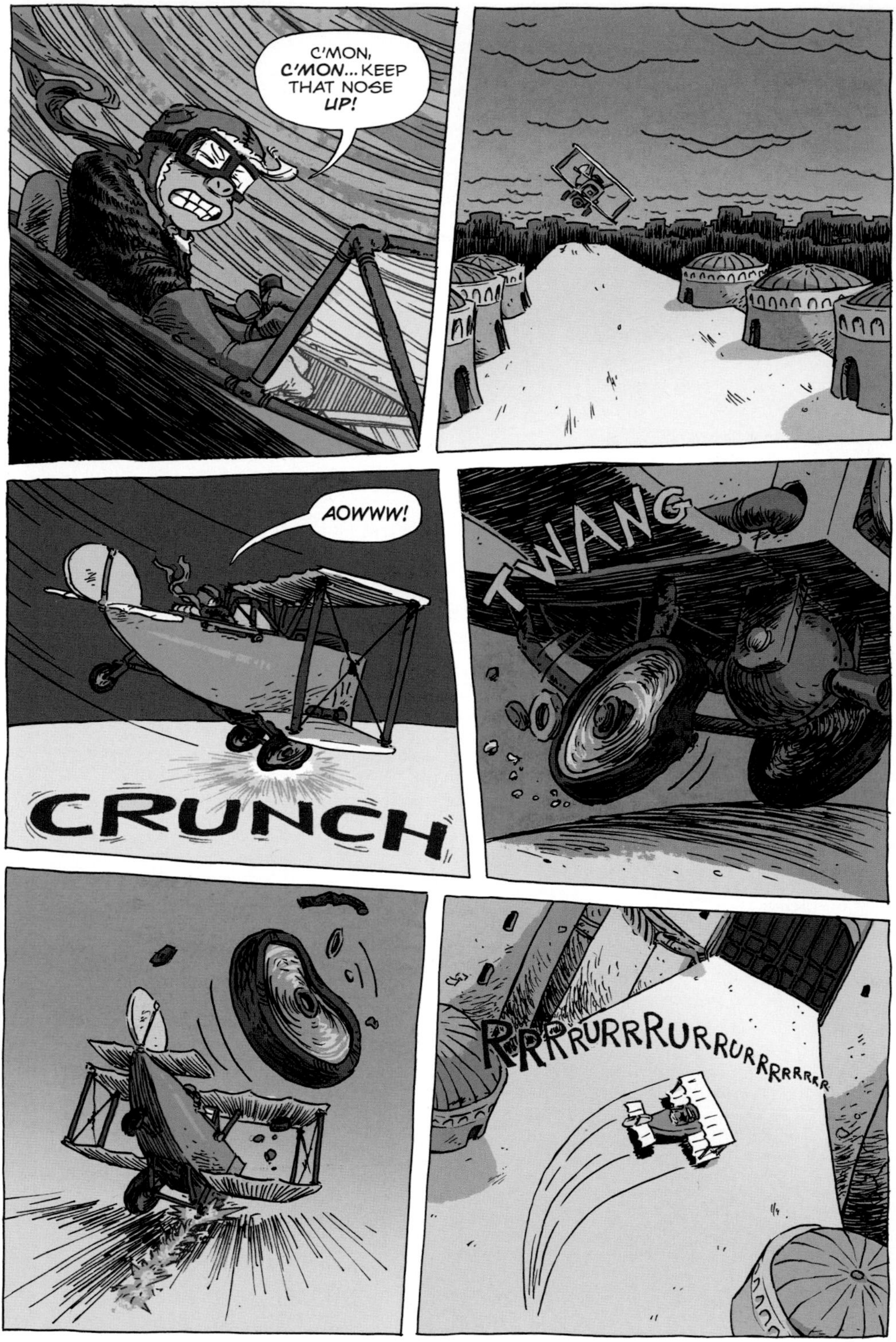
C'MON, C'MON... KEEP THAT NOSE UP!
AOWWW!
CRUNCH
TWANG
RRRRURRRURRURRRRRRRR

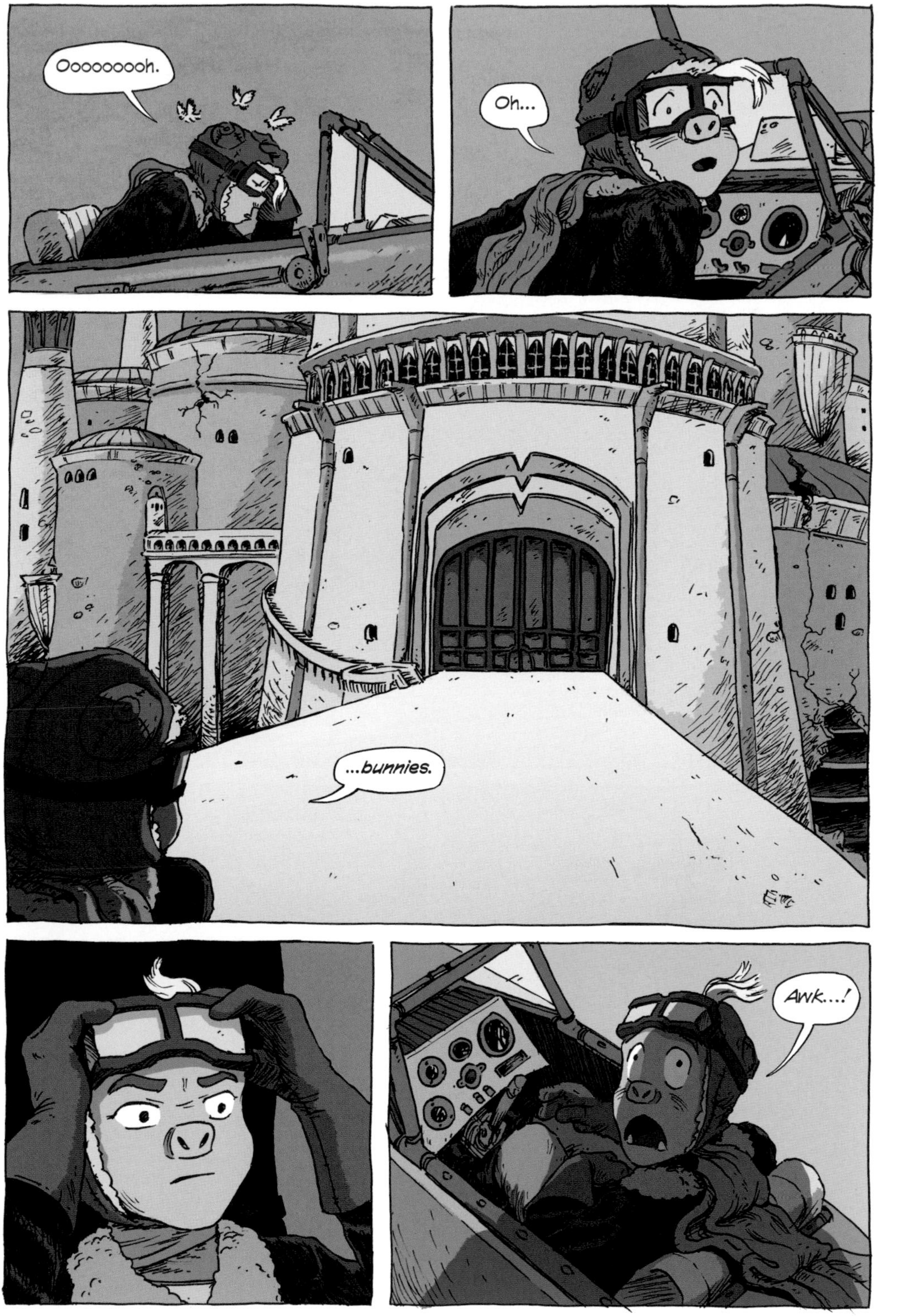
Ooooooooh.
Oh...
...bunnies.
Awk...!

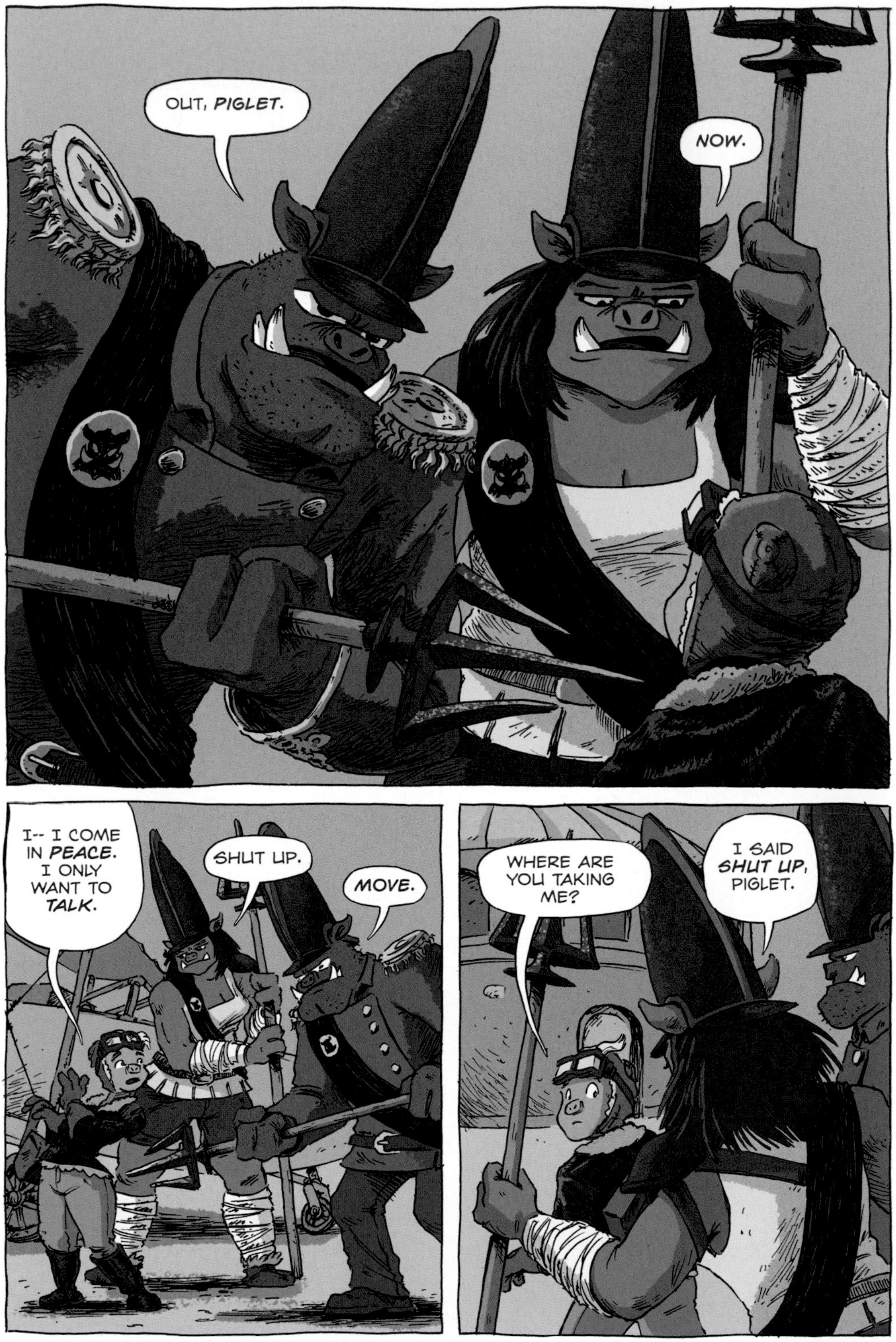
OUT, PIGLET.
NOW.
I-- I COME IN PEACE. I ONLY WANT TO TALK.
SHUT UP.
MOVE.
WHERE ARE YOU TAKING ME?
I SAID SHUT UP, PIGLET.

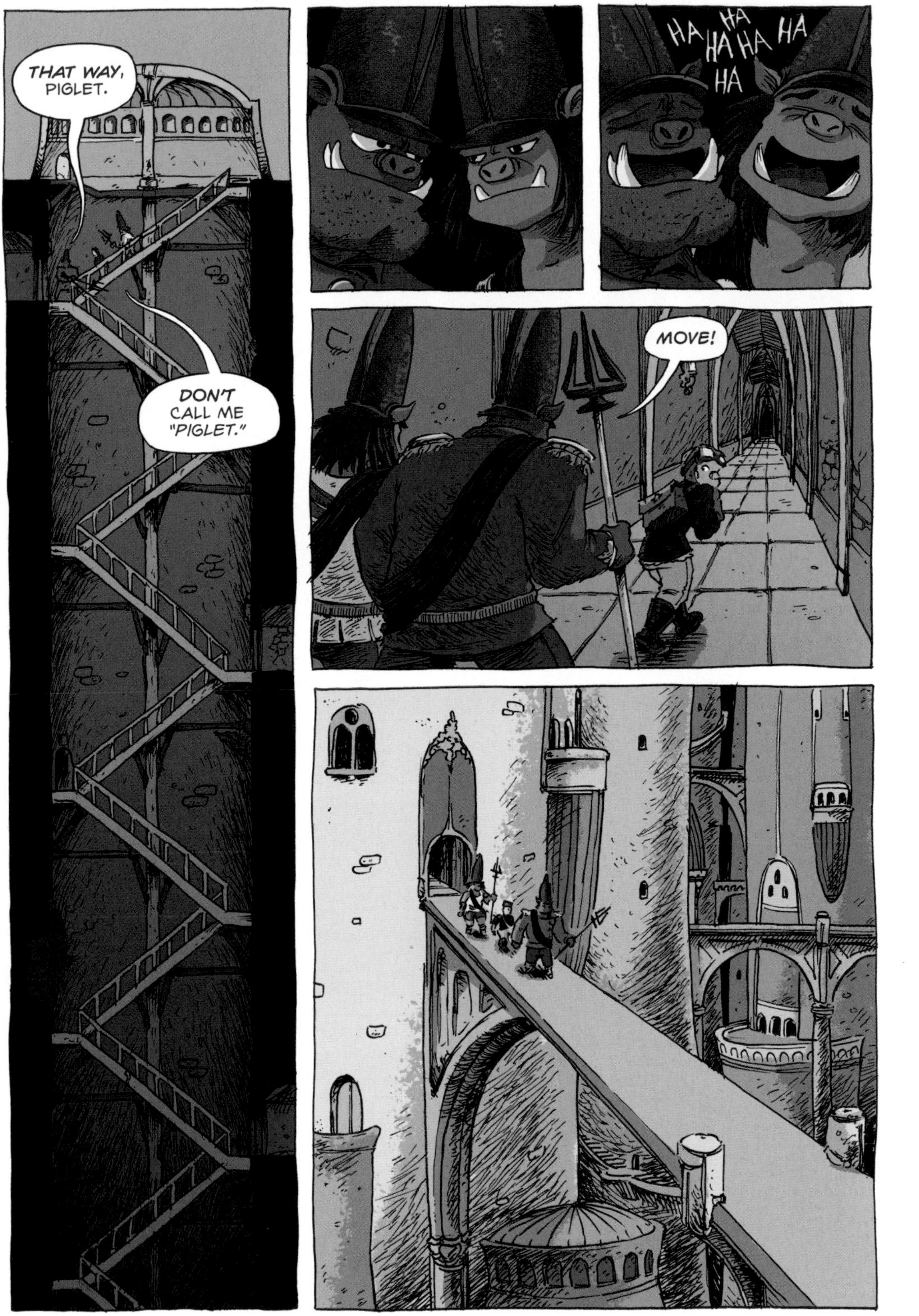
THAT WAY, PIGLET.
DON'T CALL ME "PIGLET."
HA HA HA HA HA HA HA
MOVE!

ISN'T IT QUICKER TO GO THAT WAY?

NO, LET'S TAKE A SHORTCUT THROUGH THE *ABBEY*.

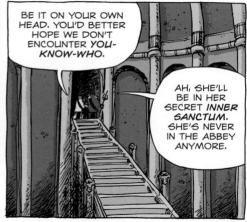

BE IT ON YOUR OWN HEAD. YOU'D BETTER HOPE WE DON'T ENCOUNTER *YOU-KNOW-WHO*.

AH, SHE'LL BE IN HER SECRET *INNER SANCTUM*. SHE'S NEVER IN THE ABBEY ANYMORE.

NOT SINCE EVERYONE LOST *INTEREST*...

SINCE *THE CHIEF* TOOK OVER.

SHE'S ONLY GOOD FOR *BINDING SPELLS* FOR HIM NOW...

THIS WAY...

MOVE!

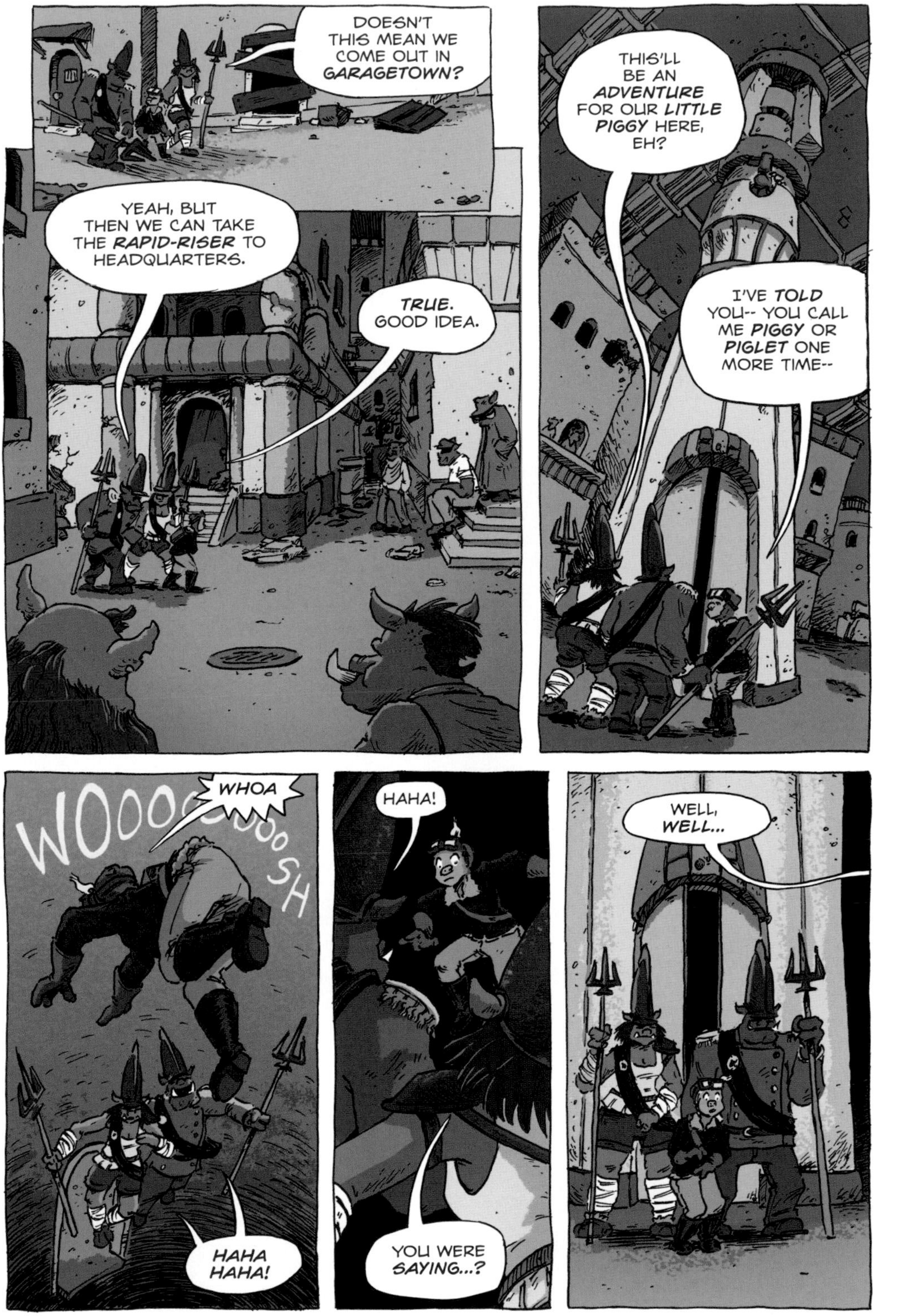
DOESN'T THIS MEAN WE COME OUT IN GARAGETOWN?
YEAH, BUT THEN WE CAN TAKE THE RAPID-RISER TO HEADQUARTERS.
TRUE. GOOD IDEA.
THIS'LL BE AN ADVENTURE FOR OUR LITTLE PIGGY HERE, EH?
I'VE TOLD YOU-- YOU CALL ME PIGGY OR PIGLET ONE MORE TIME--
WOOOOOOOOSH
WHOA
HAHA HAHA!
HAHA!
YOU WERE SAYING...?
WELL, WELL...

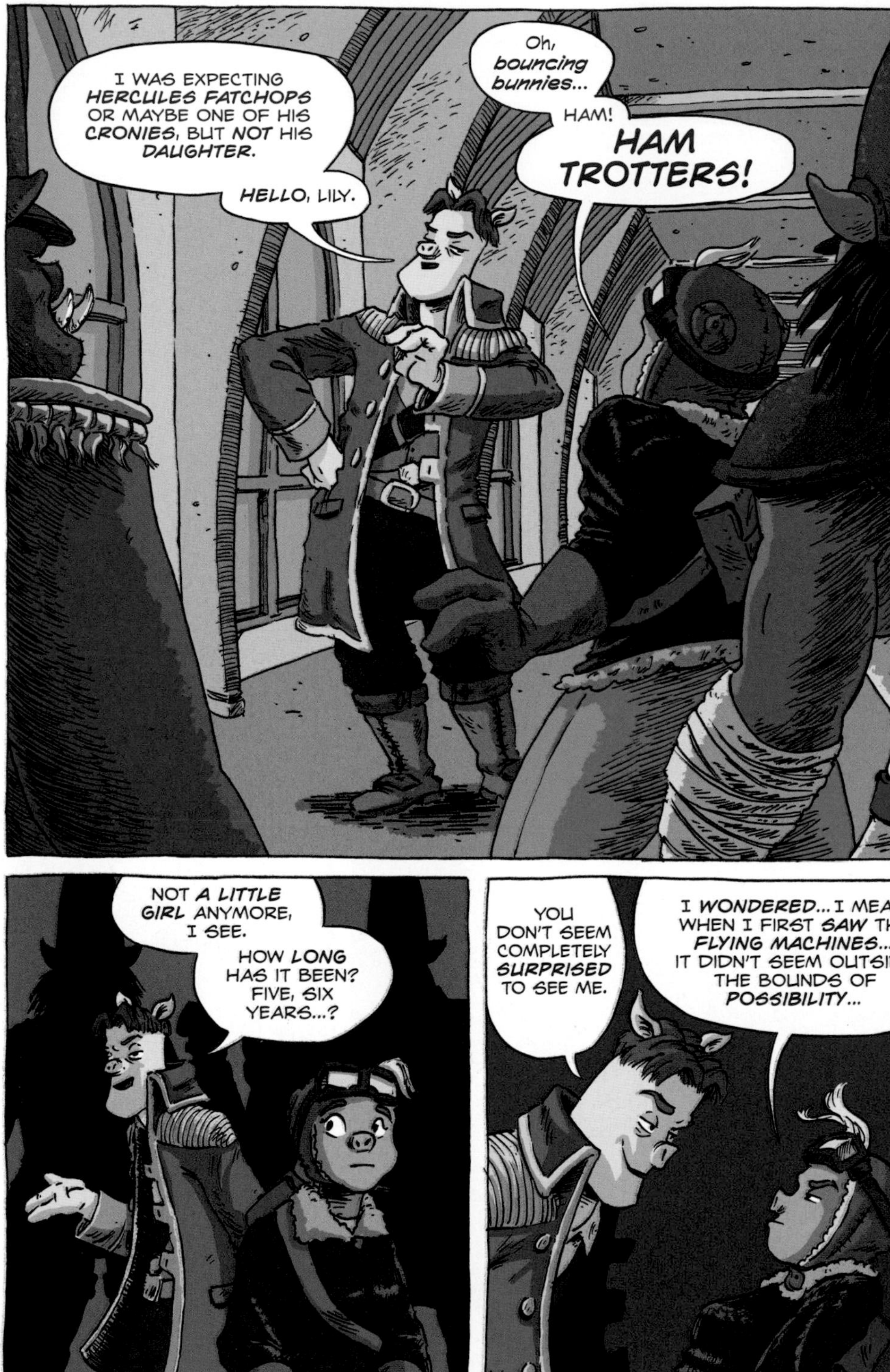
I WAS EXPECTING HERCULES FATCHOPS OR MAYBE ONE OF HIS CRONIES, BUT NOT HIS DAUGHTER.
HELLO, LILY.
Oh, bouncing bunnies...
HAM!
HAM TROTTERS!
NOT A LITTLE GIRL ANYMORE, I SEE.
HOW LONG HAS IT BEEN? FIVE, SIX YEARS...?
YOU DON'T SEEM COMPLETELY SURPRISED TO SEE ME.
I WONDERED... I MEAN, WHEN I FIRST SAW THE FLYING MACHINES... IT DIDN'T SEEM OUTSIDE THE BOUNDS OF POSSIBILITY...

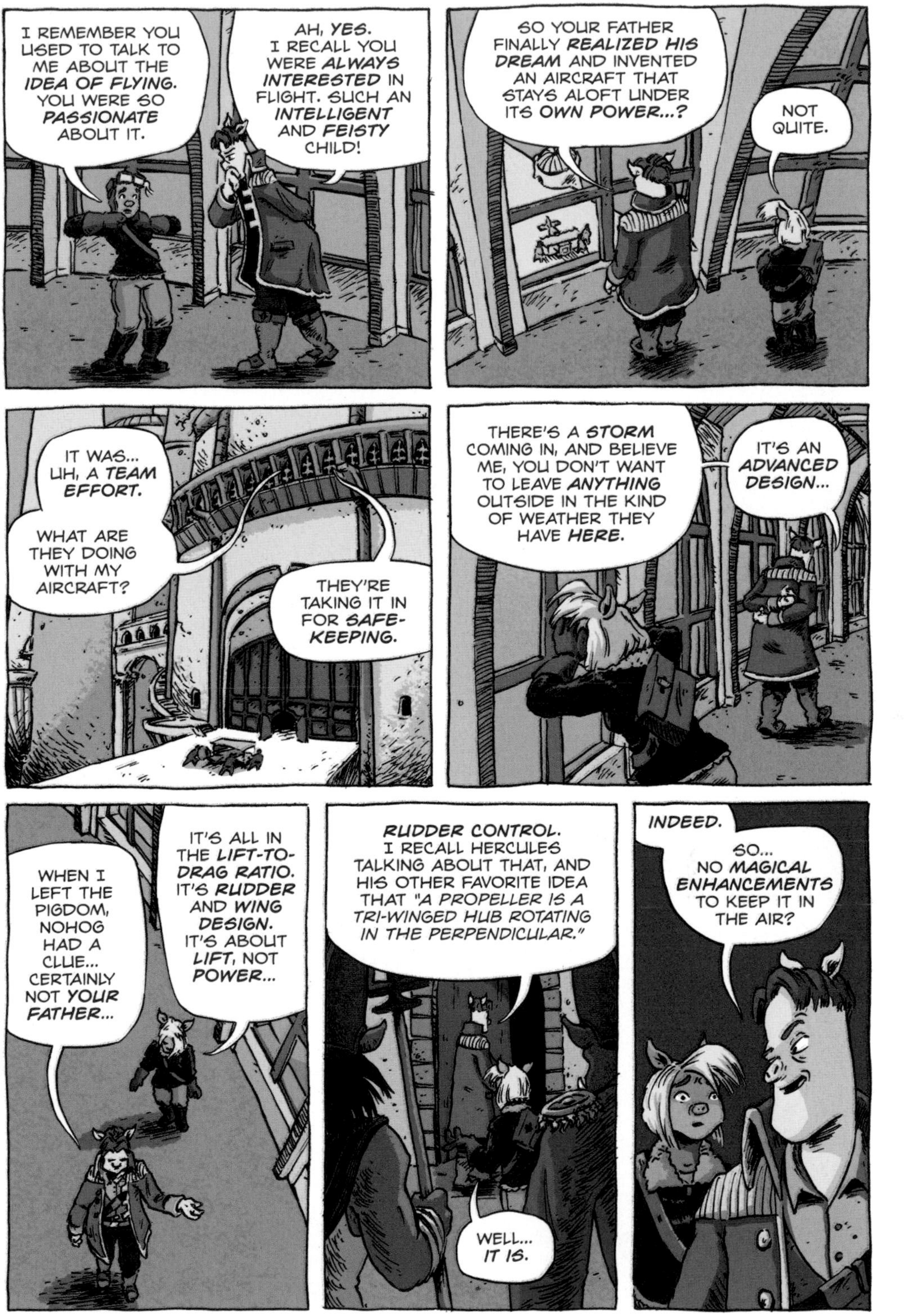
I REMEMBER YOU USED TO TALK TO ME ABOUT THE IDEA OF FLYING. YOU WERE SO PASSIONATE ABOUT IT.
AH, YES. I RECALL YOU WERE ALWAYS INTERESTED IN FLIGHT. SUCH AN INTELLIGENT AND FEISTY CHILD!
SO YOUR FATHER FINALLY REALIZED HIS DREAM AND INVENTED AN AIRCRAFT THAT STAYS ALOFT UNDER ITS OWN POWER...?
NOT QUITE.
IT WAS... UH, A TEAM EFFORT.
WHAT ARE THEY DOING WITH MY AIRCRAFT?
THEY'RE TAKING IT IN FOR SAFE-KEEPING.
THERE'S A STORM COMING IN, AND BELIEVE ME, YOU DON'T WANT TO LEAVE ANYTHING OUTSIDE IN THE KIND OF WEATHER THEY HAVE HERE.
IT'S AN ADVANCED DESIGN...
WHEN I LEFT THE PIGDOM, NOHOG HAD A CLUE... CERTAINLY NOT YOUR FATHER...
IT'S ALL IN THE LIFT-TO-DRAG RATIO. IT'S RUDDER AND WING DESIGN. IT'S ABOUT LIFT, NOT POWER...
RUDDER CONTROL. I RECALL HERCULES TALKING ABOUT THAT, AND HIS OTHER FAVORITE IDEA THAT "A PROPELLER IS A TRI-WINGED HUB ROTATING IN THE PERPENDICULAR."
WELL... IT IS.
INDEED.
SO... NO MAGICAL ENHANCEMENTS TO KEEP IT IN THE AIR?

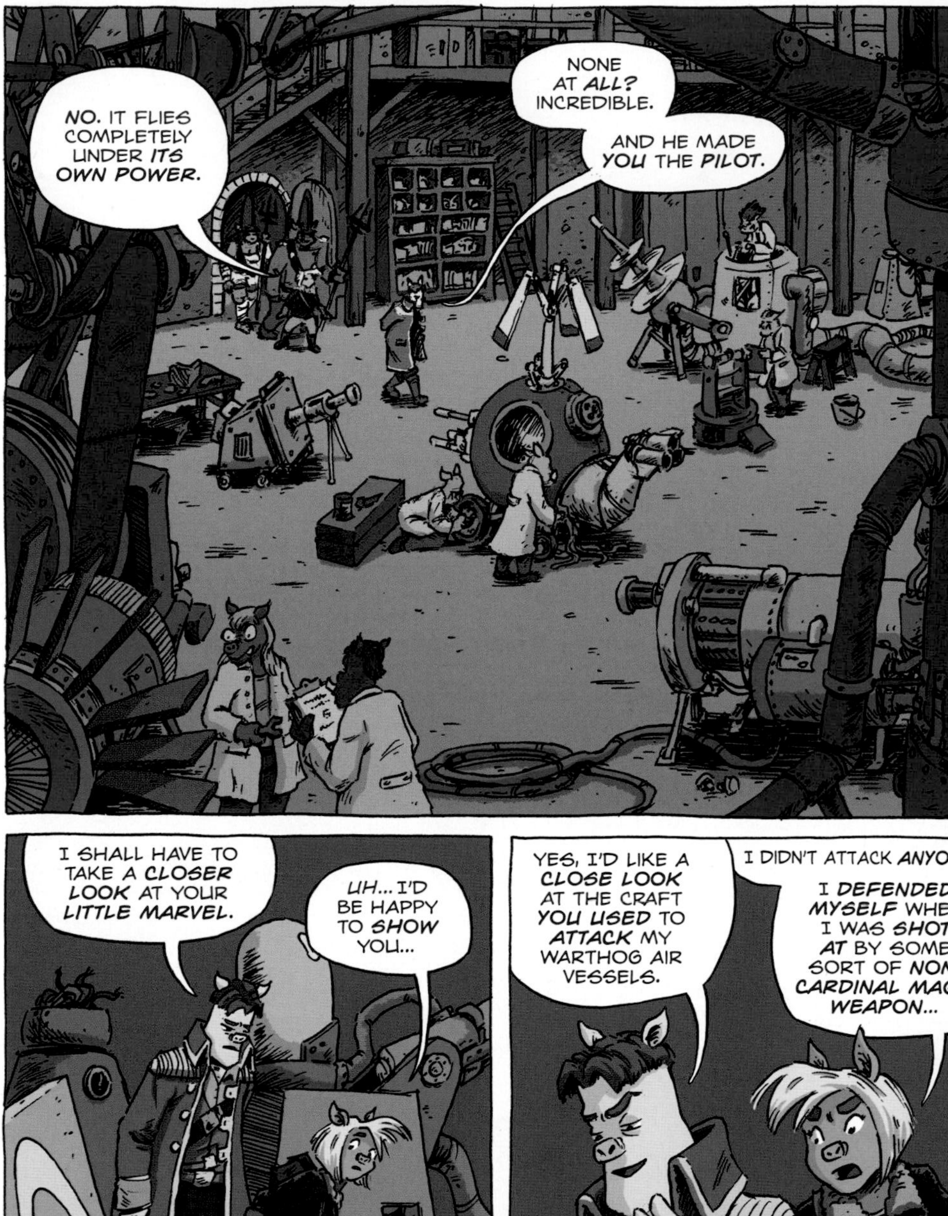
NO. IT FLIES COMPLETELY UNDER ITS OWN POWER.
NONE AT ALL? INCREDIBLE.
AND HE MADE YOU THE PILOT.
I SHALL HAVE TO TAKE A CLOSER LOOK AT YOUR LITTLE MARVEL.
UH... I'D BE HAPPY TO SHOW YOU...
YES, I'D LIKE A CLOSE LOOK AT THE CRAFT YOU USED TO ATTACK MY WARTHOG AIR VESSELS.
I DIDN'T ATTACK ANYONE!
I DEFENDED MYSELF WHEN I WAS SHOT AT BY SOME SORT OF NON-CARDINAL MAGIC WEAPON...

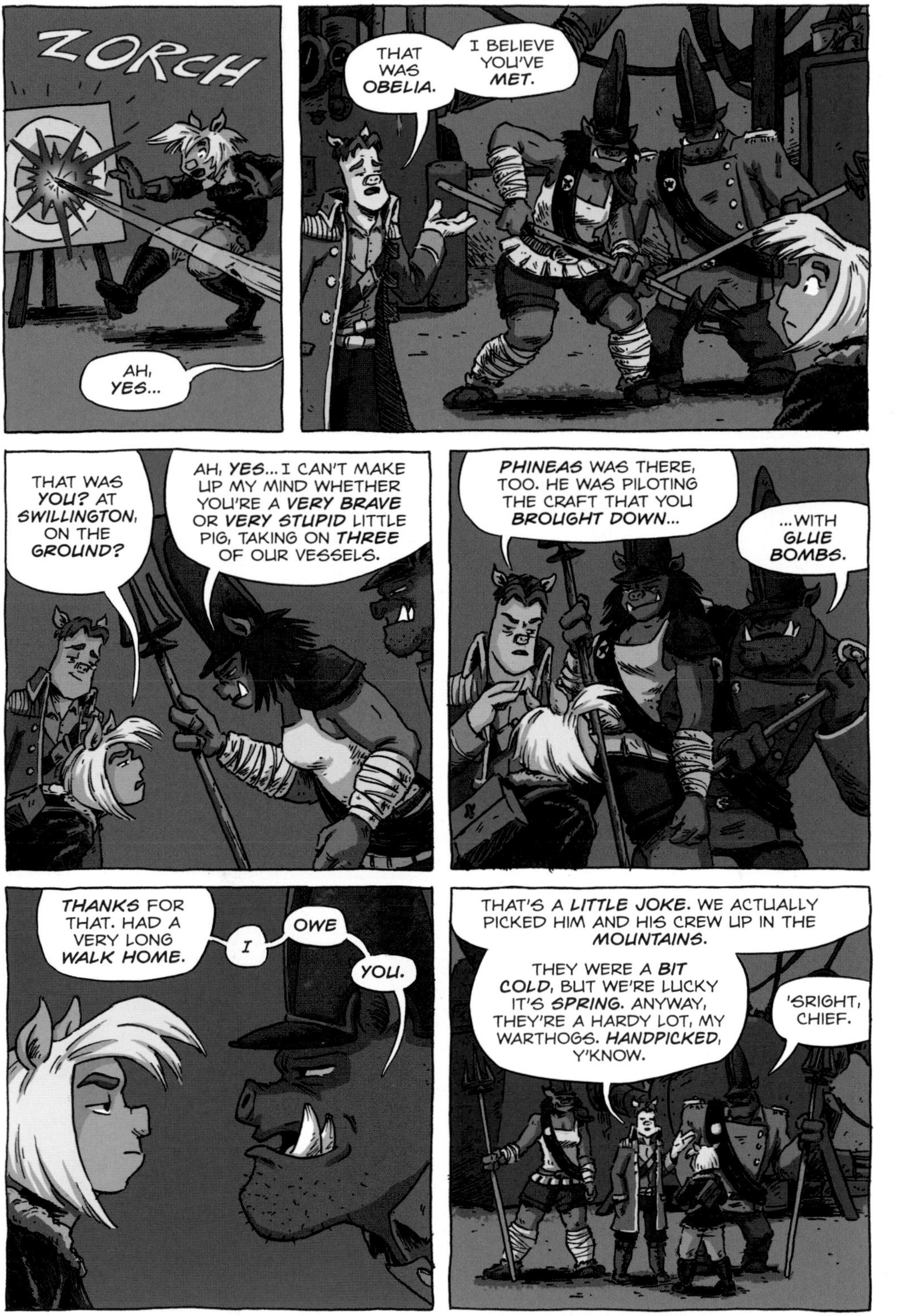
ZORCH
AH, YES...
THAT WAS OBELIA.
I BELIEVE YOU'VE MET.
THAT WAS YOU? AT SWILLINGTON, ON THE GROUND?
AH, YES... I CAN'T MAKE UP MY MIND WHETHER YOU'RE A VERY BRAVE OR VERY STUPID LITTLE PIG, TAKING ON THREE OF OUR VESSELS.
PHINEAS WAS THERE, TOO. HE WAS PILOTING THE CRAFT THAT YOU BROUGHT DOWN...
...WITH GLUE BOMBS.
THANKS FOR THAT. HAD A VERY LONG WALK HOME.
I
OWE
YOU.
THAT'S A LITTLE JOKE. WE ACTUALLY PICKED HIM AND HIS CREW UP IN THE MOUNTAINS.
THEY WERE A BIT COLD, BUT WE'RE LUCKY IT'S SPRING. ANYWAY, THEY'RE A HARDY LOT, MY WARTHOGS. HANDPICKED, Y'KNOW.
'SRIGHT, CHIEF.

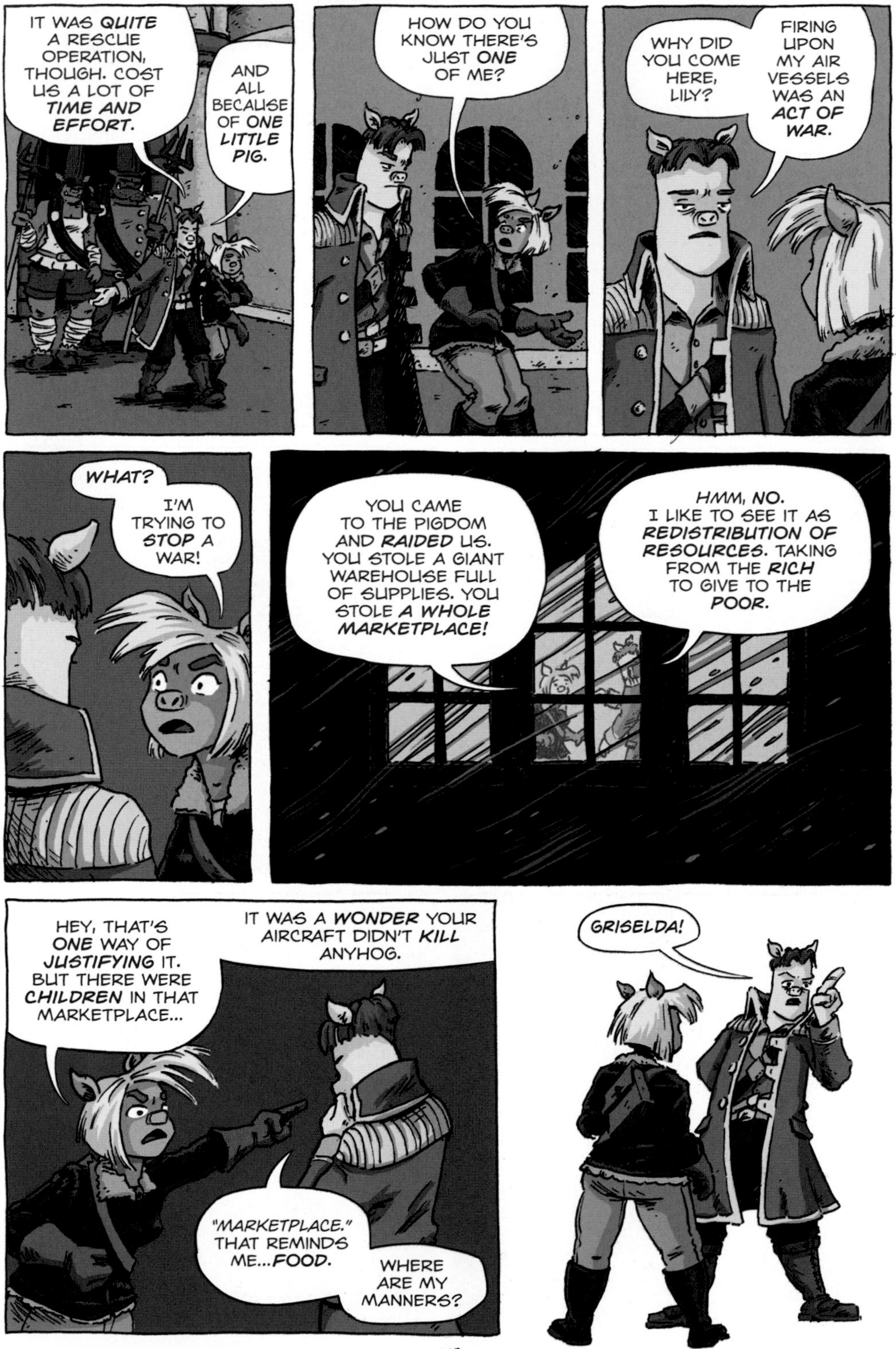

IT WAS QUITE A RESCUE OPERATION, THOUGH. COST US A LOT OF TIME AND EFFORT.
AND ALL BECAUSE OF ONE LITTLE PIG.
HOW DO YOU KNOW THERE'S JUST ONE OF ME?
WHY DID YOU COME HERE, LILY?
FIRING UPON MY AIR VESSELS WAS AN ACT OF WAR.
WHAT?
I'M TRYING TO STOP A WAR!
YOU CAME TO THE PIGDOM AND RAIDED US. YOU STOLE A GIANT WAREHOUSE FULL OF SUPPLIES. YOU STOLE A WHOLE MARKETPLACE!
HMM, NO. I LIKE TO SEE IT AS REDISTRIBUTION OF RESOURCES. TAKING FROM THE RICH TO GIVE TO THE POOR.
HEY, THAT'S ONE WAY OF JUSTIFYING IT. BUT THERE WERE CHILDREN IN THAT MARKETPLACE...
IT WAS A WONDER YOUR AIRCRAFT DIDN'T KILL ANYHOG.
"MARKETPLACE." THAT REMINDS ME...FOOD.
WHERE ARE MY MANNERS?
GRISELDA!

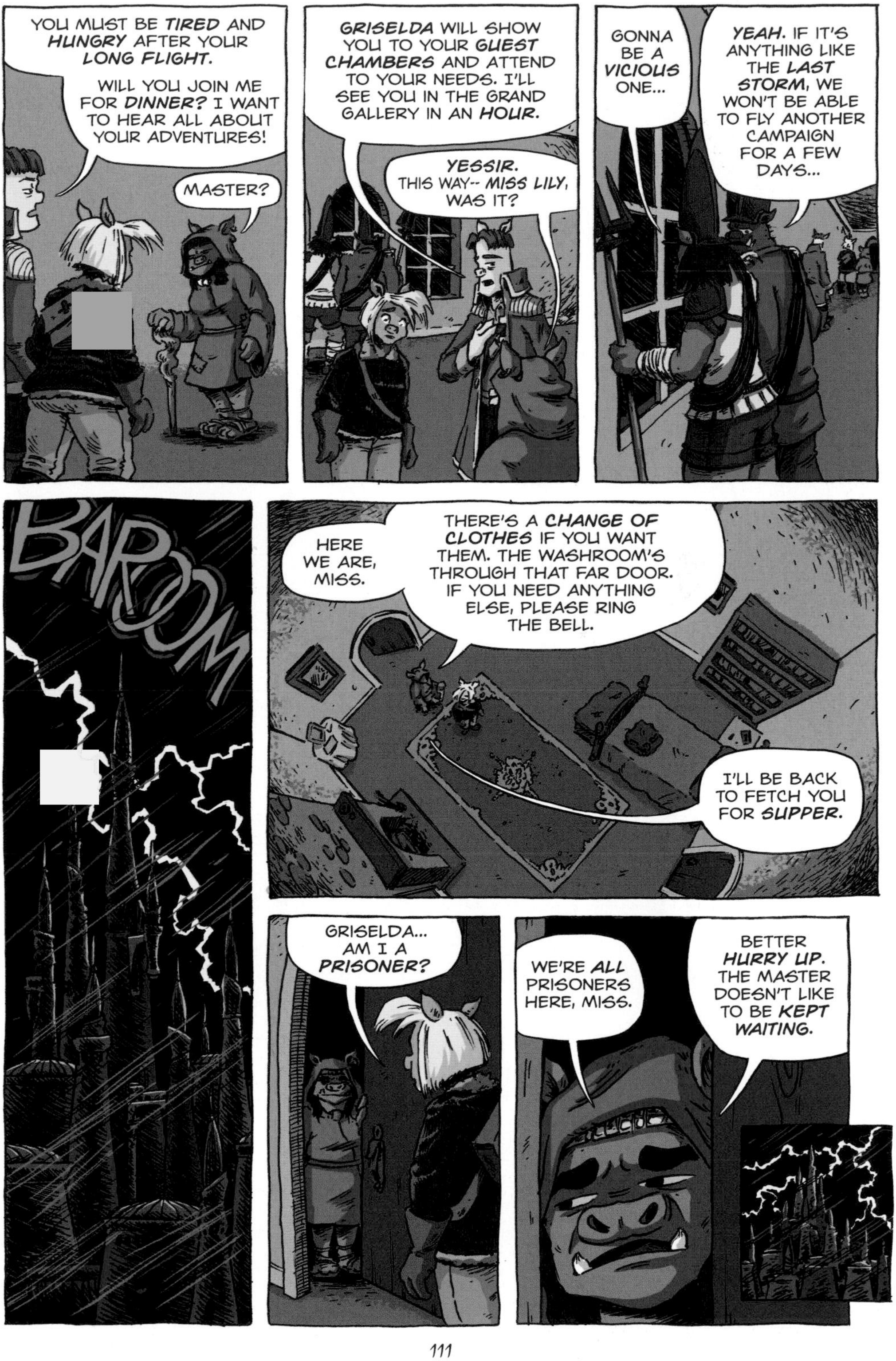
YOU MUST BE TIRED AND HUNGRY AFTER YOUR LONG FLIGHT.
WILL YOU JOIN ME FOR DINNER? I WANT TO HEAR ALL ABOUT YOUR ADVENTURES!
MASTER?
GRISELDA WILL SHOW YOU TO YOUR GUEST CHAMBERS AND ATTEND TO YOUR NEEDS. I'LL SEE YOU IN THE GRAND GALLERY IN AN HOUR.
YESSIR. THIS WAY-- MISS LILY, WAS IT?
GONNA BE A VICIOUS ONE...
YEAH. IF IT'S ANYTHING LIKE THE LAST STORM, WE WON'T BE ABLE TO FLY ANOTHER CAMPAIGN FOR A FEW DAYS...
BAROOM
HERE WE ARE, MISS.
THERE'S A CHANGE OF CLOTHES IF YOU WANT THEM. THE WASHROOM'S THROUGH THAT FAR DOOR. IF YOU NEED ANYTHING ELSE, PLEASE RING THE BELL.
I'LL BE BACK TO FETCH YOU FOR SUPPER.
GRISELDA... AM I A PRISONER?
WE'RE ALL PRISONERS HERE, MISS.
BETTER HURRY UP. THE MASTER DOESN'T LIKE TO BE KEPT WAITING.

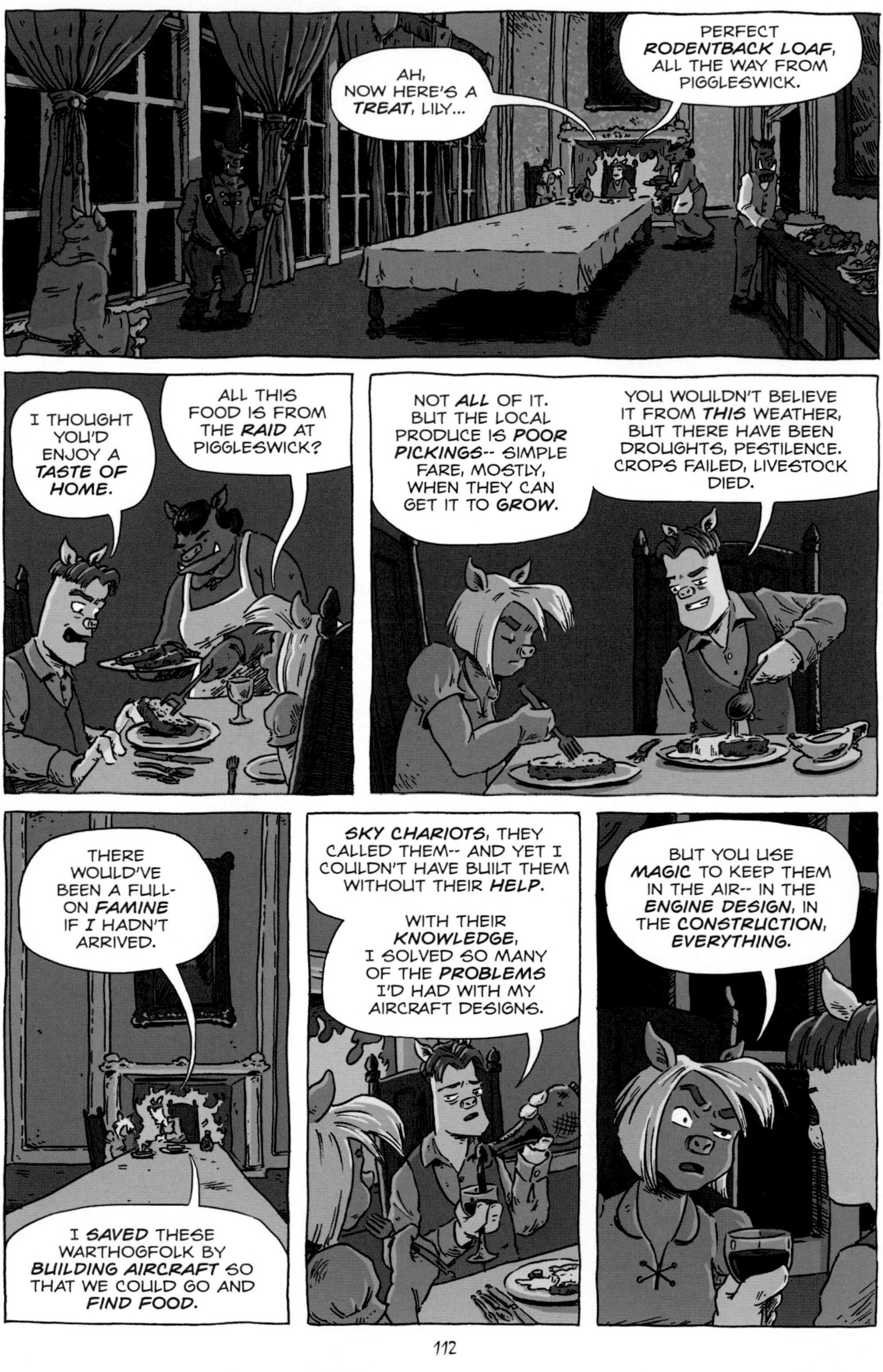
AH, NOW HERE'S A TREAT, LILY...
PERFECT RODENTBACK LOAF, ALL THE WAY FROM PIGGLESWICK.
I THOUGHT YOU'D ENJOY A TASTE OF HOME.
ALL THIS FOOD IS FROM THE RAID AT PIGGLESWICK?
NOT ALL OF IT. BUT THE LOCAL PRODUCE IS POOR PICKINGS-- SIMPLE FARE, MOSTLY, WHEN THEY CAN GET IT TO GROW.
YOU WOULDN'T BELIEVE IT FROM THIS WEATHER, BUT THERE HAVE BEEN DROUGHTS, PESTILENCE. CROPS FAILED, LIVESTOCK DIED.
THERE WOULD'VE BEEN A FULL-ON FAMINE IF I HADN'T ARRIVED.
I SAVED THESE WARTHOGFOLK BY BUILDING AIRCRAFT SO THAT WE COULD GO AND FIND FOOD.
SKY CHARIOTS, THEY CALLED THEM-- AND YET I COULDN'T HAVE BUILT THEM WITHOUT THEIR HELP.
WITH THEIR KNOWLEDGE, I SOLVED SO MANY OF THE PROBLEMS I'D HAD WITH MY AIRCRAFT DESIGNS.
BUT YOU USE MAGIC TO KEEP THEM IN THE AIR-- IN THE ENGINE DESIGN, IN THE CONSTRUCTION, EVERYTHING.

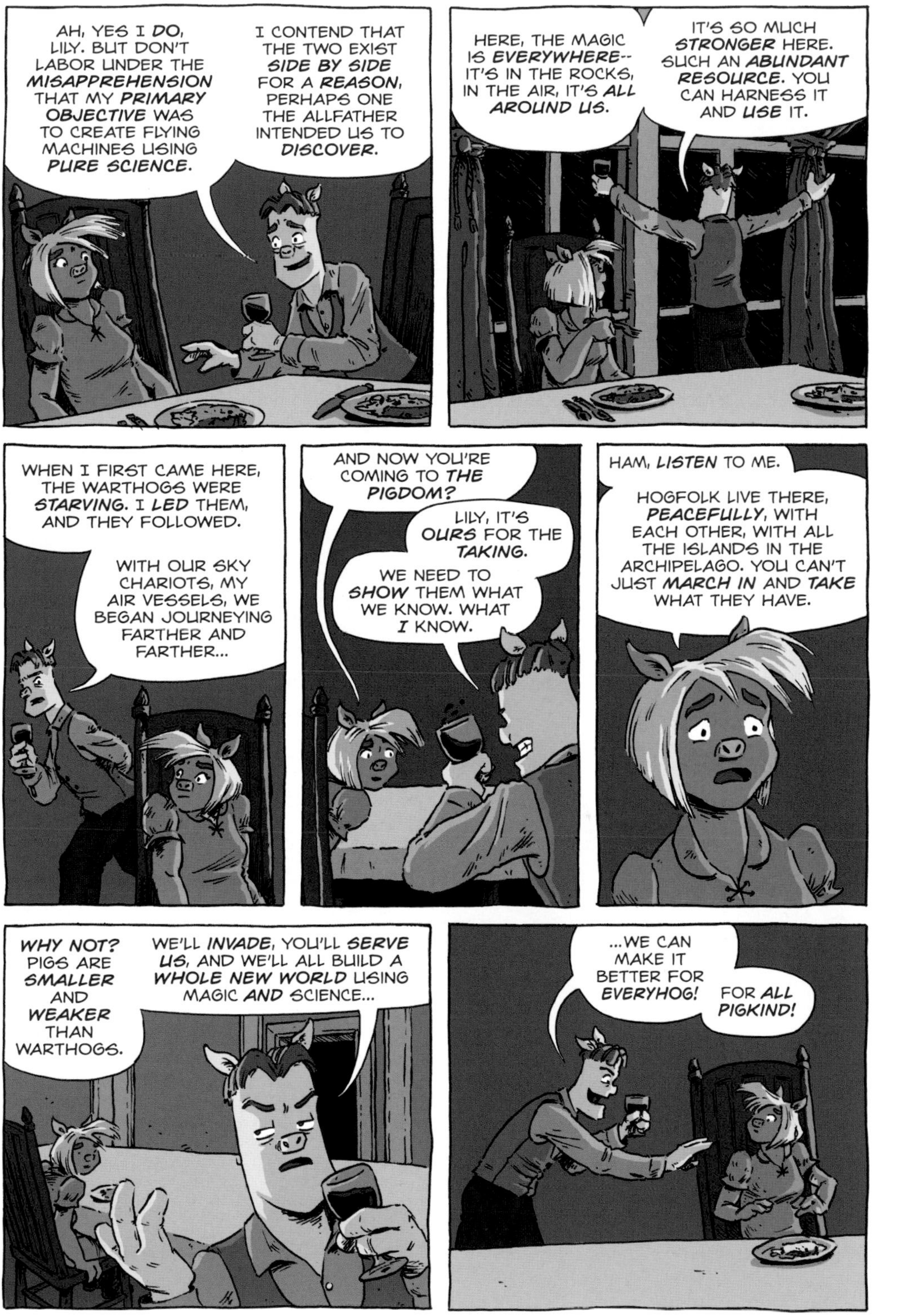
AH, YES I DO, LILY. BUT DON'T LABOR UNDER THE MISAPPREHENSION THAT MY PRIMARY OBJECTIVE WAS TO CREATE FLYING MACHINES USING PURE SCIENCE.
I CONTEND THAT THE TWO EXIST SIDE BY SIDE FOR A REASON, PERHAPS ONE THE ALLFATHER INTENDED US TO DISCOVER.
HERE, THE MAGIC IS EVERYWHERE-- IT'S IN THE ROCKS, IN THE AIR, IT'S ALL AROUND US.
IT'S SO MUCH STRONGER HERE. SUCH AN ABUNDANT RESOURCE. YOU CAN HARNESS IT AND USE IT.
WHEN I FIRST CAME HERE, THE WARTHOGS WERE STARVING. I LED THEM, AND THEY FOLLOWED.
WITH OUR SKY CHARIOTS, MY AIR VESSELS, WE BEGAN JOURNEYING FARTHER AND FARTHER...
AND NOW YOU'RE COMING TO THE PIGDOM?
LILY, IT'S OURS FOR THE TAKING.
WE NEED TO SHOW THEM WHAT WE KNOW. WHAT I KNOW.
HAM, LISTEN TO ME.
HOGFOLK LIVE THERE, PEACEFULLY, WITH EACH OTHER, WITH ALL THE ISLANDS IN THE ARCHIPELAGO. YOU CAN'T JUST MARCH IN AND TAKE WHAT THEY HAVE.
WHY NOT? PIGS ARE SMALLER AND WEAKER THAN WARTHOGS.
WE'LL INVADE, YOU'LL SERVE US, AND WE'LL ALL BUILD A WHOLE NEW WORLD USING MAGIC AND SCIENCE...
...WE CAN MAKE IT BETTER FOR EVERYHOG!
FOR ALL PIGKIND!

SORRY. JUST WANTED TO SAY THAT YOU'RE AN *INSPIRATION*... TO *ME*, AND, UH, MY *ENGINEERS*.

DON'T TRY TO *SWEET-TALK ME*, GIRL...

I'M NOT. IT'S *TRUE*.

YOU KNOW WHY I CAME HERE, LILY? I CAME BECAUSE IT *CALLED* ME. I COULD *FEEL* IT.

I *FLEW* HERE.

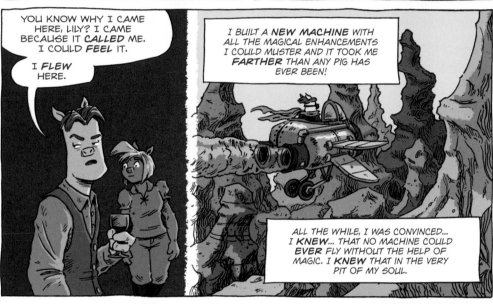

I BUILT A *NEW MACHINE* WITH ALL THE MAGICAL ENHANCEMENTS I COULD MUSTER AND IT TOOK ME *FARTHER* THAN ANY PIG HAS EVER BEEN!

ALL THE WHILE, I WAS CONVINCED... I *KNEW*... THAT NO MACHINE COULD *EVER* FLY WITHOUT THE HELP OF MAGIC. I *KNEW* THAT IN THE VERY PIT OF MY SOUL.

THEN *YOU* FLY IN HERE WITH THAT MACHINE OF YOUR FATHER'S... PROVING THAT IT *IS* POSSIBLE.

BY THE ALLFATHER, YOU ARE YOUR *FATHER'S DAUGHTER*, ALL RIGHT.

I DON'T *AGREE* WITH HIM ON *EVERY DETAIL*. I'M *SURE* THERE'S A WAY OF MIXING *BOTH DISCIPLINES* TO GET A *BETTER RESULT*.

ONE OF MY, ER-- *ASSISTANTS* WOULD *AGREE* WITH YOU. BUT I THINK HE MIGHT HAVE AN ISSUE WITH THE *TYPE* OF MAGIC YOU USE.

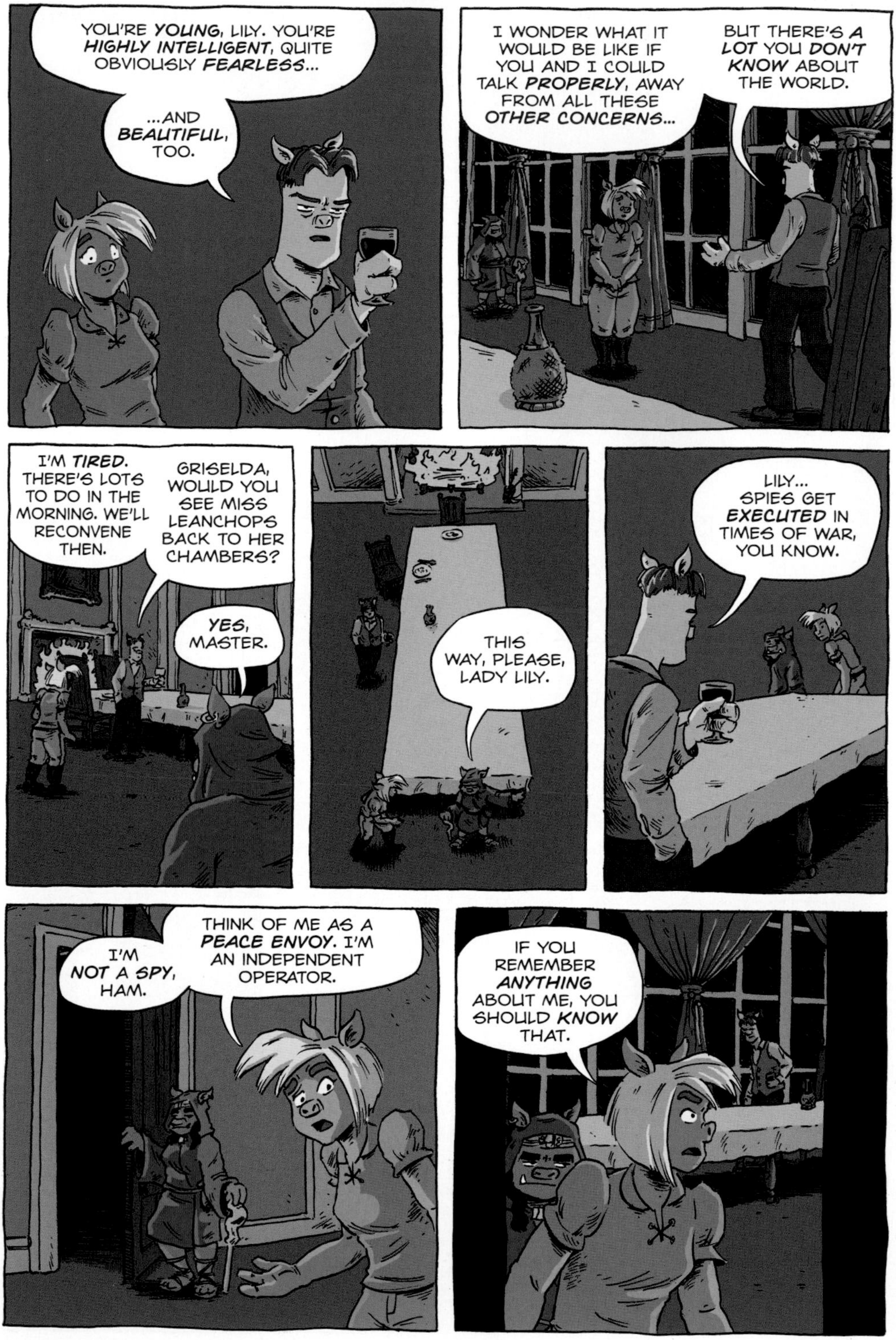
YOU'RE YOUNG, LILY. YOU'RE HIGHLY INTELLIGENT, QUITE OBVIOUSLY FEARLESS...
...AND BEAUTIFUL, TOO.
I WONDER WHAT IT WOULD BE LIKE IF YOU AND I COULD TALK PROPERLY, AWAY FROM ALL THESE OTHER CONCERNS...
BUT THERE'S A LOT YOU DON'T KNOW ABOUT THE WORLD.
I'M TIRED. THERE'S LOTS TO DO IN THE MORNING. WE'LL RECONVENE THEN.
GRISELDA, WOULD YOU SEE MISS LEANCHOPS BACK TO HER CHAMBERS?
YES, MASTER.
THIS WAY, PLEASE, LADY LILY.
LILY... SPIES GET EXECUTED IN TIMES OF WAR, YOU KNOW.
I'M NOT A SPY, HAM.
THINK OF ME AS A PEACE ENVOY. I'M AN INDEPENDENT OPERATOR.
IF YOU REMEMBER ANYTHING ABOUT ME, YOU SHOULD KNOW THAT.

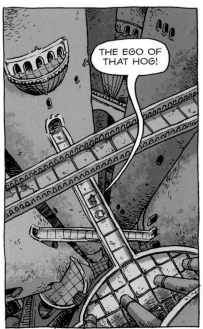

THE EGO OF THAT HOG!

THIS PLACE IS *INCREDIBLE!*

WAIT, GRISELDA... THIS ISN'T THE WAY WE CAME...

NO, MILADY. WE'RE TAKING THE *SCENIC* ROUTE.

WHY?

HEY, IF IT ISN'T A LITTLE *PIGGY-WIGGY!*

A *PIGGY* AND A *DWARFHOG!*

I HEARD A *RUMOR A LITTLE PINK PIGLET* FLEW IN.

AS IF PIGS KNEW HOW TO *FLY!*

PLEASE LET US PASS.

WHAT IF WE *DON'T,* DWARFHOG?

WHERE ARE YOU GOING IN SUCH A HURRY?

STAY. *ENTERTAIN* US!

WON'T ASK AGAIN.

NO. PLAY WITH US!

STAY *BEHIND* ME, MILADY.

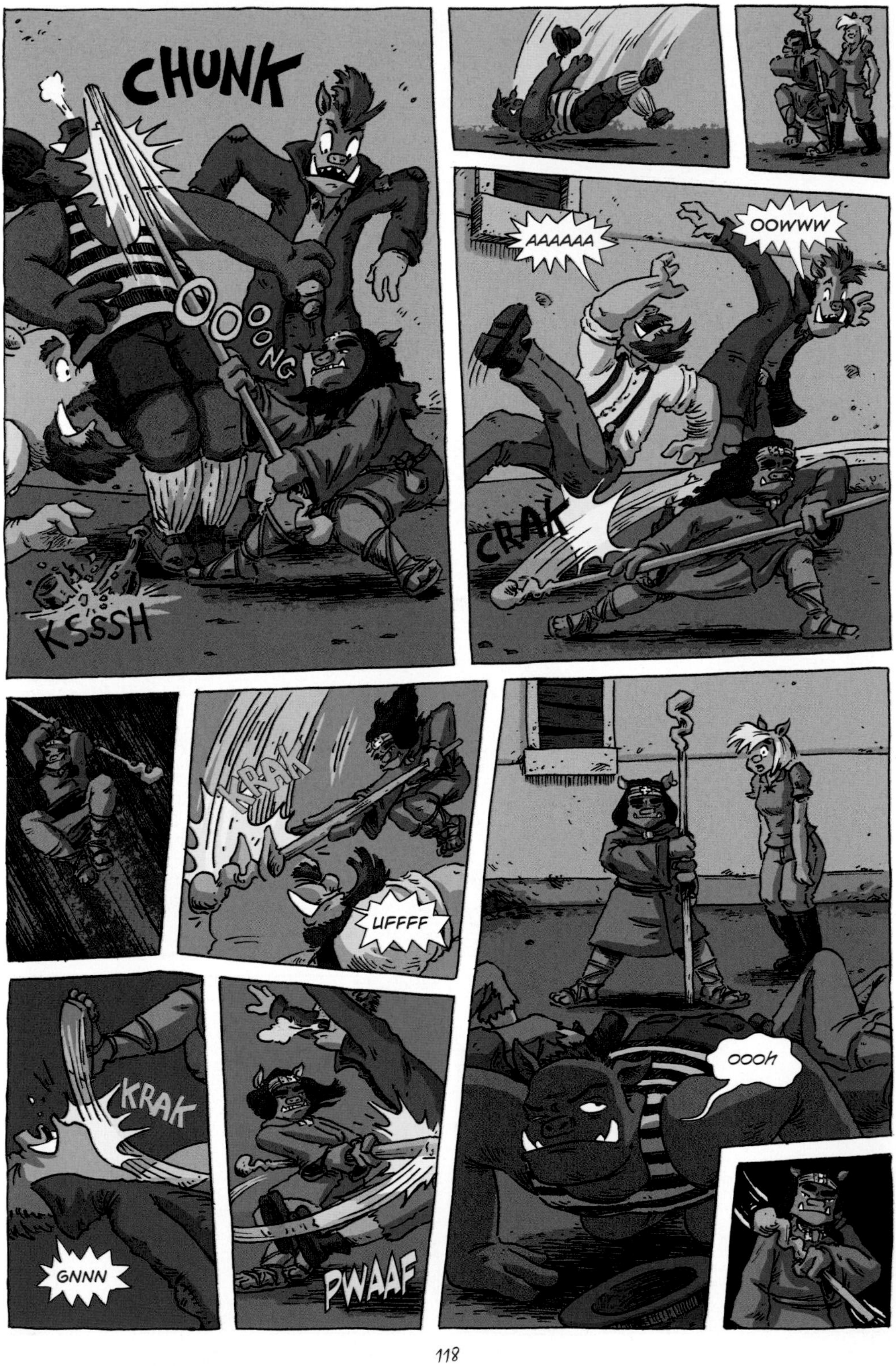
CHUNK
OOOONG
KSSSH
AAAAAA
OOWWW
CRAK
KRAK
UFFFF
KRAK
GNNN
PWAAF
oooh

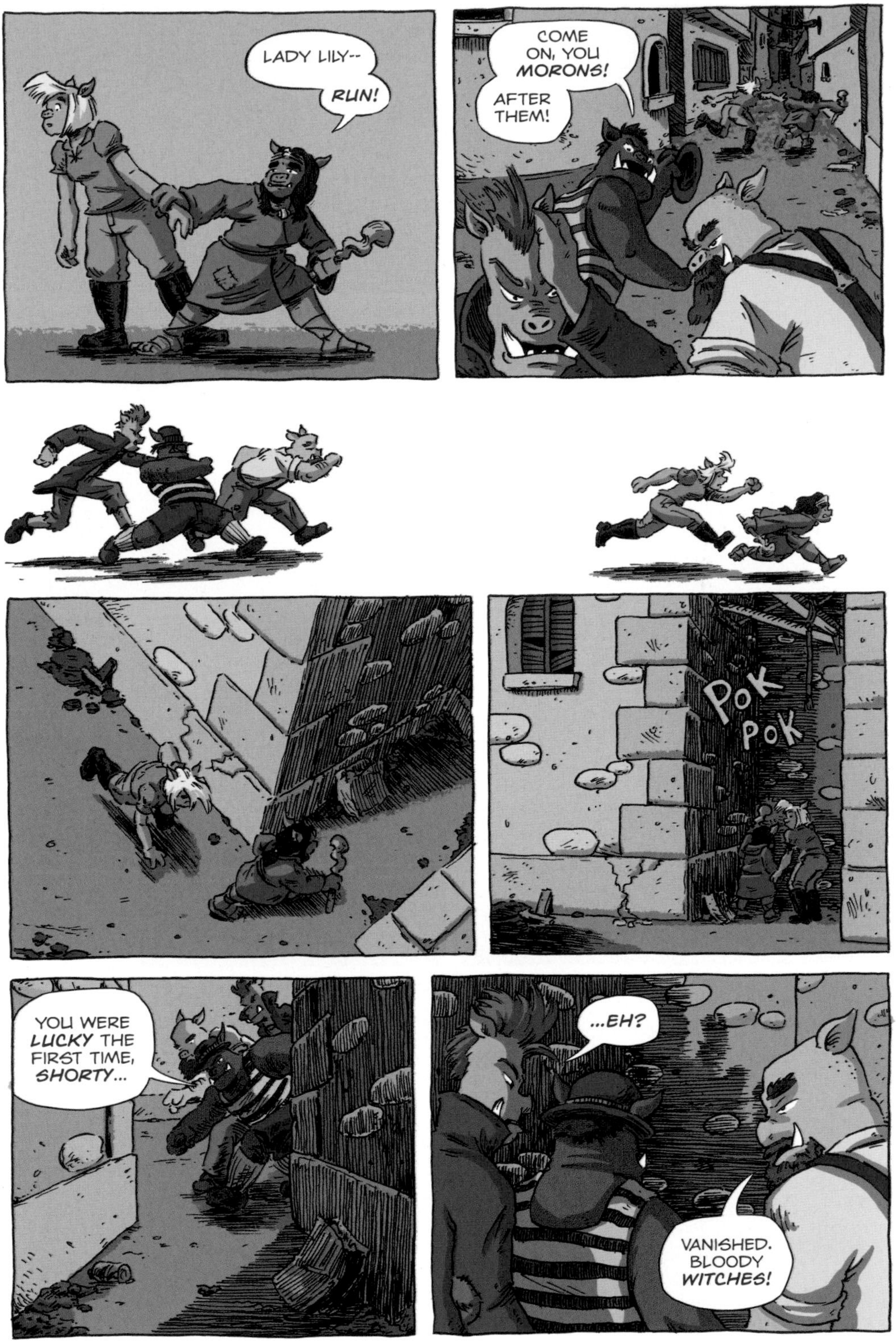
LADY LILY--
RUN!
COME ON, YOU MORONS!
AFTER THEM!
POK POK
YOU WERE LUCKY THE FIRST TIME, SHORTY...
...EH?
VANISHED. BLOODY WITCHES!

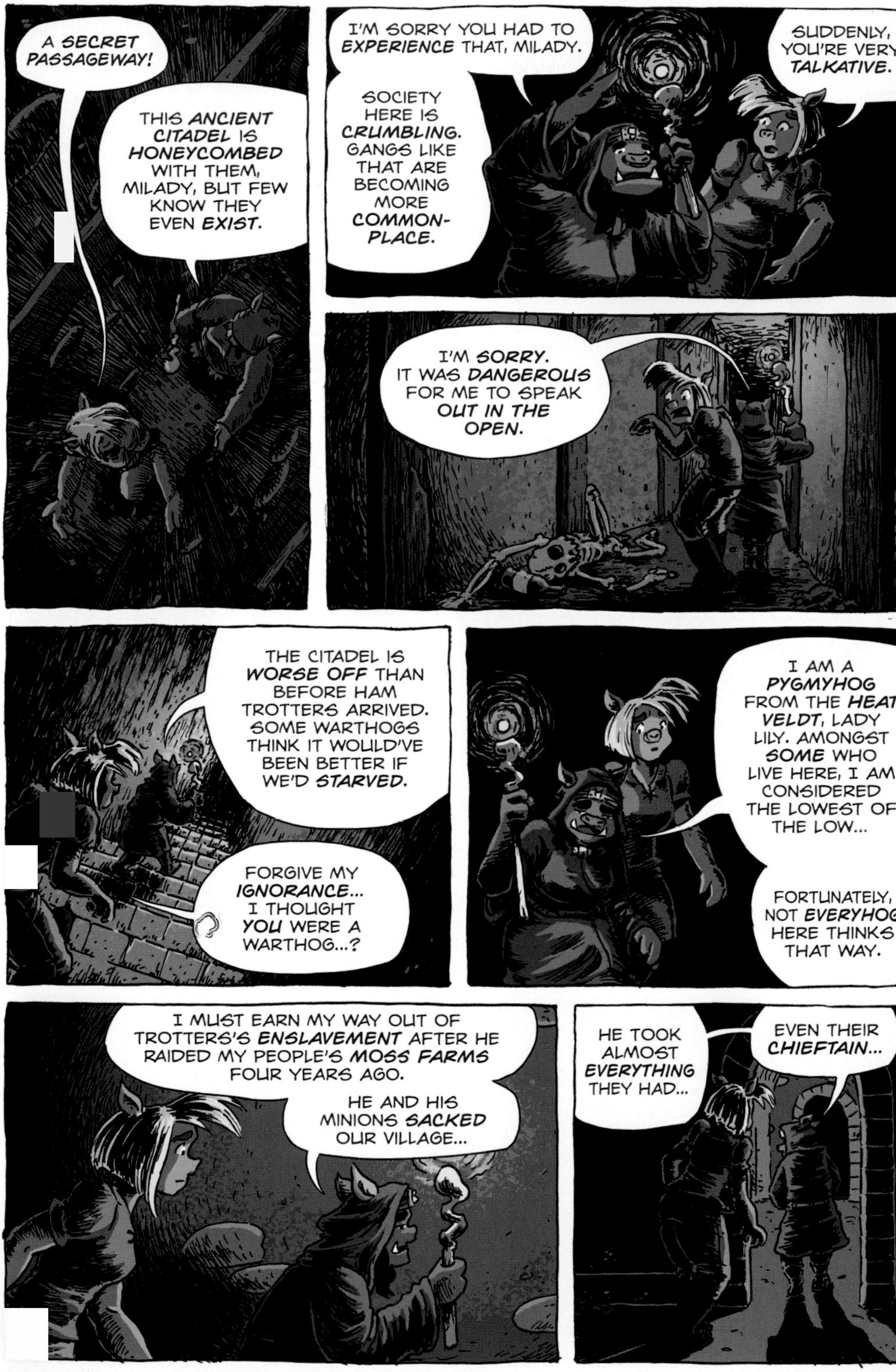
A SECRET PASSAGEWAY!
THIS ANCIENT CITADEL IS HONEYCOMBED WITH THEM, MILADY, BUT FEW KNOW THEY EVEN EXIST.
I'M SORRY YOU HAD TO EXPERIENCE THAT, MILADY.
SOCIETY HERE IS CRUMBLING. GANGS LIKE THAT ARE BECOMING MORE COMMON-PLACE.
SUDDENLY, YOU'RE VERY TALKATIVE.
I'M SORRY. IT WAS DANGEROUS FOR ME TO SPEAK OUT IN THE OPEN.
THE CITADEL IS WORSE OFF THAN BEFORE HAM TROTTERS ARRIVED. SOME WARTHOGS THINK IT WOULD'VE BEEN BETTER IF WE'D STARVED.
FORGIVE MY IGNORANCE... I THOUGHT YOU WERE A WARTHOG...?
I AM A PYGMYHOG FROM THE HEAT VELDT, LADY LILY. AMONGST SOME WHO LIVE HERE, I AM CONSIDERED THE LOWEST OF THE LOW...
FORTUNATELY, NOT EVERYHOG HERE THINKS THAT WAY.
I MUST EARN MY WAY OUT OF TROTTERS'S ENSLAVEMENT AFTER HE RAIDED MY PEOPLE'S MOSS FARMS FOUR YEARS AGO.
HE AND HIS MINIONS SACKED OUR VILLAGE...
HE TOOK ALMOST EVERYTHING THEY HAD...
EVEN THEIR CHIEFTAIN...

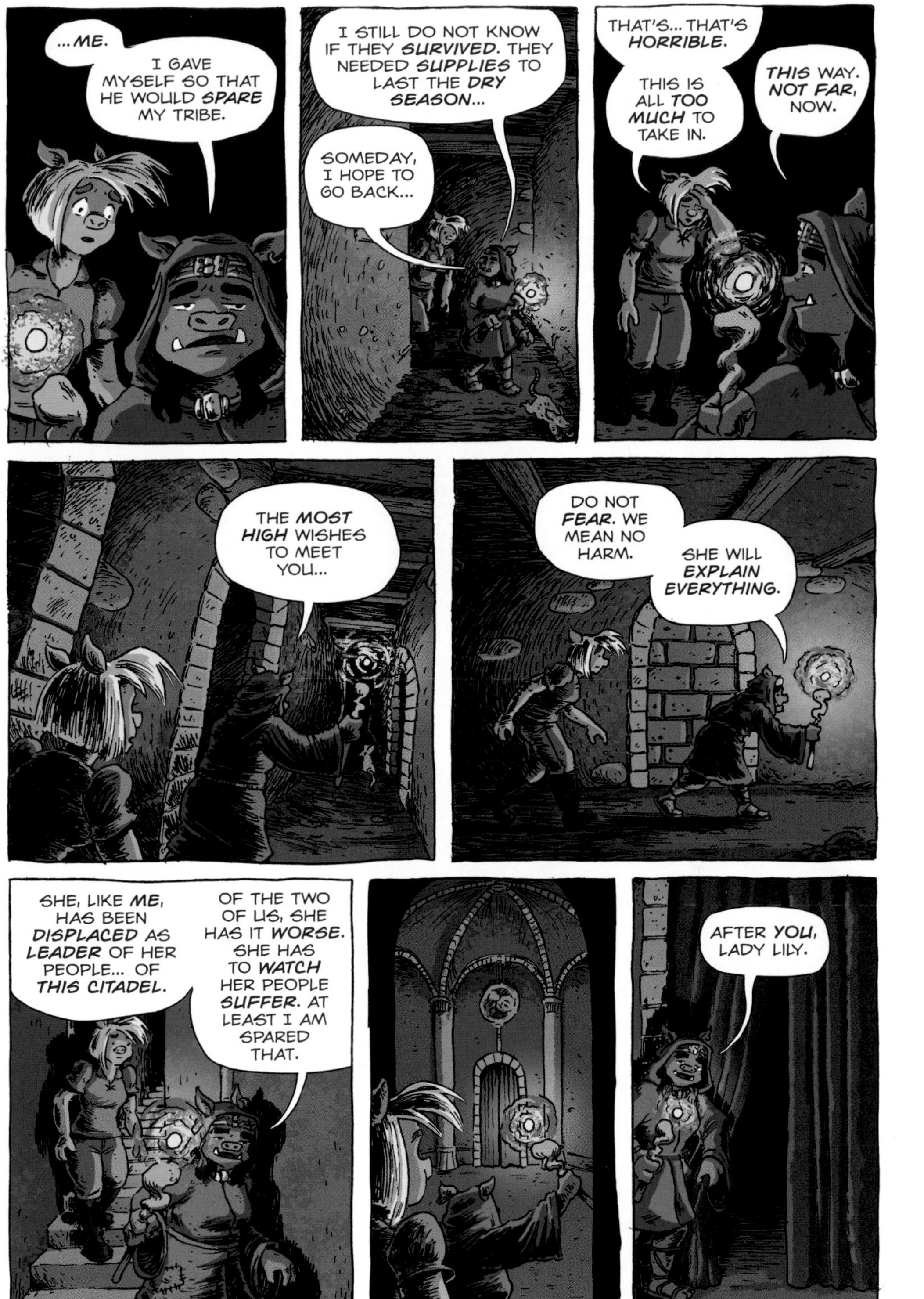
...ME.
I GAVE MYSELF SO THAT HE WOULD SPARE MY TRIBE.
I STILL DO NOT KNOW IF THEY SURVIVED. THEY NEEDED SUPPLIES TO LAST THE DRY SEASON...
SOMEDAY, I HOPE TO GO BACK...
THAT'S... THAT'S HORRIBLE.
THIS IS ALL TOO MUCH TO TAKE IN.
THIS WAY. NOT FAR, NOW.
THE MOST HIGH WISHES TO MEET YOU...
DO NOT FEAR. WE MEAN NO HARM.
SHE WILL EXPLAIN EVERYTHING.
SHE, LIKE ME, HAS BEEN DISPLACED AS LEADER OF HER PEOPLE... OF THIS CITADEL.
OF THE TWO OF US, SHE HAS IT WORSE. SHE HAS TO WATCH HER PEOPLE SUFFER. AT LEAST I AM SPARED THAT.
AFTER YOU, LADY LILY.

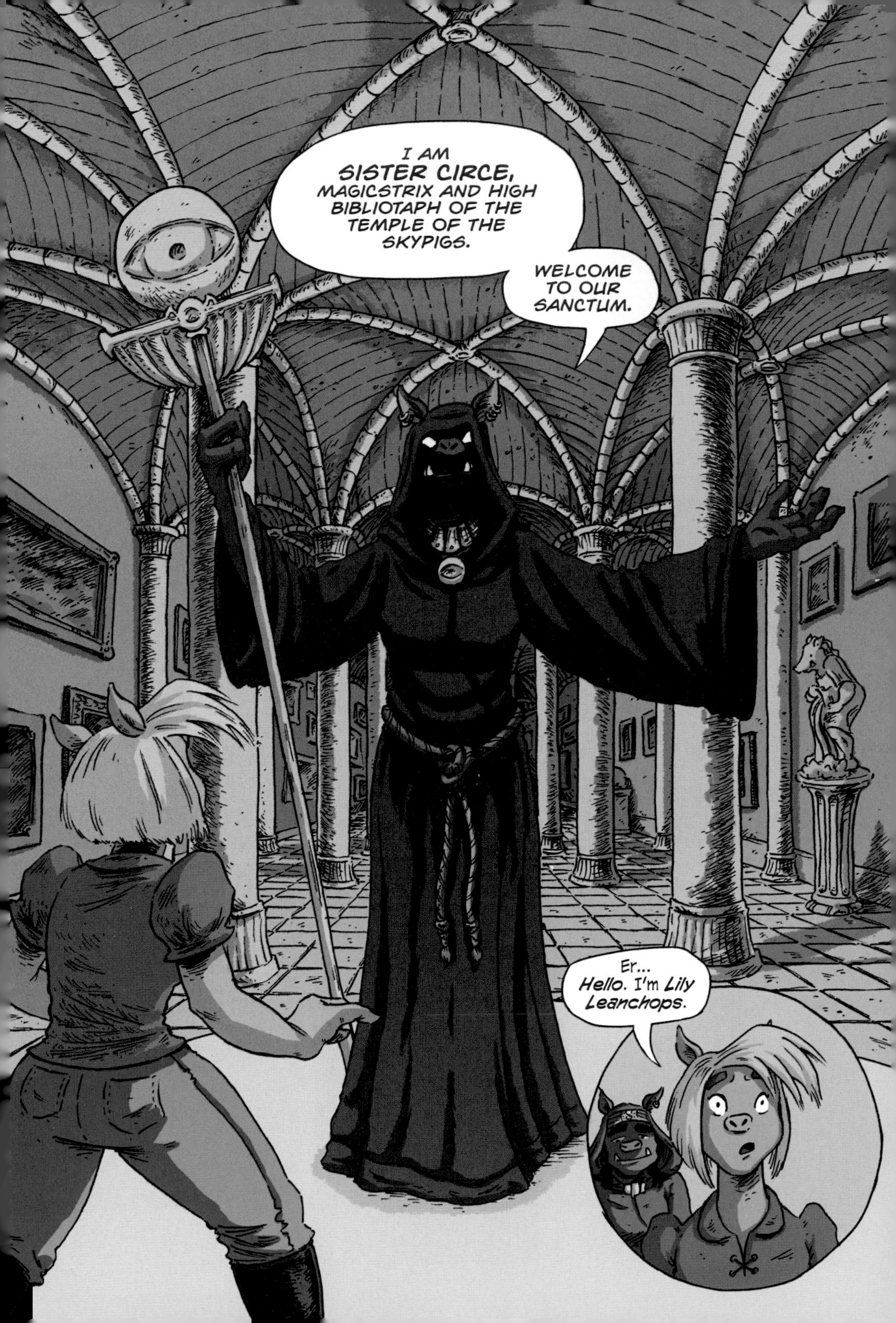

I AM **SISTER CIRCE,** MAGICSTRIX AND HIGH BIBLIOTAPH OF THE TEMPLE OF THE SKYPIGS.
WELCOME TO OUR SANCTUM.
Er... *Hello.* I'm *Lily Leanchops.*

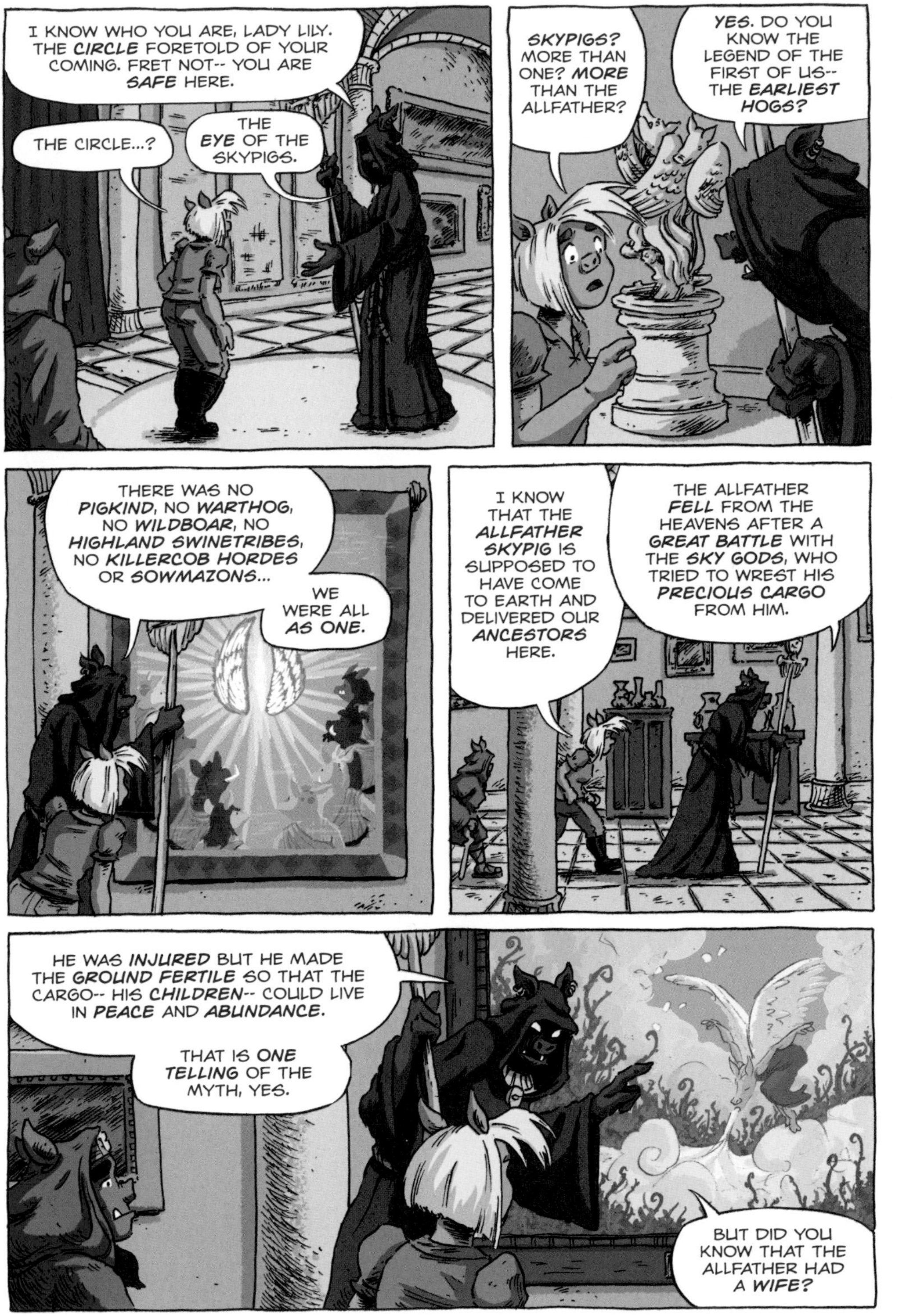
I KNOW WHO YOU ARE, LADY LILY. THE CIRCLE FORETOLD OF YOUR COMING. FRET NOT-- YOU ARE SAFE HERE.
THE CIRCLE...?
THE EYE OF THE SKYPIGS.
SKYPIGS? MORE THAN ONE? MORE THAN THE ALLFATHER?
YES. DO YOU KNOW THE LEGEND OF THE FIRST OF US-- THE EARLIEST HOGS?
THERE WAS NO PIGKIND, NO WARTHOG, NO WILDBOAR, NO HIGHLAND SWINETRIBES, NO KILLERCOB HORDES OR SOWMAZONS...
WE WERE ALL AS ONE.
I KNOW THAT THE ALLFATHER SKYPIG IS SUPPOSED TO HAVE COME TO EARTH AND DELIVERED OUR ANCESTORS HERE.
THE ALLFATHER FELL FROM THE HEAVENS AFTER A GREAT BATTLE WITH THE SKY GODS, WHO TRIED TO WREST HIS PRECIOUS CARGO FROM HIM.
HE WAS INJURED BUT HE MADE THE GROUND FERTILE SO THAT THE CARGO-- HIS CHILDREN-- COULD LIVE IN PEACE AND ABUNDANCE.
THAT IS ONE TELLING OF THE MYTH, YES.
BUT DID YOU KNOW THAT THE ALLFATHER HAD A WIFE?

EVEN OF *OBELIA* AND *PHINEAS*. EVEN *THE ARMY OF FOOLS* WHO ANSWER TO THEM.

EVEN SUCH AS THEY. EVEN *HAM TROTTERS*.

THIS IS SHE--

THE DISTANT, ANCESTRAL *MOTHER* OF US *ALL*.

THE ALLMOTHER *VANISHES* FROM MANY OF THE *ANCIENT TEXTS* THAT WERE CARRIED FORTH TO DISTANT LANDS-- BUT WE MAINTAIN THE *OLDER STORIES* HERE, IN THE TEMPLE.

SO IT IS SAID, THE ALLMOTHER BIT OFF HER OWN WINGS AND PARTED FROM HER LOVE, THE ALLFATHER, TO STAY ON *SOLID GROUND* AND TEND TO HER CHILDREN, WHILE HE RETURNED TO THE SKY.

IS THAT *TRUE*?

LADY LILY, IT IS *MYTH*. EVEN OUR RECORDS HERE IN THE CITADEL DO NOT GO BACK TO THE *BEGINNING OF HISTORY*.

IT WAS RETOLD *MANY TIMES*, FROM GENERATION TO GENERATION, BEFORE IT WAS EVER *WRITTEN DOWN*.

TRUTH IS REVEALED THROUGH *INTERPRETATION* OF MYTH, WHICH IS AS IT SHOULD BE.

EVEN IF THERE IS AN ALLFATHER SKYPIG ABOVE... AND *I* BELIEVE THERE *IS*... AND EVEN IF MY GREATEST, GREAT-GRANDMOTHER WAS THE ALLMOTHER SKYPIG, WE MUST STILL BE *RESPONSIBLE* FOR OUR OWN ACTIONS.

THIS IS WHERE I HAVE *ERRED* WITH *HAM TROTTERS.* I SHOWED HIM *POWER...*

MAGIC HAS *CRAZED* AND *CONSUMED* HIM AND NOW HE IS *OBSESSED* WITH WHAT IT BRINGS TO HIS INVENTIONS.

THAT'S NOT *YOUR* FAULT.

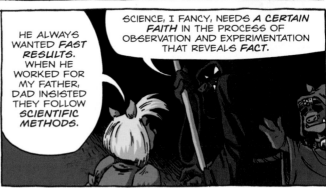

HE ALWAYS WANTED *FAST RESULTS.* WHEN HE WORKED FOR MY FATHER, DAD INSISTED THEY FOLLOW *SCIENTIFIC METHODS.*

SCIENCE, I FANCY, NEEDS *A CERTAIN FAITH* IN THE PROCESS OF OBSERVATION AND EXPERIMENTATION THAT REVEALS *FACT.*

UM... THE DIFFERENCE BETWEEN *MAGICAL* AND *SCIENTIFIC APPROACHES* SEEM FAIRLY *SIMPLE* TO ME. *SCIENCE* IS EVERYTHING YOU'VE *TESTED AND DISCOVERED...* AND EVERYTHING YOU *BUILD* FROM WHAT YOU'VE LEARNED *LASTS.*

ANYTHING YOU BUILD WITH MAGIC IS *SHORT-LIVED.*

INDEED. SCIENCE AND MAGIC ARE MORE *ALIKE* THAN MANY *ACKNOWLEDGE.*

BUT THE SHORT-LIVED QUALITY OF MAGIC SUGGESTS...?

THAT IT IS A *TOOL.*

MAGIC IS IMPERMANENCE. *EVERYTHING* IS IMPERMANENT, BUT MAGIC IS THE PRESENT, THE *NOW.* SCIENCE BUILDS *BRIDGES INTO THE FUTURE.* AND IT IS *THE FUTURE* THAT WE MUST *PROTECT.*

TROTTERS FOUND US WHEN WE WERE **WEAK**.

THE LAND WAS **BLIGHTED**. SUDDENLY WE COULDN'T **SUSTAIN** OURSELVES.

OUR **ONCE-PROUD CIVILIZATION** HAD SUFFERED **DISASTER** AFTER **DISASTER**.

THE DAYS WERE **DARK**. WE WERE **AILING**.

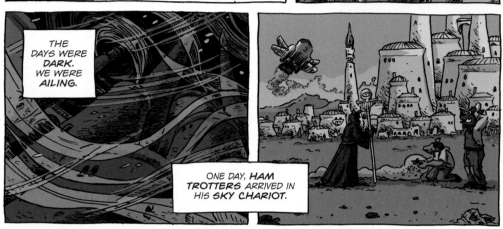

ONE DAY, **HAM TROTTERS** ARRIVED IN HIS **SKY CHARIOT**.

IT **CRASHED**, HE WAS **INJURED**. WE TOOK HIM IN AND NURSED HIM BACK TO HEALTH...

TROTTERS TALKED, AND PROMISED TO **HELP**. HE PROMISED **BETTER THINGS** TO **ALL WARTHOGS**.

WE WERE **DESPERATE**... BUT I WAS **FOOLISH**.

I INVITED HIM IN. I **TRUSTED** HIM.

I SAW THAT HE HAD HIS OWN BASIC APTITUDE WITH MAGIC, AND I **GUIDED** HIM, TAUGHT HIM TO **HONE** HIS ABILITIES.

HE **DID**, ALL THE WHILE SEEDING RUMOR AND **MISTRUST** AGAINST THE **LEADERSHIP** OF THIS CITADEL. AND WHEN HE SAW HIS MOMENT, HE SEIZED **CONTROL**.

MY HOGFOLK **TURNED AWAY** FROM THE **OLD WAYS**...

THEY NEEDED **HOPE**...AND TROTTERS **GAVE** THEM HOPE.

FALSE HOPE, BY THE SOUNDS OF IT.

AND NOW HE PLANS TO **TAKE OVER** THE PIGDOM...

HE ALREADY **TOLD** YOU THIS? SUCH **CONFIDENCE**.

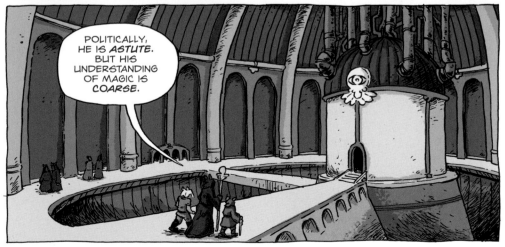

POLITICALLY, HE IS **ASTUTE**. BUT HIS UNDERSTANDING OF MAGIC IS **COARSE**.

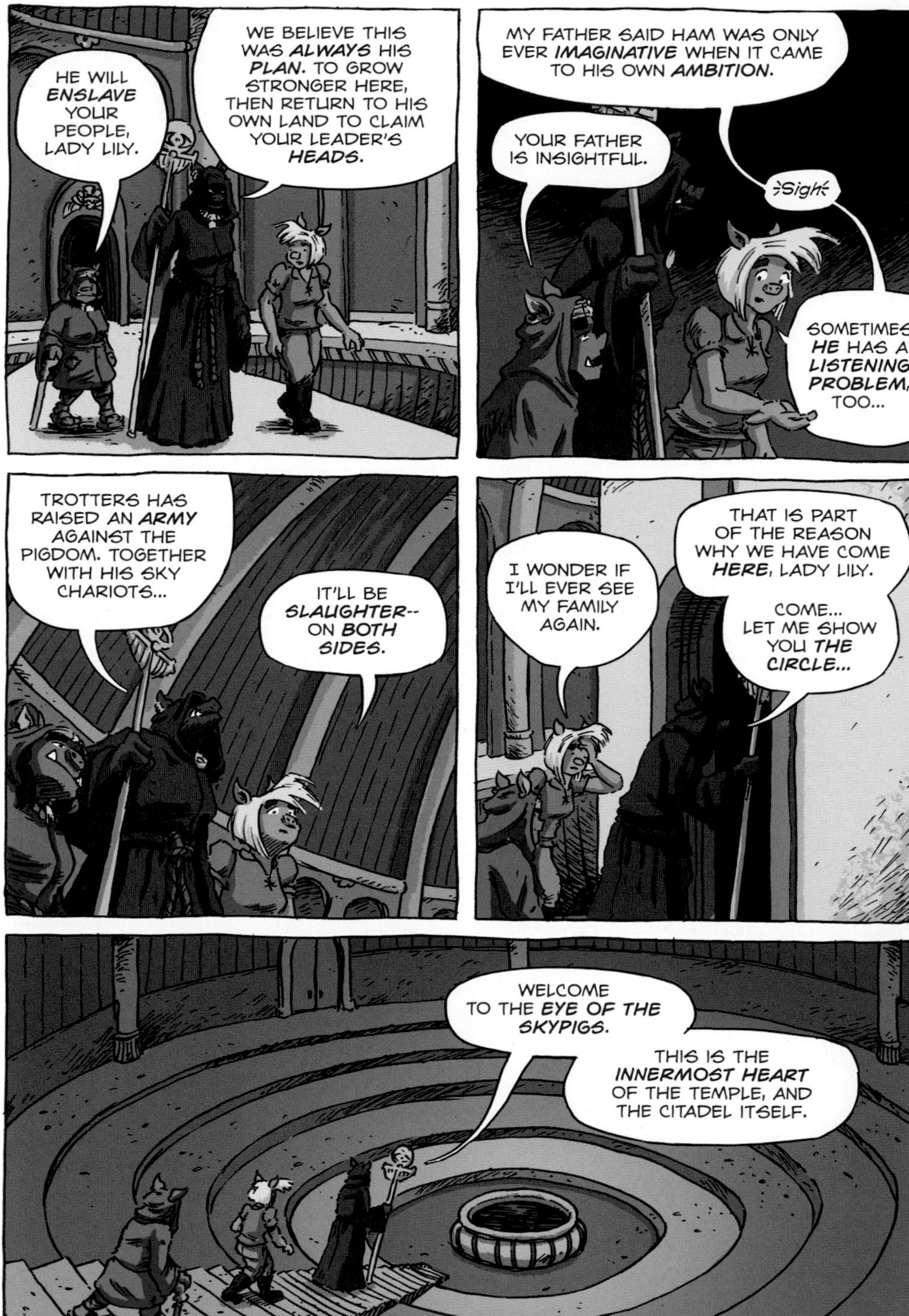

HE WILL ENSLAVE YOUR PEOPLE, LADY LILY.
WE BELIEVE THIS WAS ALWAYS HIS PLAN. TO GROW STRONGER HERE, THEN RETURN TO HIS OWN LAND TO CLAIM YOUR LEADER'S HEADS.
MY FATHER SAID HAM WAS ONLY EVER IMAGINATIVE WHEN IT CAME TO HIS OWN AMBITION.
YOUR FATHER IS INSIGHTFUL.
Sigh
SOMETIMES HE HAS A LISTENING PROBLEM, TOO...
TROTTERS HAS RAISED AN ARMY AGAINST THE PIGDOM. TOGETHER WITH HIS SKY CHARIOTS...
IT'LL BE SLAUGHTER-- ON BOTH SIDES.
I WONDER IF I'LL EVER SEE MY FAMILY AGAIN.
THAT IS PART OF THE REASON WHY WE HAVE COME HERE, LADY LILY.
COME... LET ME SHOW YOU THE CIRCLE...
WELCOME TO THE EYE OF THE SKYPIGS.
THIS IS THE INNERMOST HEART OF THE TEMPLE, AND THE CITADEL ITSELF.

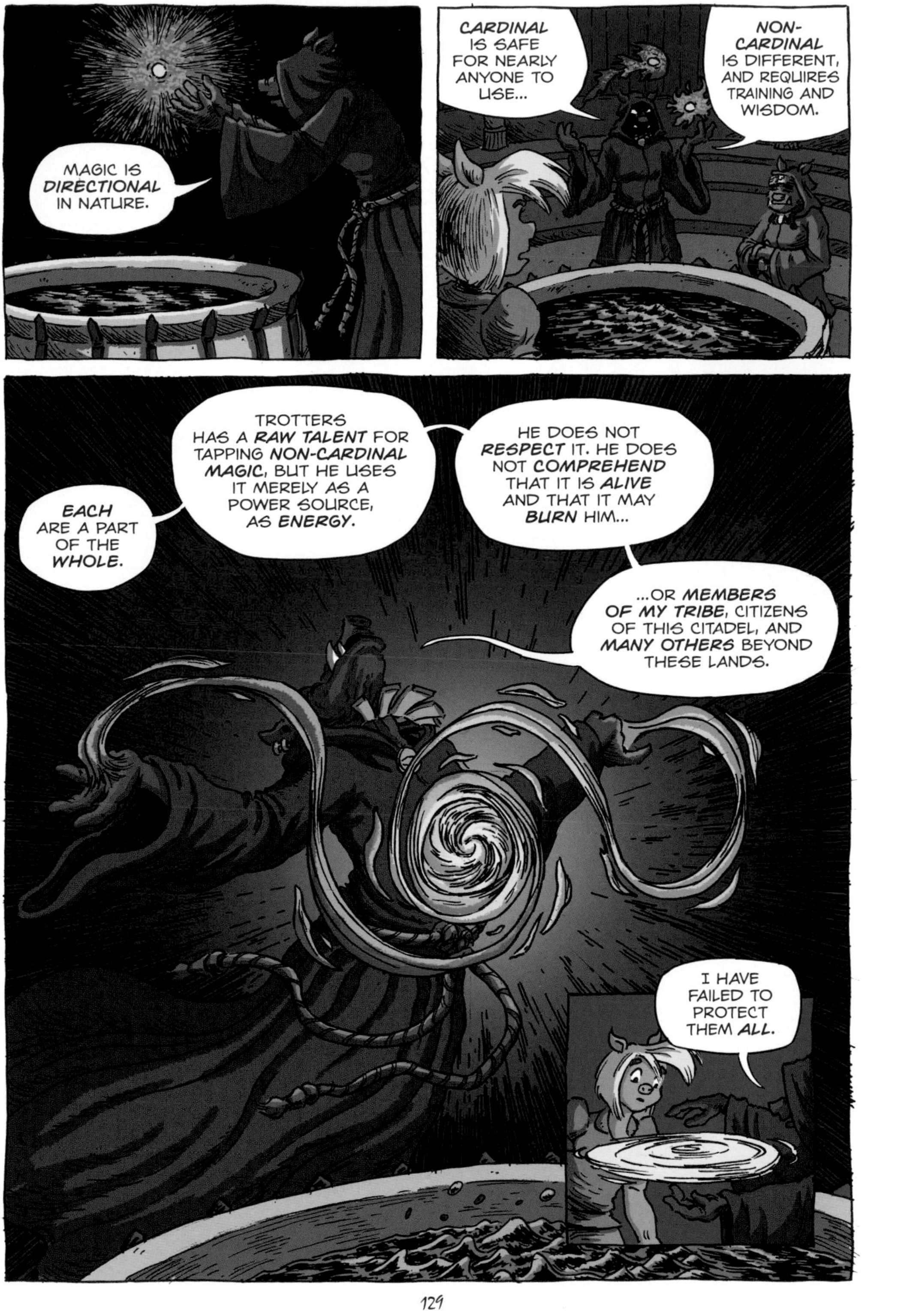
MAGIC IS DIRECTIONAL IN NATURE.
CARDINAL IS SAFE FOR NEARLY ANYONE TO USE...
NON-CARDINAL IS DIFFERENT, AND REQUIRES TRAINING AND WISDOM.
EACH ARE A PART OF THE WHOLE.
TROTTERS HAS A RAW TALENT FOR TAPPING NON-CARDINAL MAGIC, BUT HE USES IT MERELY AS A POWER SOURCE, AS ENERGY.
HE DOES NOT RESPECT IT. HE DOES NOT COMPREHEND THAT IT IS ALIVE AND THAT IT MAY BURN HIM...
...OR MEMBERS OF MY TRIBE, CITIZENS OF THIS CITADEL, AND MANY OTHERS BEYOND THESE LANDS.
I HAVE FAILED TO PROTECT THEM ALL.

WE CANNOT CHANGE THE *PAST*, AND THE *FUTURE* IS *UNWRITTEN*, SO THE ONLY ASPECT OF LIVING WE HAVE INFLUENCE OVER IS THE *PRESENT*.

THERE IS ALWAYS THE *CONSTANCY OF CHANGE*, THE *CERTAINTY OF CHANCE AND RENEWAL*. BUT WE MUSTN'T ABANDON *WISDOM* FOR *WAR*.

WHAT SHOULD I *LOOK FOR*, LADY LILY? *WHO?*

IS THIS HOW YOU *KNEW* I WAS COMING HERE? CAN IT TELL THE *FUTURE?*

NO. IT IS NOT AN ORACLE OF *PREDICTION*, EXACTLY... MORE OF *DEEPENED PERCEPTIONS*.

IT WILL SHOW US YOUR *LOVED ONES*, PERHAPS...

DAD! HE LOOKS SO TIRED.

DAD, WHY WOULDN'T YOU LET ME *HELP* YOU?

AUNTIE SASHA! SHE'S A *MOTHER* TO ME... SHE'S SO LOVELY. SHE KNOWS MAGIC, YOU KNOW!

I CAN FEEL THAT SHE'S AN *ADEPT*...

IS THERE A WAY WE CAN *HEAR* WHAT THEY'RE SAYING?

STRANGE. WE SHOULD ALREADY BE ABLE TO. YOUR EMOTIONAL CONNECTION TO THEM IS *STRONG*. AND YET...

WHAT'S HAPPENING...?

THERE IS... *INTERFERENCE*...

ARCHIE!

NO. SOMETHING ELSE...

I MUST *CONTAIN--*

CIIIIRCCEEEE...

SHROOOM

130

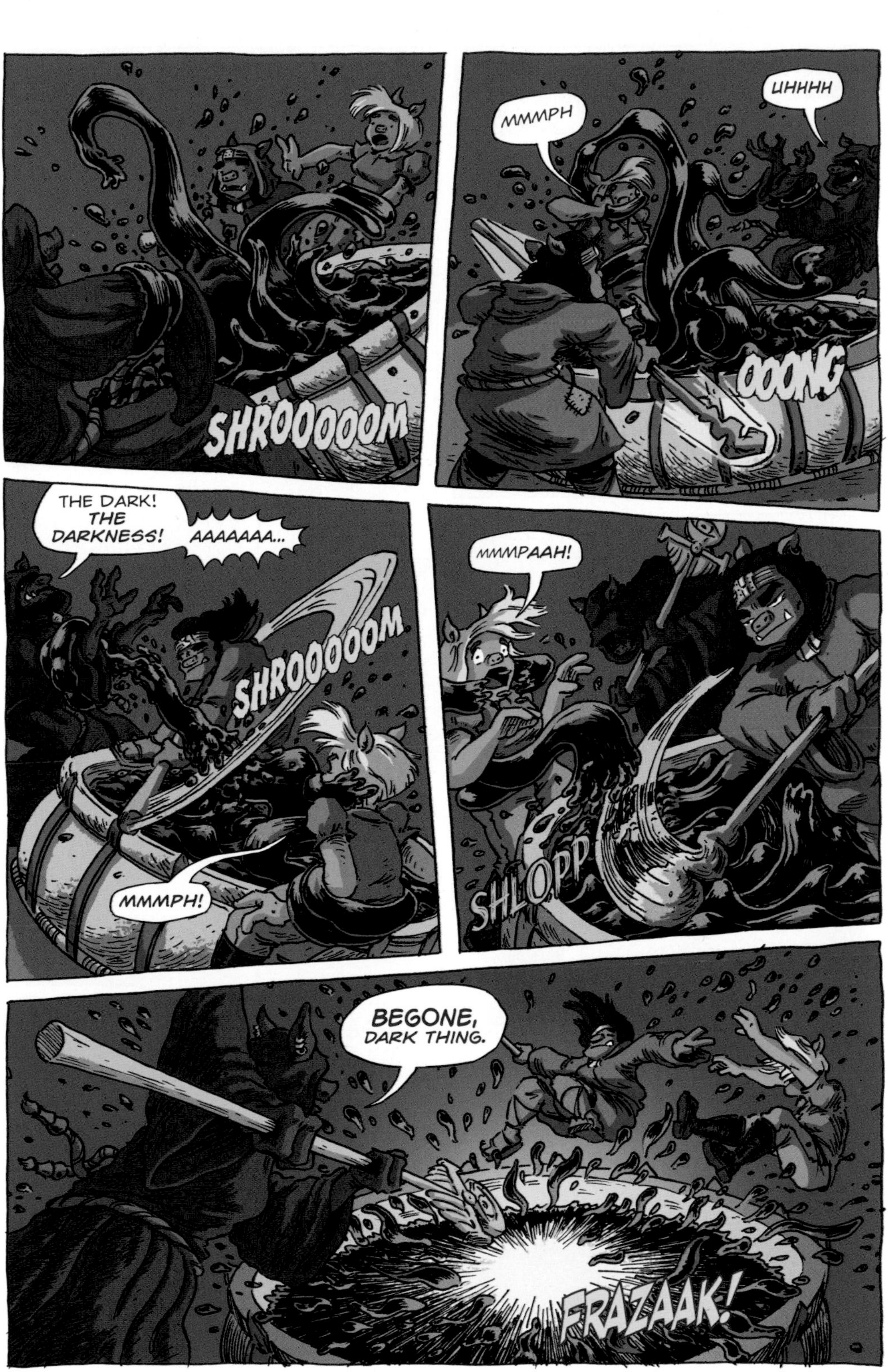
SHROOOOOM
MMMPH
UHHHH
OOONG
THE DARK! THE DARKNESS!
AAAAAAA...
SHROOOOOM
MMMPH!
MMMPAAH!
SHLOPP
BEGONE, DARK THING.
FRAZAAK!

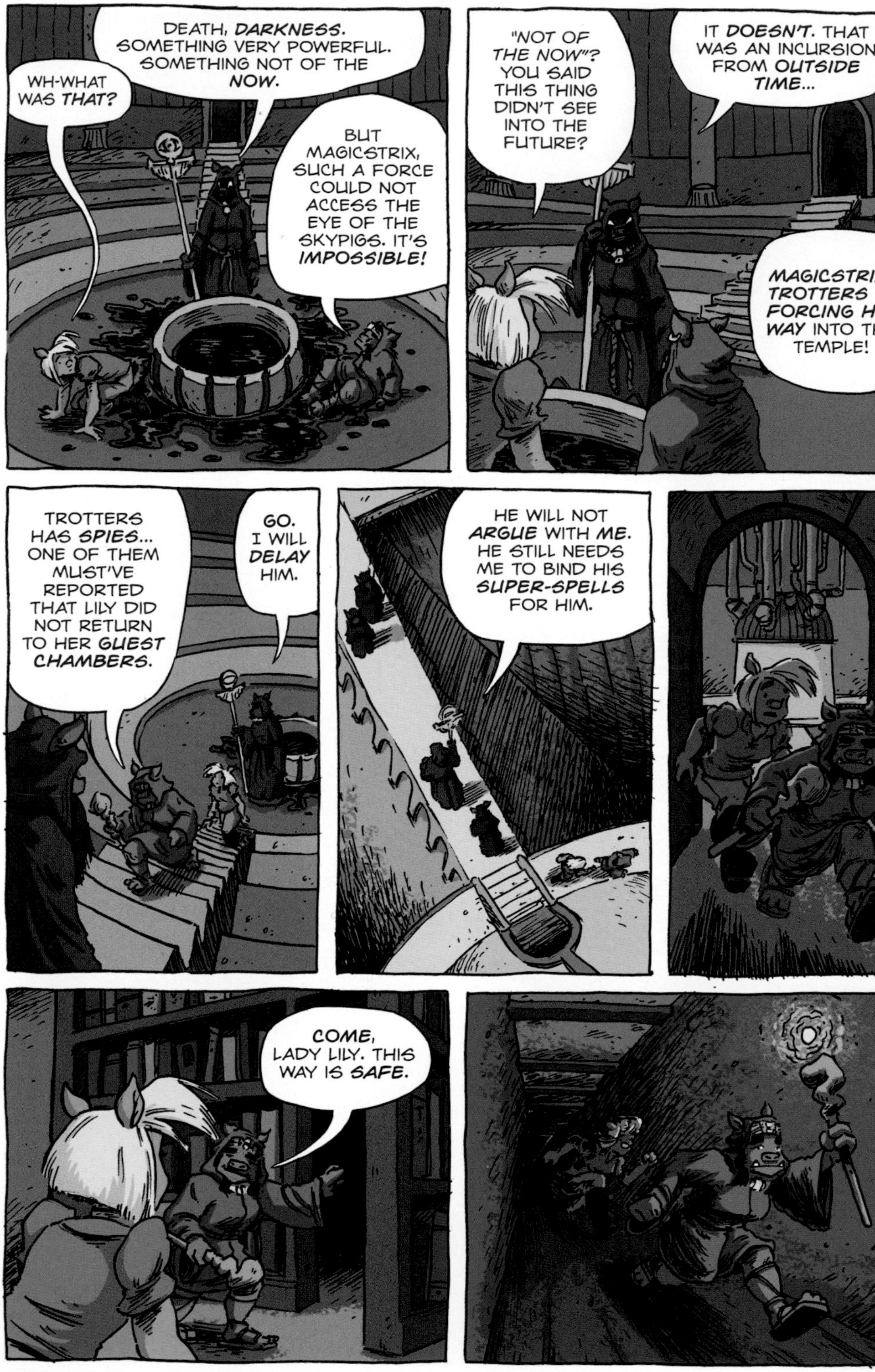
WH-WHAT WAS THAT?
DEATH, DARKNESS. SOMETHING VERY POWERFUL. SOMETHING NOT OF THE NOW.
BUT MAGICSTRIX, SUCH A FORCE COULD NOT ACCESS THE EYE OF THE SKYPIGS. IT'S IMPOSSIBLE!
"NOT OF THE NOW"? YOU SAID THIS THING DIDN'T SEE INTO THE FUTURE?
IT DOESN'T. THAT WAS AN INCURSION FROM OUTSIDE TIME...
MAGICSTRIX! TROTTERS IS FORCING HIS WAY INTO THE TEMPLE!
TROTTERS HAS SPIES... ONE OF THEM MUST'VE REPORTED THAT LILY DID NOT RETURN TO HER GUEST CHAMBERS.
GO. I WILL DELAY HIM.
HE WILL NOT ARGUE WITH ME. HE STILL NEEDS ME TO BIND HIS SUPER-SPELLS FOR HIM.
COME, LADY LILY. THIS WAY IS SAFE.

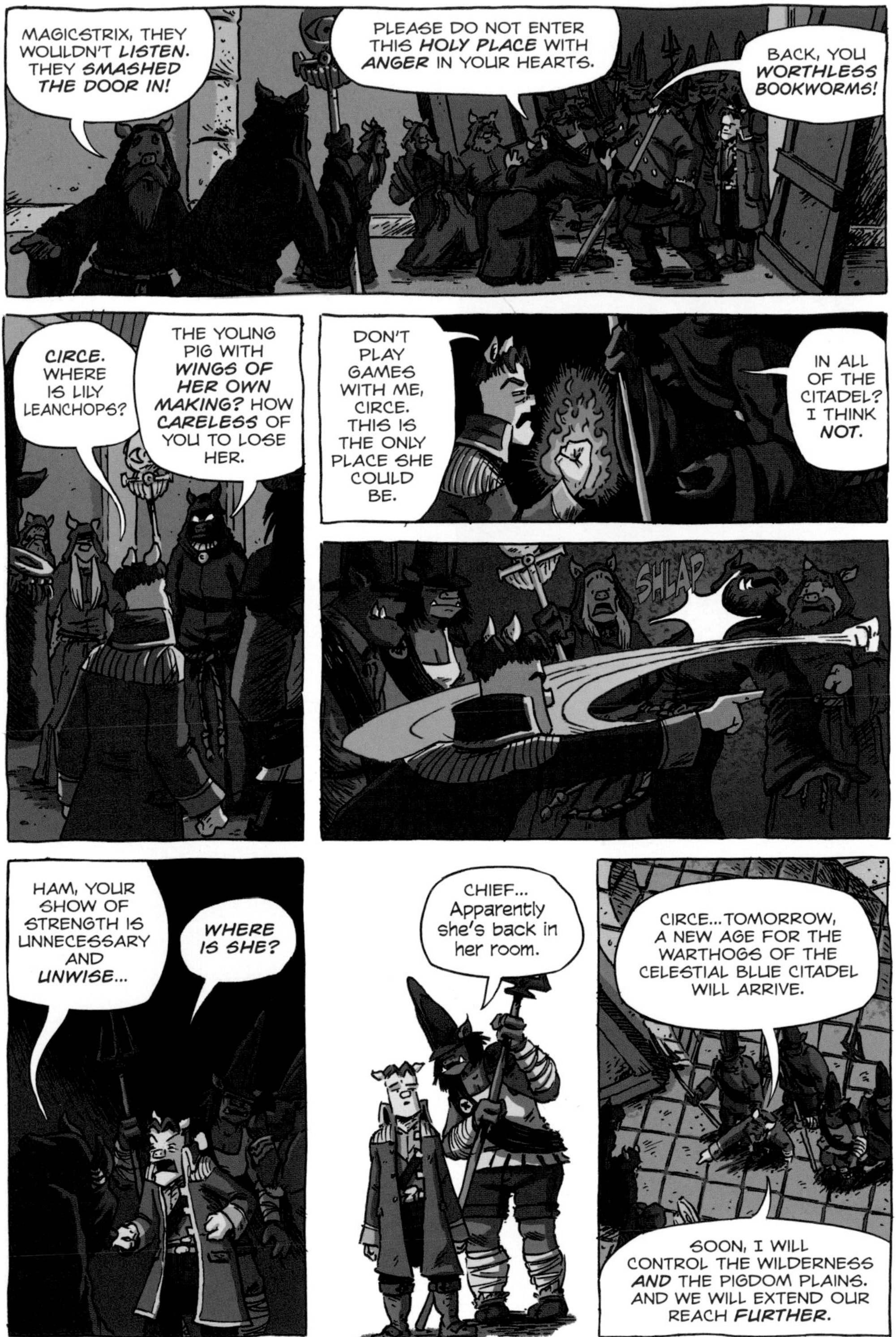
MAGICSTRIX, THEY WOULDN'T LISTEN. THEY SMASHED THE DOOR IN!
PLEASE DO NOT ENTER THIS HOLY PLACE WITH ANGER IN YOUR HEARTS.
BACK, YOU WORTHLESS BOOKWORMS!
CIRCE. WHERE IS LILY LEANCHOPS?
THE YOUNG PIG WITH WINGS OF HER OWN MAKING? HOW CARELESS OF YOU TO LOSE HER.
DON'T PLAY GAMES WITH ME, CIRCE. THIS IS THE ONLY PLACE SHE COULD BE.
IN ALL OF THE CITADEL? I THINK NOT.
SHLAP
HAM, YOUR SHOW OF STRENGTH IS UNNECESSARY AND UNWISE...
WHERE IS SHE?
CHIEF... Apparently she's back in her room.
CIRCE...TOMORROW, A NEW AGE FOR THE WARTHOGS OF THE CELESTIAL BLUE CITADEL WILL ARRIVE.
SOON, I WILL CONTROL THE WILDERNESS AND THE PIGDOM PLAINS. AND WE WILL EXTEND OUR REACH FURTHER.

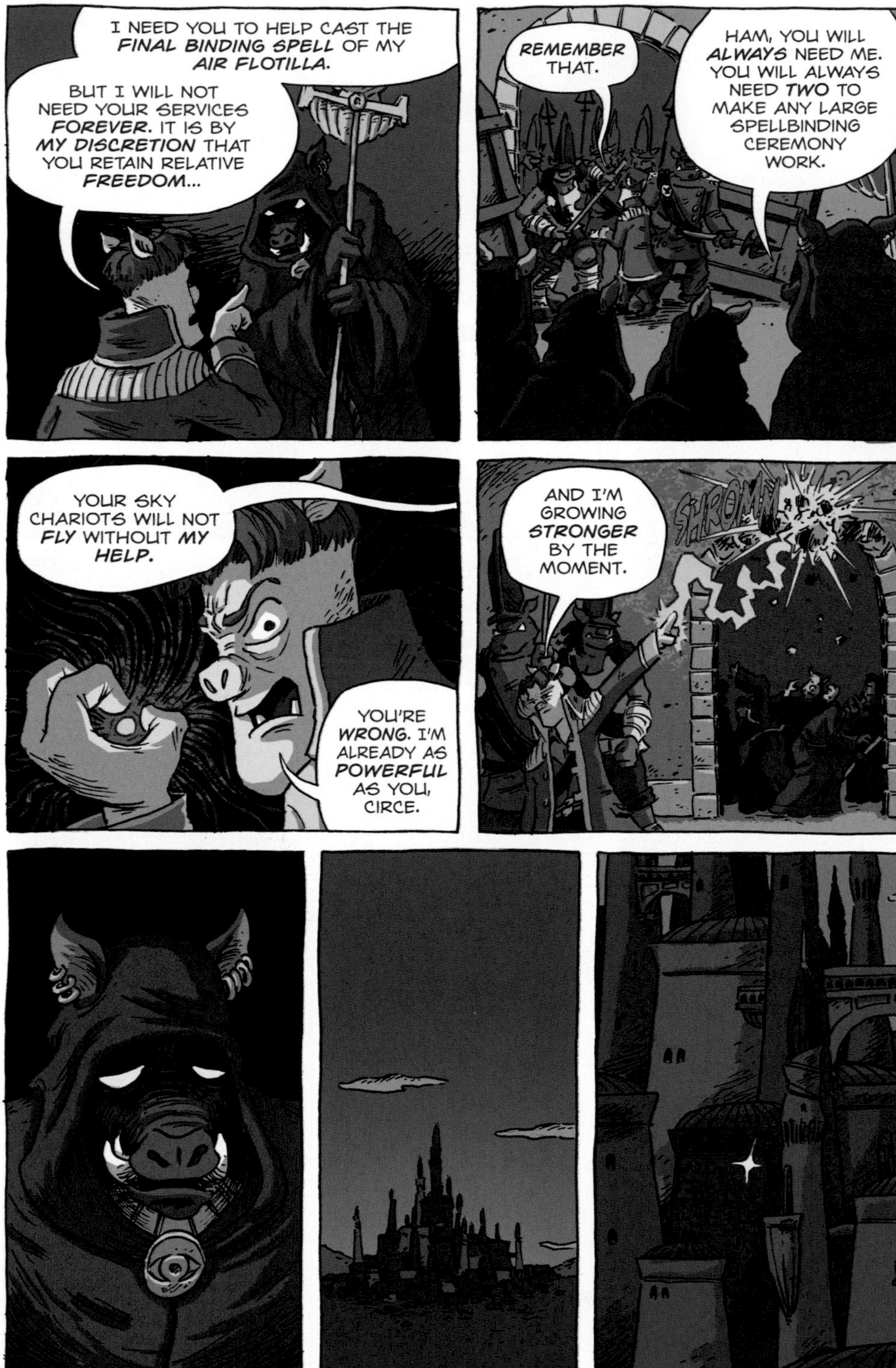
I NEED YOU TO HELP CAST THE FINAL BINDING SPELL OF MY AIR FLOTILLA.
BUT I WILL NOT NEED YOUR SERVICES FOREVER. IT IS BY MY DISCRETION THAT YOU RETAIN RELATIVE FREEDOM...
HAM, YOU WILL ALWAYS NEED ME. YOU WILL ALWAYS NEED TWO TO MAKE ANY LARGE SPELLBINDING CEREMONY WORK.
REMEMBER THAT.
YOUR SKY CHARIOTS WILL NOT FLY WITHOUT MY HELP.
YOU'RE WRONG. I'M ALREADY AS POWERFUL AS YOU, CIRCE.
AND I'M GROWING STRONGER BY THE MOMENT.
SHROMM

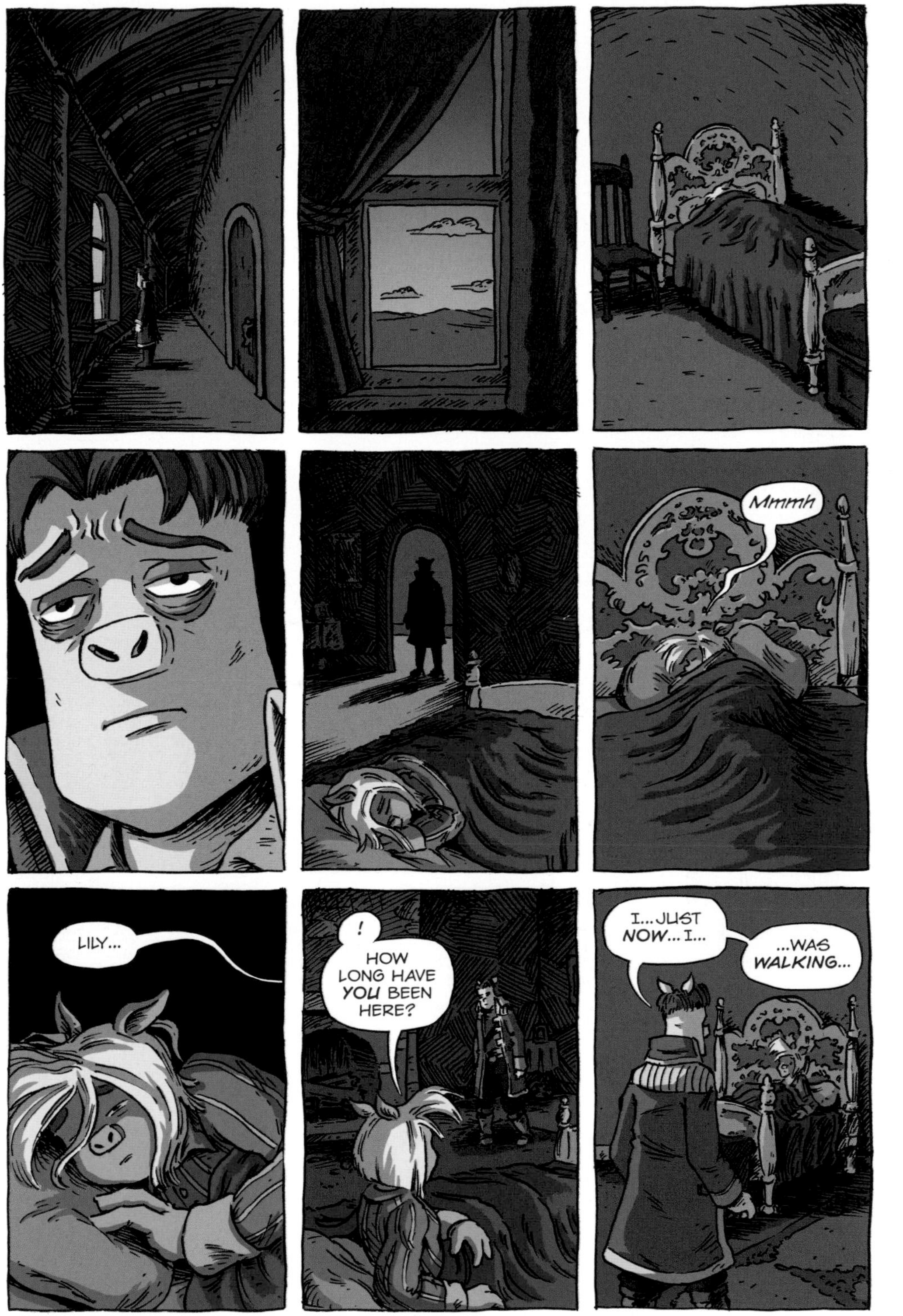
Mmmh
LILY...
!
HOW LONG HAVE YOU BEEN HERE?
I... JUST NOW... I...
...WAS WALKING...

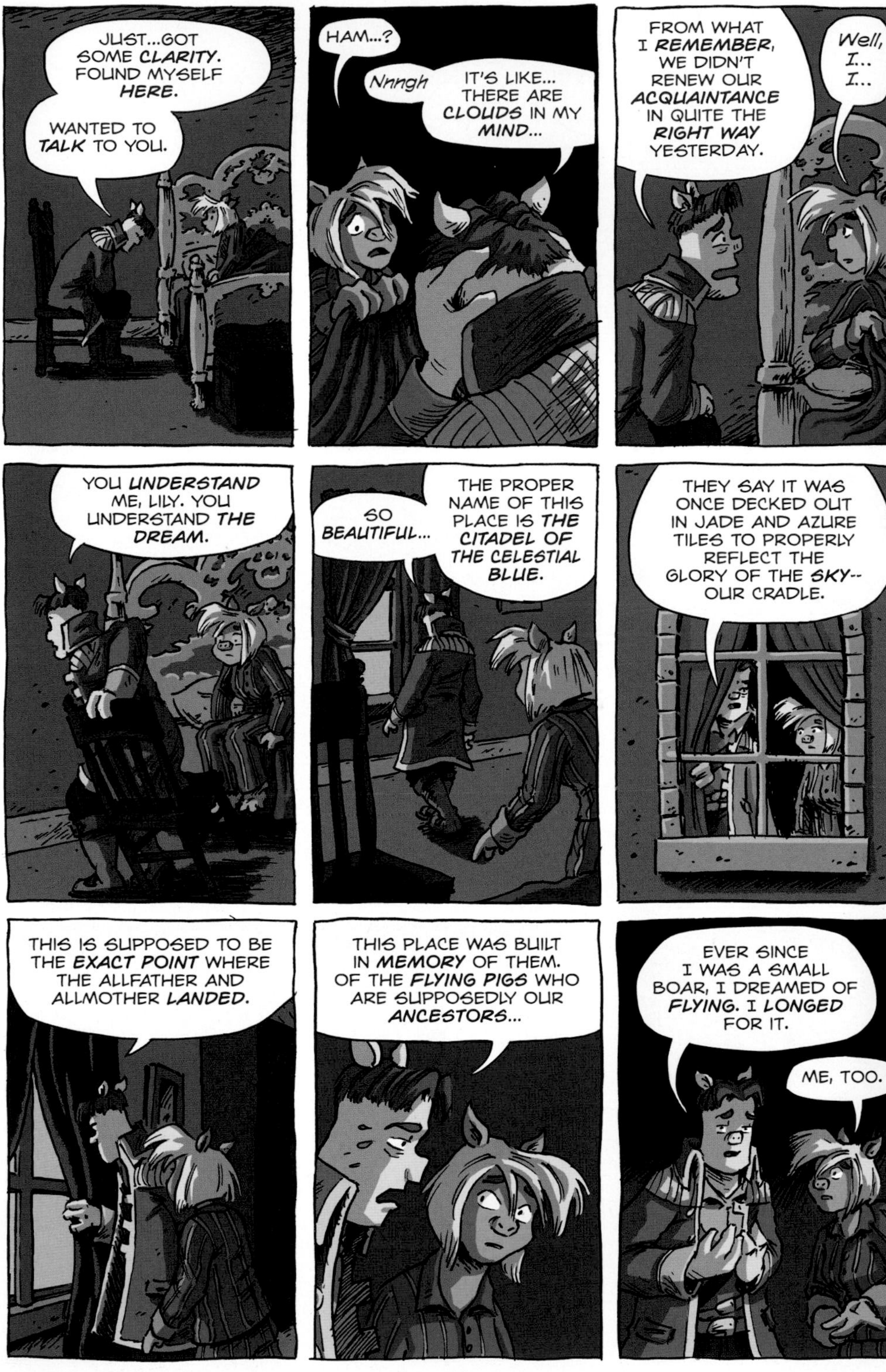
JUST...GOT SOME CLARITY. FOUND MYSELF HERE.
WANTED TO TALK TO YOU.
HAM...?
Nnngh
IT'S LIKE... THERE ARE CLOUDS IN MY MIND...
FROM WHAT I REMEMBER, WE DIDN'T RENEW OUR ACQUAINTANCE IN QUITE THE RIGHT WAY YESTERDAY.
Well, I... I...
YOU UNDERSTAND ME, LILY. YOU UNDERSTAND THE DREAM.
SO BEAUTIFUL...
THE PROPER NAME OF THIS PLACE IS THE CITADEL OF THE CELESTIAL BLUE.
THEY SAY IT WAS ONCE DECKED OUT IN JADE AND AZURE TILES TO PROPERLY REFLECT THE GLORY OF THE SKY-- OUR CRADLE.
THIS IS SUPPOSED TO BE THE EXACT POINT WHERE THE ALLFATHER AND ALLMOTHER LANDED.
THIS PLACE WAS BUILT IN MEMORY OF THEM. OF THE FLYING PIGS WHO ARE SUPPOSEDLY OUR ANCESTORS...
EVER SINCE I WAS A SMALL BOAR, I DREAMED OF FLYING. I LONGED FOR IT.
ME, TOO.

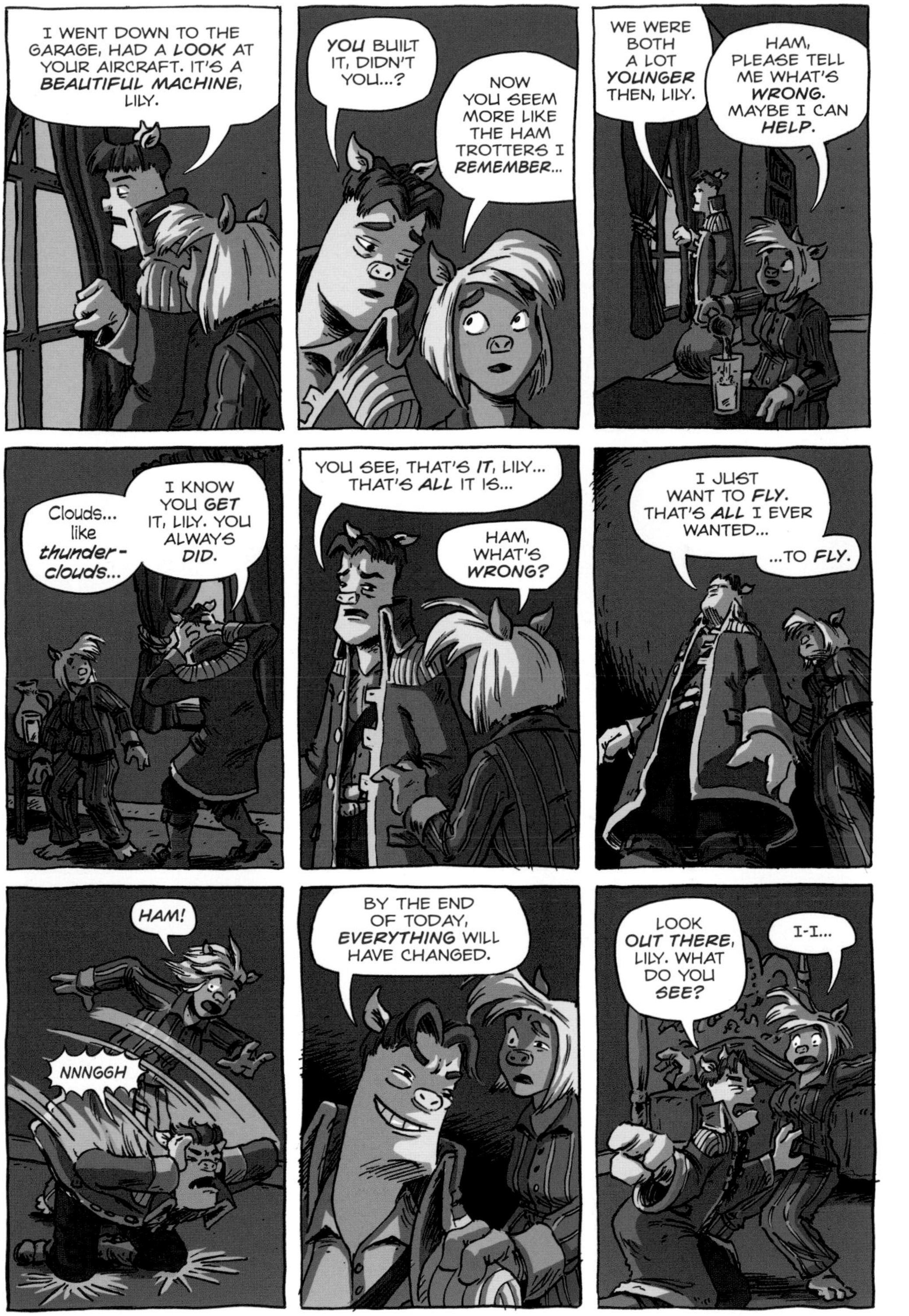
I WENT DOWN TO THE GARAGE, HAD A LOOK AT YOUR AIRCRAFT. IT'S A BEAUTIFUL MACHINE, LILY.
YOU BUILT IT, DIDN'T YOU...?
NOW YOU SEEM MORE LIKE THE HAM TROTTERS I REMEMBER...
WE WERE BOTH A LOT YOUNGER THEN, LILY.
HAM, PLEASE TELL ME WHAT'S WRONG. MAYBE I CAN HELP.
Clouds... like thunder-clouds...
I KNOW YOU GET IT, LILY. YOU ALWAYS DID.
YOU SEE, THAT'S IT, LILY... THAT'S ALL IT IS...
HAM, WHAT'S WRONG?
I JUST WANT TO FLY. THAT'S ALL I EVER WANTED...
...TO FLY.
HAM!
NNNGGH
BY THE END OF TODAY, EVERYTHING WILL HAVE CHANGED.
LOOK OUT THERE, LILY. WHAT DO YOU SEE?
I-I...

NO CLOUDS! THE WEATHER'S GOOD!

DO YOU KNOW HOW *RARE* THAT IS FOR THIS WILDERNESS? *PERFECT* FLYING WEATHER... LIKE THE STORM CLEARED ALL THE *DUST* AWAY.

IT'S A GOOD OMEN! YOU CAN SEE *FOREVER!*

YOU SEE, LILY, *TODAY* IS *THE DAY.*

TODAY IS THE DAY *WE INVADE THE PIGDOM PLAINS!*

HAM... NO!

JOIN ME, LILY. BE ON *THE WINNING SIDE!*

IMAGINE WHEN YOUR FATHER SEES US *BOTH* SOARING IN ON THE KIND OF AIRCRAFT HE CAN ONLY *DREAM* OF INVENTING!

JUST *IMAGINE* HIS *HUMILIATION!*

HAM, YOU'RE HURTING MY ARM.

AS WELL AS THE *SKY CHARIOTS*, THERE IS A *GROUND FORCE* OF WARTHOGS WAITING IN THE MOUNTAINS. ONCE THE AIR FLOTILLA HAS TAKEN OUT ALL RESISTANCE, I'LL SEND UP *A FLARE.*

HAM, PLEASE LET GO OF ME.

THAT'S THE *SIGNAL* FOR THEM TO SWARM DOWN AND *INVADE.* THE PIGDOM WILL NEVER KNOW WHAT'S *HIT* IT.

HAM...

LET GO.

OH *NO...*

BY THE *WINGED ONE*, THE *CLOUDS*... THEY'VE CLEARED!

LILY, *LISTEN* TO ME...

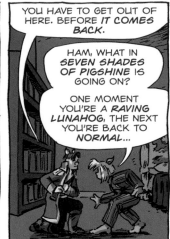

YOU HAVE TO GET OUT OF HERE. BEFORE *IT COMES BACK.*

HAM, WHAT IN *SEVEN SHADES OF PIGSHINE* IS GOING ON?

ONE MOMENT YOU'RE A *RAVING LUNAHOG*, THE NEXT YOU'RE BACK TO *NORMAL...*

NO TIME TO EXPLAIN. YOU NEED TO *WARN THE PIGDOM* ABOUT THE INVASION.

HERE, IF ANYHOG TRIES TO *STOP* YOU, FLASH THIS *SIGNATURE* AT THEM.

YOUR AIRCRAFT IS IN THE MAIN COURT GARAGE *BENEATH* US. TAKE THE MAIN RAPID-RISER ALONG THE CORRIDOR.

RUN, WARN THE PIGDOM...

HHKKKKKKK

GO, LILY. CAN ONLY *RESIST* IT FOR A *SHORT TIME...*

OH!

LOOK OUT, LADY LILY...!

WHERE D'YOU THINK YOU'RE GOING IN SUCH A *HURRY*, PIGGIKINS?

≥whew≤

TO GET *HELP*. YOUR *CHIEF* IS HAVING SOME KIND OF FIT.

A FIT?

SEE FOR YOURSELVES. YOU'D BETTER LOOK AFTER HIM, OR ELSE THERE'LL BE *HELL TO PAY!*

CHIEF!

CHIEF, WHAT'S *WRONG?*

ARE YOU ALL RIGHT?

I THINK, PERHAPS, AN *ESCAPE* IS BEING MADE...?

YEAH. AND I'M VERY *GRATEFUL* FOR YOUR HELP.

NOW *HIT ME OVER THE HEAD* AND I'LL SAY YOU *OVERPOWERED* ME.

I CAN'T DO *THAT!*

YOU *HAVE* TO! OTHERWISE MY COVER AS A LOYAL, VANQUISHED SERF WILL BE *BLOWN.*

COME *WITH ME.*

TO THE GARAGE?

NO, SILLY. TO THE *PIGDOM PLAINS!*

BAM BAM

OPEN THIS DOOR!

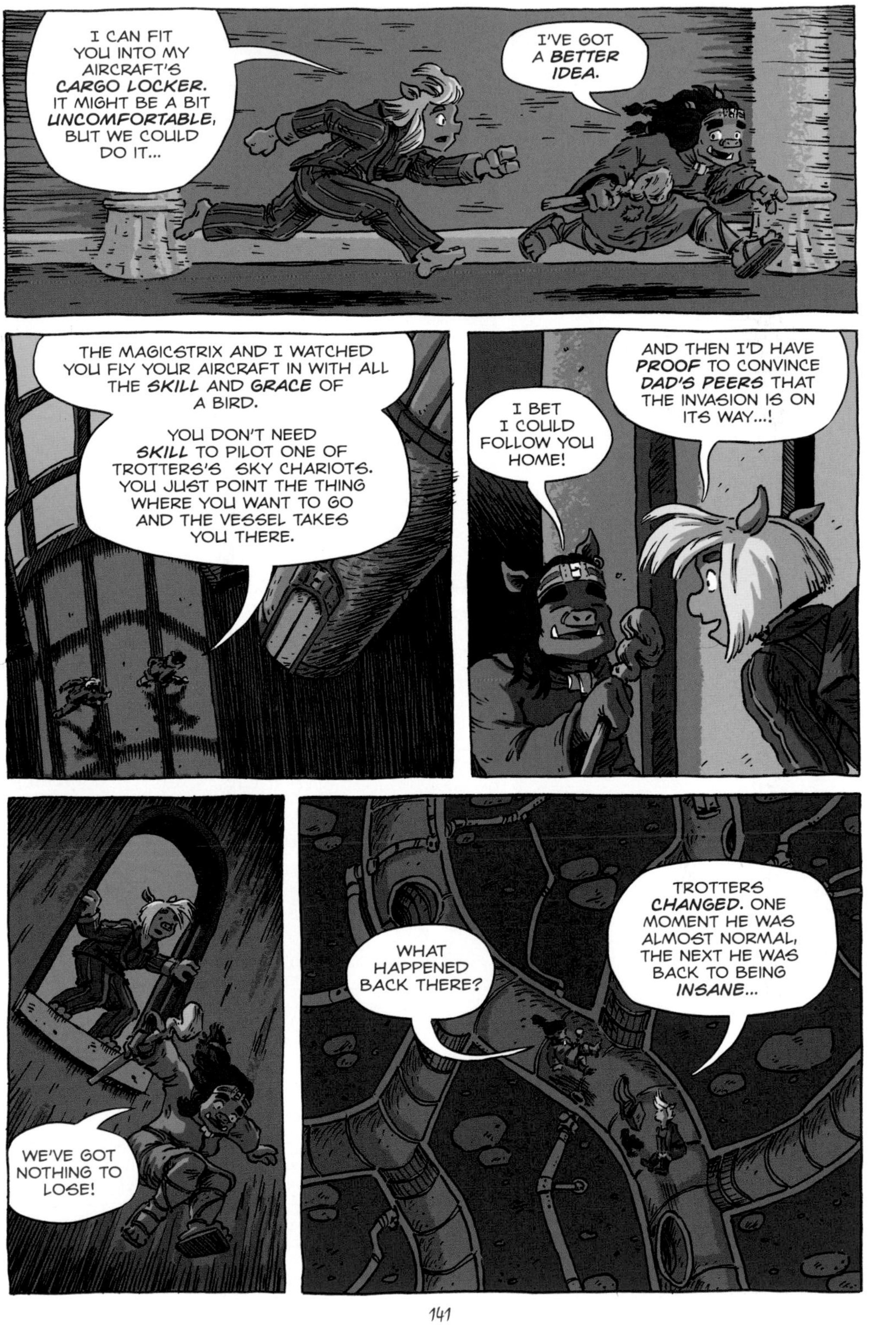
I CAN FIT YOU INTO MY AIRCRAFT'S CARGO LOCKER. IT MIGHT BE A BIT UNCOMFORTABLE, BUT WE COULD DO IT...
I'VE GOT A BETTER IDEA.
THE MAGICSTRIX AND I WATCHED YOU FLY YOUR AIRCRAFT IN WITH ALL THE SKILL AND GRACE OF A BIRD.
YOU DON'T NEED SKILL TO PILOT ONE OF TROTTERS'S SKY CHARIOTS. YOU JUST POINT THE THING WHERE YOU WANT TO GO AND THE VESSEL TAKES YOU THERE.
I BET I COULD FOLLOW YOU HOME!
AND THEN I'D HAVE PROOF TO CONVINCE DAD'S PEERS THAT THE INVASION IS ON ITS WAY...!
WE'VE GOT NOTHING TO LOSE!
WHAT HAPPENED BACK THERE?
TROTTERS CHANGED. ONE MOMENT HE WAS ALMOST NORMAL, THE NEXT HE WAS BACK TO BEING INSANE...

TROTTERS IS CONSUMED BY *NON-CARDINAL MAGIC*. IT *INFECTS* EVERYTHING HE DOES.

...SOMETHING *WORSE*.

I'VE HEARD STORIES LIKE THAT FROM MY AUNTIE SASHA...

BUT *NO*... THIS IS... DIFFERENT. SOMETHING *MORE*...

NOHOG ABOUT. DON'T THINK THE ALARM'S BEEN *RAISED* YET.

LET'S GO *THIS* WAY... FEWER GUARDS.

MAYBE WE CAN MAKE IT TO THE GARAGE WITHOUT BEING SEEN.

WE'RE OUT OF LUCK. THOUGHT THIS *BACK WAY* INTO THE GARAGE WOULD BE *UNGUARDED*.

LEAVE THIS TO ME.

HEY, YOU!

THIS AREA'S *OFF-LIMITS* TO CIVILIANS.

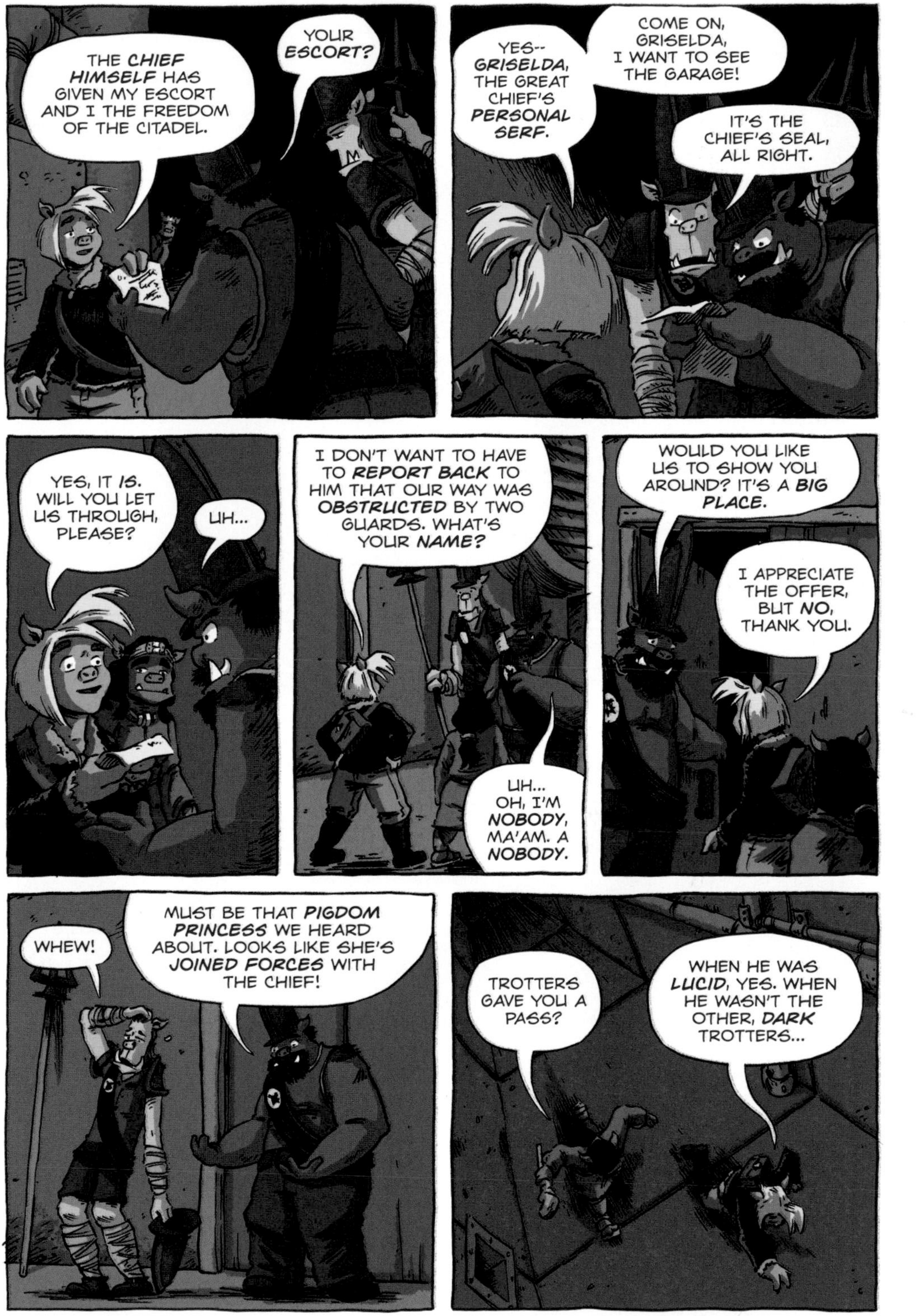
THE CHIEF HIMSELF HAS GIVEN MY ESCORT AND I THE FREEDOM OF THE CITADEL.
YOUR ESCORT?
YES-- GRISELDA, THE GREAT CHIEF'S PERSONAL SERF.
COME ON, GRISELDA, I WANT TO SEE THE GARAGE!
IT'S THE CHIEF'S SEAL, ALL RIGHT.
YES, IT IS. WILL YOU LET US THROUGH, PLEASE?
UH...
I DON'T WANT TO HAVE TO REPORT BACK TO HIM THAT OUR WAY WAS OBSTRUCTED BY TWO GUARDS. WHAT'S YOUR NAME?
UH... OH, I'M NOBODY, MA'AM. A NOBODY.
WOULD YOU LIKE US TO SHOW YOU AROUND? IT'S A BIG PLACE.
I APPRECIATE THE OFFER, BUT NO, THANK YOU.
WHEW!
MUST BE THAT PIGDOM PRINCESS WE HEARD ABOUT. LOOKS LIKE SHE'S JOINED FORCES WITH THE CHIEF!
TROTTERS GAVE YOU A PASS?
WHEN HE WAS LUCID, YES. WHEN HE WASN'T THE OTHER, DARK TROTTERS...

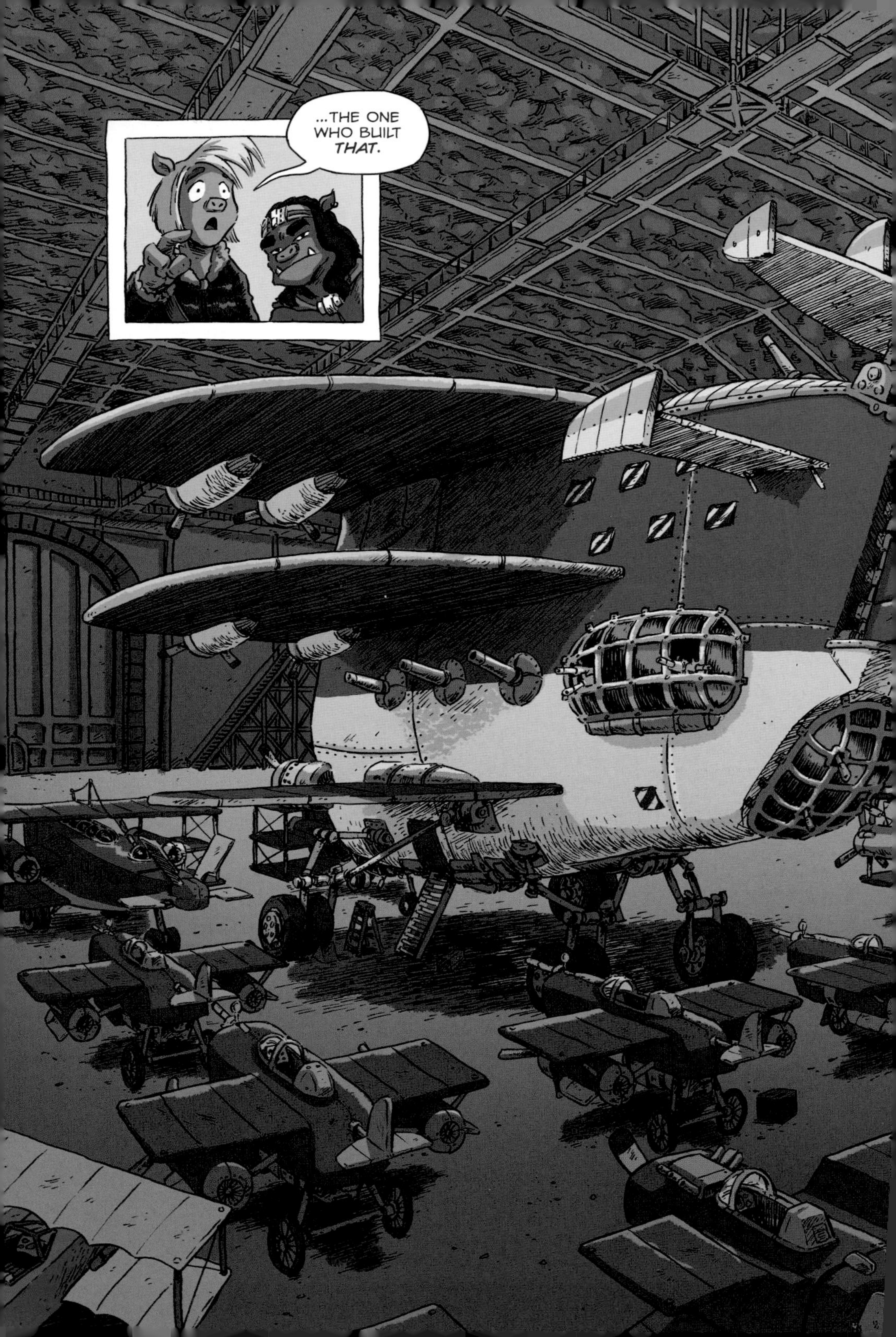
...THE ONE WHO BUILT *THAT*.

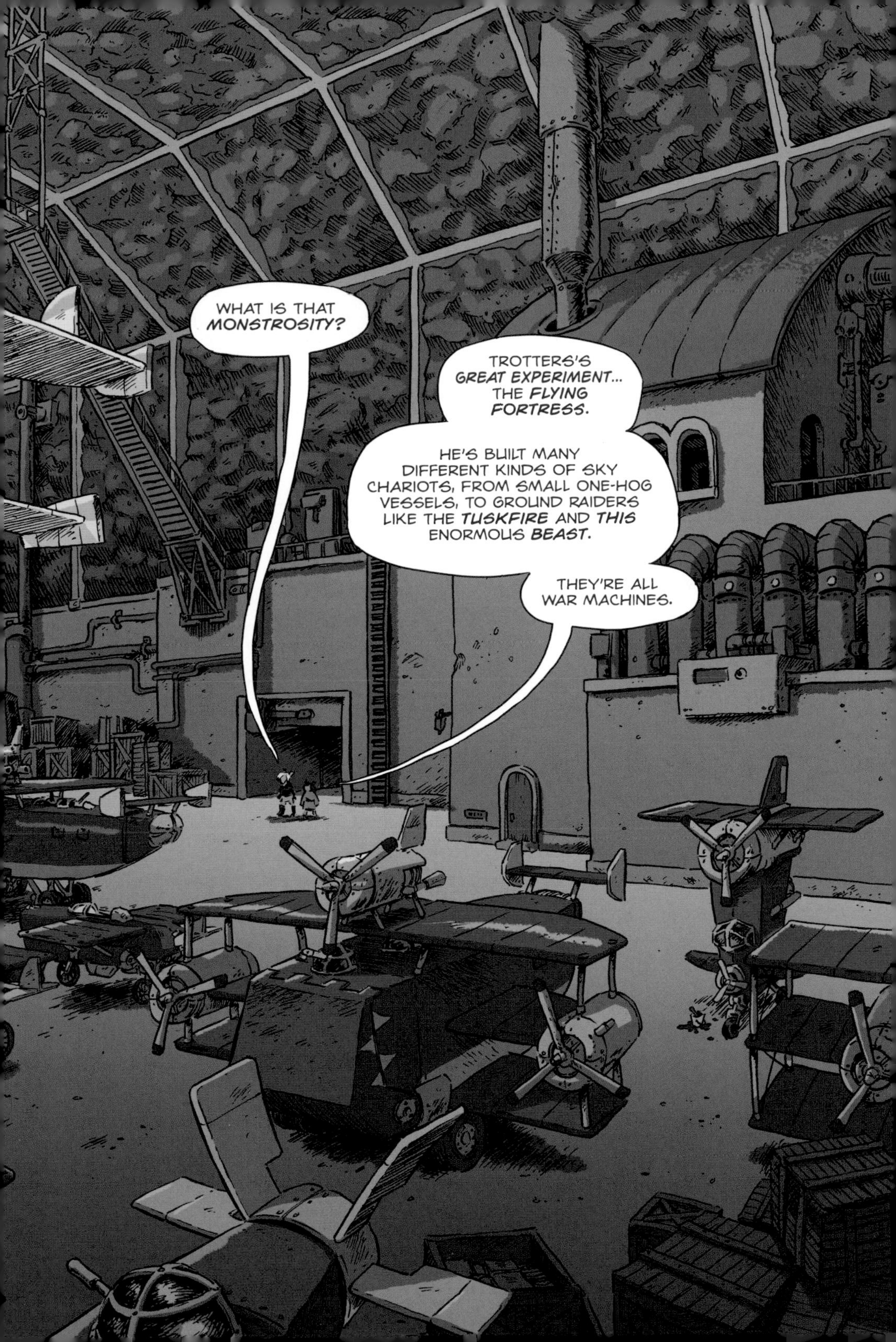
WHAT IS THAT MONSTROSITY?
TROTTERS'S GREAT EXPERIMENT... THE FLYING FORTRESS.
HE'S BUILT MANY DIFFERENT KINDS OF SKY CHARIOTS, FROM SMALL ONE-HOG VESSELS, TO GROUND RAIDERS LIKE THE TUSKFIRE AND THIS ENORMOUS BEAST.
THEY'RE ALL WAR MACHINES.

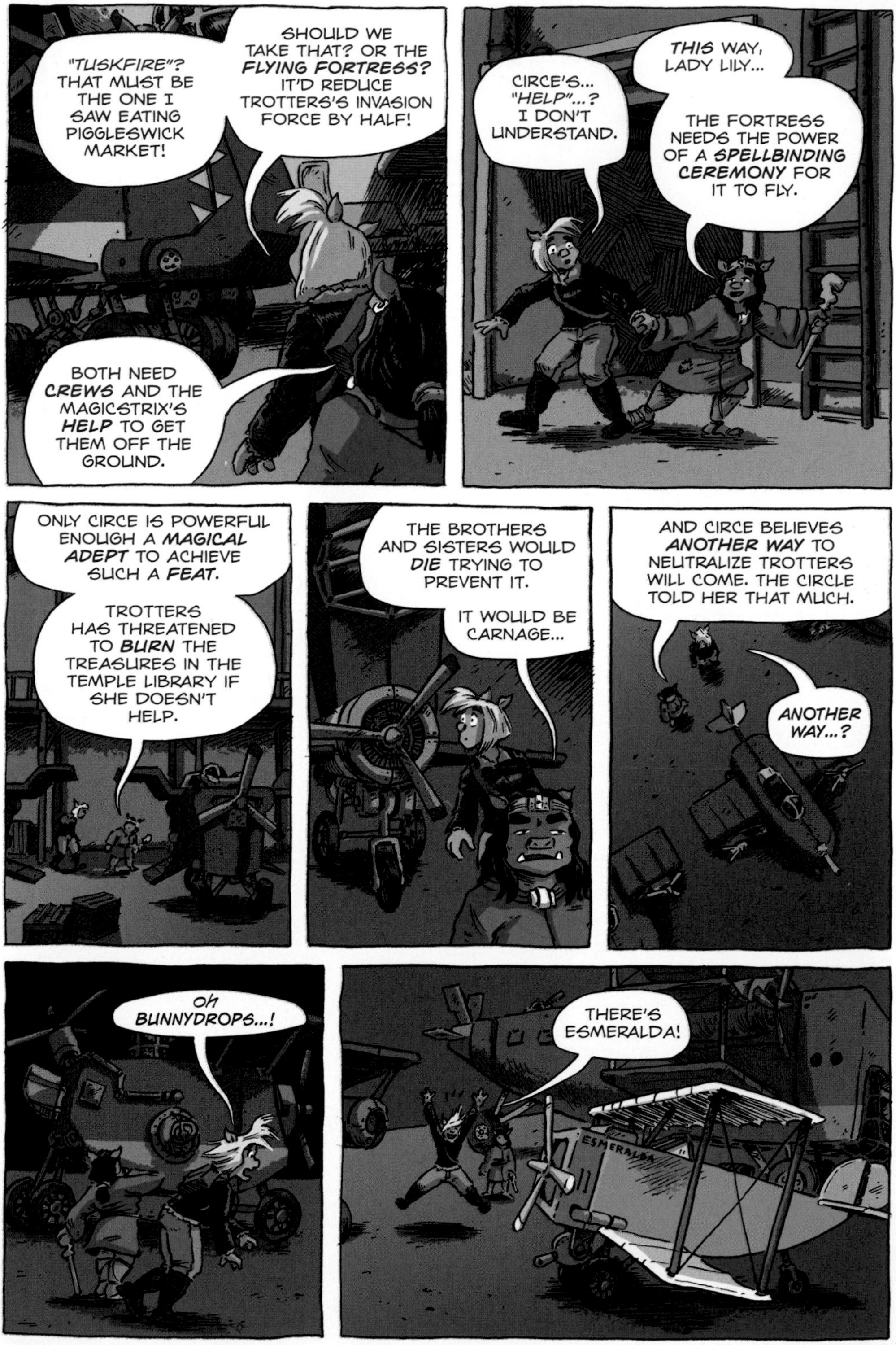
"TUSKFIRE"? THAT MUST BE THE ONE I SAW EATING PIGGLESWICK MARKET!
SHOULD WE TAKE THAT? OR THE FLYING FORTRESS? IT'D REDUCE TROTTERS'S INVASION FORCE BY HALF!
BOTH NEED CREWS AND THE MAGICSTRIX'S HELP TO GET THEM OFF THE GROUND.
CIRCE'S... "HELP"...? I DON'T UNDERSTAND.
THIS WAY, LADY LILY...
THE FORTRESS NEEDS THE POWER OF A SPELLBINDING CEREMONY FOR IT TO FLY.
ONLY CIRCE IS POWERFUL ENOUGH A MAGICAL ADEPT TO ACHIEVE SUCH A FEAT.
TROTTERS HAS THREATENED TO BURN THE TREASURES IN THE TEMPLE LIBRARY IF SHE DOESN'T HELP.
THE BROTHERS AND SISTERS WOULD DIE TRYING TO PREVENT IT.
IT WOULD BE CARNAGE...
AND CIRCE BELIEVES ANOTHER WAY TO NEUTRALIZE TROTTERS WILL COME. THE CIRCLE TOLD HER THAT MUCH.
ANOTHER WAY...?
oh BUNNYDROPS...!
THERE'S ESMERALDA!
ESMERALDA

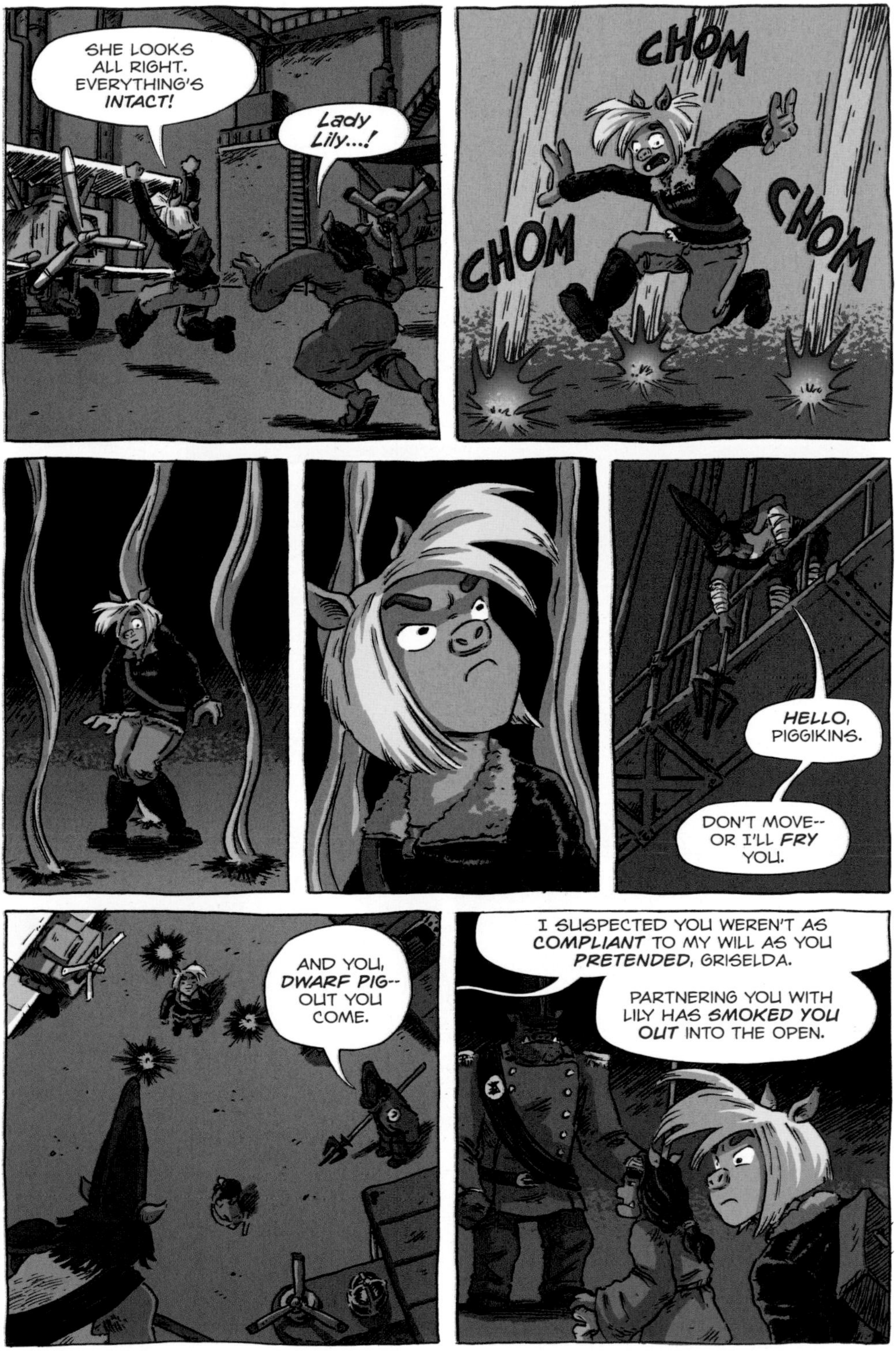
SHE LOOKS ALL RIGHT. EVERYTHING'S *INTACT!*
Lady Lily...!
CHOM
CHOM
CHOM
HELLO, PIGGIKINS.
DON'T MOVE-- OR I'LL *FRY* YOU.
AND YOU, *DWARF PIG*-- OUT YOU COME.
I SUSPECTED YOU WEREN'T AS **COMPLIANT** TO MY WILL AS YOU *PRETENDED*, GRISELDA.
PARTNERING YOU WITH LILY HAS **SMOKED YOU OUT** INTO THE OPEN.

AND, MY DEAR LILY, DID YOU *REALLY* THINK I'D LET YOU GET AWAY TO *WARN* THE PIGDOM?

HAM, PLEASE *LISTEN*. YOU'RE NOT WELL. YOU'VE BEEN *TAKEN OVER* BY SOMETHING...

...YOU DON'T KNOW WHAT YOU'RE *DOING!*

ON THE CONTRARY... I KNOW *EXACTLY* WHAT I'M DOING.

OH, I *FORGOT*. YOU'RE NOT SO *PROUD* THAT YOU WON'T USE *MAGIC SHIELDING*, EH?

NO!

JUST HAVE TO USE *EXTRA POWER...!*

SHRAAAK

SHRAAAK

HAM! STOP IT, *PLEASE!*

SHRAAAK

FOOOOM

YOUR RUDDER IS *BROKEN.* YOU WON'T FLY NOW.

WHO CREATED THE *PROTECTION SPELL* ON YOUR AIRCRAFT?

NOHOG *YOU* KNOW.

TELL ME! I WANT TO KNOW HOW IT COULD BE THAT STRONG.

I'LL *FIND OUT,* ANYWAY. BUT IF YOU TELL ME NOW, NOHOG WILL *SUFFER.*

ENOUGH.

TROTTERS, YOU STILL NEED MY *COOPERATION* FOR THE *BINDING CEREMONY.*

AND I WILL NOT GIVE IT IF THIS *VILE COERCION* CONTINUES.

DO NOT *PROVOKE* ME, CIRCE...

CHIEF...

THE *CREWS* ARE HERE. TIME FOR YOUR *SPEECH.*

OF COURSE!

THROW THOSE TWO IN A *CELL,* PHINEAS. WE'LL FIGURE OUT WHAT TO DO WITH THEM LATER.

DESTINY AWAITS!

149

WELL, WHAT ARE YOU *WAITING* FOR, CIRCE? LET'S GET STARTED!

THE *SPELLBINDING CEREMONY*... NOW YOU'LL SEE WHAT POWERFUL MAGIC *REALLY IS*.

IN THE *HEAT VELDT*, WE KNOW SOMETHING OF MAGIC, TOO. BUT IT SEEMS SO MUCH *MORE POWERFUL* IN THIS PLACE.

WHEN I FIRST ARRIVED IN THIS CITADEL AS A *"GUEST"* OF TROTTERS, I WAS *SHUNNED*.

NOT OUT OF *CRUELTY*, MORE OUT OF *EMBARRASSMENT*. BECAUSE, SUDDENLY, I WAS *VISIBLE*, A REPRESENTATIVE OF EVERYTHING THAT WAS BEING *STOLEN FROM AFAR*, HERE IN THE WARTHOGS' MIDST.

I'M A REMINDER OF WHAT THE WARTHOGS' SURVIVAL TACTICS *COST*.

BUT CIRCE AND HER FOLLOWERS *ALWAYS* SHOWED ME FRIENDSHIP.

FOR ALL HER *POWER*, CIRCE ALWAYS PUTS KINDNESS AND CONSIDERATION BEFORE OTHER CONCERNS.

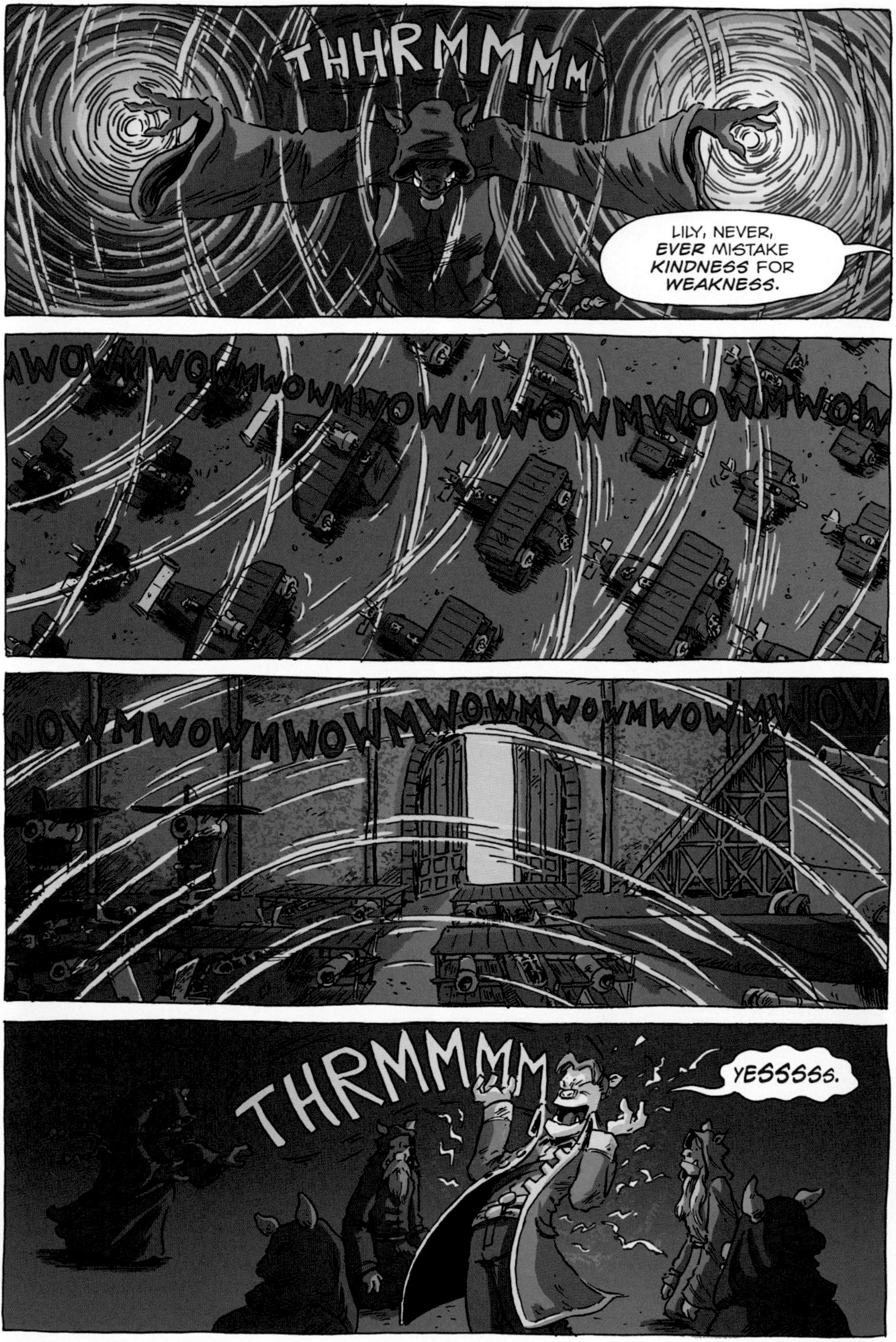
THHRMMMM
LILY, NEVER, EVER MISTAKE KINDNESS FOR WEAKNESS.
WOWMWOWMWOWMWOWMWOWMWOWMWOW
WOWMWOWMWOWMWOWMWOWMWOWMWOW
THRMMMM
YESSSSS.

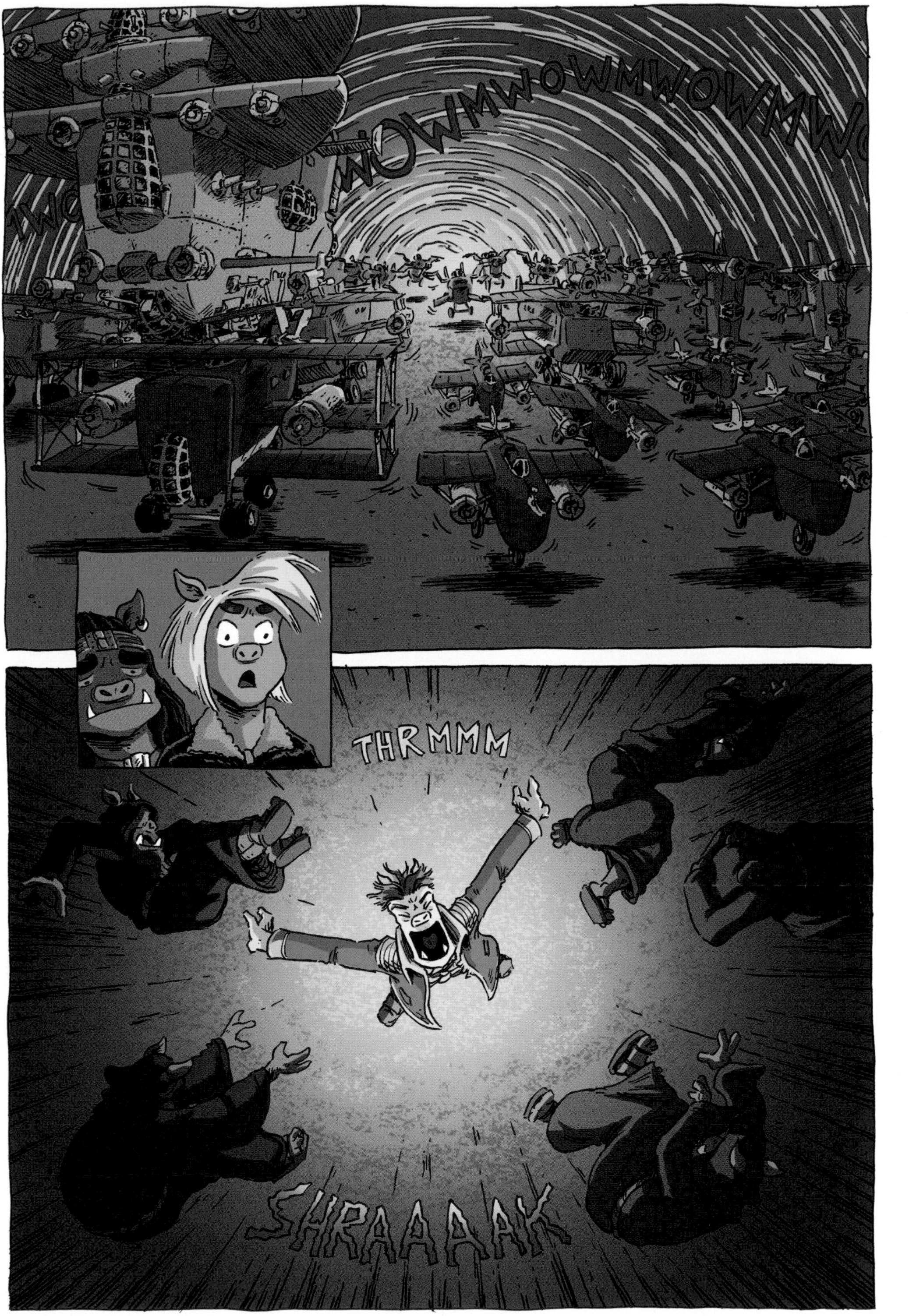
WOWMWOWMWOWMWO
THRMMM
SHRAAAK

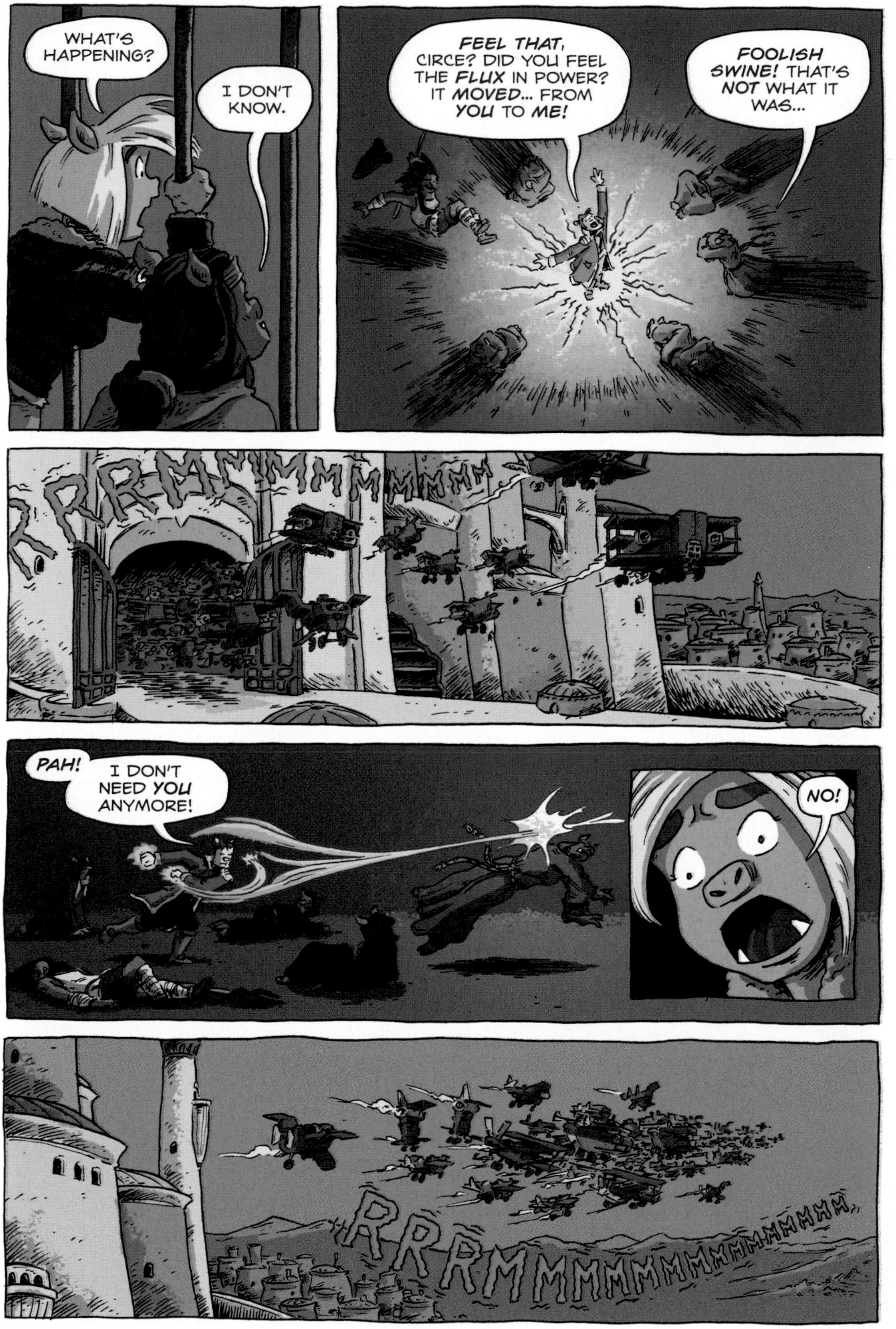
WHAT'S HAPPENING?
I DON'T KNOW.
FEEL THAT, CIRCE? DID YOU FEEL THE FLUX IN POWER? IT MOVED... FROM YOU TO ME!
FOOLISH SWINE! THAT'S NOT WHAT IT WAS...
RRRMMMMMMMMMM
PAH!
I DON'T NEED YOU ANYMORE!
NO!
RRRMMMMMMMMMMMMMMMMMMMMMMMH

I CAN FEEL *POWER* COURSING THROUGH MY VEINS...

COME, *PHINEAS,* OBELIA...

DESTINY AWAITS!

WHAT HAVE YOU DONE?

OBELIA... *SPEAK* TO ME!

SHE'S *ALIVE.*

PHINEAS, I NEED YOU ON THE BRIDGE OF THE FLYING FORTRESS.

WE NEED *HER,* TOO!

SHE'S NOT GOING ANYWHERE. WE'LL MAKE DO. *COME ON*... SHE'LL BE *FINE!*

DESTINY AWAITS!

THRRRM

WELL DONE, LINUS!

WE MUST HELP THE *MOST HIGH.* SHE'S *HURT.*

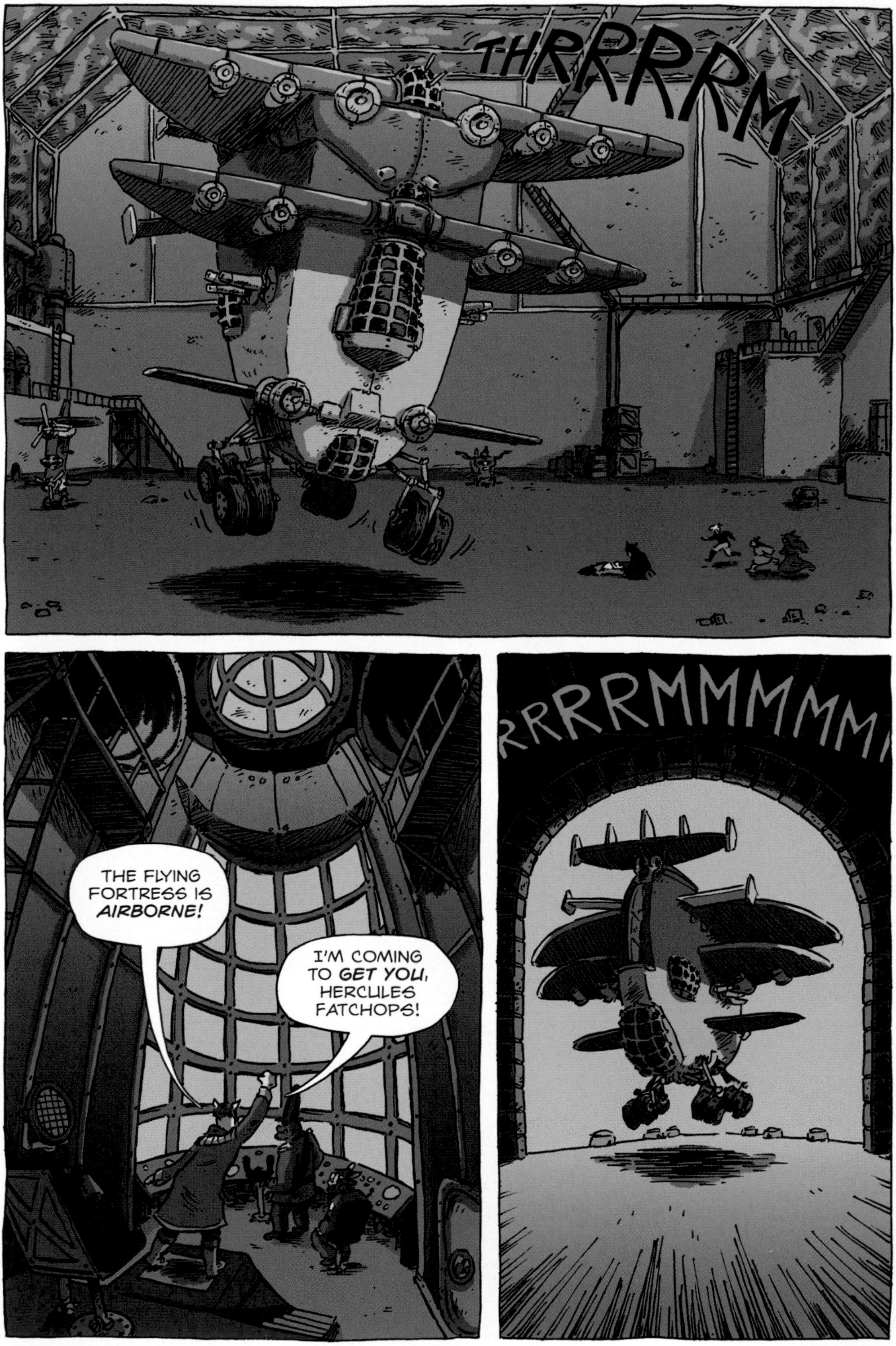
THRRRRM
THE FLYING FORTRESS IS AIRBORNE!
I'M COMING TO GET YOU, HERCULES FATCHOPS!
RRRRMMMMMM

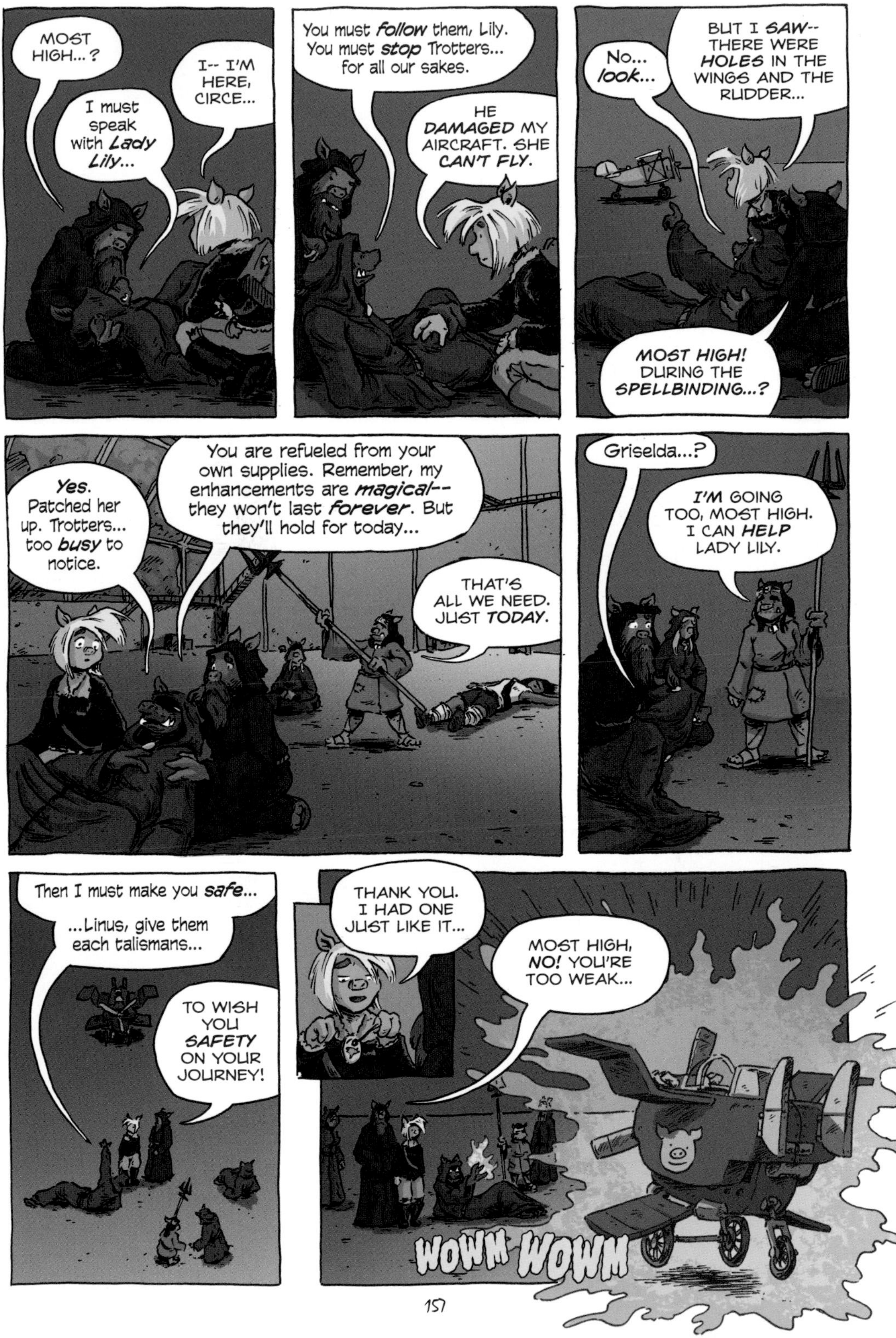
MOST HIGH...?
I must speak with *Lady Lily*...
I-- I'M HERE, CIRCE...
You must *follow* them, Lily. You must *stop* Trotters... for all our sakes.
HE *DAMAGED* MY AIRCRAFT. SHE *CAN'T FLY*.
No... *look*...
BUT I *SAW*-- THERE WERE *HOLES* IN THE WINGS AND THE RUDDER...
MOST HIGH! DURING THE *SPELLBINDING*...?
Yes. Patched her up. Trotters... too *busy* to notice.
You are refueled from your own supplies. Remember, my enhancements are *magical*-- they won't last *forever*. But they'll hold for today...
THAT'S ALL WE NEED. JUST *TODAY*.
Griselda...?
I'M GOING TOO, MOST HIGH. I CAN *HELP* LADY LILY.
Then I must make you *safe*...
...Linus, give them each talismans...
TO WISH YOU *SAFETY* ON YOUR JOURNEY!
THANK YOU. I HAD ONE JUST LIKE IT...
MOST HIGH, *NO!* YOU'RE TOO WEAK...
WOWM WOWM

MOST HIGH...! CIRCE!

GO. I WILL ATTEND TO HER.

hhhhhh

MAY I BORROW YOUR WATER?

WHA--?

SPLOOSH!

WAKEY-WAKEY!

YOU'RE GOING TO TELL US WHAT HAM'S *FLIGHT PATH* IS.

WHAT...?

THEY'RE GONE, HONEY.

NO!

YES. YOUR BOARFRIEND AND YOUR PRECIOUS CHIEF *LEFT YOU BEHIND.*

I WON'T ASK TWICE. WHAT'S THEIR *HEADING?*

THEY'RE HEADING INTO *THE PIGDOM* VIA THE *SNAGJAW PASS.*

LOCK HER UP, AGATHA.

SNAGJAW PASS...?

SHORTEST ROUTE OVER THE MOUNTAINS, BUT *TREACHEROUS* AND OFTEN *OBSCURED BY CLOUDS.*

HERE...

I KNOW IT. WE CALL IT THE **ALLFATHER'S PASS** IN THE PIGDOM. IT'S A DIFFERENT ROUTE FROM THE ONE I CAME IN THROUGH...

LOOKS LIKE IT'S THE **SAME ROUTE** THEY USED WHEN THEY DID THEIR FIRST **SCOUTING RUN.** WHICH WILL TAKE THEM RIGHT OVER...

...MY HOUSE...

Linus... get me to the Temple. There is something else I must do...

MOST HIGH, YOU MUST **REST...**

HERE-- SPARE PAIR OF **GOGGLES.** YOU'LL NEED THEM UP THERE.

I WILL SEE YOU IN THE SKY, LADY LILY. I WILL WATCH YOUR BACK.

I'LL MAKE YOU A DEAL. WE BOTH COME OUT OF THIS **ALIVE,** WILL YOU STOP CALLING ME "LADY LILY"...?

DEAL. I WILL THINK OF SOMETHING APPROPRIATE...

TAKE **GOOD CARE,** CHILDREN...

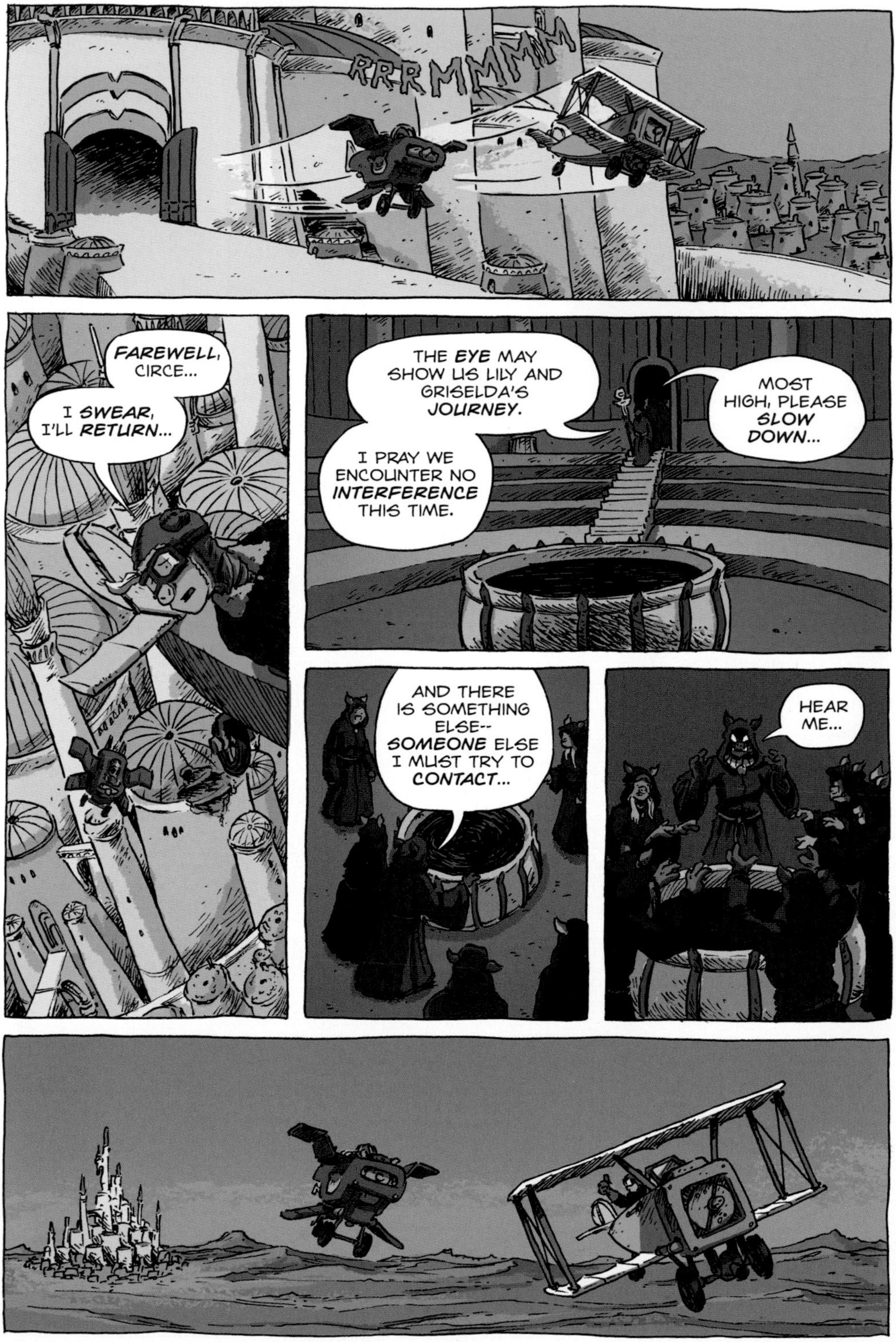
RRRMMMMM
FAREWELL, CIRCE...
I SWEAR, I'LL RETURN...
THE EYE MAY SHOW US LILY AND GRISELDA'S JOURNEY.
I PRAY WE ENCOUNTER NO INTERFERENCE THIS TIME.
MOST HIGH, PLEASE SLOW DOWN...
AND THERE IS SOMETHING ELSE-- SOMEONE ELSE I MUST TRY TO CONTACT...
HEAR ME...

WE HAVE TO *CATCH UP* TO THEM BEFORE THEY GET TO THE SNAGJAW PASS!

...Because we'll *lose* them in those clouds...

COME ON NOW, ESMERALDA. I KNOW YOU'VE BEEN THROUGH A LOT, BUT YOU'RE *TOUGH!*

LET'S APPLY SOME OF THE *ADVANTAGES* OF *SCIENCE...*

RRRMMMM

WWWRRRRRR

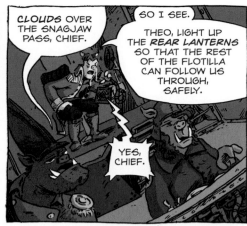

CLOUDS OVER THE SNAGJAW PASS, CHIEF.

SO I SEE.

THEO, LIGHT UP THE REAR LANTERNS SO THAT THE REST OF THE FLOTILLA CAN FOLLOW US THROUGH, SAFELY.

YES, CHIEF.

...WE'RE GOING FIRST.

CHIEF!

162

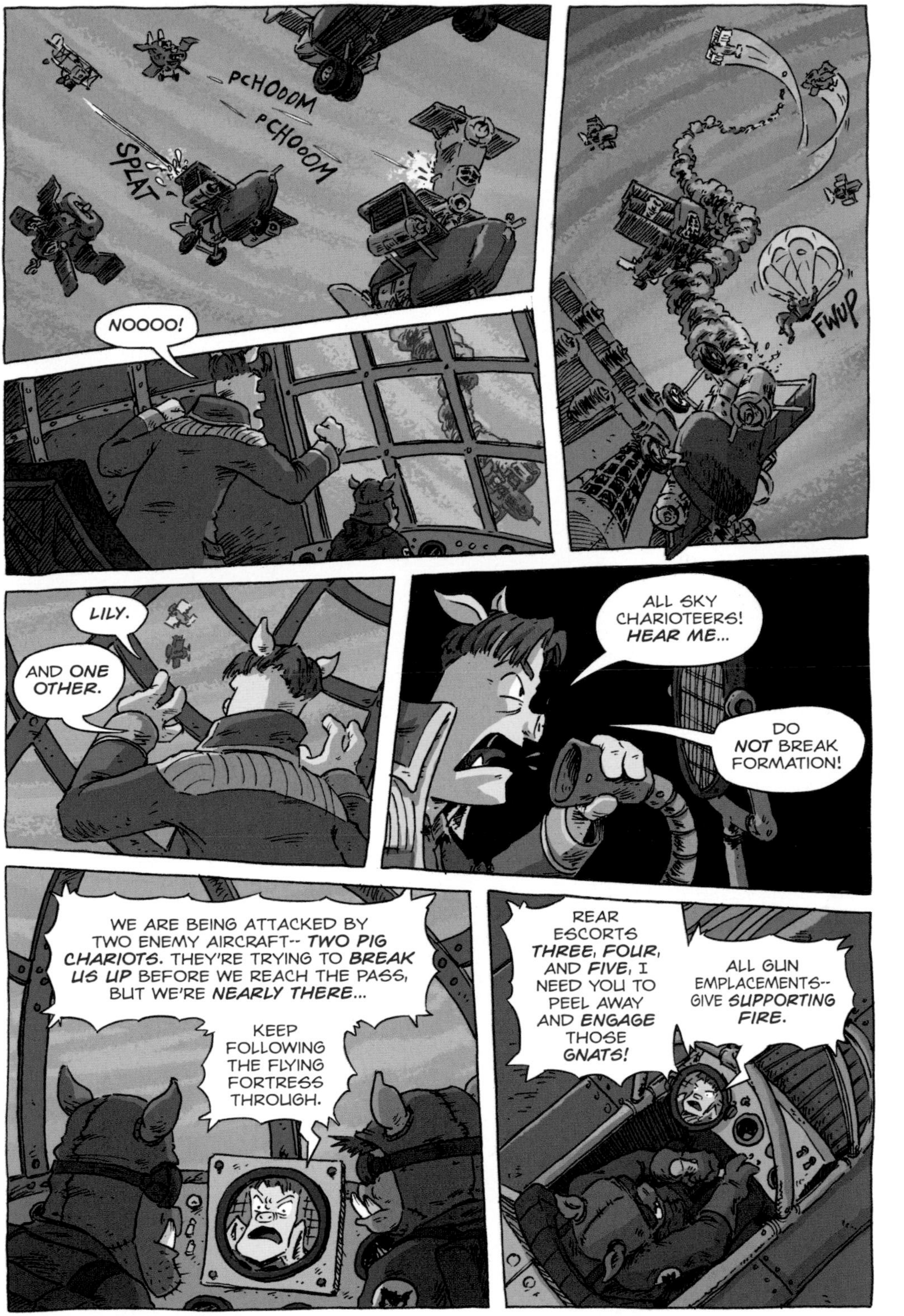
PCHOOOM
PCHOOOM
SPLAT
NOOOO!
FWUP
LILY.
AND ONE OTHER.
ALL SKY CHARIOTEERS! HEAR ME...
DO NOT BREAK FORMATION!
WE ARE BEING ATTACKED BY TWO ENEMY AIRCRAFT-- TWO PIG CHARIOTS. THEY'RE TRYING TO BREAK US UP BEFORE WE REACH THE PASS, BUT WE'RE NEARLY THERE...
KEEP FOLLOWING THE FLYING FORTRESS THROUGH.
REAR ESCORTS THREE, FOUR, AND FIVE, I NEED YOU TO PEEL AWAY AND ENGAGE THOSE GNATS!
ALL GUN EMPLACEMENTS-- GIVE SUPPORTING FIRE.

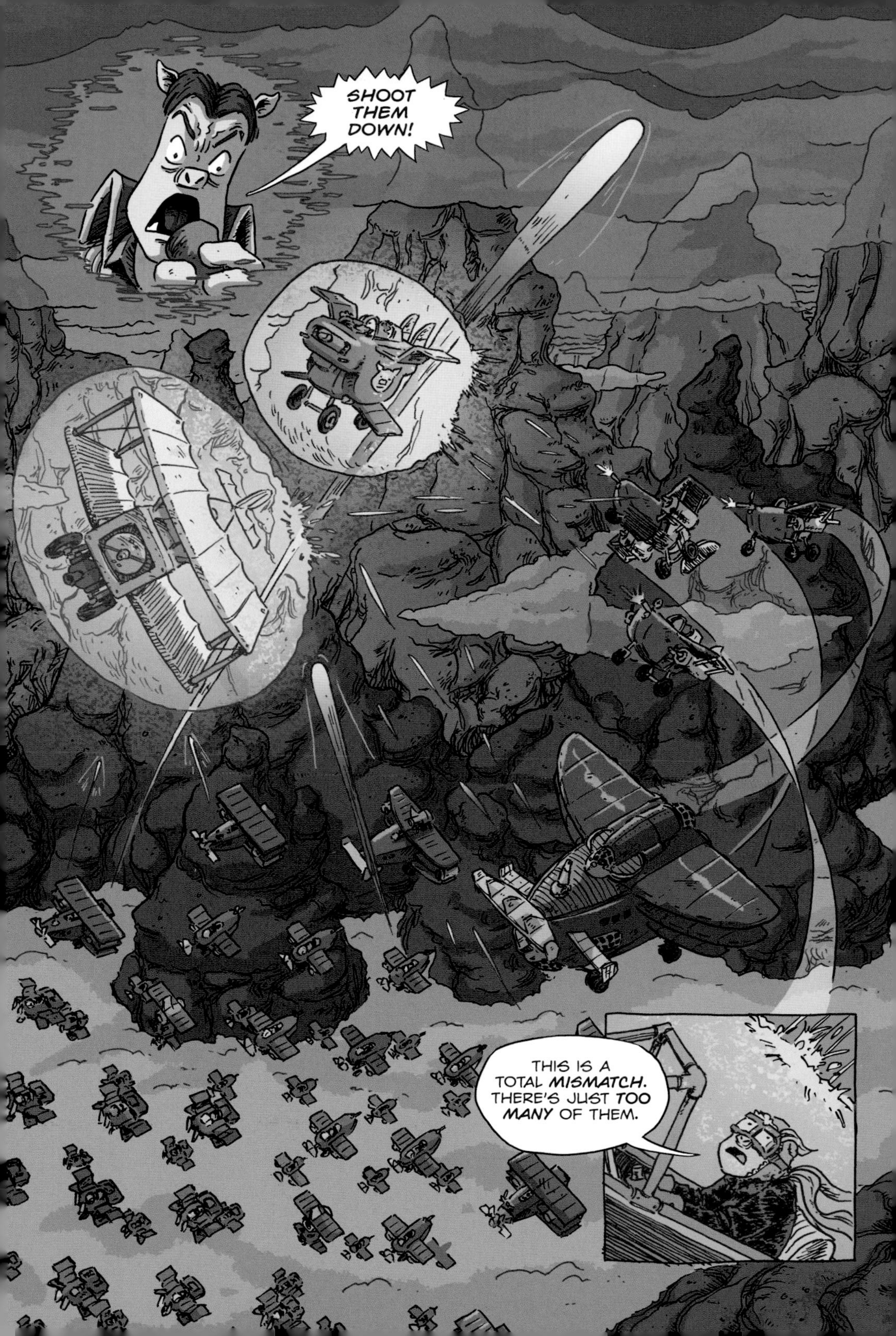
SHOOT THEM DOWN!
THIS IS A TOTAL MISMATCH. THERE'S JUST TOO MANY OF THEM.

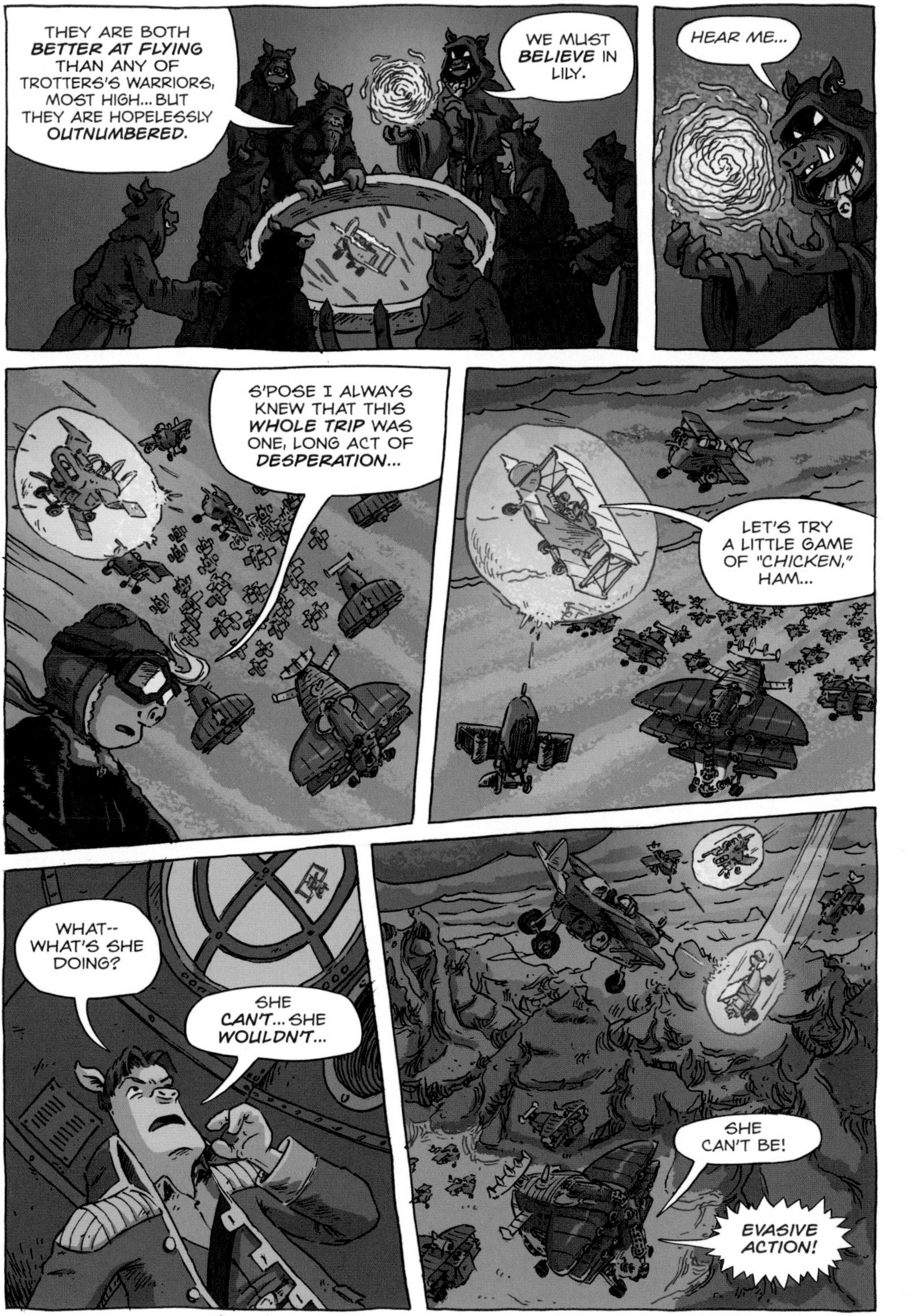
THEY ARE BOTH BETTER AT FLYING THAN ANY OF TROTTERS'S WARRIORS, MOST HIGH... BUT THEY ARE HOPELESSLY OUTNUMBERED.
WE MUST BELIEVE IN LILY.
HEAR ME...
S'POSE I ALWAYS KNEW THAT THIS WHOLE TRIP WAS ONE, LONG ACT OF DESPERATION...
LET'S TRY A LITTLE GAME OF "CHICKEN," HAM...
WHAT-- WHAT'S SHE DOING?
SHE CAN'T... SHE WOULDN'T...
SHE CAN'T BE!
EVASIVE ACTION!

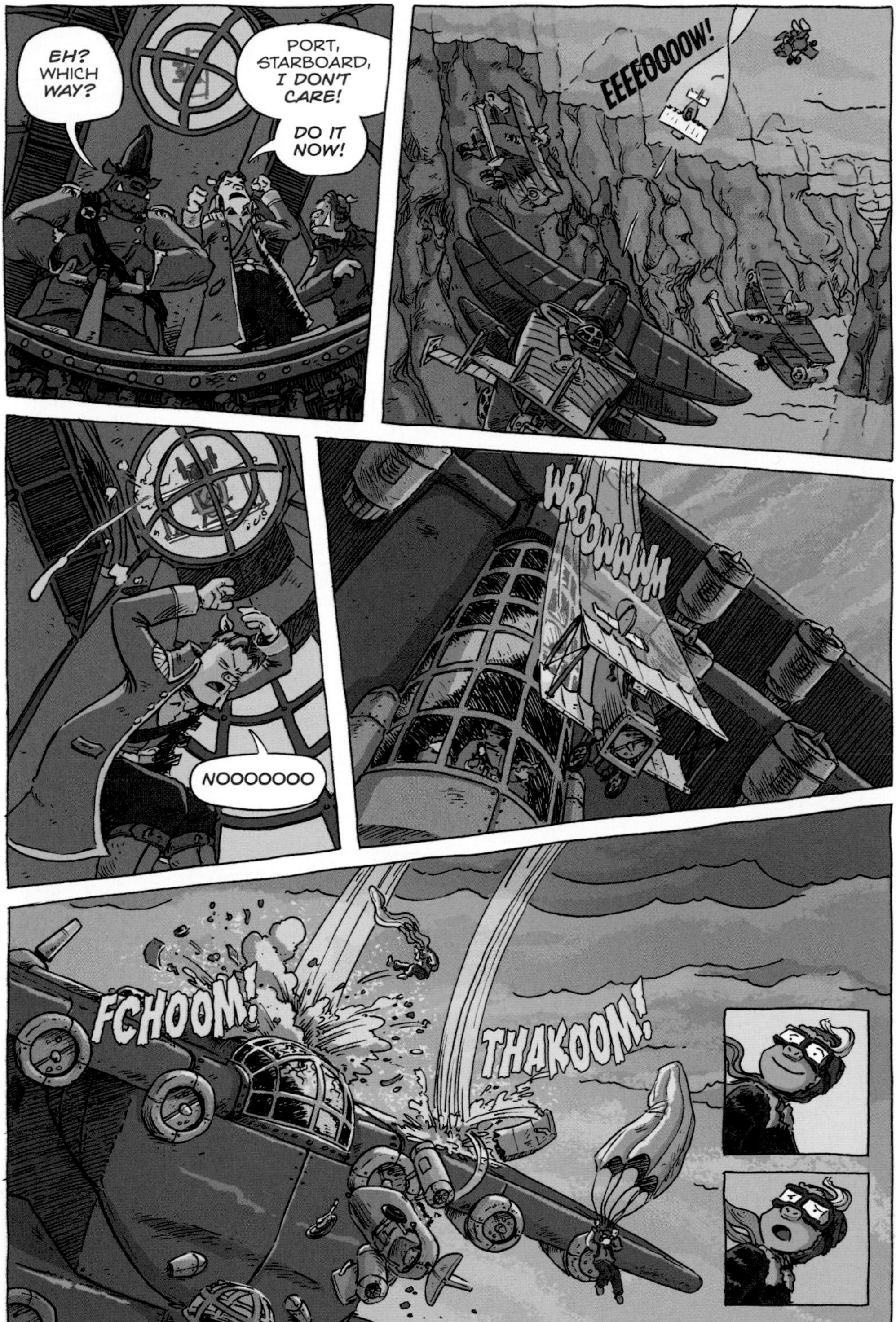
EH? WHICH WAY?
PORT, STARBOARD, I DON'T CARE!
DO IT NOW!
EEEEOOOOW!
WROOWWWM
NOOOOOOO
FCHOOM!
THAKOOM!

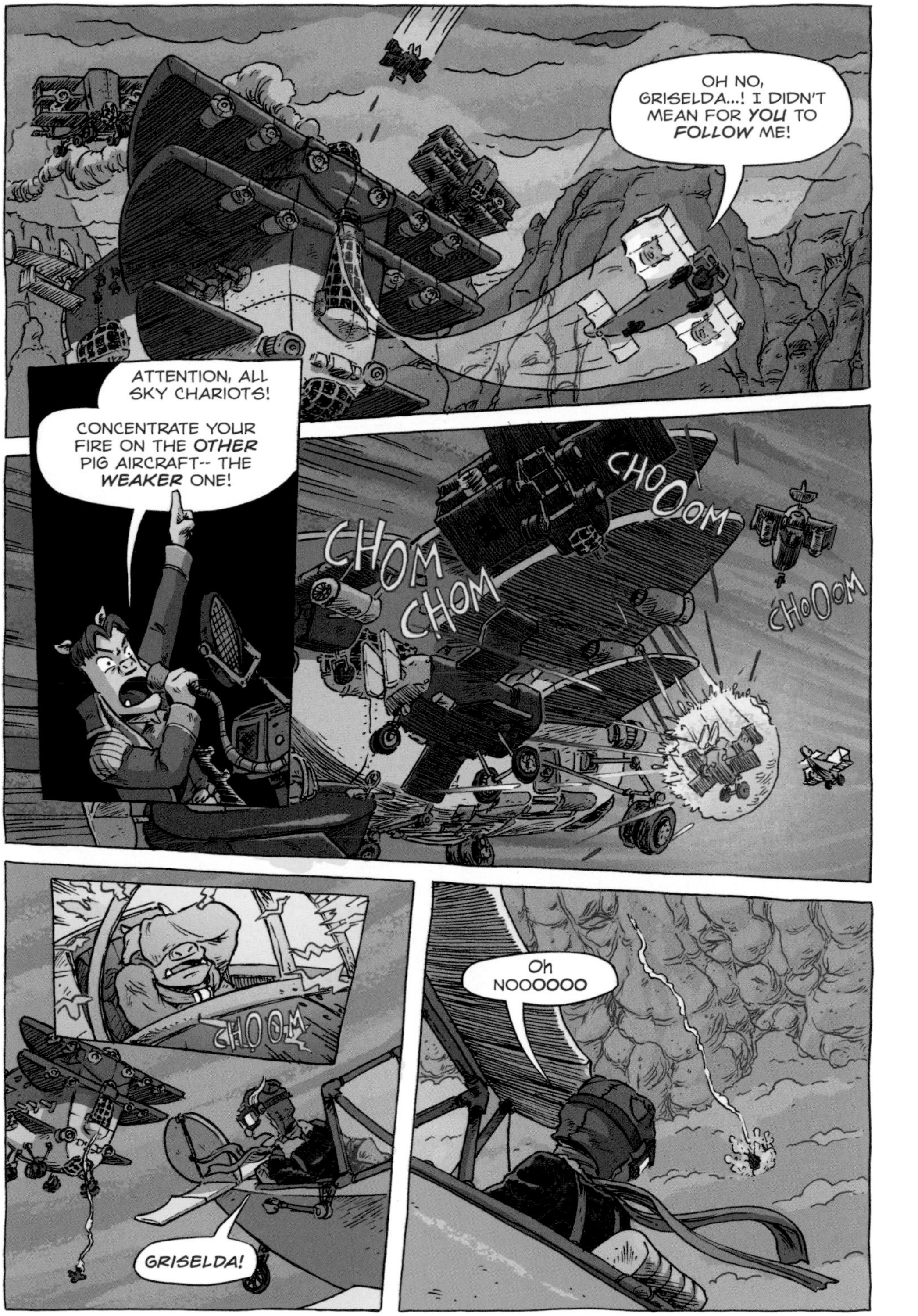
OH NO, GRISELDA...! I DIDN'T MEAN FOR **YOU** TO **FOLLOW** ME!
ATTENTION, ALL SKY CHARIOTS!
CONCENTRATE YOUR FIRE ON THE **OTHER** PIG AIRCRAFT-- THE **WEAKER** ONE!
CHOOOM
CHOM CHOM
CHOOOM
CHOOM
GRISELDA!
Oh NOOOOOO

INTERFERENCE. THE EYE IS CLOUDING...

ONE DOWN!

SKY CHARIOTS-- CONCENTRATE FIRE ON THE *SECOND* PIG AIRCRAFT.

CHIEF, WE'RE ABOUT TO ENTER THE PASS!

YES, THAT *IS* THE PLAN!

WHAT, *TWO* SKY CHARIOTS, AT THE *SAME* TIME?

WE CAN'T *BOTH* FIT! WE HAVE TO GO THROUGH THE PASS *SINGLE FILE!*

KR-A-A-AAK

TUSKFIRE, YOU'RE *OFF COURSE!* DECREASE SPEED!

NO TIME TO CORRECT--

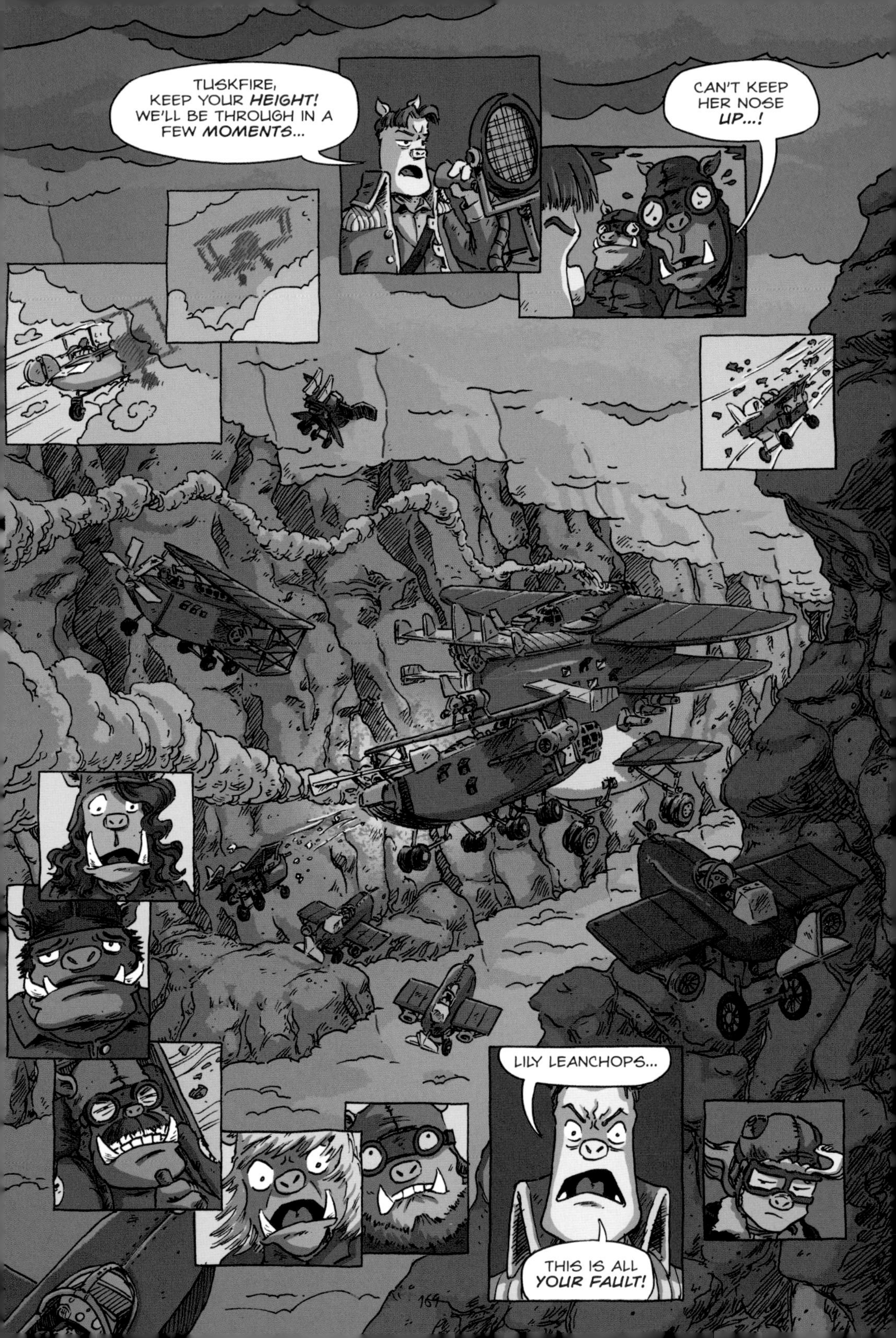
TUSKFIRE, KEEP YOUR HEIGHT! WE'LL BE THROUGH IN A FEW MOMENTS...
CAN'T KEEP HER NOSE UP...!
LILY LEANCHOPS...
THIS IS ALL YOUR FAULT!

170

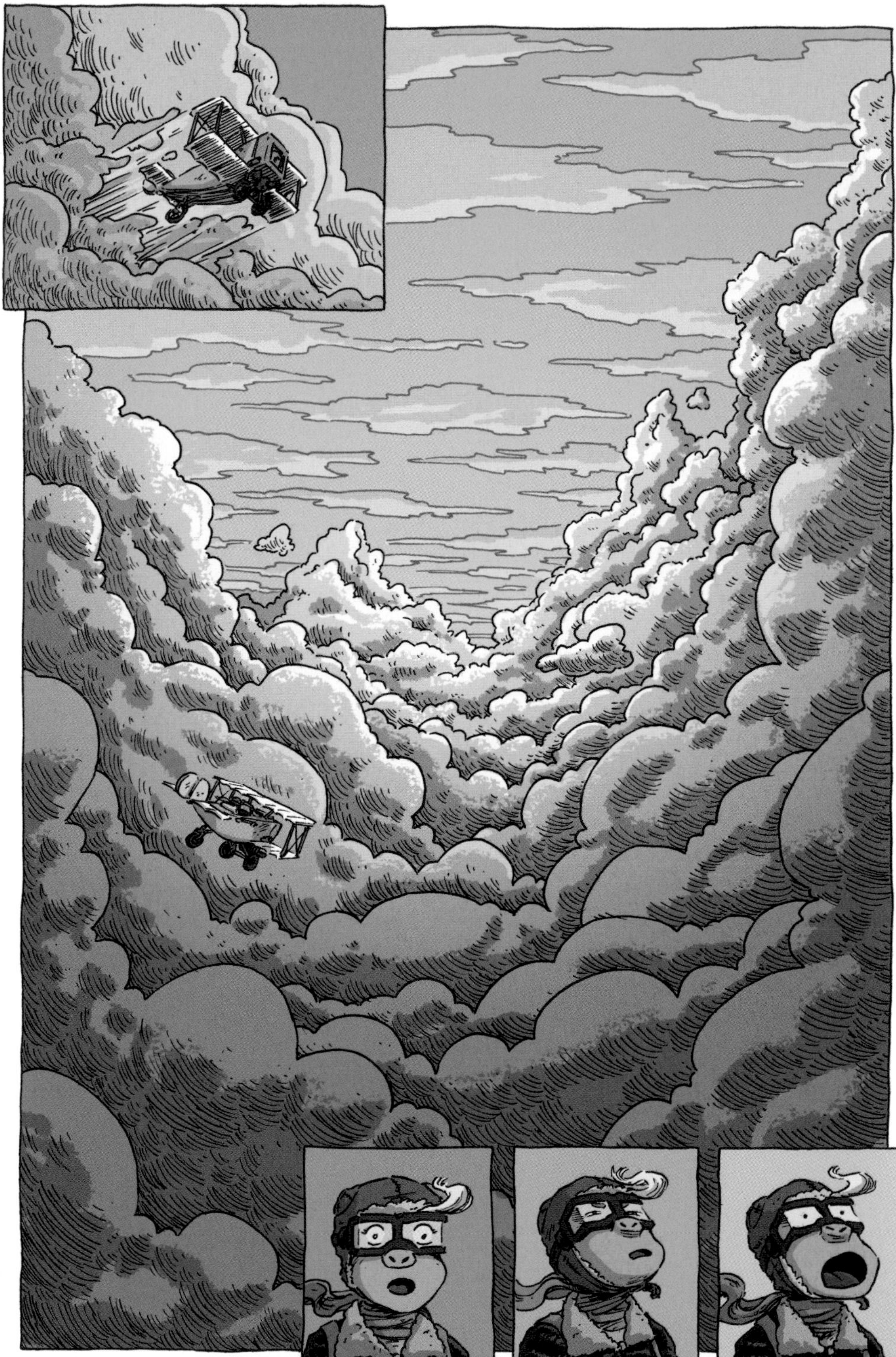

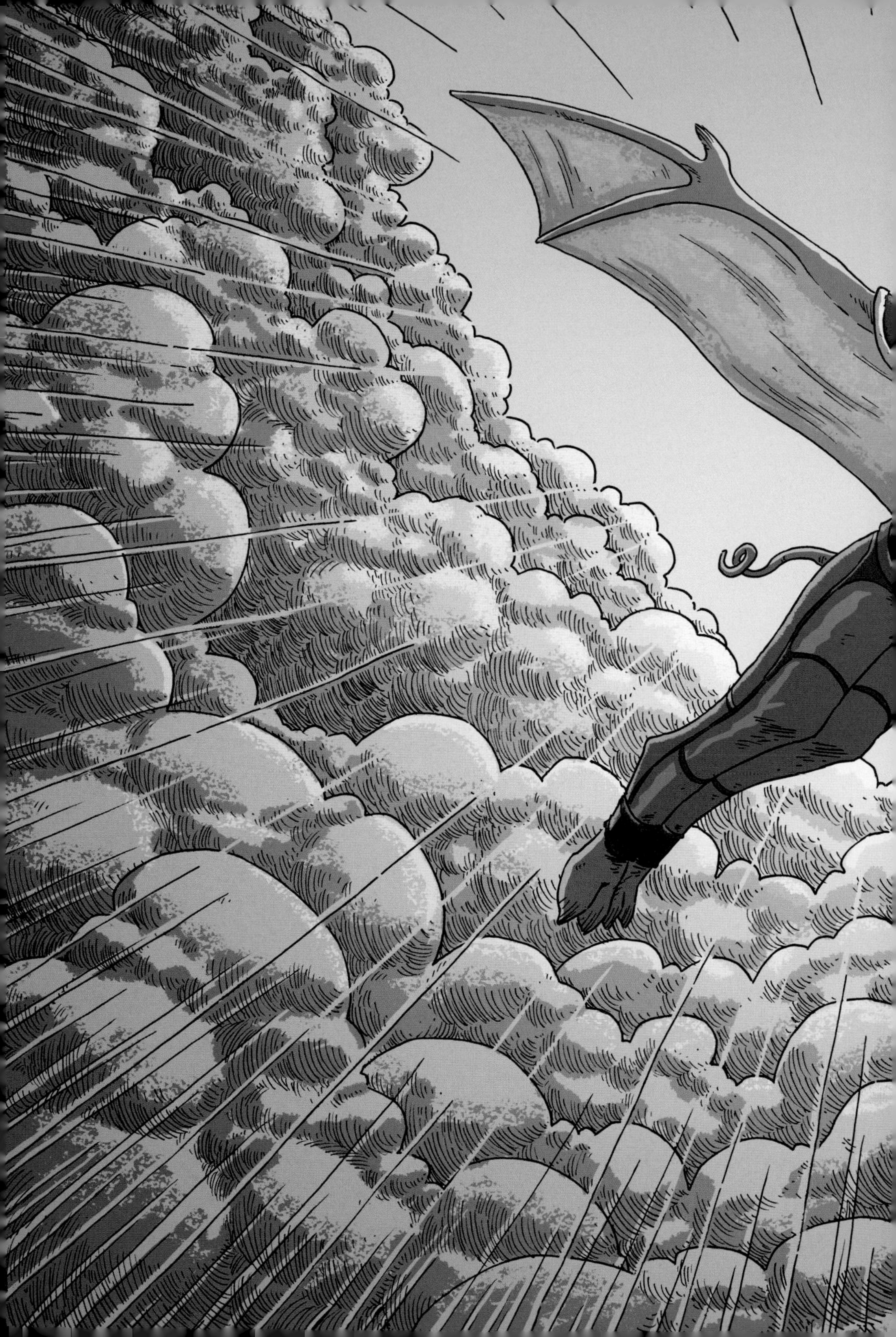

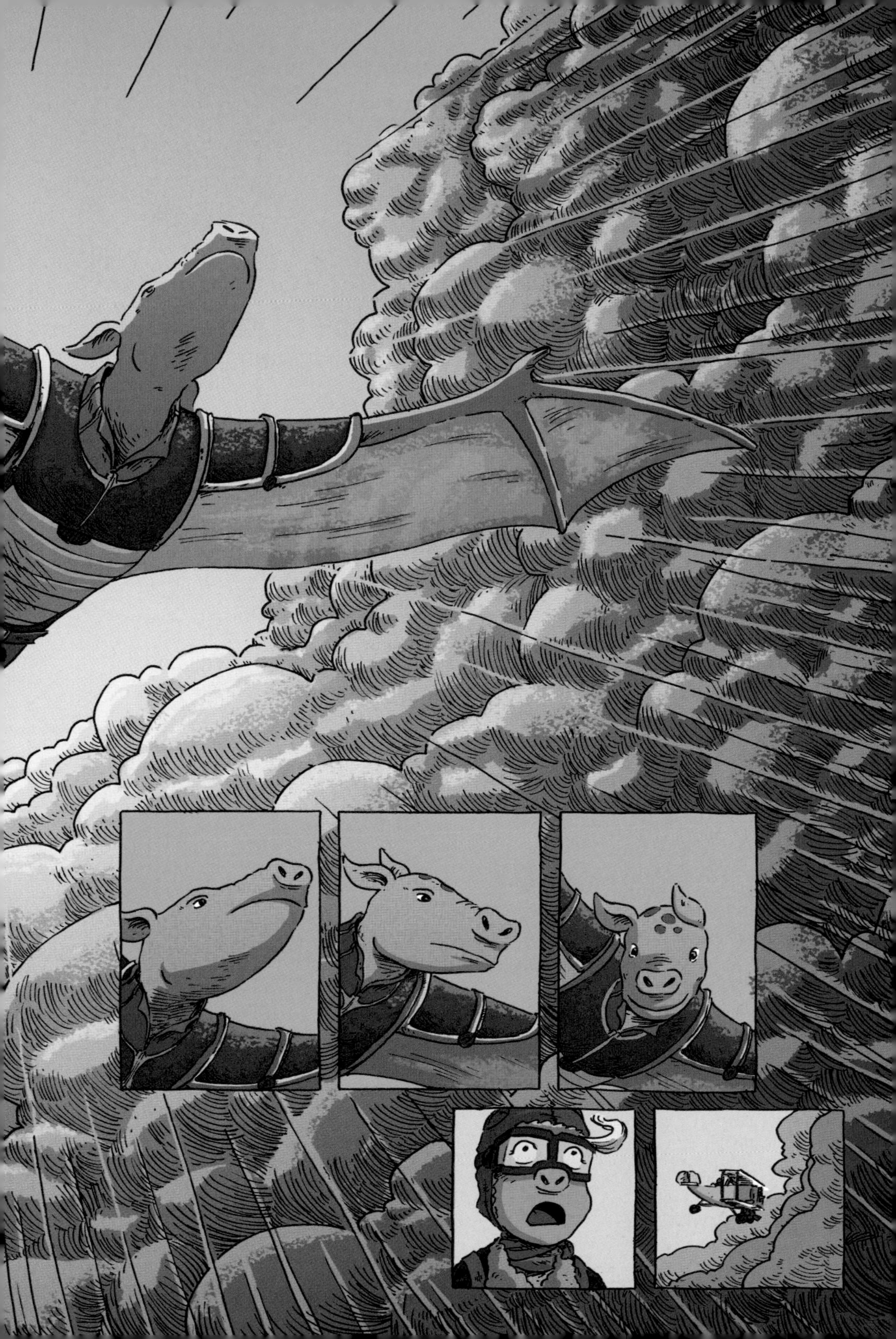

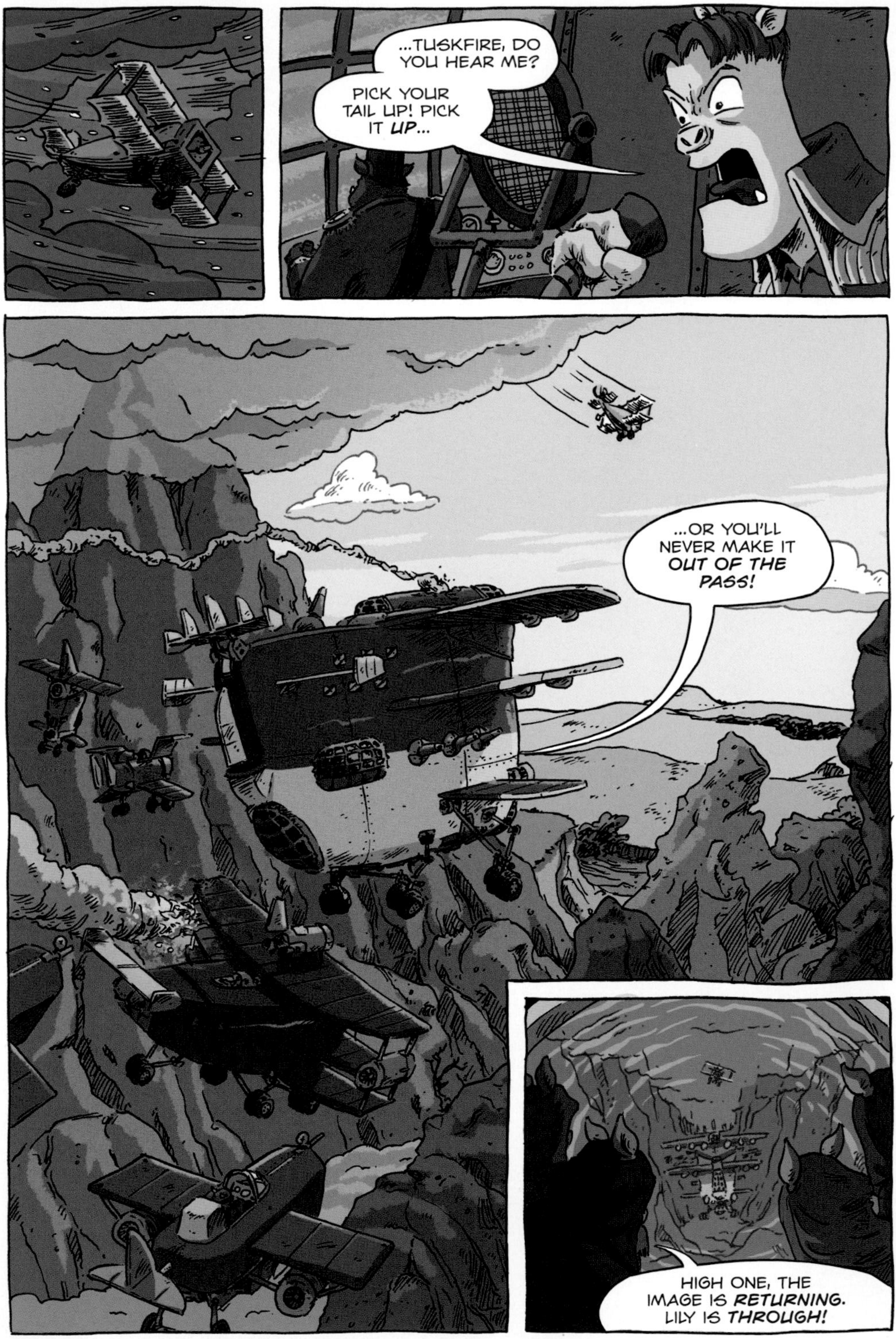

...TUSKFIRE, DO YOU HEAR ME?
PICK YOUR TAIL UP! PICK IT UP...
...OR YOU'LL NEVER MAKE IT OUT OF THE PASS!
HIGH ONE, THE IMAGE IS RETURNING. LILY IS THROUGH!

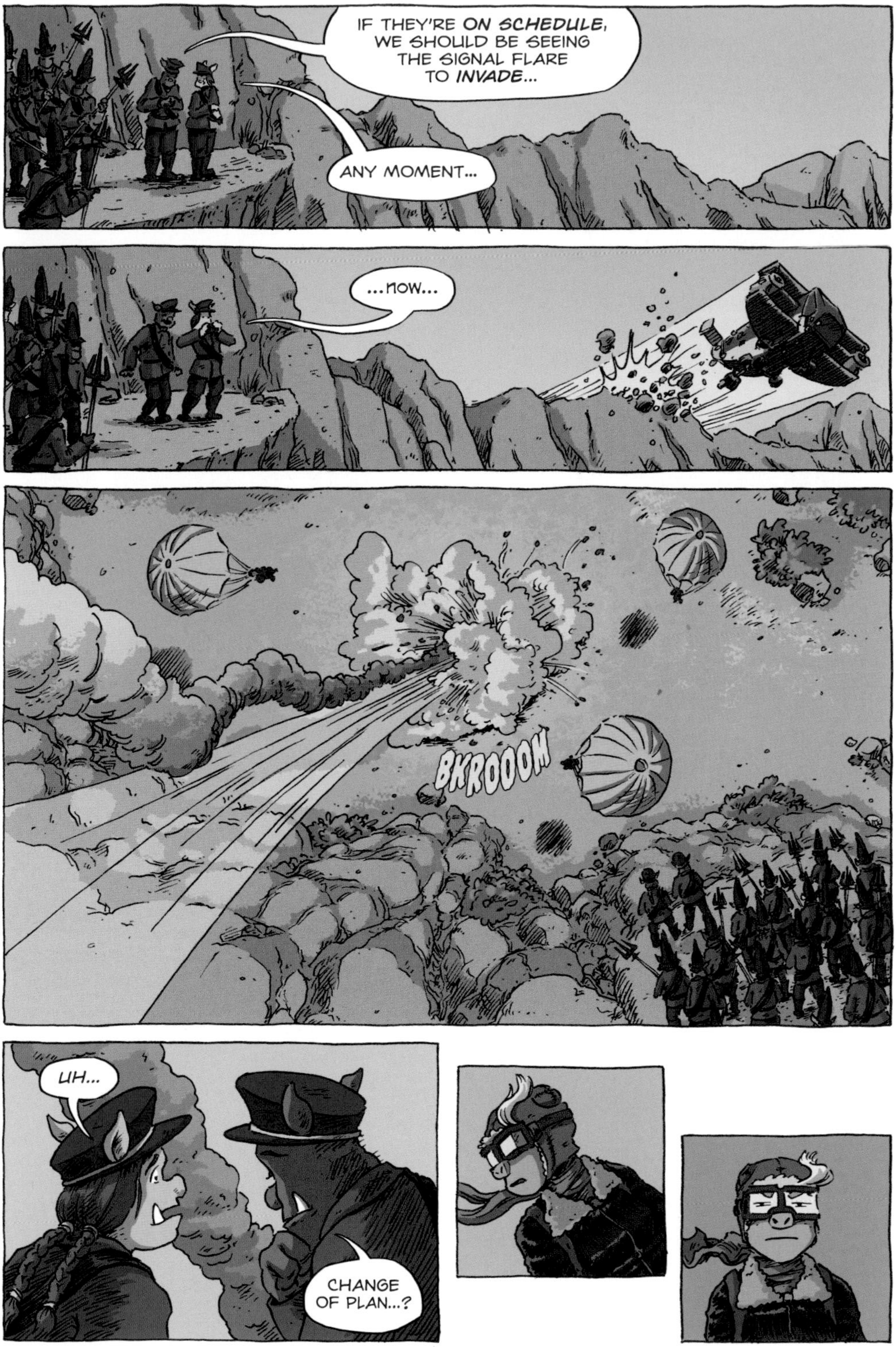
IF THEY'RE ON SCHEDULE, WE SHOULD BE SEEING THE SIGNAL FLARE TO INVADE...
ANY MOMENT...
...NOW...
BKROOOM
UH...
CHANGE OF PLAN...?

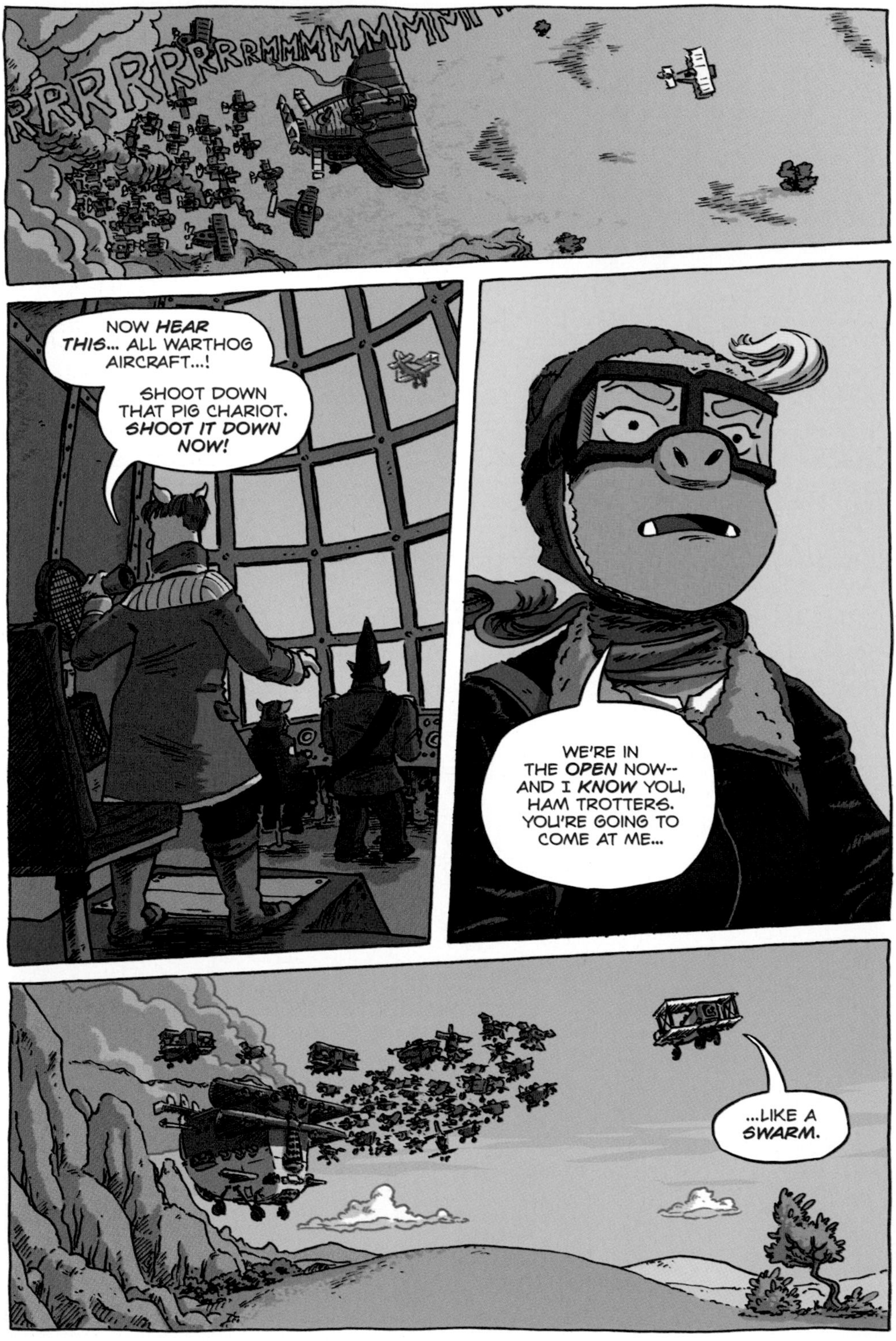
RRRRRRRRRMMMMMMMMM
NOW **HEAR THIS**... ALL WARTHOG AIRCRAFT...!
SHOOT DOWN THAT PIG CHARIOT. ***SHOOT IT DOWN NOW!***
WE'RE IN THE **OPEN** NOW-- AND I **KNOW** YOU, HAM TROTTERS. YOU'RE GOING TO COME AT ME...
...LIKE A **SWARM.**

WAIT... HOW MANY AIRCRAFT HAS HAM GOT?

LOOK AT HER! SHE'S *INSANE!* SHE'S GOING TO GET *SWATTED* OUT OF THE SKY, BUT SHE'S HEADING STRAIGHT *FOR* US!

YOU HAVE TO ADMIRE HER *COURAGE.* SHE NEVER GIVES--

uuuup

BCHOOM

WHA... HAPPENED?

WE WERE ATTACKED FROM THE REAR.

WE'RE LOSING *ALTITUDE.* NEED TO CORRECT OUR COURSE...

FROM THE *REAR?* BY WHAT...?

BY *THOSE.*

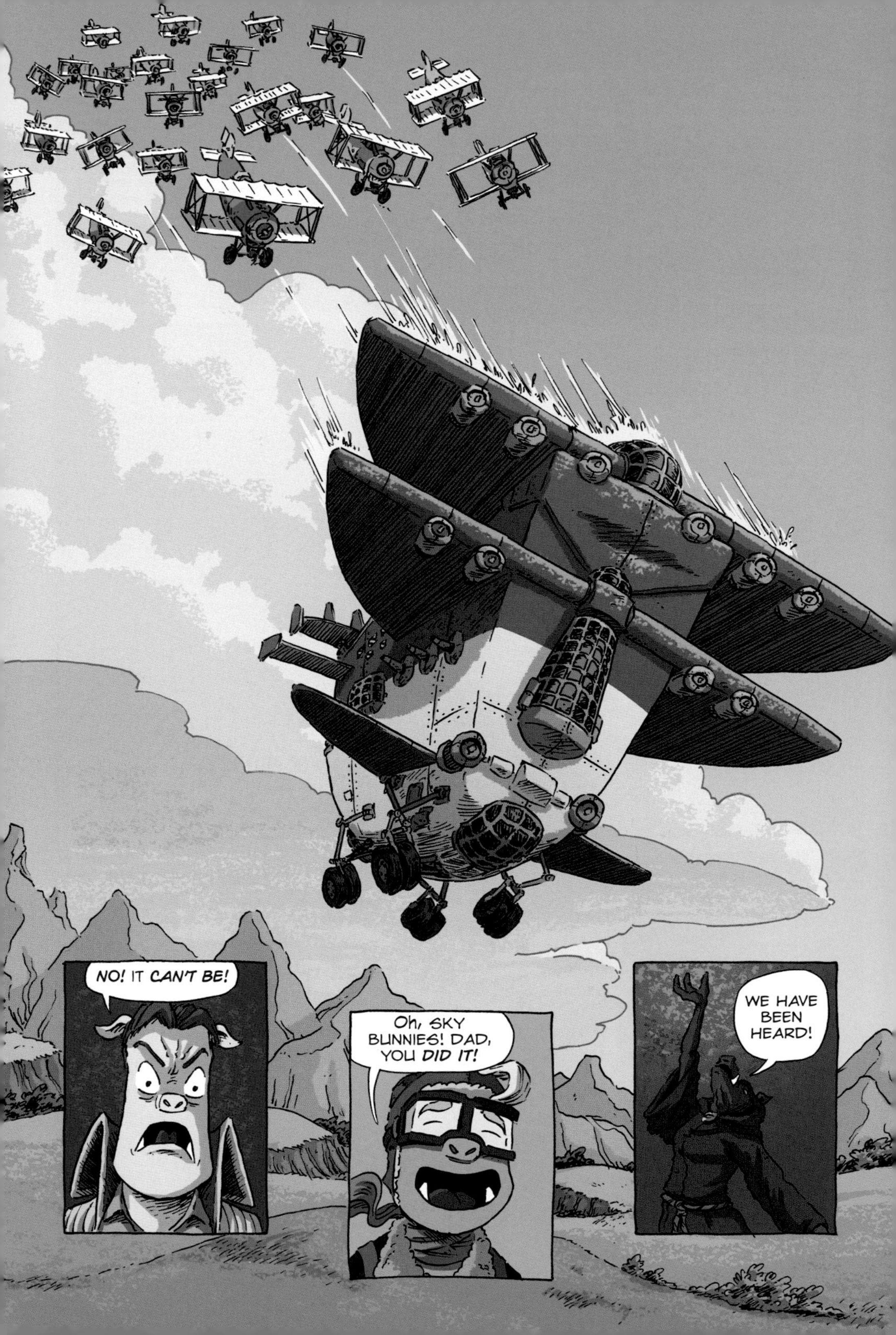
NO! IT CAN'T BE!
Oh, SKY BUNNIES! DAD, YOU DID IT!
WE HAVE BEEN HEARD!

LILY, CAN YOU HEAR ME? ARE YOU ALL RIGHT?

DAD! Oh, I'VE NEVER BEEN *SO ALL RIGHT!*

CAN YOU JOIN US?

NO. TOO MANY OF HAM'S FORCES BETWEEN YOU AND ME...

AND I'VE ALREADY PICKED UP A *HANGER-ON...*

HOLD ON, LILY. WE'LL GET TO YOU AS FAST AS WE CAN.

THAT'S *HIM.* I KNOW IT IS! IT'S *HERCULES FATCHOPS!* EVEN THE WAY HE FLIES IS *ARROGANT...*

HE MUST'VE SWALLOWED HIS *PRIDE* AND USED *MAGIC* TO BUILD THIS FLEET SO QUICKLY!

WARTHOGS, CONCENTRATE YOUR FIRE ON THE *LEAD PIG* AIRCRAFT...

CHIEF, WE'RE TAKING A *PUMMELING* HERE!

THEY CAME OUT OF *NOWHERE!*

CHIEF, WE NEED TO *FALL BACK,* REGROUP.

OUR *SURPRISE ATTACK* ISN'T MUCH OF A *SURPRISE!*

PHINEAS, SET COURSE FOR THE LEAD PIG AIRCRAFT. I'LL MAN THE MAIN GUNS *MYSELF.*

CHIEF...!

DO IT!

WHO'S THAT?!

CHOM CHOM

THANK YOU, WHOEVER YOU ARE!

WHOEVER HE IS, I CAN'T *SHAKE* HIM.

AND I CAN'T EVEN GET CLOSE TO THE OTHER PIGDOM AIRCRAFT...

GRISELDA!

OH, I'M SO *HAPPY* TO SEE Y--

AAACK.

KEEP YOUR MIND ON THE JOB, LILY...!

PCHOW

MOST HIGH, IS THERE ANY WAY WE CAN *HELP* THEM?

IT IS *FAR*, AND I AM *WEAK*... I MUST SAVE MY ENERGY FOR *COMMUNICATION*...

THIS WILL *PLAY OUT* THE WAY IT *MUST*...

ALL UNITS! CONCENTRATE YOUR FIRE ON THE *BIGGEST* WARTHOG AIRCRAFT!

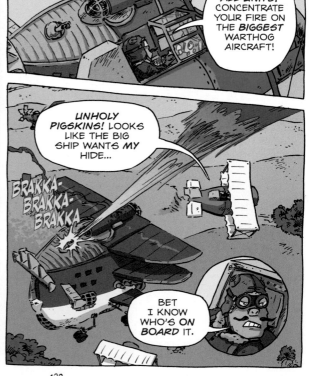

UNHOLY PIGSKINS! LOOKS LIKE THE BIG SHIP WANTS *MY* HIDE...

BRAKKA-BRAKKA-BRAKKA

BET I KNOW WHO'S ON BOARD IT.

CHIEF! YOU'RE *SHOOTING UP* OUR OWN AIRCRAFT!

THEY'RE IN THE WAY.

YOU'RE *CRAZY!*

NO. I SEE THE *BIGGER PICTURE...*

BIGGER REWARDS. *NOTHING* MUST GET IN MY WAY.

ENOUGH!

NOOOOO!

DAD!

THE *TRICKBOX...!*

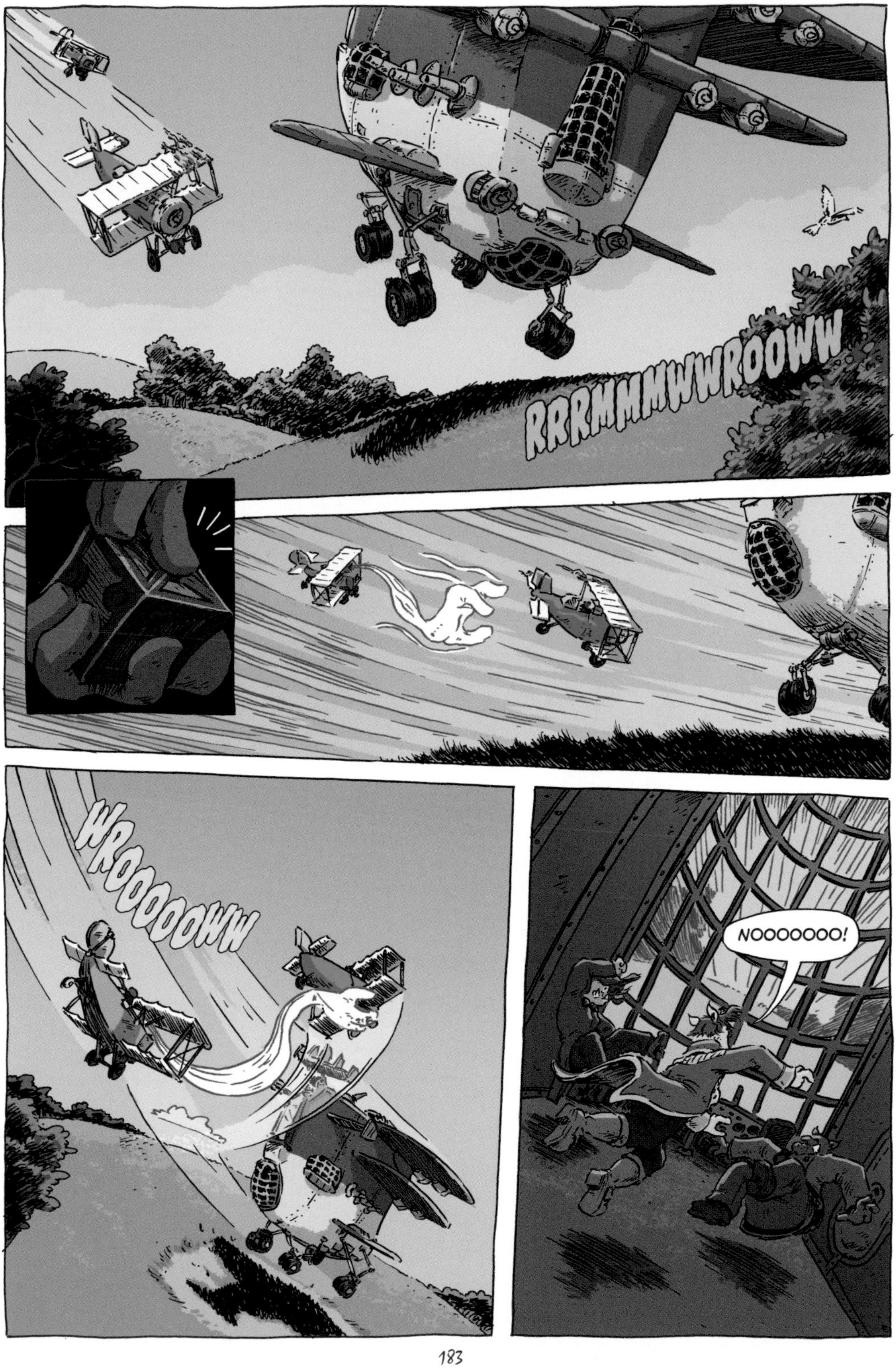
RRRMMMWWROOWW
WROOOOOWW
NOOOOOOO!

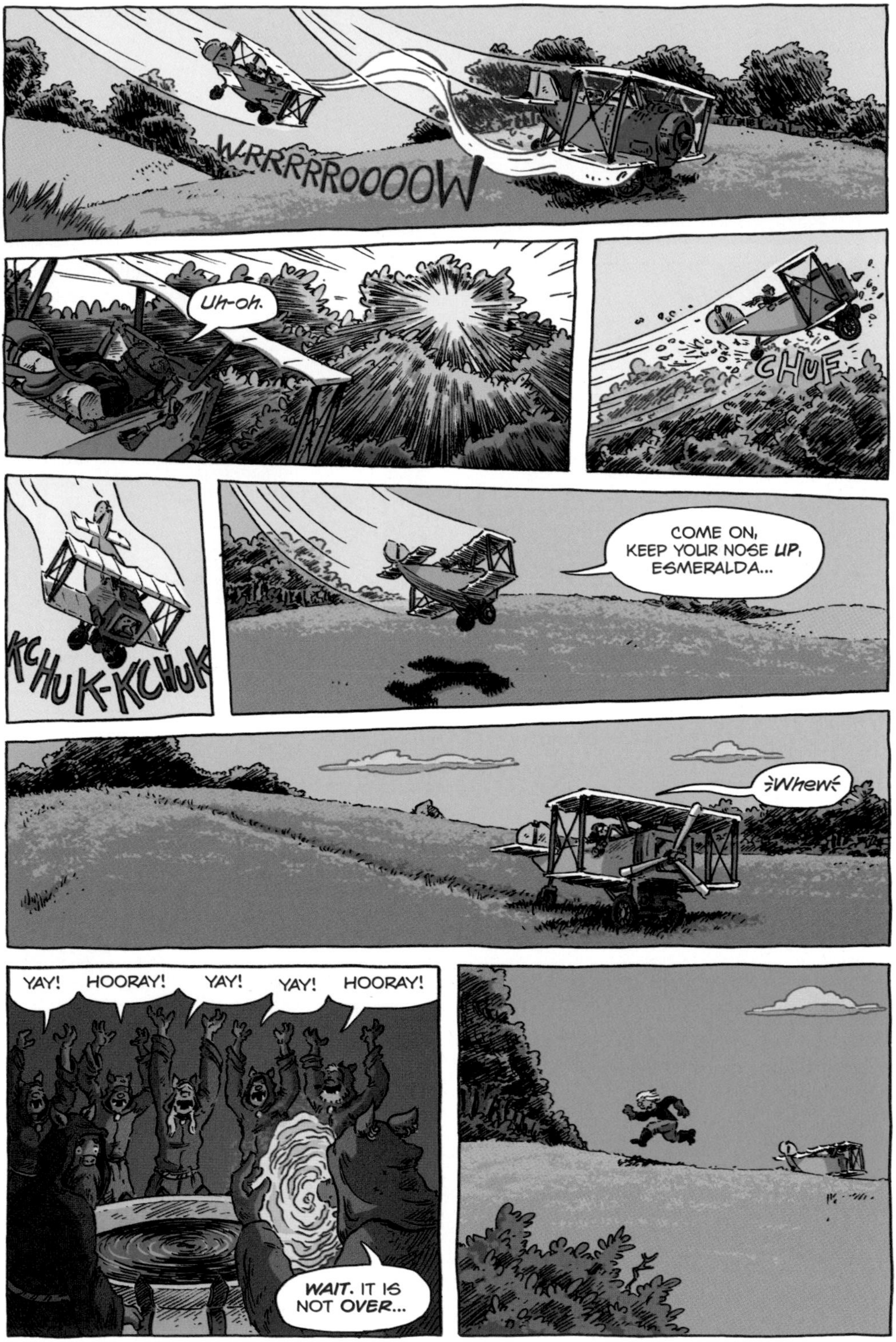
WRRRRROOOOW
Uh-oh.
CHUF
KCHUK-KCHUK
COME ON, KEEP YOUR NOSE UP, ESMERALDA...
Whew
YAY!
HOORAY!
YAY!
YAY!
HOORAY!
WAIT. IT IS NOT OVER...

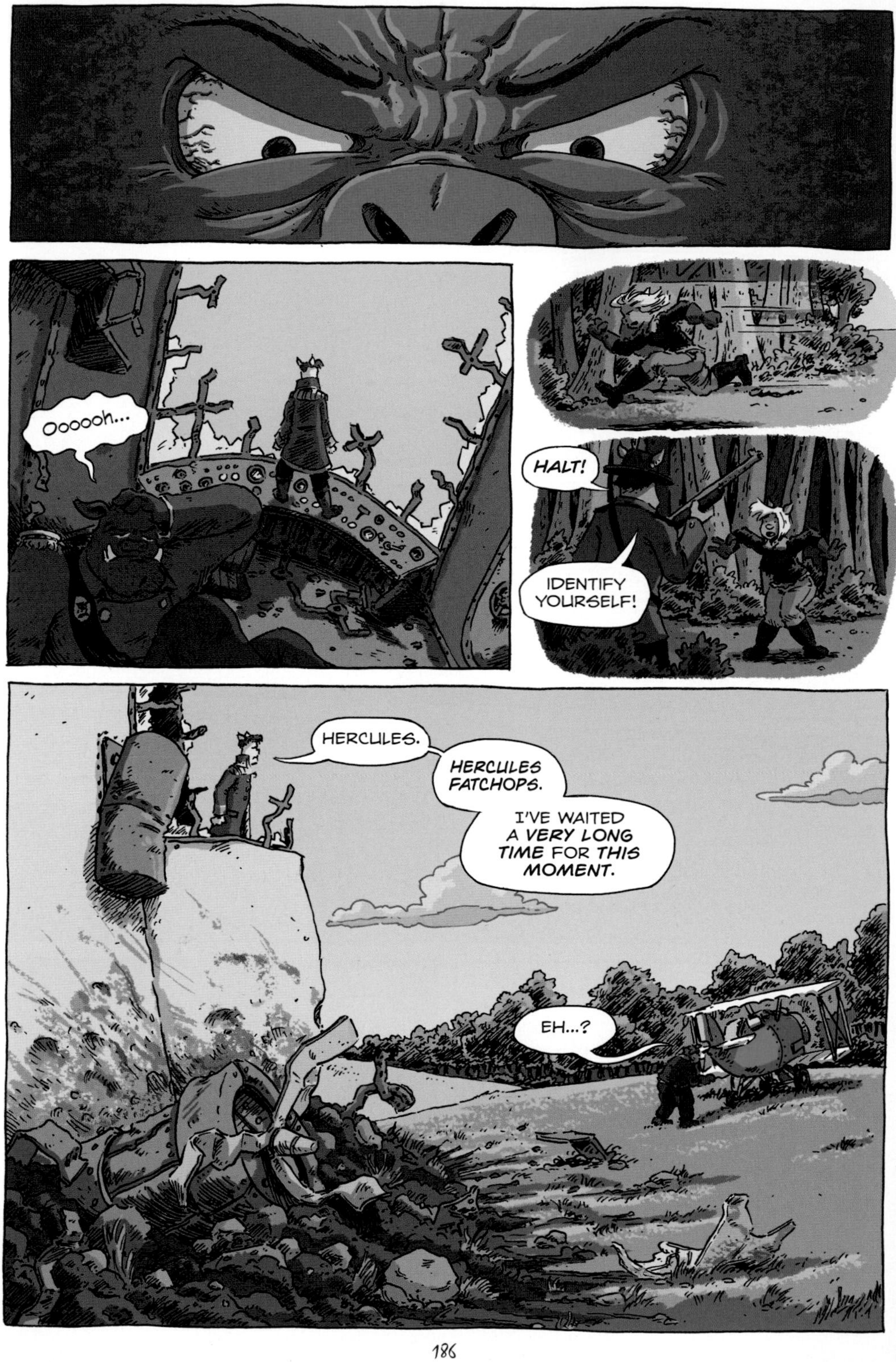
Oooooh...
HALT!
IDENTIFY YOURSELF!
HERCULES.
HERCULES FATCHOPS.
I'VE WAITED A VERY LONG TIME FOR THIS MOMENT.
EH...?

STAND DOWN, SOLDIER. D'YOU *KNOW* WHO THAT IS?

THAT'S *LILY LEANCHOPS*, HERCULES FATCHOPS'S DAUGHTER, ALSO KNOWN AS *AERIAL HONKER...*!

MA'AM!

What...?

IT'S ALL RIGHT, LILY. THE *WHOLE PIGDOM* KNOWS. I'M AFRAID A REPORTER LEAKED YOUR-- ER, "SECRET IDENTITY"...!

YEAH, YOU'RE FAMOUS!

YOU WOULDN'T *BELIEVE* WHAT'S HAPPENED IN THE LAST COUPLE OF DAYS...

ARCHIE! SASHA...? HOW CAN YOU *BE* HERE?

A *FRIEND* GUIDED US-- *CIRCE*. I'VE BEEN IN COMMUNICATION WITH HER VIA THE *NETWORK OF THE MYSTIC CIRCLES*. SHE TIPPED US OFF TO HAM TROTTERS'S *PLANS...*!

MRS. WIGGSLY AND HER SON ARE OUR *CONSULTANTS* ON MAGIC...

OKAY-- *WHAT?* THAT'S *LOVELY*, AND I'M OVERJOYED TO SEE YOU, BUT WE HAVE TO GET TO MY DAD...!

LILY, *WAIT...*!

NO TIME.

LILY!

ARCHIE, STOP *RIGHT NOW!* DO YOU *HEAR* ME?

LIKE MINDS ACROSS THE MOUNTAINS *HEARD YOU*, HIGH ONE.

THEY DID, INDEED!

BE CAREFUL, LILY. THERE IS STILL *GREAT DANGER...*

HAM TROTTERS! I SUPPOSE IT *HAD* TO BE YOU, DIDN'T IT? YOU ALWAYS DID *OVERUSE* MAGIC...

SORRY...

...DON'T WANT TO *HEAR* IT.

NO!

AAAH!

KZRAAAK

THAT THE BEST YOU'VE GOT?

WHAT'S THIS? SORCERY...?

NOT SORCERY, NOT MAGIC-- *SCIENCE.*

HOGWASH! I JUST BLEW YOU OUT OF THE SKY...

INDEED-- THROUGH *SHEER FORCE,* OLD BOY. HAD NO MEANS OF *DEFLECTING* IT.

THIS DEVICE IS SOMETHING I RIGGED UP AT EVEN SHORTER NOTICE THAN THE PIGDOM'S AIRCRAFT FLEET.

IT'S DESIGNED TO EITHER DEFLECT OR STORE AND *REROUTE* MAGICAL ENERGY...

...LIKE SO.

HMM. HERE ON THE GROUND, I THINK WE'RE A BIT MORE *EVENLY MATCHED*...

I ALWAYS TRIED TO TEACH YOU NOT TO *BLUDGEON* WHEN A *MERE TAP* WILL DO.

NO! YOU NEVER KNEW *ANYTHING* ABOUT MAGIC!

NOT SO. MY SISTER *SASHA* IS A *MAGICAL ADEPT.* I LEARNED A FEW TRICKS GROWING UP WITH HER...

SHE, AND A WHOLE TEAM OF *CARPENTERS* AND MAGICAL ADEPTS, HELPED ME ASSEMBLE THE FLEET THAT *INTERCEPTED* YOU.

THAT'S *TEAMWORK,* DEAR BOY.

THIS IS SCIENCE.

SCIENCE!

SCIENCE AND *MAGIC* COEXIST. MAYBE *A BALANCE OF BOTH* IS DESIRABLE.

MY *DAUGHTER* TAUGHT ME THAT.

I'LL *KILL YOU* WITH MY BARE HANDS!

AAARGH!

DIIIIIE!

189

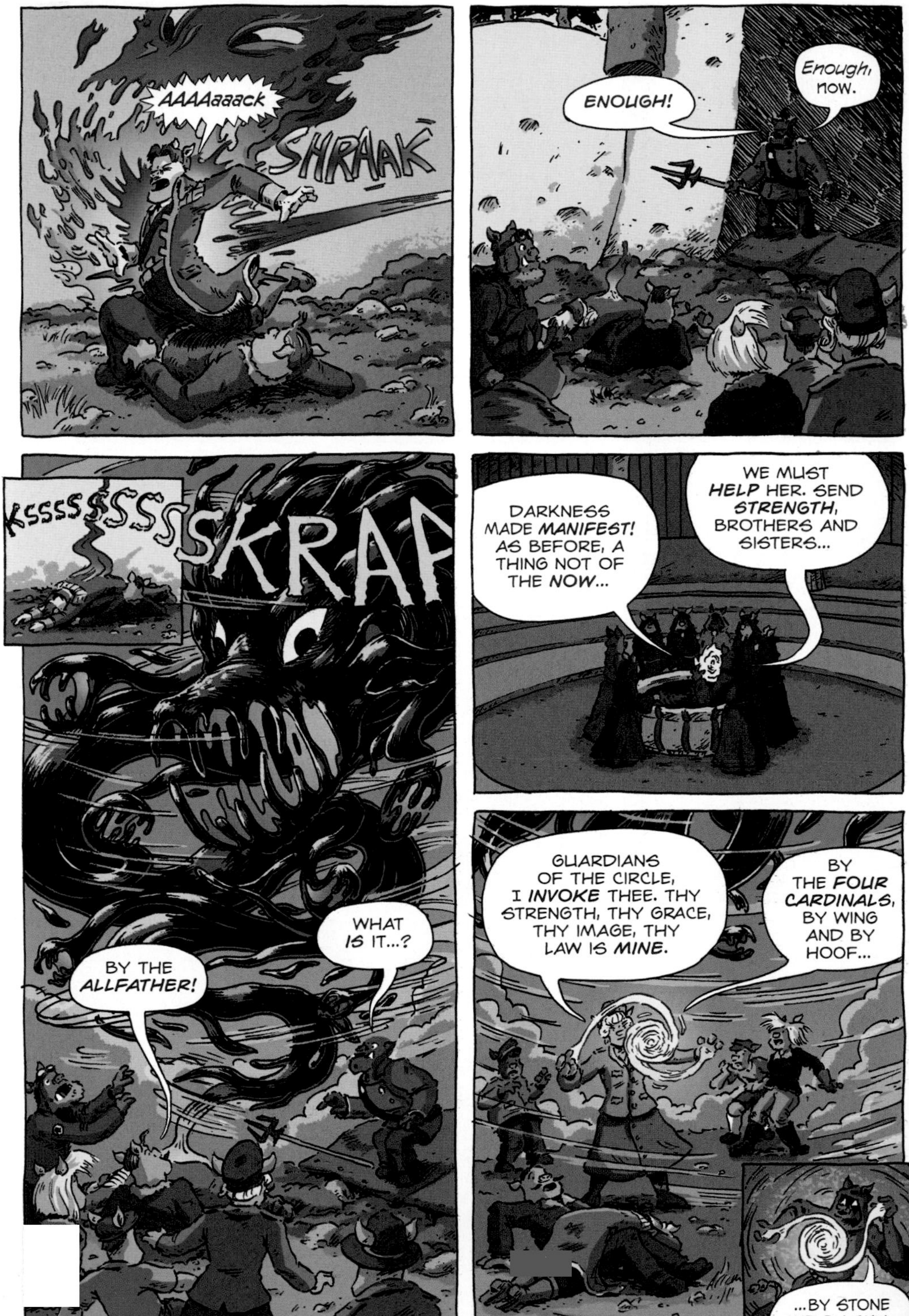

AAAAaaack
SHRAAK
ENOUGH!
Enough, now.
KSSSSSSSSS
SKRA
BY THE ALLFATHER!
WHAT IS IT...?
DARKNESS MADE MANIFEST! AS BEFORE, A THING NOT OF THE NOW...
WE MUST HELP HER. SEND STRENGTH, BROTHERS AND SISTERS...
GUARDIANS OF THE CIRCLE, I INVOKE THEE. THY STRENGTH, THY GRACE, THY IMAGE, THY LAW IS MINE.
BY THE FOUR CARDINALS, BY WING AND BY HOOF...
...BY STONE AND BY SKY...

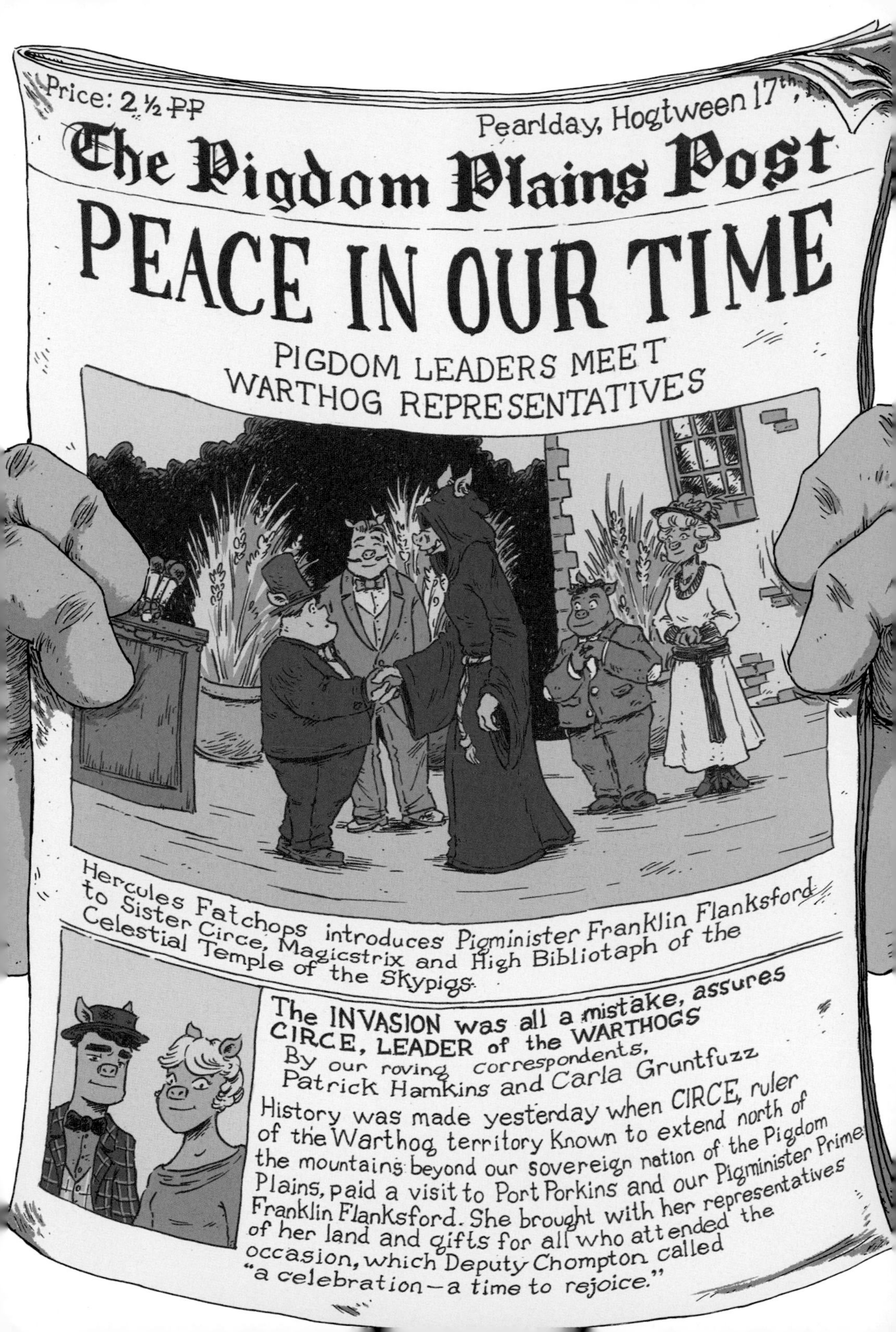
Price: 2½ PP
Pearlday, Hogtween 17th,
The Pigdom Plains Post
PEACE IN OUR TIME
PIGDOM LEADERS MEET WARTHOG REPRESENTATIVES
Hercules Fatchops introduces Pigminister Franklin Flanksford to Sister Circe, Magicstrix and High Bibliotaph of the Celestial Temple of the Skypigs.
The INVASION was all a mistake, assures CIRCE, LEADER of the WARTHOGS
By our roving correspondents, Patrick Hamkins and Carla Gruntfuzz
History was made yesterday when CIRCE, ruler of the Warthog territory known to extend north of the mountains beyond our sovereign nation of the Pigdom Plains, paid a visit to Port Porkins and our Pigminister Prime Franklin Flanksford. She brought with her representatives of her land and gifts for all who attended the occasion, which Deputy Chompton called "a celebration—a time to rejoice."

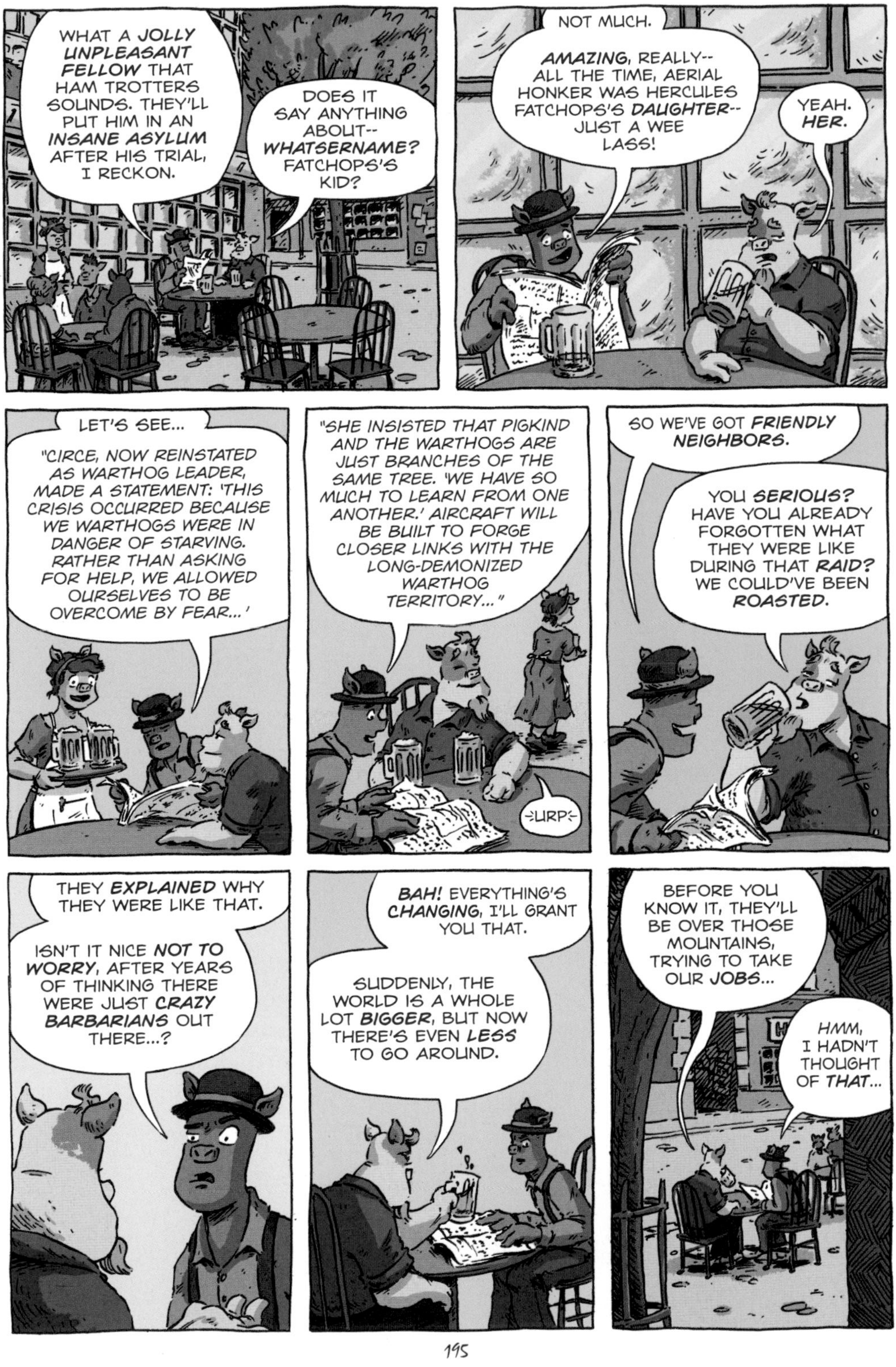
WHAT A JOLLY UNPLEASANT FELLOW THAT HAM TROTTERS SOUNDS. THEY'LL PUT HIM IN AN INSANE ASYLUM AFTER HIS TRIAL, I RECKON.
DOES IT SAY ANYTHING ABOUT-- WHATSERNAME? FATCHOPS'S KID?
NOT MUCH.
AMAZING, REALLY-- ALL THE TIME, AERIAL HONKER WAS HERCULES FATCHOPS'S DAUGHTER-- JUST A WEE LASS!
YEAH. HER.
LET'S SEE...
"CIRCE, NOW REINSTATED AS WARTHOG LEADER, MADE A STATEMENT: 'THIS CRISIS OCCURRED BECAUSE WE WARTHOGS WERE IN DANGER OF STARVING. RATHER THAN ASKING FOR HELP, WE ALLOWED OURSELVES TO BE OVERCOME BY FEAR...'
"SHE INSISTED THAT PIGKIND AND THE WARTHOGS ARE JUST BRANCHES OF THE SAME TREE. 'WE HAVE SO MUCH TO LEARN FROM ONE ANOTHER.' AIRCRAFT WILL BE BUILT TO FORGE CLOSER LINKS WITH THE LONG-DEMONIZED WARTHOG TERRITORY..."
URP
SO WE'VE GOT FRIENDLY NEIGHBORS.
YOU SERIOUS? HAVE YOU ALREADY FORGOTTEN WHAT THEY WERE LIKE DURING THAT RAID? WE COULD'VE BEEN ROASTED.
THEY EXPLAINED WHY THEY WERE LIKE THAT.
ISN'T IT NICE NOT TO WORRY, AFTER YEARS OF THINKING THERE WERE JUST CRAZY BARBARIANS OUT THERE...?
BAH! EVERYTHING'S CHANGING, I'LL GRANT YOU THAT.
SUDDENLY, THE WORLD IS A WHOLE LOT BIGGER, BUT NOW THERE'S EVEN LESS TO GO AROUND.
BEFORE YOU KNOW IT, THEY'LL BE OVER THOSE MOUNTAINS, TRYING TO TAKE OUR JOBS...
HMM, I HADN'T THOUGHT OF THAT...

IT'S A *WHOLE NEW WORLD*, ISN'T IT?

YES.

YOUR FATHER'S *HAPPY*.

HE LOVES A *BIG PROJECT*. THERE'S TALK OF *TRADE AGREEMENTS* AND EXCHANGES BETWEEN THE PIGDOM AND THE WARTHOGS...

YES, HE'S ALREADY BUTTING HEADS WITH THE PIGMINISTER PRIME ABOUT HOW TO *HANDLE* IT ALL. SLUDGEWELL'S *BACKING HIM* UP! HE'S GOT A NEW *BEST FRIEND*.

WELL, I'M GLAD CIRCE REQUESTED *YOU* AS A *LIAISON*. YOU'LL TALK SOME *SENSE* INTO THEM.

AND HOW ARE *YOU*?

YOU'VE BEEN VERY *QUIET* EVER SINCE YOU CAME BACK...

IT'S YOUR FRIEND, ISN'T IT? *GRISELDA...*?

MM.

SHE DIDN'T COME BACK. SHE WAS SUPPOSED TO COME *HERE* WITH *ME*, TO THE PIGDOM...

I *KNOW* I SAW HER... SHE *SAVED MY LIFE*.

I'M SURE SHE TRIED TO FLY BACK *HOME*, WHILE SHE HAD THE *CHANCE*...

SHE'S OUT THERE SOMEWHERE...

SASHA, I SAW THINGS UP THERE THAT I CAN'T *EXPLAIN*. BUT SOMEHOW, THEY *MADE SENSE*.

NONE OF THIS, DOWN HERE, MAKES *ANY* SENSE TO ME.

THEY'RE ALL FALLING OVER THEMSELVES TO BE *A PART* OF THIS *BRAVE NEW WORLD*.

WITHOUT *YOU*, THEY WOULDN'T BE SO *INSPIRED*, LILY.

WITHOUT GRISELDA, *I* WOULDN'T BE HERE.

I NEED TO GO AND LOOK FOR HER. I NEED TO *FIND OUT*.

I KNOW.

BUT PLEASE *COME BACK* TO US. I DON'T THINK I COULD BEAR TO *LOSE* YOU.

I WILL.

THIS IS MY *HOME BASE* WITH MY *CHIEF ENGINEER*!

HER FIRST *TEST FLIGHT*! WHERE SHALL I TAKE HER...?

ESMERALDA II IS READY TO GO!

198

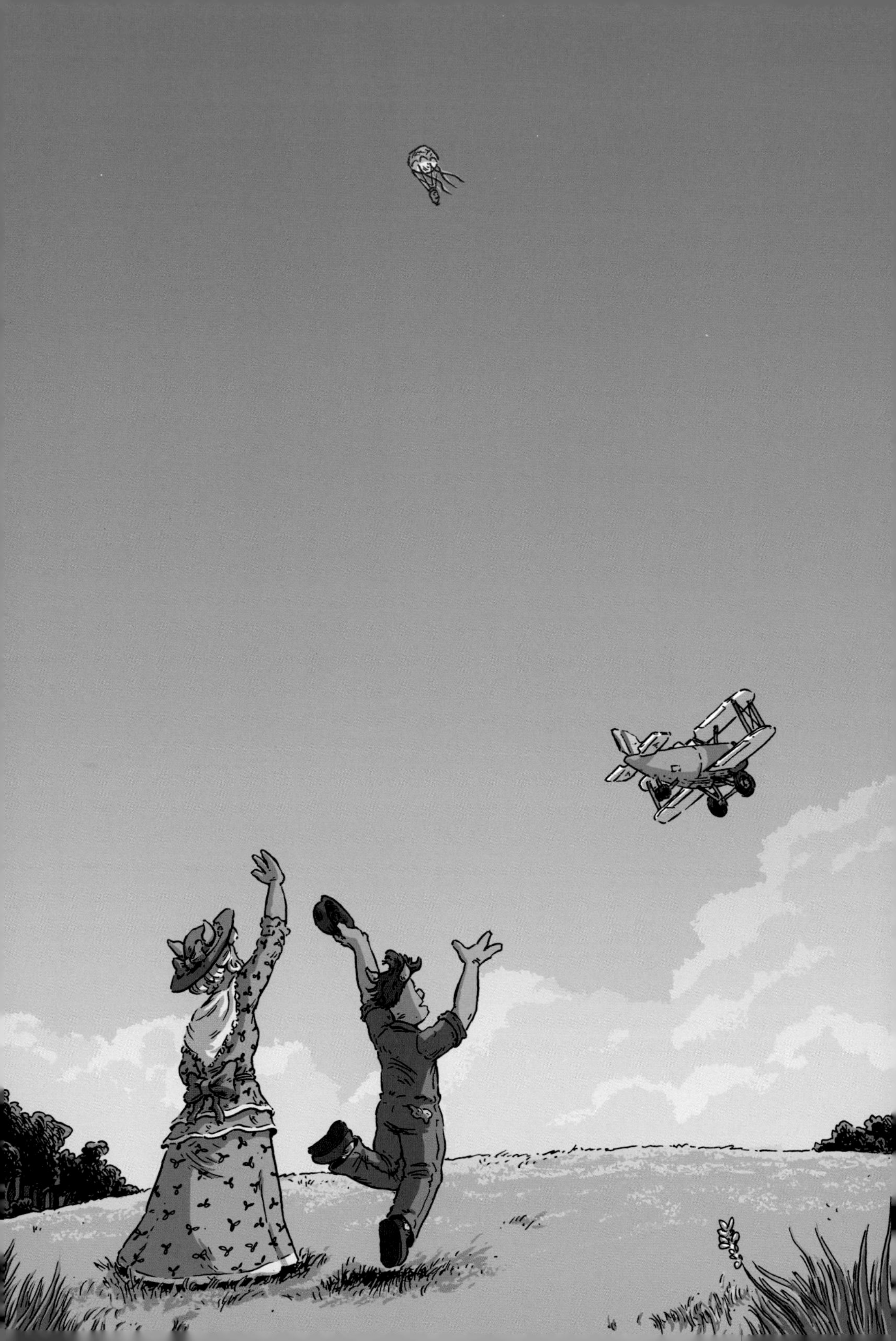

I'LL JUST HAVE TO BIDE MY TIME...!

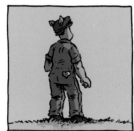

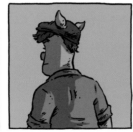

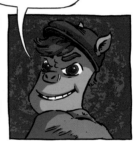

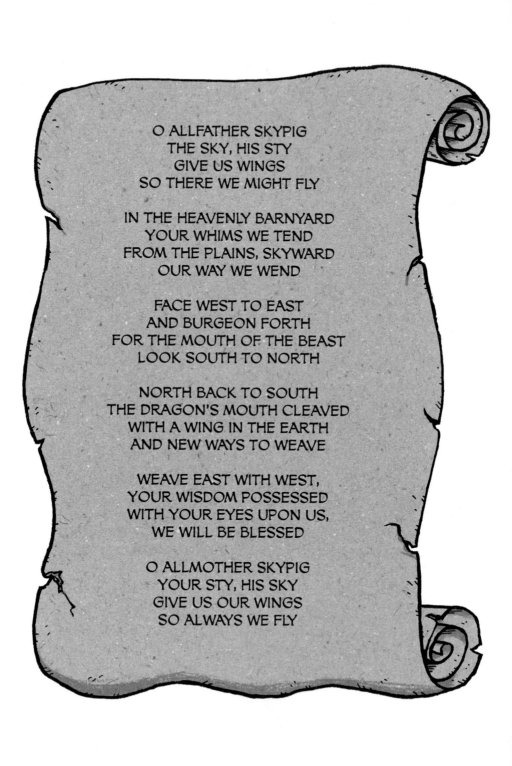

O ALLFATHER SKYPIG
THE SKY, HIS STY
GIVE US WINGS
SO THERE WE MIGHT FLY

IN THE HEAVENLY BARNYARD
YOUR WHIMS WE TEND
FROM THE PLAINS, SKYWARD
OUR WAY WE WEND

FACE WEST TO EAST
AND BURGEON FORTH
FOR THE MOUTH OF THE BEAST
LOOK SOUTH TO NORTH

NORTH BACK TO SOUTH
THE DRAGON'S MOUTH CLEAVED
WITH A WING IN THE EARTH
AND NEW WAYS TO WEAVE

WEAVE EAST WITH WEST,
YOUR WISDOM POSSESSED
WITH YOUR EYES UPON US,
WE WILL BE BLESSED

O ALLMOTHER SKYPIG
YOUR STY, HIS SKY
GIVE US OUR WINGS
SO ALWAYS WE FLY

For Nadia

Thank you, Angela Watson and all the Abadzis family for your love and support. I'm not me without you. Thanks to Ed, Nikki, Cas, John, Luciana, Alan, Glenn, Wallis, Rachael, Steve, Josh, Jim, Sean, and Gary for all the distance management and for being you. Thanks to Kirsty for all the good sense and to Sally for still being the best listening ear.

Special thanks also to Kevin, Melissa, Garth, Ruth, Charlie, Jaime, Jon, Alex, Si, Greg, other Greg, Sebastian, and Jules for being there. Big thanks to Lewis for the portrait.

Very special thanks to Jerel and Mark, who believed a pig can fly.

—Nick Abadzis

Lewis Trondheim and Brigitte Findakly

Thanks to Jesse Lonergan, Roho, Kimball Anderson, and the wonderful comics community of the BCR.

Thanks to those always inspiring artists who make machines fly: Mattias Adolfsson, Charles A. A. Dellschau, Hayao Miyazaki, and Ian McQue.

Thanks to Laurel Lynn Leake and Alex Campbell for your marvelous talent and perseverance. Special thanks to Katie Armour, to all my friends, and to my loving family whose love and support carry me through.

And thanks to Nick and Mark, who opened up a whole new world to me.

—Jerel Dye

Jesse Lonergan

First Second

New York

Published by First Second
First Second is an imprint of Roaring Brook Press,
a division of Holtzbrinck Publishing Holdings Limited Partnership
175 Fifth Avenue, New York, New York 10010

Library of Congress Control Number: 2016945556

Paperback ISBN: 978-1-62672-086-2
Hardcover ISBN: 978-1-62672-743-4

Our books may be purchased in bulk for promotional, educational, or business use. Please
contact your local bookseller or the Macmillan Corporate and Premium Sales Department at
(800) 221-7945 ext. 5442 or by e-mail at MacmillanSpecialMarkets@macmillan.com.

First edition 2017
Printed in China by Toppan Leefung Printing Ltd., Dongguan City, Guangdong Province

Penciled with 2H Faber Castell 9000 Pencil and inked with Copic Multiliner SP pens
on Strathmore Smooth Bristol paper. Colored digitally in Photoshop.

Paperback: 10 9 8 7 6 5 4 3 2 1
Hardcover: 10 9 8 7 6 5 4 3 2 1